MW01123722

Rivers Ebb

Also by Jim H. Ainsworth

Rivers Crossing
2005 Novel

In the Rivers Flow
2003 Novel

Biscuits Across the Brazos
2001 Memoir

Rivers Ebb

A Novel

Jim H. Ainsworth

First Edition

Third book in the *Follow the Rivers Trilogy*

This is a work of fiction. All the characters, names, incidents,
organizations and dialogue in this novel are either the products of
the author's imagination or are used fictitiously.

ISBN 978-0-9679483-6-2

Library of Congress Control Number: 2006910313

Designed by Darron Moore, **MOORE OR LESS DESIGN**

Printed in the United States of America

Season of Harvest Publications
Texas

Dr. Fred Tarpley, Editor

For Teadon ...

A daddy who showed me how a firm hand can harmonize
with tenderness and unconditional love.

Thank You—

to my readers evaluation group~Terry, June, Rosalie, Jan,
Shelly, Damon

to Fred Tarpley~ not just for the width and depth of his
knowledge, but for his unflappable good humor
and enthusiasm

to Dr. O. Gaynor Janes, son of Dr. Olen Janes, for his advice
about things medical and stories about his father.

About the *Follow the Rivers Trilogy*...

Excerpts from *In the Rivers Flow* & *Rivers Crossing* -the first and second books in the trilogy

Griffin Rivers

"Flow is the difference between the way things are and they way they ought to be."

"... the fact is that a man has a lot more control over his thinkin' and his body than most folks ever use. The flow's all about using that power more."

Gray Boy Rivers

"I guess Tuck's death took the starch out of it for me—made it seem kinda foolish. ... Where was it then?"

Rance Rivers

"You know what Papa would say? He'd say the Rivers flow is in the same place it always was—in your heart and in your head. It's easy to believe when things are going your way. It's when they're not—that's when you have to believe."

Jake Rivers

"It's somethin' that kinda comes over you when you least expect it, ain't it?"

Author's note...

We each have our little lifeboats in the river of life. When we stay in the flow, pay attention, and use our gifts, we can stay in sync with other lifeboats, dodge sharp rocks, navigate sharp turns, make it through rapids—even survive a waterfall. It's when we stop navigating that we run into the banks, paddle against the flow, collide with dangerous things in the river—or take the wrong turns.

We all face rapids and waterfalls—most of us will capsize at least once, but when we stay in the flow, we will also be lifted to blissful joy, the highest levels of confidence, and supreme, perfect happiness.

Now, the third book in the trilogy—*Rivers Ebb*.

Rivers Ebb

1   The Marines took Jake Rivers' big brother, marriage
took his sister, and God took his little brother. Old age
was taking his grandfather; hard times had taken his
home. Even Shy, his dog, took up with Bo Creekwater, a man
whose mental age had grown further and further behind his
physical age. A deep sense of sadness settled over Jake as he
watched his Marine brother, Gray Boy, ride away in that
Trailways bus. He had never felt so lonely. It was the day
after Christmas, and Jake wanted to go home, but there was
no home to go to. Rance and Mattie, his parents, had left the
dying Christmas tree in the living room and headed west.
Stopping at the Klondike cemetery to say goodbye to little
brother Tuck filled the cab of his father's '56 Chevy pickup
with gloom.

     Buzzards floated above the pickup as Jake left the old
graveyard. Bone-picking birds were supposed to glide across
the sky on warm, sunny days and stay on fence rails or dead
tree limbs on cold, wet days like this one. But there they were,
circling—waiting to pick the bones of the life he was leaving
behind.

     When he saw Commerce, Texas in his rearview mirror,
nervousness set in. He had pulled a trailer a few times, but

never much farther than Cooper to ride in a parade or a rodeo grand entry. His daddy or brother had always been in the seat beside him on those trips. Jake's learner's permit required it. It still did. Every police and Highway Patrol car made Jake twitch a little.

The map spread on the pickup seat showed that Amarillo was clear across Texas. He had started to regret letting Gray Boy talk him into *crossing the river* again. Papa Griff and his daddy had urged Jake to "always stay in the flow, between the banks." His big brother was supposed to be with him all the way to Amarillo, but Gray Boy had overstayed his leave and had to catch the bus out of Cooper to get back to base on time. Jake had been cajoled again by his older brother. "You ain't big enough to drive this little pickup and trailer for eight or ten hours by yourself? Hell, all you gotta do is sit there and hold the wheel; maybe shift gears once in awhile."

Jake's confidence lifted a little when he reached Nocona. There was almost no traffic to bother him, and he could see for miles. The sky seemed bigger, somehow. He liked the names of the towns he was passing through. Cowboy country. Towns named after Indian chiefs and famous cowboys. As the air grew thinner, he pulled his hat down, glanced at his boots, and began to feel like a cowboy hauling his horse across the country. He adjusted the pillow under him and sat taller and straighter. He imagined himself as a traveling calf roper, pulling his horse to Amarillo and points beyond, wherever the rodeo circuit took him.

Rance and Mattie had told him that Wichita Falls was the last really big town before Amarillo. He knew that his new home was on the other side of Amarillo, but he didn't know how far west it was. He imagined people staring at him as he caught all the red lights in the middle of downtown Wichita Falls. Jake stepped out at the last one and walked back to check on his horse. *Let `em have a good look.*

A real cowboy in a new two-toned white and aquamarine

'58 Ford pickup with red pinstripes pulled alongside. Jake tried not to stare at the matching covered two-horse trailer behind the Ford. The horse (not cattle) trailer had four wheels, a bulldog hitch, running lights, and was pinstriped in red to match the pickup. The cowboy nodded and smiled.

As Jake looked through the trailer's window at the blanketed horse all snug and dry inside, he worried that Scar was cold. Jake's gelding was riding in an open-topped stock trailer with two wheels, pulled along by a bouncing, noisy linchpin attached to the pickup's bumper. The horse had a good coat of winter hair, but it was bitter cold, misting a little, and the wind had picked up. The melodious rumble of the Ford's twin pipes echoed off the street as it pulled away, and Jake scrambled to make it through the green light.

Rance had told him to let the horse out of the trailer every two or three hours for exercise. Jake knew that was overdue as he left Wichita Falls, but he had not found the perfect place to stop. As he pulled into Chillicothe, he saw it—a service station with a big driveway and an open lot beside it where he could walk the horse.

"Fill 'er up." Jake nodded at the station attendant.

The forty-ish man wore a baseball cap that had been baby blue before grease and oil took it. He stuck the nozzle into the Chevy's gas tank and pulled the trigger. He rolled his shoulders and hunched up from the wind as he jerked his head toward the pickup's hood. "Check the oil?"

The smell of gasoline blew past Jake's nose. He could almost feel a gasoline mist in the air and taste the fuel. Jake hesitated. "Guess we better." He pulled the pin from the trailer gate, and Scar ran backward, sliding on the concrete as he stepped out of the trailer. Jake barely avoided being hit by the gate and the horse. *What's got into him?* Aggravated, he grabbed the lead rope and jerked it as he headed toward the vacant lot. The rope tightened and slid across Jake's palm. He turned to see Scar stretching his legs and squatting into a familiar stance. The horse was about to pee all over the man's driveway. Jake hated to, but he turned back to kick him. He wanted the horse to stand up and walk to the dirt lot to take care of his business.

"How'd you like to be kicked when you're about to take a piss?" The station attendant's brow was furrowed into a frown, but the corners of his mouth seemed ready to turn up.

"Guess I wouldn't. Sure will splash everywhere, though. I'll clean it up when he's through. I forgot he refuses to pee in a trailer. Guess he's been holding it a long time." Jake headed for the wound water hose. It was hard and brittle to the touch.

"You won't do it with that. Froze up. Likely to break right off in your hands." The man turned to watch the quarter-a-gallon gas run up to $2.75. "I've had worse in this driveway. Some fool yesterday drove in here with his oil pan scraping the pavement. Must've dropped four quarts of oil right where that horse of yours is pissing. Now that shit is slick. Horse piss...it'll run off. 'Sides, it'll be covered with snow by dark."

"Snow?" Jake was relieved when the splashing finally stopped, and the horse straightened, back hooves stepping into the wetness. The wind now carried a mixture of gasoline, horse pee, and something spoiled. "You expectin' snow? How much?" The prospect of snow around Christmas in Delta County would have brought a smile to Jake's face. Driving a strange highway to his new home in Oldham County brought different emotions.

"Askin' how much it's gonna snow in Texas is like askin' how high's the moon. Radio's givin' six to nine inches." The man jerked his head toward the station.

Inside, Jake backed up to the butane heater and put his hands across his butt. He eyed the candy and chips under the glass counter. Light coats of dust eased his temptation. "How much I owe you?"

"Two-seventy-five. I tried to get her to take three even, but she just wouldn't. Don't like to spill a man's gas on the pavement just to even things out."

"Yessir." Jake pulled the twenty his father had given him for the trip and handed it over. He hated to break it. It was the first big bill he had carried since he hauled hay for Hack Gentry last year. The memory of Hack's drowning caused a little spasm in his throat. Probably one of the reasons Jake had to give up the only home he had ever known.

Jake stuffed the change deep into his left front pocket, keeping it separate from his own billfold stash. Rance and Mattie did not know he had almost twenty dollars saved up from working for Hack. He pulled the door open.

"Where you headed, kid?"

Jake stepped back inside and pushed the door shut. "Other side of Amarillo. Don't know exactly the name of the place, if it's got one. Just know Oldham County and Deaf Smith, somewhere around Hereford."

"Where you from?"

"East of here. Northeast Texas. "

The man's face still held a question.

"Little over an hour northeast of Dallas. Delta County. Near Cooper ... Klondike ... Commerce."

The man did not show a flicker of recognition at the towns Jake knew like the back of his hand. "Got a brother that lives in Texarkana. Know exactly where you're talkin' about. Be a lot different where you're goin'."

"So I hear."

"How you gonna find your new place?"

"My daddy drew me a little map with miles on it. I haven't really studied it yet. Figured I'd get past Amarillo, eat something, then study the map."

"What's your daddy's name?'

"Rance Rivers."

"Knew some Rivers out by Ranger. You any kin? What

did your daddy do back there?"

Jake did not know which question to answer first. "My granddaddy originally came from out around Ranger before they moved to where we been livin'. Back in Delta County, we had a dairy farm, ran a few cows, planted a little cotton back there. Daddy drove heavy equipment for the county when drought took the dairy."

"Seems strange to be coming this direction if you're runnin' from drought. Hell, it ain't rained here since 1950. Just snows. I know Oldham County. May be a dairy farm or two, but I doubt it. He'll likely raise wheat and maize out there. Gonna irrigate?"

Jake put his hand on the door. He felt the conversation getting over his head. He knew one thing about farmers—he wasn't going to be one. "Daddy says half the place is dry and half irrigated. We're just leasin' the place. I'm hopin' we can run a few cattle, too." Jake pulled the door open and felt the wind push. "I'll sure clean up that mess if you got any water. I got a bucket."

"Nope. Let the snow do it. Be careful. Road's likely to get slick."

"If you don't mind my askin', what's that smell in the air here?"

"Don't even notice it anymore, myself, but it's probably silage. See them silos across the street? Grain's been fermentin' in there since summer. Ought to smell it when it's hot."

"I'll bet." Hamburgers and pan-fried onions overtook the silage as he stepped outside and pulled his Levi jacket collar up. He should have brought a bigger coat. Jake figured he would ignore the hunger pains a while longer ... give him something to look forward to. As he pulled away, he eyed the tin-foil-covered biscuits his grandfather had stuffed into his hand when he left that morning. He sure hated to leave that old man behind. Eating those two biscuits seemed like saying goodbye to his Papa Griff for good. Besides, he didn't have anything to drink with the biscuits. He decided to keep them for a while. He could drink when he stopped for a good meal.

2 It started spitting a little moisture around Childress, but Jake wasn't worried. At Goodnight, he played a little game of trying to figure out which house suited the grand-old-man-of-cattle. Rance had said the Charles Goodnight place could be seen from 287, but Jake had no idea where it was. He settled on an old two-story just outside of town. He was staring back at it when he felt a little hesitation in the tires. Maybe the horse had shifted, trying to dodge the wind and rain. When it happened again, he knew he was spinning a little. Jake had driven in mud, and his father had shown him how to maneuver over ice, but he had never actually done it. Rance whispered in his ear. *Don't hit the brakes; just let off the foot feed and let her ease back.* Jake was a little tense now.

Clarendon. Running about fifty. Snowing pretty good. Claude. Fields white—windshield wipers working steady—snow building up on the hood—speed about forty-five. At Amarillo, Jake was bad hungry and his horse was white, blinking away the sting of snow and wind. He knew he was probably in trouble, and Rance and Mattie would be worried sick. Maybe come looking for him. He didn't want that, but he had to stop and get his bearings, let the horse out again.

9

He needed to be out of Amarillo to do that.

He felt something inside him change when the saw the Route 66 sign. The Mother Road—that's what his grandfather had called it. Even Mrs. Plaxco, his freshman teacher, had talked about it when she was trying to make him feel better about leaving. She said something about John Steinbeck naming it that. Jake wished he could remember what it was she had said, but he wasn't having any of it. Too stubborn. He was mad about leaving and wanted his daddy, his teacher, and everybody else to know it. Something about being on 66 connected him to Papa Griff and his daddy. Like he had been here before. Like he was leaving the east behind.

Hunger pains were stabbing him, and he thought he had run out of towns when he saw it—the tall sign stood stubborn against the wind and snow. *Jesse's Café–Homemade Pies.* The city limit sign said Wildorado. Lights inside suggested warmth and good food. He parked a good distance from the front of the café to avoid a repeat embarrassment when he unloaded Scar. A horse peeing outside a service station was one thing, but a café was something else.

The wind's strength surprised him when he opened the truck door. He had to hold it to keep it on the hinges. He imagined folks inside the café laughing as he put his shoulder against it to close it. Griffin had surrounded a bucket of water and a bucket of sweet feed in the pickup bed with a couple of spare tires. Jake had forgotten to offer his horse water at Chillicothe. Some cowboy. He broke the ice on the water and set both buckets beside the trailer. He took the pin out of the gate and held on as the wind carried him back. Scar backed out like a gentleman this time. The horse sniffed the water before wolfing down the feed.

Jake dropped the lead rope and dodged the wind as best he could on the side of the pickup. Scar sniffed the water again and pawed the ground beside it. Jake ran over to keep him from tipping it over. "Damn. Ain't no more water, Boy.

You stupid enough to knock over what you got?" The horse sniffed again, put his muzzle in the cold water and sipped.

Jake walked him around a little before tying the lead rope to the trailer with a nice slipknot. It was late afternoon, but the smell of sausage frying drifted out as a man in pointed boots walked out of the café. His jeans were stuffed into the boots' stovepipe tops with mule-ear pulls. He pulled his hat down hard and trotted toward a pickup loaded with bales of hay. He had barely removed his hand from the doorknob before Jake turned it, figuring that his entry would not be as noticeable if it coincided with the man leaving. Jake did not like to be stared at.

His shyness did not deter the people inside Jesse's Café. All eyes turned toward him as he wiped his boots on the mat. Jake's smile was apologetic toward the waitress behind the counter as the snow started melting into puddles at his feet. "Come on in, cowboy. Don't worry about them wet boots." Her eyebrows slanted toward the row of men sitting on stools at the counter. "These old farts usually track in a lot worse than snow."

Jake felt his face warm a little, but a sense of welcome came to offset it as the men smiled. He glanced toward the single open stool at the counter but decided on a booth, justifying his shyness with the need for space to fold out his map. The men all turned to look. Their faces showed more friendliness than curiosity. One man twirled his barstool completely around to face Jake and let his boots touch the floor. "You're welcome to join us at the bar, young man. I already heard all the stories these old boys can tell. I'm bettin' you got some better ones."

"Much obliged, but I need to sit over here so I can watch my horse through the window." Jake knew he must look strange. He knew well enough that he was not old enough to be driving alone, much less hauling a horse in a snowstorm. He was fourteen but had been told too often that he looked twelve.

He put an elbow on the table and picked up a menu out of a wire stand. He looked at it without seeing it. He turned the round knob on the small coin machine that hung on the wall, pretending to read the song cards as they rolled. Jake wanted to put in a nickel and play one, but decided it would bring too much attention. He was looking around for the actual jukebox when she appeared at the booth, tablet and pencil ready. "What'll it be, handsome?"

"Uh, could I get a cheeseburger basket?" As the words tumbled out, Jake realized just how green he was. He could not recall eating in a restaurant alone; could not recall ordering from a menu more than once or twice. His experience with restaurants was limited to standing outside an order window at the Cooper Dairy Queen after a Little League game. He could not recall ever ordering anything other than what he had just recited to the waitress ... well, maybe a malt or ice cream cone at Miller's Drug.

The thought made him thirsty. He called after her. "Ma'am, could I get a Coke with that?"

"Sure, Hon." She flashed a smile at Jake over her shoulder. He thought he saw her wink at one of the stool-sitters. Jake managed to look her in the eye and felt a little tingle when she looked right back. She was pretty and there was mischief in those eyes. The boy liked the woman. She stirred something in him he barely recognized.

Jake finished one of the best meals of his life and pushed back the empty plate just in time for the waitress to replace it with a saucer full of pie. His face warmed again, wondering if the pie came with the burger basket. He stared at the pie, impressed with meringue that stood as tall as the coffee cup beside it. He was embarrassed to ask why coffee and pie had been placed in front of him. His shame was made worse when she kept standing there.

"What kinda' pie is that?" Jake felt stupid before the last word left his mouth.

"Chocolate. I guessed you to be a chocolate kinda fella."

Jake cut a small piece, worried about a meringue mustache. He wiped his mouth with the paper napkin and smiled up at her. "Yes ma'am. Chocolate's my favorite." Lemon meringue was really his favorite, but he thought saying chocolate sounded more polite. Jake watched as she removed the dishtowel from her shoulder. She picked up the used plate, wiped the table and gave him another of those sweet smiles. She seemed a saucy blend between his mother and his sister, but still a lot different than either. Jake's feelings about her had nothing to do with family.

He finished the pie and took the last sip of Coke. He didn't like coffee, but turned up the cup and drank it dry. He hated to leave but knew he was going to have to find a house he had never seen in a place he had never been. With the snow slowing him down, he would probably have to do it in the dark.

He spread the road map and his daddy's smaller hand-drawn map on the table and started trying to connect them. Rance had drawn a triangle showing Vega on the northeast point, Adrian on the northwest, and Hereford on the southeast. A star almost in the middle identified their new home. Jake just about had it figured out when he felt the table move. The fellow who had invited him to sit at the counter was sitting across from him. "How old's your gelding?" The man was doing what Rance and Griff had always told Jake to do—looking him straight in the eye. Jake didn't notice people's eyes too often, but this man's eyes were a different kind of blue, like faded blue jeans that had turned shiny from wear. The eyes glistened and held some type of yearning, like he knew Jake or needed something from him—almost like the man was about to cry. There was something about him that Jake liked.

"Six, be seven in the spring."

"Usin' horse?"

Jake took a guess about what the man meant by using. "We herded a few cows on him. Papa Griff ... my grandfather, says he's got lotsa cow in him. I mostly just rode him up and down country roads."

"Looks like a cow horse." The man shifted in the seat and smiled as if he were thinking of more questions. "He a blood bay?"

Jake hesitated, figuring this man to be an expert on horse color. "I don't really know. My daddy says he's a light bay and a vet close to where we live says he's closer to a light than a blood bay. You ever hear of Dr. Ben Green?"

"A man can't go to many horse sales without hearing of or running into Ben K. Green. I imagine Dr. Green is right." He chuckled. "Course, it's hard to tell much about a horse covered with snow."

Jake was embarrassed. "Yessir. Wish I had a blanket, but we just didn't figure on any snow when we started."

"Come a long way?"

"Almost five hundred miles so far."

"Got far to go?"

"That's what I'm trying to figure out. Best I can tell from Daddy's map, our new place is just inside the county line between Deaf Smith and Oldham."

"None of my business, but I live around here. Be glad to give you a hand."

Jake slid the map across the table. "I'd appreciate it."

The man studied it for a few minutes. "You ain't far from home, Son. You're already in Oldham County ... but don't get excited. From the looks of your rig, I'd say you're from East Texas, and counties out here are a lot bigger with a lot less people. Oldham itself is bigger than Rhode Island."

The man smiled as Jake's eyes widened. Rhode Island was a whole state. "You still got nearly fifty miles to get where you're going. Just stay on 66 through Vega. You'll see some grain elevators a few miles out on your right. Turn on the first dirt road. South is the only way it goes. Keep going about twelve or fifteen miles until it doglegs right. If this map is right, your place is right on the corner after that right turn."

Jake wasn't sure what a grain elevator looked like. Dirt road had also struck a nerve. Likely to be muddy. "Appreciate it. Does that road have a name or number?"

"Naw, but you can't miss it. Just turn right past the grain elevators."

"Right?"

The man stood and winked. "Meant to say turn left, right after the elevators. Made that clear as mud, didn't I? If you see a sign that says Adrian City Limits, turn around and come back, else you'll find yourself in New Mexico. Good luck, cowboy, and take care of that horse." He stuck out a big hand.

Jake shook the hand, thanked him again, left a nickel on the table, and took his check to the counter. Cheeseburger basket—thirty-five cents—Coke—ten cents. It seemed a little high, but Jake took out a dollar, making sure the waitress noticed the wad of bills in his pocket. "What about the pie and coffee?" he asked.

She handed Jake his change and pointed toward a departing pickup. "That fella you were talking to ... the pie is on him." Jake's first taste of the Panhandle. Sweet. He stepped outside and slapped himself on the leg, regretting not doing the manly thing—for letting timidity rule his life again. He should have introduced himself to the man and asked his name. Papa Griff and Rance, even Gray Boy, were frowning.

3 Halfway between Vega and Adrian, Jake decided that
the tall concrete silos in the distance had to be grain
elevators. He eased back and made a slow left turn onto
the dirt road, ready to make ruts. It was getting dark and the
wind had died enough for him to hear the snow crunch under
the Chevy's tires. He had never driven on snow, and the
quiet soothed him. Even the linchpin wasn't making as much
noise. Except for the crunching, he could have been on a
paved road. The tension in his shoulders eased as he relaxed
his grip on the wheel.

After what seemed like an hour, he started to tense
again. He had seen no lights, no houses, no signs of life. He
imagined Rance finding his frozen body in the light of day.
Blowing snow had stacked up against the barbed wire fence
lines on each side of the road, trapping huge tumbleweeds.
This country seemed frozen in time, trapped.

He hated himself for forgetting to check his odometer
when he left 66. Sure that he was driving into uninhabited
snow-desert, he slowed and watched both sides of the road for
signs of life. Then he saw it—a dim flicker. A small house,
Quonset-hut barn, a single cottonwood tree. *That must be*

home. No—wrong side of the road. Jake thought of stopping and
asking for help, but decided against it. Didn't want to be
the butt of jokes tomorrow. Just as he was about to give up
and go back to Vega, the dogleg-right renewed his faith in the
man back at the café and his father's map. He slowed and
shifted into second as he made the turn. A small frame house
sat on the right, dim light coming from the windows. The
house seemed to have no back or front, appeared to have been
dropped there as a temporary shelter. Jake drove the pickup
and trailer past the side before he saw it.

The Rivers' chartreuse-and-white '55 Ford sat in a large
yard. The cab, hood, and trunk were covered with snow, but
enough was visible to recognize. He pulled in the yard and
straightened the trailer behind him, figuring he was pointing
west, hoping his father was not too angry. He pulled the door
handle and pushed. Stuck. Jake slid across the seat and tried
the other one. Stuck. He was about to give it a good shove
when Rance knocked on the driver's door. His father's face
was distorted through the iced window, but Jake saw the smile
and recognized the snow-covered hat. *It's a strange place, but I
am home.*

Rance shielded his lighted Zippo with both hands as he
ran it along the door handle. Ice and snow fell into the seat
and yard as he pulled the door open. "You all right?"

Jake palmed the baseball on the seat and picked up Griff's
biscuits. "Yessir. Snow slowed me down some."

"Better get inside and hug your mama. She's about to
have a heart attack."

"Where do I put the horse?"

"I'll feed him and put him up. You get on inside." Jake
was about to open the back or front door to his new home;
he didn't know which, when his father called. "We got a dry
place for Scar. First time he's ever really had a place to get in
out of the weather."

"Yessir. He'll like that, I reckon. He's had a hard

trip." Rance's voice had a sort of plea in it that Jake did not recognize. He looked up at a clearing sky. A still windmill, coated with snow in the moonlight, stared back as if Jake were an intruder in its domain. He had never been that close to a windmill.

Jake stepped into a small hut-like enclosure attached to the house. A few bricks served as a floor, but the hut was still cold. He opened a door, stepped inside and looked around in the sparse light. He saw the light's source through a door to his right. A coal-oil lantern sat on the old gray and chrome Formica table his grandfather hated, but his mother loved. That tiny room must be the kitchen. Mattie emerged from another room, carrying a second lantern. "Jake, I've been worried sick." The lantern cast a soft glow across his mother's pretty face and made her dark hair seem blacker than the night.

She held the lantern with one hand and hugged him with the other, and hands-full, he clumsily hugged back.

"We ain't got any electricity way out here in the middle of nowhere?" Jake did not try to hide his I-told-you-so tone.

"We had lights until about an hour ago, but the storm must have taken down a line. Electric company has to cover miles and miles of line out here looking for a break. You hungry?"

Jake shrugged, considering whether to mention the burger, fries, and pie. He knew Mattie wanted to fix him something. "I ate on the road." Jake felt big for his britches, a hero home from the wars.

"Your daddy went to the Amarillo bus station to look for you when it started snowing. Called Camp Lake store to see if anybody saw y'all leave. Nobody did. He's been driving up and down the road between here and Amarillo all evenin' lookin' for you."

"Don't know how I missed him. I came right down 66. Probably when I stopped to eat."

"Gray Boy get off all right?"

Jake nodded. "Yep." No need to upset her anymore than she already was.

Rance stomped his brogans inside the door and hung his hat and coat on a rack. Jake recognized the rack from the old house but could not remember where it had hung. Rance grinned at Jake again, and it made Jake feel warm. "Your mama tell you I been goin' up and down the road lookin' for you?"

"Yessir."

"Don't see how I missed you at the Amarillo bus station."

"Me neither."

Rance glanced at Mattie. Jake suspected that they knew Gray had left from Cooper and not Amarillo—knew that Jake had never been to the Amarillo bus station—that he had driven all the way alone. Rance shook his head as he stared at his brogans. "Your mama show you around yet?"

"Can't see anything." Jake was determined to continue his useless resistance against something that had already happened—to prove that he was right.

"I imagine we'll have to deal with that for a day or two. Where's my flashlight, Mattie?"

Rance took the lantern from the kitchen table and used it to nod toward the room Mattie had come from. "This is the living room." Jake resisted any expression of interest. Rance swept a Naugahyde couch and rocker with the lantern's dim light. "We got some new furniture." Brown saddles had been stitched in the middle of the couch and rocking chair backs. Half wagon wheels adorned both ends of the couch and both sides of the chair. Rance pointed the lantern toward a dark lamp. Jake ran his finger along a roping cowboy stitched into the lampshade and tried not to show his approval.

Mattie walked into a room off the living room's left. "This is your room, Jake."

Jake's eyes widened when he saw the bookcase headboard

instead of his old iron one. Mattie moved the sliding door
on one end. It stuck a little. He tried to ignore that the end
had already been bent and that it looked a lot like cardboard.
"They call these Hollywood bedroom suites. Bookcase
headboards. You can put your stuff in these little cases and
slide the door to."

Mattie had already placed Jake's books in the headboard
bookshelves—all four of them. His wooden saltshaker and
peppershaker made to look like tiny books sat beside the real
books. Tuck's bronzed boots were there, too. Jake placed his
mounted homerun baseball beside them and remembered
the biscuits still in his hand. "You got an empty jelly jar or
something with a lid?"

Mattie walked back into the kitchen and returned with a
Mason jar. Jake dropped the tin-foiled covered biscuits into
the jar and screwed the lid down tight. He placed the jar
beside Tuck's boots. Mattie did not ask. She switched on a
small reading lamp that Jake did not recognize. "Forgot about
the electricity being off. You can read at night now—right here
in your own bed instead of reading by that old naked bulb
hung from the ceiling like you did back home."

Jake knew he was being coddled—was ashamed that he
liked it. Mattie held the lantern over his matching dresser as
he opened each drawer. His clothes had been folded and
neatly placed inside. He gave up and smiled when he closed
the last drawer. "Looks like you already got me settled in."

"Come in here, Jake." Rance stood inside a small, narrow
room. "This old house was built before many people out here
had running water, but they added this bathroom later."

The room seemed like an outhouse attached to the house
as an afterthought, reminding Jake of the porch his father had
added to their old farmhouse at Klondike. The flushing
sound brought another smile. The shower made of galvanized
tin was primitive, but it sure beat a number-two washtub.
There was no tub. Jake smiled again as the commode refilled.

"That's nice. Sure would hate to have to run to the outhouse on a night like this."

It wasn't very funny, but their laughter gushed out as if held back for months. For the first time, Jake recognized the heavy guilt his parents felt for taking him out of school midway through his freshman year. There was no more need to show them how much he resented it.

They showed him their bedroom, with the same old bed and dresser, before moving back to the kitchen. They sat at the kitchen table and stared awkwardly across the lamp at each other, feeling trapped by the weather and afraid to speak about what they all feared. They were a new family now—reduced from six to three, and it made them feel like strangers. The conversation got clumsy after Jake told them about the trip. They told him that the previous renters had just walked away from the place. Something about health problems and a rattlesnake bite. He opened the door to the same old Frigidaire. "Dang. This thing is full."

Mattie smiled and nodded toward the still-dark big room where Jake had entered the house. "The people who leased this place before us sold us their freezer and a whole beef, too. It's almost forty miles to the nearest grocery store, and no telling when you can get snowed in out here." She tried to make it sound exciting.

Jake walked into the dark room and ran his hand along the horizontal white freezer. "What is this room?"

Rance followed him and shined his flashlight around. The room was filled with odds and ends that Mattie had not found a place for. "I think they used it for sort of a cook shack—a big room to eat in. One of the neighbors told us there used to be a big harvest table in here where farm and ranch hands would sit down to eat in the old days. I think they cooked outside on an open fire."

Jake liked that thought. "Really?"

"Said they used to gather cattle here after winter wheat

grazin'. They'd drive `em to loadin' pens south of here. I imagine lots of cowboys have sat around this room in its day."

"How old is this house?"

Mattie walked in to stand in the dark. "Not as old as the one back home. Nothing out here is very old. Sixty or seventy years ago, this country was mostly just Comanches and a few cattlemen. A lot of the pioneers that settled this country are still here. I imagine this house was built in the late thirties or early forties."

Jake was tired all of a sudden. He stretched and yawned. "That shower got hot water?"

Rance handed him the flashlight. "You bet. Heater runs on gas."

Jake closed the door to his room—something he had not been able to do in the old house. He liked the privacy. He took the second shower of his life and looked for clean underwear. Mattie had laid out a pair of new flannel pajamas on his bed. He never slept in pajamas, but the room was already cold. The closed door had blocked the heat from the Dearborn in the living room. Jake slipped on the pajama bottoms and looked out the window beside his bed. Moonlit snow. Ice on the windows. He crawled in and pulled up the covers. They seemed warm. Jake ran his hand along the cover and felt the wires of his first electric blanket. The electricity had not been off long enough for it to cool.

He put his hands behind his head and stared at the ceiling. The house was not as drafty as the old one. Seemed to smell better, too. No mildew; no rat pee; no rats running along the ceiling or scratching the walls. But he still felt strange ... lost ... adrift. Maybe if he had made the trip with his parents ... but meeting them here, in a strange place, made it all different somehow. Tuck was dead, Gray Boy was gone to the Marines, and Trish was married. His sister and brothers had been part of Jake's identity. He used them to relate to his parents. Their shared heritage in Klondike and Delta County had bound them together. Now, that was gone, too. Jake felt as if he had not seen Rance and Mattie for a long time, and they had changed. What was it that made them seem like strangers? Jake tried to put aside his own selfishness and see things from their point of view. Then he knew. They were strangers here and afraid, just like him.

4 Jake put his feet on the cold vinyl-covered floor and pulled on the flannel pajama tops before walking to the bathroom. He was surprised that his room was not much colder than it had been when he went to bed. Mattie must have left the stove on by accident. Daylight allowed a closer inspection. He stared at himself in the medicine cabinet mirror, ran his finger along the dark spots in the sink. The commode was nice and white, looked almost new. He ran a brush through his flattop and picked up a toothbrush. Brushing teeth inside instead of on the porch was going to be nice. Store-bought Pepsodent had replaced his usual baking soda and salt. He turned the faucet to wet his toothbrush. Nothing. He put both hands on the sink and stared at himself in the mirror. "Damn. Last night was just a dream. We ain't really got running water."

"Who you talking to in there?" Mattie poked her head inside his bedroom. You need to use the bathroom, you'll have to go outside."

Jake grimaced, considering himself long past the age when his mother should be discussing his bathroom habits. "What's the matter with the water?"

"Frozen, but Rance says he knows how to fix it. You need to hurry up and help him before breakfast."

Coddling was over. He yawned and looked out his bedroom window as he buttoned his Levis. A movement caught his attention and he wiped away the fog on the ice-covered window. Sunlight reflecting off the snow and ice gave Jake a prismatic, uncertain view, but he thought he saw a man standing beside the windmill stock tank. Still disoriented in this new environment, he rubbed his eyes and looked again. The man was naked from the waist up and was breaking the ice on the water tank with a sledgehammer. Jake watched as the man pulled off his boots, pants and underwear. He hung them on a post with his shirt and stepped into the ice water. Jake rubbed the window again, not believing his eyes. The man dropped underwater and came up, shaking water from his dark hair. Droplets sparkled in the morning sun as they flew from his hair and skidded across the ice. He stepped out of the tank, shook himself like a wet dog, and put his clothes back on.

Jake dressed and walked into the living room. The floor was soft and warm from the Dearborn heater. He reached down and ran his hand across brown carpet. A wooden-board-pattern made the carpet look like a plank floor. Jake liked it. The house walls were sheetrock painted the color of brown chicken eggs. The walls looked warmer than the warped pine boards of their old house. Mattie had laid his wool work coat, a pair of new lined gloves, and his dirty dairy cap on the floor beside the stove. Their warmth soothed him as he walked through his parents' bedroom and stepped outside.

Sun reflecting off the snow blinded him at first. He waded snow to the side of the house to get a better look at the man, but there was no sign of him. Feeling watched, Jake stepped behind the largest butane tank he had ever seen and melted a little spot in the snow. He put a gloved hand over his eyes and saw Rance walking toward a small house under the windmill with a five-gallon bucket. The air was light, clear, and sharp and Jake felt a momentary sense of elation. Tuck was probably whispering in his ear. He and Tuck had played all day in snow not half this deep a short time before Tuck died.

Snow was up to Rance's knees, and the bucket was leaving a trail in it. "Come over to the well house, Jake, and we'll thaw out the water."

Jake followed his daddy into a tall cinderblock building beside the windmill. A water tank sat atop the building with a pipe leading from the windmill. Jake's elation evaporated when he stepped inside. The walls and floor were black and smelled of wet soot and diesel. Rance set the bucket of diesel on the floor and struck a match. "Stand back a little, Jake. This will be your job next time." Rance dropped the match into the diesel. A small flame, then black smoke boiled up from the bucket.

Jake watched the smoke rise and drift through a small window next to the roofline. "What is that? What's it supposed to do?"

"Diesel. Don't flame up like gasoline. It'll warm up this little building and thaw out the pipes that supply water to the house." Rance pointed to a water pipe poking through a wall. "By the time we're though with breakfast, we'll have running water."

Jake could not believe they were going to walk off and leave a fire going inside the building. "You mean the people that lived here before had to do this every time it got below freezing?" It seemed dumb to Jake. "I need to stay here and watch it?"

"Nothing to catch on fire in here. Come on. Let's eat. We got lots of work to do." Lots of work sounded familiar to Jake, but depressing.

Jake hung back. "You go ahead. I just want to look at

where I live for a little bit." He stepped on the trailer fender, pulled himself up, and looked around. The house had been painted at least once, probably when it was built. Some white paint was left, but the flakes shook in the wind, trying to turn loose. The white looked dull compared to the snow. Mixed with the unpainted parts of the boards, it all blended into a motley gray thing, the color of nothing—the color of his new life. The rectangular house appeared as an afterthought, an intrusion that tried not to be noticed by the field crops and pasture surrounding it. He could see no path or walkway to the front of the house. The hut Jake had entered last night hid the back door. Mattie had called it the dirty-boots-hut. Jake thought it looked like a good places for possums to hide— or a rattlesnake. There were no porches.

A lonesome mesquite stood stubbornly between the road and the house, as if it had survived by its own wits, unwanted and uncared for by previous occupants of this desolate place. Jake thought of the chinaberry tree in the side yard at their old home—the grass under it worn down from many family sittings under its shade. He could not see why anyone would want to sit in the dirt under that mesquite and suffer through dust clouds brought by every passing car in the summer. The old house had been old, unpainted, and drafty, but Jake missed it.

He looked west across the sand in a long equipment yard at a building that could have been a garage or shop—maybe both. It looked better than the house. The sides had been plastered with something that was probably stucco, but it looked like leftover concrete. Sliding garage doors faced the large yard between the house and the shop. He wondered why his father had not parked the car inside. A couple of fuel tanks stood at one end, snow up to their hoses. Jake made a mental note to tell his buddies about the tall snowdrifts, and then wondered if he would ever see them again, or if they would care. A snow-covered tractor sat beside the tanks. Jake could not tell what kind it was, only that it was bigger than anything they had ever owned. Their old Case sat beside the big tractor, looking like a child's tricycle.

As he looked up and north through the diesel smoke coming from the well house, he read Aermotor-Chicago on the windmill tail. Seemed strange to Jake that something way out here in the Panhandle of Texas would be made in Chicago. Probably had something to do with Route 66. Papa Griff had said that Chicago was where the road began. The big stock tank's frozen top, except for the broken spot where the man had bathed, reflected the morning sun's rays. A few yards farther north, Jake saw a barn with a corral. Probably where Scar was all snug and warm. Also probably where the man had disappeared.

Jake felt better. Maybe some cattle went with the stock tank and corral. Creosote crossties made a sturdy corral fence that contrasted with the barbwire lots back home. A long alley led to a chute with a headgate in one corner. The loading ramp was higher than any Jake had ever seen. Good for loading cattle into eighteen-wheelers, he figured. He saw himself horseback, herding cattle into that alley. Another pen without corners had been built just west of the barn. Old tires had been stacked on light pole posts and spread along the rails of this round pen. Jake figured it was for breaking wild horses.

The barn grabbed him. It had a loft like their old hay barn, but this one had a window—a real glass one, not just an opening for loading hay. The red paint on the barn had faded to a comfortable patina that looked like something out of a western picture show to Jake. He forgot about breakfast, pulled down a strand of barbed wire to cross the yard fence and look in the loft. Mattie's call for breakfast stopped him.

5 "What kinda tractor is that?" Jake made an ambiguous nod toward the west window as he stared at the bacon-grease eggs in his plate. The eggs held no interest for him and the tractor only slightly more.

"W-9. The Super M is inside the shop. It's got a few problems." Rance poured some ribbon-cane syrup on his barely-cooked biscuits.

"Is Scar in the red barn?" Jake cut off a slice of butter from the oval mold and slipped it between the halves of a brown biscuit. He wondered how his mother had managed to come up with churned butter without a cow.

"Yep. There's a nice little stall in there. Good feed room, too. Rat-proof. Too much trouble to stall a horse all the time, but it's a good place for Scar to sleep when it's wet or cold."

Jake pushed around the eggs, chased red-eye gravy around the plate with his biscuit before taking the last bite. He wanted to give his father every chance to mention the man who bathed in ice water. "Guess I'll go find that feed room and give Scar a little oats. Any hay in that loft?"

"No hay in the loft. String stays there when he's between

jobs."

"String?"

Rance smiled. "Harvey Stringfellow. Everybody calls him String. You'll see why when you meet him."

"Is he out there now?"

"Was yesterday. Can't keep up with his comin's and goin's. If he's not there now, he won't be gone long. He's lookin' after the bank's cattle this winter. In the spring, he generally wanders up to some of the spreads along the Canadian River to work roundup. Usually stays for shippin' in the fall, then winters somewhere around here."

Jake looked toward his mother to see if she understood what his father had said. He knew that he sure didn't. Mattie laughed. "Didn't take your daddy long to take on Panhandle talk, did it?"

Jake's confusion showed. "Why's he staying in our barn?"

Rance saucered-and-blowed his coffee. "It's not our barn. We just get the use of the barn and the fenced twenty acres beside it in exchange for lookin' out for things when String ain't here. Bank said we could let a few of our stock graze the pasture as long as there's plenty of grass to go around."

Jake brightened. "We got stock?"

Rance pulled the makin's from his overalls pocket and began to roll a cigarette. "Bout the only stock we got now is your horse. Shame to let ten sections of land go to waste, though. If we bring in some good wheat in the spring, I plan on borrowin' some more money and buyin' a few cattle to run with the bank's."

Jake made the calculations in his head. "Ten sections is 6,400 acres. Right? How many cows are they runnin'?"

"String says they just have about fifty head right now. Bank's not really in the cattle business. They just repossessed the land and the cattle from the people who lived here before we did."

"How come the bank didn't take the whole place?"

Rance stood and reached for his hat. He looked at Mattie as he answered. "Cause we took the farm land."

Jake followed his father outside. "So our place stops right outside the yard?"

Rance nodded. "This little narrow strip where the house and shop sits is our home. He pointed a little south and a lot west. "See that winter wheat over there? We farm the half section that starts right there and another section about six miles up the road and to the south. They call the other place Section Nine."

"Whoa. Just under a thousand acres." Jake jerked his thumb toward the red barn. "Am I gonna bother String if I go feed my horse?"

"Guarantee he ain't in the loft. When it's daylight, String is outside."

"Yeah. He's an outside type of man, for sure. I saw him taking a bath in that tank a while ago."

Rance laughed as Jake walked through a wooden gate in the north fence. A small length of rope made into a loop held the gate to a set-post. Jake stepped through the gate, replaced the loop, and started toward the barn. The tank-bather was leading Scar into the corral. The man used his hand to brush hay off the horse's back, then ran his hand along Scar's front leg before lifting his hoof. Jake stood on a rail and watched.

"Your horse?" String spoke without turning or looking up. He was using a pocketknife to peel a small curl off Scar's hoof.

"Yep. Got him for my birthday a few years back." Jake was a little irritated at the liberties the man was taking with his horse—not to mention that he had stripped naked where his mother might have seen him.

String stood, folded the knife blade, and put it back into his pocket. He was stooped a little, but not much. Standing straight, he would have probably been nearly six feet. From the side, he looked as thin as a slice of bacon. Not even as thick as Jake. A worn-out dusty black hat covered a thick head of hair that looked to be still wet. Jake guessed the hair to be red when dry. The rest of him had that red-complected look. "I was just peeling a little hang-nail off of him. Might have turned into a problem later. Hope it was all right with you to turn him out. He looked like the type to hold his water in tight places."

Jake smiled. "He is. Won't pee in a trailer. He never had a stall before, so I guess he felt the same way about it."

"The way I see it, a horse that won't make water where he sleeps is pretty smart. He's kinda got that Mustang look. Used to own a horse that favored yours a lot. He was about as tough and quick as any I ever owned. Name's Harvey Stringfellow. You must be Jake."

Jake climbed down and shook the offered hand. "Yessir." Jake stared at the man's boots. One pants leg hung in a boot top revealing soft-yellow leather tops like his grandfather wore. The vamps were muddy brown.

"Rance tells me you may have your granddaddy's way with horses."

Jake was taken aback. Measuring up to his father or grandfather in at least one thing had always been his dream. "Guess I'm a few years away from that. You know Papa Griff?" Jake was surprised. It seemed as if the stories his grandfather had told of the Panhandle had been just that—stories. He guessed String to be in his late thirties, too young to have been friends with his grandfather in those early days.

"Mostly through my daddy, but I remember him pretty good. That old man hung up his spurs yet?"

Jake's mind went back to the night before last. Sleeping on a pallet beside his grandfather's bed, moonlight had captured Griff's spurs hanging on the wall of his bedroom in town. "He had to move to town when we sold the place, or at least that's what my aunts wanted him to do. He don't even own a horse right now. No car, either."

String rolled a piece of straw between his fingers and stared at the ground. "Hate to hear that. Liked to watch Griff set a horse. He taught me a thing or two when I was a boy. I've seen him rope lots of steers and climb lots of windmills. He used to grease that one right over there."

Jake looked at the windmill with new interest. "Papa lived here?"

"No, but during the thirties, when times got tough, he worked as a range rider sometimes."

"Range rider?" Jake had visions of a lone cowboy, riding fences, gathering strays, and fighting rustlers.

"Yep. When cattle work got scarce, he'd hook up with a driller or a windmiller and take up ridin' from ranch to ranch, a beer can full of grease tied to his saddle, climbin' and greasin' windmills. I was just a boy, but I remember my daddy tellin' about the time he ran into a big wasp nest out on the Matador. Most men would've fell fightin' `em off, but he just let `em sting till he could get his hat off and beat `em off with one free hand. He went ahead and finished the greasin' before he came down."

"Where'd they sting him?"

"Wasps seem to head right for your face and eyes. That's why they've killed more than a few range riders."

"From the bites?"

"Usually from falling off a windmill tower." String chuckled under his breath. "Your granddaddy's face was pretty swoll-up. Eyes were slits. My daddy had a bottle of cheap whiskey in his saddlebags. Griff just took a couple of hits off that old bottle, rolled out his bedroll, and went right to sleep. Daddy drank the rest of the bottle ... out of pure sympathy, he said."

"I never heard that story."

"I probably shouldn't have mentioned about the whiskey and all." String slapped his leg like Jake often did to punish himself for doing something he was sorry for. "Your granddaddy was a top hand. He teach you how to rope?"

"Not really. We had mostly dairy cattle, and Daddy wouldn't let us rope ˋem for practice. Said it got the calves all stirred up. Didn't have a ropin' pen to rope stocker cattle." Jake did not want to mention that he had roped from a horse in front of this real cowboy.

A sorrel horse with a blaze face ambled out and stuck his head under String's arm. His mane was roached, and his tail had been trimmed to his hocks. He stood over fifteen hands, a few inches taller than Scar. Jake felt his heart sink as he made the comparison between the two horses. Scar's long black mane, tail, and forelock made him look like a Shetland pony beside the big, sleek sorrel. String ran a thumb between the big horse's eyes down to his muzzle and nodded toward Scar. "Well, looks like you got the horse for it, and there's more'n a few ropin' pens out here. I have been known to rope out of this one. Takes two men ˋcause you got to chase ˋem in the pasture. You goin' to school at Adrian?" The sorrel followed String back toward the barn like a puppy.

Jake heard the big Oldsmobile 98 float into the yard. He turned to watch as he answered. "Hereford, I think. I have to finish an ag course that they don't have in Adrian. What's your horse's name?"

String grinned. "Pink. Yours?

Jake grinned. "Scar."

"I recall an old radio show that had a horse named Scar."

"Doc Sixgun. That's where I got the name."

JD and Bess Boggs were already out of the car. Bess, one of Mattie's eight sisters, headed for the house and JD, dressed in an expensive Stetson and kangaroo boots that Jake figured to be custom made, walked toward the shop and Rance. Bob Lee, their son, waved once as he danced his way through the snow toward Jake and Sting. Jake's cousin had always carried twenty or thirty pounds of extra weight, but it was evenly distributed. Seven years older than Jake, Bob Lee had been more Gray Boy's friend than his, but his mere presence was usually enough to make Jake laugh. Bob Lee found something funny in almost everything.

He grabbed Jake's belt and tugged as if to pull him off his perch on the fence rail. "Jaker Ridge." Bob Lee's voice echoed across the flat, snow-covered prairie. It was neither high nor low; it just carried through the light air easily. "How you like Panhandle weather so far? You probably ain't ever seen this much snow."

String came out with a saddle under one arm and a blanket in his hand. He slowed when he saw Bob Lee nimbly take the fence rail beside Jake. "Well, look what the dogs drug up that the cats wouldn't have."

Bob Lee grinned, showing perfect white teeth and a smile that seemed to envelop his whole body. He was hatless as usual, showing off his wavy, corn silk hair. "String. How's things in the skinny world?"

"Looks like you ought to consider a visit there." String rubbed the horse's back with the blanket, shook it and put in on. "Surprised to see your white ass out of bed this time of day."

Bob Lee chuckled. "Man works late, he deserves a little extra shut-eye on some mornin's." He pointed toward the hole in the ice that was starting to crust over again. "You been bathin' with the goldfish again? They gonna think your goober is bait one of these days and bite it plumb off."

"Not a chance. Can't find it myself on mornings this cold. Fish sure as hell can't.'"

Jake was too curious not to ask. "Why are there goldfish in that water tank?"

"They keep the water from gettin' scummy." Bob Lee answered.

"Do I need to feed `em?"

"Hell, no. Don't feed `em. Defeats the purpose. We

want `em hungry enough to eat what the cows drop out of their mouths and off their noses."

String dropped a hand through the thin crust of ice and splashed a little water toward Bob Lee. "Chasin' whores in Amarillo passin' for work these days? Me and Jake was just passin' the time talkin' about his school when we was rudely interrupted. I was about to tell Jake that Adrian's got their own ropin' pen and rodeo team." String looked at Jake, but nodded toward his cousin. "I went to school there. Bob Lee, here, can probably tell you more about Hereford."

Bob Lee shook his head. "String is referring to the fact that I just got out of there by the skin of my teeth."

String laughed out loud. "Skin of your teeth, my ass. They threw your sorry butt out because they got tired of you." He rested both arms on the horse's back. "What do you think, Jake, about a boy lets his parents dress up for graduation and take him to town for the ceremonies before he tells `em he ain't gonna make that walk across the stage."

Jake had already heard the story. Bob Lee stories were a constant source of amusement and sorrow for Mattie and her sisters.

String's actions were so effortless, it seemed that the big sorrel dressed himself in blanket, saddle, breast harness, and bridle. He mounted and made the horse side-pass toward them as they sat on the fence. He pulled his hat brim toward Jake. "Hereford, they say, is one of the best schools in the state. Tough, too. I wish you good luck." String rode away before Jake could ask another question. Jake thought of Papa Griff as he watched him take his leave.

They sat around the kitchen table, drinking coffee and smoking cigarettes, Rance plainly ill at ease with the interruption to his workday. It was not his practice to sit in the house in the middle of the day, but he could not be rude to his company. JD and Bess had been responsible for getting them the lease on the farm. JD still farmed and ranched several sections and had progressed into grain storage and shipment. He propped one boot across his knee, and Jake tried to examine the boots without being noticed. They seemed to be made out of one piece of soft, orange leather with no visible line between the uppers and the vamps. JD noticed Jake's interest in his boots. "Had those made in Amarillo last summer. Your daddy tell you what I got over at my place?"

"No sir." Jake looked toward his father. Rance stared at his coffee cup.

"A cotton patch."

Jake did not know what he was expected to say. "Thought y'all didn't raise cotton out here."

"Don't usually. I just planted some to prove I could. Need somebody to harvest it. "

Jake kept his silence. JD put both elbows on the table and leaned toward him. "Been saving that cotton since I found out you were coming. You and your brother were one hell of a pair at pickin' cotton as I recall."

Jake felt all eyes on him and his face turning red. Getting away from cotton patches had been the single bright spot in leaving East Texas. Pulling an entire cotton patch alone seemed like cruel punishment.

JD saw the anger and frustration in Jake's eyes. "I'll pay you five dollars a hundred. I figure there's a thousand pounds in the patch."

That was more than twice what Jake had ever earned in the cotton patch. With everyone staring, Jake felt like the butt of a joke and could not make the mental calculations. He looked to Rance for help.

"It's up to you, Jake. The fifty bucks will be yours to keep. I figure you can pull the whole patch in about five good days."

Fifty bucks—five days. He knew he would shame his parents if he declined. Before he could say yes, JD pulled a hundred out of his pocket and slid it across the table to Jake. "You're driving a hard bargain, Jake. Tell you what, I need that cotton out of there. Should have been gone months ago. You pick up that hundred, and we have a deal."

Jake smiled and slipped the hundred into his pocket. They all laughed.

Bess reached across the table and patted Jake's hand. "So you're going to Hereford." She had the same hair and facial features as Mattie, but she looked as if she was hiding some physical pain.

Jake nodded and dreaded what was sure to come.

"Well, I know it's tough to change schools, but you'll do just fine."

Bob Lee shifted his bulk in a chair that was too small. "I already told Uncle Rance and Aunt Mattie not to be too hard on him. Hereford ain't like that Podunk school he's been goin' to. Straight A's there will be more like B's and C's here."

Bob Lee's words scared Jake, but he was grateful for the lowered expectations. Mattie and Rance visibly stiffened and Bob Lee noticed. He looked toward Rance at the end of the table. "Now Unc, I ain't sayin' Jake ain't smart. Just don't be too hard on him for awhile."

Rance gave a wincing smile. JD stood and stared a hole in his son. "Just cause your sorry ass was too lazy to graduate don't mean other boys can't. Let's go, Bess. This boy been settin' on his ass too long. We got work to do."

6 Working in the shop beside his father brought mixed feelings for Jake. It was almost like working outside without being in the cold or rain. The shop smelled of oil, grease, diesel, and gasoline. Jake did not particularly like the smells, but the big propane stove, the concrete floor, and dry air made it seem snug—especially when he compared it to the dairy barn back home. Jake had forced himself to learn how to change oil, filters, and spark plugs, even fix flats, but the workings of engines remained mysteries that made him feel stupid. Rance and Gray usually swapped opinions, even argued about what was wrong and how to repair it. Jake had no opinions; he just handed his daddy the tools he needed.

He did like the fact that they now had three tractors, a grain truck, and a '49 GMC pickup purchased from the bank when they had leased the farm. He was a little disillusioned when Rance told him that they all needed work—some of it major. Still, the shop's warmth made Jake feel secure in his new insecure world. A place to hide—a temporary respite from what he knew was ahead.

It had warmed up some, but snow was still on the ground and drifted against fencerows on the first day that they did not go to the shop. Jake was almost numb with sadness and fear as he dressed for his first day at Hereford High School. A sty had almost closed his right eye and turned the lid an angry red overnight. Jake saw it as a bad sign on a worse day. Fearing that his voice would break, he avoided speaking to either of his parents. They respected his emotions and kept their distance.

As he stepped into the pickup with his father, the Adrian bus passed less than thirty feet from the front door of their house. Frustration showed on Jake's face as he watched the bus pass. Eight miles from the house, down dirt roads that made turns at sharp angles instead of curving roads that followed creek beds or timberlines like Jake was used to, Rance finally stopped the truck. "They say this is where the bus will pick you up every morning."\

"You gonna have to drive me all this way every day?"

"Don't see a way around it. We live in Adrian's district, not Hereford's."

Jake stared out the window, anger and resentment welling. Even though he could see where the earth met the sky across the flat prairie, he was pretty sure he could not find his way back to the house without help. The land was divided into blocks here, not like Delta County, where boundary lines had often been decided decades before by the placement of a bois d'arc post or wild trees that had grown along a meandering creek or river. There were plenty of landmarks there to tell where you were. Here, it all looked the same—big square patches of farmland without markers. The wind whistled as it blew hard enough to move some of the snow piled up against the fences. The road was already dry enough for particles of dust to cling to the once-pristine snow. The dirty snow reminded Jake of how this move had dirtied up his life. "How will I get home?"

Rance turned to stare at Jake. "The same way you got here, Jake. Your mother or I will pick you up."

"Seems like a lot of trouble." Jake put his nose against the side window. "What would you say about me just quittin' school? I could help you on the farm. Don't see how you can farm that much land by yourself."

Rance stared straight ahead. The small lines in his forehead disappeared and his ears moved a little as he tightened his scalp and clenched his jaw. "Don't talk stupid, Jake. You're good in school and you're gonna finish. I can make out till you get home to help. Your mother can drive a tractor if we need her to." There was a long silence before he spoke again. "Besides, farming here is not the same as it was back home. These big tractors cover a lot more ground a lot quicker."

"I still have a thousand pounds of cotton to pick." The hundred was more money than Jake had ever had, but the cotton patch had grown to plantation size in his head. Another pickup stopped at the dirt road intersection. Two boys stepped out, and the driver waved at Rance as he drove away. Jake stared at the two boys as they braced themselves against the wind. "Who's that?"

"That was Leland Wells drivin' off. Expect those are his boys. Leland's the one that told me where to meet the bus. His boys have to do the same thing you're doin'."

"Guess if they can stand in the cold, I can too. No use in you waitin' around." Jake stepped out and walked toward the boys. Rance watched until Jake turned back to look at him. He nodded at Jake and lifted his index finger from the wheel before he pulled away.

Jake felt abandoned. He hunched his shoulders and put his hands in his Levis as he approached the boys. He wished for something heavier than the Levi jacket, but thought his wool coat looked stupid. Rance had made a mistake—these boys were definitely not brothers. The older one was dark with a wide face and straight, coarse black hair like Rance's. His shoulders were broad and squared-off, and his body tapered down to a slim waist and big legs. The younger boy came to the other one's shoulders, was freckled-faced and had red hair. His shoulders sloped, and a band the size of a bicycle inner tube hung above his waist and spilled slightly over the waist of his Levis.

"Hidy. I'm Jake Rivers." Jake's meek greeting could barely be heard above the wind. He made a mental note to stop saying hidy. It sounded like hick or baby talk. From now on, he would say hi or hey or hello.

The big boy inspected Jake, focusing on his loafers and white socks. The stare made Jake's ankles cold. The boy's wide, dark face finally broke into a half-grin. Jake noticed small caramel-colored spots on his teeth. "Nocona Wells. This is Jelly."

"Nice to meet you." Jake turned to the smaller boy. "Jelly who?"

The smaller boy adjusted the black glasses on his nose. "Jerry Wells, stupid. What's wrong with your eye?" More brown spots on his teeth.

The smile disappeared from Jake's face, and he squared off in front of the red-faced boy. "Is it Jerry or Jelly?"

"Shut up, Jelly." The bigger boy turned to Jake. "He thinks you're supposed to know we're brothers because we both catch the bus here. His name is Jerry, but you can see why we call him Jelly."

"He saw us both get out of the same pickup." Jelly glared at Nocona.

"I told you to shut up, piss-ant. Just because we got out of the same pickup don't mean we're brothers."

Jake relaxed a little as he took a liking to Nocona. "Y'all catch the bus here every day?"

"We do now. Used to drive to school till my daddy took my car keys."

"You got a car?"

"Yep."

Jelly interrupted. "It's a '55 Chevy. Cherry red with red and white rolled and pleated upholstery."

Jake took a closer look at the boys. Both were dressed in boots that looked expensive. Both wore coats that looked like colorful Indian blankets. Their shirts had long flowing yokes in the front with pearl snaps. He ignored Jelly and spoke to Nocona. "How old are you?"

"Sixteen. I'm a sophomore."

Jake saw the bus approaching long before he heard it. "Why'd your daddy take the keys?"

Nocona's smile grew wider as he stepped through the bus door. "Found some beer in the trunk."

The bus was half empty. Not wanting to appear as a new kid alone, Jake stayed close to Nocona, examining the faces on the bus as he made his way down the aisle. Farm kids mostly, better dressed than most of the kids who rode the bus back home. The thin air carried the smell of hair oil, soap, and breakfast. Nocona stopped near the back and started to sit as Jelly elbowed his way into a window seat beside him. Nocona looked at Jake and shook his head. Jake took the seat just behind them and across the aisle, wishing for Gray Boy. He would never have sat beside him, but he had not realized how comforting it was to have a big brother close by.

From behind, he studied Nocona. There was something about him that Jake could not figure. Nocona's look was almost as handsome as his own brother's, but menacing. His face was broad, almost too broad, as was his mouth. He clinched his teeth when he smiled. The smile was engaging, intimidating, and irreverent. Nocona Wells looked a little like a thug, but he was perfectly groomed and smelled of cologne and talcum powder. When the morning sun came through the bus window and glazed the side of Nocona's face, Jake knew. Straight, coarse black hair and Bo Creekwater's facial features—Nocona was an Indian—probably full blood. But how could a full-blood Indian have a brother like Jelly?

45

Nocona told him how to find the principal's office and walked away as soon as they stepped off the bus. Jake stared at the huge brick buildings and large campus. At Klondike, he had known the schoolyard, the gym, and all of the classrooms by heart—every corner and crevice. He knew every teacher and every member of their families. All of his classes had been in the same room. Here, he wondered if he could find his way to classes in different rooms. If it had not been forty miles, he would have walked home. The principal scolded Jake for being late to pick up his schedule and told him he would have to hurry to avoid being late for his first class. Jake disliked the man before he opened his mouth. Afterward, he hated him.

He scrambled through the day, always on the verge of throwing up or crying. At the last period, a public address system startled him. The hated principal announced that the entire high school would gather in the auditorium for general assembly before going home. He followed the crowd to the auditorium. At Klondike, kids gathered in the gym on such occasions. Students there stood in their socks on the hardwood floor to hear presentations from the stage beside the basketball court. Hereford's auditorium was like the biggest picture show Jake had ever seen.

One of the last to enter, he selected an empty row and an aisle seat. He was still alone on the row when the principal started to speak from the stage down front. The principal paused and frowned as the front door opened and slammed against the wall. A herd of boys stampeded down the aisle and piled over Jake. Most of them stepped on his shoes, smiling those mottled-tooth smiles that Jake had noticed all day. They took all the remaining seats on Jake's row. The last boy, tall and blond with dark eyelashes, stood in the aisle beside Jake. His hair was wet. He tapped Jake on the shoulder. "You're in my seat, Freshman."

Jake's face flushed. Was freshman written all over his

face? New kid? The auditorium grew quiet as the principal
stopped his talk, and Jake felt eyes on him as he looked up at
the boy. "We got assigned seats in here?"

"Freshmen don't. I do, and you're in it." No mottled
teeth on this kid as he smiled down at Jake.

"And you are?"

"You don't get to ask, Sonny Boy, but you'll hear soon
enough that you pissed off Mike Drager. Now move."

Jake looked in front and back and across the aisle. All
the seats were taken. Eyes full of pity and amusement stared
back at him. As he stood and turned to go to the back of
the auditorium he felt a hand push him, and he stumbled
and fell to one knee. Mike Drager was snickering. Jake felt
himself shriveling in front of the whole school. He did not
want this, but all of his choices had been taken away. Gray
Boy whispered in his ear and Jake's pent-up anger and shame
exploded. He turned and ran toward the boy.

He hit him in the chest with his shoulder, and they fell
down in the aisle. Jake remembered what his father and
brother had told him. When you have to fight a big kid, hit
first and keep hitting. Jake came up on top and hit the boy
square in the face. Pain shot through his knuckles all the way
to his elbow. Jake felt some satisfaction as blood oozed from
the boy's nose. Jake's deep despair welled up in his eyes as
he felt the whole school against him. He drew back to hit
the kid with his other hand. Before he could swing, Drager's
leg caught Jake's outstretched arm and rolled him off. Their
positions reversed before Jake knew what was happening.
He felt two knees in his chest. The air left his lungs as a fist
glanced off his cheek and his nose and across the sty on his
eyelid.

Jake saw the principal shouting above him, but the ringing
in his ears was too loud to hear what he was saying. He knew
that the man he intensely disliked had just deflected the blow
that would have broken his nose. The big man pulled Drager

to his feet and held him while Jake struggled to stand, gasping for air. Harsh but pitiful sounds from his throat echoed through the auditorium, shattering the hush that had fallen. He had never known such humiliation.

The principal told Drager to sit in the seat Jake had left empty and guided Jake to a seat in the back. He put a forefinger in Jake's chest. "I'll see you in my office first thing in the morning. Be there an hour before the first class begins." Jake did not look up. Shrinking with each terrible minute, he did not hear anything that was said during the orientation session. Staring at the floor, he sensed that the session was over only when other kids started filing out. He joined the crowd and made his way to the exit.

Feeling something rise in his throat, he looked for a bathroom. As he stepped out into the cold air, his nausea eased. Through the crowd, he saw school buses and made his way toward them. An elbow shot out and stung his ribs as a foot pushed between his own. Jake stumbled and fell into a rose garden beside the sidewalk. His face stung from thorn scratches when he jumped up. When he touched his cheek, his fingers came back streaked with blood.

7 By the time Jake spotted Jelly Wells laughing and waving at him through the bus window, the bus was already leaving. Chasing it down and banging on the door brought a fitting close to the worst day of school in his life. He felt only slightly better as he saw a grinning Nocona Wells beckon to him from the back of the bus. Jake plopped down beside him and took a deep breath.

"You get those scratches from Snake Drager?"

Jake took out a handkerchief and wiped at the blood. "Fell into some rose bushes by the auditorium door."

"Fell or pushed?"

"Tripped and pushed."

"How do you like good old Hereford High School so far?"

Jake shook his head. "Why do you go here? Don't you live in the Adrian district like I do?"

"I was wondering the same thing about you."

"I have to go here to finish out half a year in Ag ... if I can make it. I want to quit, but I'd have to run away from home to get that done."

"I go here because my parents think bigger is better. I got lots of friends that go to Adrian, though. I'm going next year, whether they like it or not. They don't like it, I **will** leave home."

Jake felt better. Nocona had made up his mind. He was going to Adrian, too. He could stand Hereford if he knew there was an end to it in five months. Misery loved company, and he seemed to have company in Nocona.

Nocona poked him in the ribs with his elbow. "What made you decide to take on Mr. Tough Guy on the first day?"

Jake thought he heard a hint of admiration in Nocona's voice. "Who was he?"

Nocona lowered his voice. "Mike Drager. Bad news for you is, he'd be on this bus right now if he wasn't having basketball practice or something."

"He rides the same bus we do? Great." Jake let that additional burden settle on his shoulders before choking out a reply. "Didn't figure him for a country kid."

"Just about everybody around here is a farmer. His daddy's one of the biggest farmers in Deaf Smith County."

"Why'd you call him Snake, and why are we whispering?"

Nocona chuckled. He pointed to a girl in the bench seat just in front of theirs. "Ask her why they call him Snake."

Jake hesitated. Nocona gave an encouraging nod toward the girl. "Go ahead."

Jake did not want to, but he was afraid to let Nocona know he was too bashful. He lightly touched the girl's sweater-covered shoulder, and she turned to face him. Jake found her attractive. She had dark brown hair with eyes to match, and they twinkled. Her mouth curved into a bashful smile as she waited for Jake to speak. "Hi. I'm Jake Rivers. Nocona here says you can tell me why they call Mike Drager, Snake."

The girl turned abruptly toward the front without answering. Jake caught a flicker of crimson on her cheek and neck as she turned. He looked at Nocona and held his palms up as he whispered, "What kinda trick you playin'?"

Nocona laughed out loud. Jake felt tricked and alone again. "What did you get me into?"

"Hell, you picked a fight with the captain of the school basketball team today. What are you worried about his sister for?"

"He's captain of the basketball team? That's his sister?"

"He's the school stud in just about every sport I can think of—and yes, that is his sister. Cute and nice, ain't she?"

Jake stared out the window as they approached the drop-off point. His mother was waiting in the '55 Ford. She had already moved to the passenger side of the seat. He was relieved his daddy had not come. He needed to explode and could not do that in front of Rance. Jake slammed the door and stared straight ahead as he popped the clutch on the Ford. The tires spun as he backed out onto the road.

Mattie leaned forward. "What happened to your face?"

Jake looked in the rearview mirror. His face was scratched, the sty was turning his eyelid inside out, and his nose had turned a little blue. "You didn't see the sty when I left this mornin'?"

"I saw the sty, Jake, but what about those scratches and that bruise?"

Jake's voice dripped with sarcasm. "Got into a fight with the captain of the basketball team." Mattie took a deep breath and leaned back. She did not say anything until they were pulling into the yard. "It's not like you to fight, Jake. I don't want to go through what we did with Gray."

Jake cut the engine and pushed against the wheel with both hands. "I hate this school, Mama. It's ten times bigger than Klondike. I want to quit. Everybody says I can't even pass there, anyway."

Mattie's eyes flared. "Who says you can't pass?"

"You told me yourself that Aunt Bess said not to expect me to make good grades. Bob Lee said I would be lucky to pass. Even String said it was one of the toughest schools in the state."

"Yes, they all said that. You know what I said back? I said you most certainly would pass—that Klondike was a good school, and if you made straight A's there, you would do it again in Hereford. Schools in East Texas are just as good as the ones out here."

Jake slammed the steering wheel with his open palm, bringing back memories of how it hurt to hit Mike Drager in the nose. "Why would you go and say something like that? It's hard enough without your goin' and tellin' everybody I'm gonna make straight A's. Hell, Mother, I barely found my way to class today. Couldn't even find the right bus to get on to come home. I left all my books in a damn locker that I don't even know how to open."

"Watch your mouth, Jake. You're not too big for me to take a belt to."

Jake slammed the car door and walked into the house. He turned on the television, plopped down in the new rocker, and waited for his mother to come to comfort or confront him.

Mattie let him cool down before she turned off the television and sat on the footstool in front of him. She put a hand on each of Jake's knees. "Your daddy and me have put up with your sass because we feel sorry for you, but that's over now. Jake, I know it's tough. It's tough for me, too. I have no friends out here except my sister. But you know who has it toughest of all?" She did not wait for an answer. "It's your daddy. He has to learn a new way of farming. He has to overhaul almost every piece of equipment on the place. He has to fix fence, repair well motors and learn how to irrigate. He's farming ten times the amount of land we had back home with different crops, different equipment, different soil, and different weather."

Jake, bewildered, just nodded. "And without the only son who could really help him."

"But you know what he talks about every time we're alone? He wants to know just one thing. 'How's Jake makin' out? It's really tough on him and I hate it.' He doesn't complain about his many problems. Just ... 'how is Jake doin'?'"

For the third time in one terrible day, Jake's eyes began to fill against his will.

Mattie raised both hands and slapped him lightly on both knees as she cried with him. "He told me about your threatening to quit school this morning. You shocked him, but you don't fool me. You're just feelin' sorry for yourself, tryin' to get attention. You won't ever quit school. It's not in you. You'll finish high school just like you did grade school— with some of the best grades in your class."

Jake shook his head. "I don't think so, Mama."

"I know you better than you know yourself, Jake. You're having a tough time, but you never give up. It's not in you. You can't stand to be beat. Now you change your clothes and get on over to Section Nine in that old pickup. Your daddy wants you to bring him some oil for the Super M before you go pull bolls. It uses about five gallons a day, but he can't take time to fix it yet."

Clothes changed, Jake stepped out the back door. Mattie called him back. "Jake, your daddy needs you more than he's willing to admit. It's time to stop whining and start acting like a man."

Jake knew that his mother was wrong about his finishing high school with some of the best grades in his class. He had always made good grades because he was afraid to fail at anything. He saw himself as a weakling who could not survive in the rear, not a champion who needed to be in front.

Alone in the pickup headed toward Section Nine, Jake's spirits lifted a little. Rance was tinkering with the Super M when he arrived. Jake drew a small line in the dirt with the sole of his boot as Rance poured the oil into the tractor. "Never saw a tractor use so much oil. We never put more than a quart in the little Case between changes."

Rance put the oilcan down and studied Jake's face. "Get in a scrape the first day of school?"

Something in his father's voice or something his mother had said caused Jake to smile. "Guess I did."

"You hold your own?"

"Hard to hold your own against the captain of the basketball team."

Rance leaned against the tractor tire and folded his arms. "Guess he'd be a lot bigger'n you."

"Twice as big."

"How big?"

Jake shrugged. "I don't know. I guess about six feet and one-seventy-five or one-eighty."

"You start it or did he?"

"I say he did. Principal will probably say I did."

"Kid outweighs you by a good forty pounds. I'm surprised you don't look worse than you do." Rance touched the light scratches on Jake's face. "He a scratcher, too?"

"That's another story."

"You can tell me about that tonight. Right now, we're burnin' daylight."

Jake looked at the partially harvested field of maize. His father had started shredding the stalks. "You gonna harvest the rest of this or just shred it all?"

"Not enough left to get a harvest crew and combines out here. Bank told me I should shred it when I borrowed the money. They own the crop, so I'm gonna do what they say." Rance climbed back into the tractor seat. "You better head on over to JD's. I need you to finish that cotton patch by this weekend so we can patch fence by the house and put up a fence around the wheat."

"Why are we fencing the wheat?"

"Got a fellow bringing cattle to graze it. Don't want his cows getting on the bank's land or out in the road."

"Yessir." Jake opened the door of the truck. "Hey, you know why a lot of the kids out here have those spots on their teeth?"

Rance smiled. "That's fluoride in the water. Most kids who grew up here have those. It's a sign of healthy teeth. Hereford is called the town without a toothache."

Jake headed east toward the Boggs home and cotton patch, passing his house on the way. Just knowing how to find Section Nine and get back home again was a boost for his confidence. Thinking about those cattle coming was more welcome news. It was past dark when he emptied his last sack in the makeshift cotton trailer that JD had put beside the patch. He marked each sack's weight on a sideboard with a grease pencil. He drew a line, entered the date, and wrote the total. Eighty-nine pounds. At this rate, he might finish by Sunday.

He was almost home, singing along with Buddy Holly and the static on the radio when the GMC made a loud clatter. Jake turned down the radio and slowed as the clatter turned into a definite knock. He knew little about engines, but he was pretty sure that the pickup had thrown a rod. He coasted to a stop on the side of the road, got out, and raised the hood.

He was leaned against a fender, shivering, when Rance's headlights found him an hour later. "What's wrong?"

"She threw a rod, I think."

Rance looked under the hood with a flashlight, and then lay down in the dirt to look underneath. "Damn. Looks like it's all the way through the pan." He came up with a handful of dirt and threw it across the road. The wind blew it back. "Beats hell out of me how a man can let his equipment get in this kind of shape. He must have been sick a long time." Rance pulled his truck in front of the GMC and backed up to the front bumper. Jake took the log chain from the pickup bed and began looking for a place to hook it. Rance jerked the chain away from him and hooked it. He had an almost desperate look in his eyes when he stood and faced Jake. "How fast were you going?"

Rance's rage made its own heat in the thin night air.

"I don't know. Probably about fifty or sixty."

"Didn't you hear the knocking?"

"I stopped as soon as I heard it."

"Why the hell would a boy your size pick a fight with a big athlete? Weren't you paying attention when Gray Boy got the shit kicked out of him by a kid who boxed in real competition? Have I raised two idiots?"

Jake folded his arms and stood in front of his father. "Guess you did."

Rance put a hand on the GMC fender and looked toward home. "Ah, hell. I'm just takin' my problems out on you. Sounds like the fight might not have been your fault and this truck sure ain't. It was just about the only thing on the place that wasn't broke. Just hope this is the last domino to fall."

They pulled the pickup home and pushed it into the shop. Jake rolled up the chain and dropped it back into the Chevy's bed. Outside under moonlight, Jake saw his daddy standing in shadows inside the shop, hands in his back pockets, staring at the damaged truck. He remembered what his mother had said about his daddy's burdens. With his own confidence shattered, he felt Rance's despair. Still, Jake could not keep from worrying about himself first. *What happens to us if Daddy breaks under the strain? What if he can't farm out here?*

Jake waited for Rance to close the shop door, and they walked toward the house together. He walked close enough to smell the mixture of sweat, dirt, grease and fear on his daddy. He needed to feel Rance's strength. "I'll go feed Scar."

Rance stopped and looked at Jake. "You get any bolls pulled?"

"Almost ninety pounds." As Jake headed toward the barn, he stopped and spoke to Rance's back. "Daddy. I hate to tell you this, but I have to be at school an hour early tomorrow."

"Why's that, Jake?"

"The fight, I guess. Principal wants to see me."

Rance shook his head and walked toward the house.

8 Jake fidgeted as he sat with both parents in front of the principal's desk. The sty had burst during the night and was starting to itch—a good sign, but the eye was still red and sore. He ran his finger across it to be sure no pus had dried and crusted. Jake felt like an ugly freak. Rance had replaced his overalls and brogans with khaki pants, matching shirt, and good boots for the meeting. Jake knew his father needed to be in the field. Students peeked through the open door as they passed down the hall. Jake was starting the day just as he had ended the last one—humiliated. Rance took out his pocket watch and checked the time. It was almost eight. He tapped Jake's knee. "This principal the same big man I met when we enrolled you here?"

"S'pose so. He's plenty big."

Rance left the room and returned with the principal a step behind. The man stared at Jake as if he did not recognize him. "Sorry for the delay, Mr. Rivers. In all the commotion yesterday, I forgot that I had told your son to be here an hour early."

Rance stared.

The principal cleared his throat, took a seat, clasped

his hands, and put both elbows on his desk. His face was smooth, white and wrinkle-free, but his hair had started to thin and recede. Jake noted with satisfaction that he would soon be bald. "It wasn't necessary for the two of you to come in, I just wanted to visit with"... he leafed through a folder ... "uh, Jake, about that little altercation yesterday."

Rance leaned forward and put a hand on the principal's desk. The hand was rust -colored and scabbed from cuts and knuckle-busting work on engines. Jake cringed when Rance spoke. "How would we have managed that, Mr....? What was your name again?"

"Meadows. James Meadows. Come again?"

"I said how would we have managed that?"

"I'm sorry. I don't follow."

"We live forty miles from here, Mr. Meadows. Jake rides the bus to school. It doesn't get here an hour early. We had to bring him because you told him to come in early."

"Yes, well, what I meant was that I did not need to meet with you, just Jake."

Rance shook his head. "What about?"

The principal's white face was beginning to get dark. He stiffened. "Jake got into a fight in the school auditorium on his first day. I just wanted to make it clear that we don't stand for that type of thing here at Hereford High. Our discipline code is very strict—and it is enforced."

Jake sensed his mother shifting in her seat. "You couldn't have had that little talk between classes or during lunch period?"

"Yes ma'am. I could have. I just thought it might take longer. I did not know at the time that Jake was a bus student." He paused to look at all three. "Jake caused quite a disruption yesterday. I thought our talk might have taken longer."

Rance looked at his watch again. "You say Jake caused this disruption. What about the other boy?"

The principal sighed and leaned back in his chair. "He's had the talk a few times before."

Mattie stood behind Jake and put her hands on his shoulders. He slumped as the air went out of him. "Mr. Meadows, this boy has been a good student since the first grade. We have never once had to be at school because of his causing a problem. Not once. If you tell us that he has developed a smart mouth or a fighting problem, we will take care of it. Just be sure before you make assumptions."

Rance interrupted. "We're new here, Mr. Meadows. Where we came from, if one of our kids had a problem at school, we were told about it, and we handled it. They knew Jake was a decent kid. They knew we are caring parents. You seem to think he's a little criminal or something."

Mr. Meadows leafed through the folder. Jake tried to read upside down. The principal finally looked up from the folder and directly at Jake. "It appears that Jake does have a clean record and excellent grades. I am sure he will do fine. I just wanted him to get off on the right foot."

In the hall outside the principal's office, Jake and his parents went in opposite directions. Jake heard the sounds of the Lone Ranger theme song coming from his English classroom. Mr. Finnegan greeted him at the door. "Late two days in succession, Mr. Rivers. You are off to an auspicious start."

Jake nodded and stared at the floor as he stepped around his teacher. Duff Finnegan's blunt talk had intimidated Jake the day before, but he liked him better than his other teachers. Jake understood little of the teacher's Navy vocabulary. A Navy man about as far from the ocean as you could get, Finnegan was not much taller than Jake, but appeared almost as wide as he was tall. Mr. Finnegan held himself at full attention as he stopped Jake from walking down the aisle to his desk. The teacher's shirt was buttoned all the way to the collar, and he would not allow a boy to enter his class with more than his collar button undone or with his shirt not tucked. Having met inspection, Jake was allowed to walk toward his desk. Finnegan's voice stopped him again. "Can you tell us the name of the music that is playing, Mate?"

Jake, his face rapidly warming, turned to face his teacher. "No sir."

"You mean to tell me that you do not recognize it?"

"I recognize it, all right. But something tells me you don't want me to say it's the theme song for the Lone Ranger show."

The teacher walked down the aisle as Jake took his seat. "Excellent response, Mr. Rivers. The tune is something written by Rossini as an overture to the William Tell opera." Mr. Finnegan made a complete circle that took in the entire class. "None of your fellow students gave more than a giggle as their answer—afraid to say Lone Ranger. This is an English class, but I want my students to leave here with a modicum of sophistication for other fine arts."

Mr. Finnegan kept walking and talking as he dropped a blue envelope on Jake's desk. A naval anchor was printed in the upper left hand corner. Jake opened the envelope and withdrew a small card. *Duff Finnegan, Chief Petty Officer, US Navy, Ret.* was printed on two lines at the top. Jake could barely read the scribbling underneath.

I read your records from Klondike School. I expect nothing less here.

Duff Finnegan

P. S. Admirable job on standing up to Mr. Drager. If you need pugilistic instructions, let me know. I boxed in the Navy.

Jake smiled. Mr. Finnegan passed again and tapped Jake's desk. "Be here on time tomorrow, Mate. I will not tolerate tardiness."

The note carried Jake through the day. He no longer felt totally alone. By the end of the day, he felt that familiar itch that told him the sty was leaving. He did something he had never done at Klondike—he carried all of his books home. Nocona kidded him about it on the bus, but Jake discovered something that night. Though he hated studying, the books took his mind off of his lack of friends and his non-existent social status at his new school. Fear, anger, and envy drove him to keep at the books. He had something to prove.

9 Jake dumped the last of JD's cotton into the trailer
Sunday afternoon. He made his marks on the sideboard
and added the last day's weighing to his running total—
nine hundred and eighty-seven pounds. He was sitting on
the cotton, admiring his accomplishment, when JD drove up
in the Olds.

Jake noticed a light layer of dust on JD's boots and a sliver
of cow manure on one heel. A diamond horseshoe ring on
his right ring finger glittered in the late afternoon sun. "Well,
by God, you picked the whole damn patch. How much you
charge me to spread it out and plow the whole shootin' match
under?"

Jake was stunned. "You mean the cotton stalks?"

"Hell, no. I mean the cotton and the stalks. I just found
out that it won't pay for the cost of deliverin' and ginnin' it.
I told `em I'd plow the shit under before I'd take what they
offered ... and by God, I will."

"Guess I ought to give your money back for pullin' it."

"Hell, no. A deal's a deal. How much you charge me?"

Jake was confused. "For what?"

"For spreading it out and plowin' it under. I don't want

to see hide nor hair of it again. That's my last damn cotton crop."

"I won't charge anything. Guess you already lost enough on it."

"Aw, hell. I just planted it ` cause I was a little homesick and wanted to win a bet I could make a crop of cotton out here. I won more on that bet than a couple of acres of cotton will bring."

Jake felt better. "What do I use to spread it and plow it under?"

"See that tractor over there?"

Jake had already inspected the shiny IH 560. "Yep."

"You think that big sumbitch will pull this trailer full of cotton?"

"Yes sir, but I don't know how to drive it."

An hour later, Jake had learned about the new glow plug start to the six-cylinder diesel engine and knew how to hook up the matching five-bottom plow. He bounced in the seat and leaned against the backrest as JD raved about something called dual torsion spring suspension. Jake looked under the seat. "Where's the battery?"

"Under the goddam hood, where it belongs."

"I just don't think I ought to drive this without checking with Daddy first."

"Hell, you got to start sometime to learn how to farm out here. Might as well start with the best and the newest. If you can tear this sumbitch up hauling that piss-ant trailer and plowin' under a little cotton, I'll take it back and make ` em give me a new one. If they won't, I'll start buyin' John Deeres."

Jake was surprised by how much he wanted to drive the big, shiny machine. "Okay. When do you want me to do it?"

JD almost grinned. "You ain't told me how much you gonna charge me."

"I won't charge you nothin'. You already paid me for the cotton. I'll do it for the experience."

"Well, what are you waiting for?"

It was dark when Jake knocked on the back door of the Boggs' house. Bess came to the door. "What is it, Jake?"

Jake looked toward the far corner of what had been the small cotton patch. "I'm stuck." He had managed to spread the cotton in the field and plow it under with the stalks, but made the mistake of plowing the whole patch to make it look uniform. He liked driving the tractor. The dark spot in the corner had not looked muddy, but it was.

JD walked to the door in his socks, sloshing amber-colored liquid and ice cubes in a small glass. Jake recognized the smell of whiskey. JD looked at his big 560 askance in the field. "Ah, hell, Jake. Don't worry about it. A man can piss on a set of duals and get stuck. We'll pull it out tomorrow. It's getting' dark. You get on home." Jake was embarrassed and apologized until Bess took his arm and led him to the Ford. Halfway home, he noticed a ten-dollar bill in the seat beside him. He did not understand it, but he now had one hundred and ten dollars for a patch of cotton that had disappeared into the ground.

Jake dreaded telling his father that he had stuck the 560 and left it there—one more failure to add to the growing list. He was breaking everything he touched. On the way home, he made up his mind to leave school and home and return to live with Uncle Seth and Aunt Tillie and his cousins. His parents might even agree to that, especially since he had stuck the 560 and blown the GMC engine. But his failure as a farmer wasn't the real reason. He was just too weak to survive being bullied and humiliated at school, even for five months. He was the butt of jokes at school and now, on the farm. Jake was miserable, had made no new friends, and spent his weekend nights watching silly television shows that he would never have watched before. He was becoming something he never thought he would be.

Jake made his confession and went straight to bed. Mattie

and Rance took the news pretty well, but he could tell they were embarrassed for him. In bed, Jake read Finnegan's note again. Maybe he could survive until summer. His mother had said that his father needed him more than he was willing to admit. Jake hated farming, but he had to prove he had not become a sissy.

Jake felt closer to his father as they strung a two-wire temporary fence across part of the wheat field the next afternoon. Rance planned to move it and the cattle gradually across the whole field. Jake felt more like a cowboy than he had since he last saw his grandfather—something about the big sky and the anticipation of cattle coming. Though it was late in the grazing season, JD had helped them to find a rancher to bring cattle to graze their winter wheat.

It was in the twenties the day the cattle were scheduled to come, and Jake planned to stay home from school to watch and help. He entered the kitchen just before five dressed in coveralls and scuffed boots that he had outgrown. Rance raised his eyebrows as he looked up from his coffee cup. "What are you doing up this early?"

Jake hesitated before taking a seat. "Cattle are coming today, aren't they?

Rance nodded. "They probably won't be here till afternoon, though."

Mattie sat a bowl of oatmeal in front of Jake. He wasn't hungry, but he poured teaspoons full of sugar on the mush until his mother touched his hand. He added a little milk from his glass and stirred. He shot his mother a look that asked for help, but she did not respond. He stared at the oatmeal. "I thought I would stay here today in case you need any help."

Rance shook his head. "No use in your missing school. You got off to such a bad start, I don't want those teachers to think you'd lay out of school for no good reason. Besides, JD says Mr. Sunday will bring plenty of cowboys to handle the cattle. Should be pretty easy. They'll head straight to the wheat from the loadin' pen. They'll be hungry and there ain't much else they can do."

Jake imagined mounted cowboys in the yard, building barriers with their horses, herding the cattle from the corral to the wheat—without him. "I never saw anything like that before, Daddy. I'd like to be here."

Rance had already stood and reached for his hat. His mind had already started the workday. Mattie called after him. "I don't see how it would hurt for him to miss one day of school."

Rance already had one foot in the yard when he heard Mattie. He stepped back in. "What happens if he gets sick and has to be out? I hear that they'll fail you if you miss more than a few days in Hereford. I don't want him to waste one."

Jake dropped his spoon against the bowl and stalked toward his room. Rance called after him. "Jake, I appreciate the offer of help. There will probably still be plenty to do after you get home. You'll need to ride the fence line and keep 'em settled. May keep you out till late tonight." Rance thought that would appease Jake, and it did a little. But, he still felt unworthy as he changed into school clothes.

He was past his anger and looking forward to saddling his horse when Mattie picked him up at the bus stop after school. He took the wheel from Mattie and started toward home. "They here yet?"

Mattie shook her head. "No. JD came by to tell us they had been delayed. Will Tom Sunday called him. Something about a few getting down in the trailer. JD says we need to get a telephone. Living way out here, I guess he's right. Your daddy said I should go into town and see about getting lines strung to our house."

Jake nodded and kept silent, trying to conceal his excitement about getting their first telephone, though he had nobody to call. "Who's Will Tom Sunday?"

"The man who's bringing the cattle." Mattie's expression softened as she looked at Jake. "JD says Will Tom lost a son about your age a year or two ago."

"How?"

"Truck wreck. JD was driving a cattle truck and swerved to avoid hitting a cow that ran into the road. It was wet and slippery and he turned the truck over."

"And the boy was ridin' with him?"

"They say he went on every trip when he wasn't in school. He was thrown out and pinned underneath something, I think. Crushed the life right out of him." Tears started to well in Mattie's eyes.

"Did you know him?"

Mattie seemed not to hear the question. "They said JD held him in his arms till the ambulance got there. The boy was talking to him when he died. He apparently doted on that boy."

"That's bad, all right."

When they reached the crossroads, they saw two big cattle trucks heading toward the house. Jake followed them home and ran into the house to change. He was saddled and mounted by the time the trucks backed up to the loading chute. Mesmerized by the familiar smell of cattle and sounds of bawling, he did not notice the man until he pulled an ear loop over Scar's ear. In his haste, Jake had failed to properly bridle his horse. He checked to see if the throatlatch was buckled. The man slapped Jake's leg, smiled and put out his hand. Jake looked down from his saddle into familiar eyes the color of shiny spots on worn, faded blue jeans. "Oh, hey. I didn't see you standing there. Never had a chance to thank you for that piece of pie." He took the offered hand and shook it firmly.

"Glad to see that my directions got you home. Name's Will Tom Sunday. Never caught yours."

"Jake Ridge Rivers."

"Glad to see you mounted. This little hoss looks better without snow on him. Okay with your daddy if you help us out? We can sure use an extra man."

Jake took a deep breath, inhaling the sweet sound of being called a man. "Just tell me what to do."

Will Tom looked toward the red barn. "Guess you know this old boy ridin' up."

Jake saw String and Pink approaching. "Yep. Didn't know he had come back. Didn't know he had gone, for that matter. Just looked up one day and he was gone."

Will Tom winked at Jake. "Cowboys don't know how to say goodbye, but you can always count on 'em to show up. You watch String—you'll learn a thing or two."

String shook Jake's hand across their saddles. "How you been, Jake? Keepin' that little pony legged-up?"

Jake did not know what legged-up meant, and he could not take his eyes off the batwing chaps that String was wearing. "Ashamed to say it, but when you left, I slowed down my ridin'."

String gave him a forgiving smile as he nodded. "It happens." He turned toward Will Tom. "Me and Jake was tryin' to get him and Scar ready for a little calf ropin'."

Will Tom looked up at Jake and stroked Scar's neck. "I told him this little horse could probably do it. Built like a barrel, moves like an athlete. How far'd you get with him?"

"Went kinda slow, just tracked a few cows in that pen over there and swung our ropes a little. Jake's roped a little before. Scar don't booger none when you swing a rope over his eyes and he stands in the box just fine."

Will Tom looked toward the loading pens. "Looks like we may get to test him here in a minute or two. Got to get to work." He took a few steps toward the pens and turned. "Jake, maybe you can get him ready to enter the rodeo at Adrian this fall."

Jake started to shake his head, but Will Tom was already walking away. Jake followed String's lead and two hours later, the cattle were grazing wheat. It was close to being the best two hours Jake had ever spent. He could see that he had not really been needed, but just filling a hole and pushing the cattle a little was good enough for him. This was what he wanted to do with the rest of his life. He let the reins drop on Scar's neck as he had seen his grandfather do many times to roll and light a cigarette. Jake had no cigarettes or the makin's, but he imagined that he did. He was startled to hear the cattle trucks start their engines. He was proud of Scar as he held his ground when air brakes released as the truck pulled alongside.

Will Sunday's elbow hung out the passenger window. He waved Jake over and stepped out on the running board. "Put out your hand." Jake obliged and Will pressed a folded ten-dollar bill into it.

"Oh, no sir. I can't take this. I was just working for my daddy. 'Sides, I didn't do much."

Will stared at Jake as he had back at Jesse's Café, like he was trying to ask a question with his eyes instead of his voice ... like he wanted something Jake had. "You were more help than you know, Jake." He pointed a hand toward the grazing cattle. "Those are my cattle. You keep 'em settled till bedtime. That's worth a lot more than ten dollars to me. You made a good hand."

Jake nodded and shoved the ten into his jeans as the truck pulled away. He had been here less than four months, and he already made one hundred and twenty dollars—more money than he had made in two years back home. His hand was still in his pocket when String and Pink appeared beside him. String was close enough to put a hand on Scar's hip. "Will Tom seems to have taken a likin' to you. He's a good man."

"Sure seems to be. You hear what he said about the

Adrian rodeo?"

"Yep. You interested?"

"Nah. I ain't good enough to rope in any rodeo."

"Like anything else, it takes lots of practice. You got some natural instincts. They just need the rough edges taken off."

"Can you help me?"

String's eyes took a faraway look. "Will when I'm here, but you know I got to make a livin'."

10 By mid-March, Jake's face and hands were tanned from the wind and winter sun. His brother's arms and shoulders looked back at him from the mirror above his bedroom dresser. He rode his horse four or five times a week and started throwing the rope at his practice dummy. He threw it from the ground and horseback, but it was frustrating not to throw at anything alive.

Though Nocona shared his own results, Jake refused to discuss his first Hereford report card on the school bus. Mattie was not in the house when he arrived, so he laid it on his dresser. He changed clothes and headed for Section Nine in the overhauled GMC.

Rance was working on the big diesel engine that pumped irrigation water when Jake arrived. The W-9 was pulling a big breaking plow by itself. Jake watched the big arm that propelled the tractor in circles by staying in a deep furrow. He started the Super M and pulled a disc behind it for two hours without adding a drop of oil. His father's engine overhaul was working. He was disappointed when Rance rigged a light off his truck battery at dark and told Jake he might not be home until past bedtime.

Jake fed and curried his horse before going into the house. He wanted String to roach his mane and trim his tail all the way to his hocks, but Rance discouraged it, saying they had no clippers to keep the mane trimmed. In the house, Mattie did not speak as he walked by. He showered and walked into the kitchen. Mattie slammed down a plate of leftovers and left him to eat alone. She brought in a basket of wet clothes and unfolded the ironing board in the big room beside the kitchen. The ironing board squeaked and rattled with each harsh bang of iron against board. A stoppered Dr Pepper bottle sprinkled his shirts with a vengeance. His mother was angry with somebody or something, and Jake decided not to ask who or why.

His surprise had been spoiled. He moved the report card to the kitchen table, went to bed and waited. Mattie started warming things up when she saw Rance's headlights turn down the road toward their house. Jake heard the drop of a single plate, glass, cup, and saucer on the Formica table. She had set the table for one. It was the third night in a row that Rance had arrived home at bedtime.

Voices raised as Rance sat down to eat his late supper. Jake felt his own temper start to rise as he judged it time for his father to take his coffee. Their voices rose and fell in urgency. Jake could not make out the words, just angry, stressed tones. Then the voices softened. He heard his mother cry out softly, and then laugh. Jake listened as his father read each subject and the grade aloud, his voice rising with each pronounced A. Mr. Finnegan had even included a sealed envelope with Mr. and Mrs. Rivers written in the English teacher's scribbling. Jake knew the blue envelope was there, had seen the navy anchor and Duff Finnegan's navy rank printed on the envelope flap. He did not know what was inside, but it felt warm in his hands. He waited for his parents to mention it. Rance knocked softly on the door to his room. Jake could not remember his father ever knocking that way before. Always just one hard rap or a shouted "Get up, Jake."

Rance eased the door open and stuck his head in the room. "You awake, Son?"

Jake pretended to be asleep but sat up enough to answer. "Yessir." The *Son* was definitely a good sign.

Mattie moved in beside Rance, and they stood at the foot of Jake's bed. She smiled to keep from crying as she waved the report card. Rance held Mr. Finnegan's envelope. Mattie could not speak. Rance pointed to the report card in her hand. "Son, we're mighty proud of that. You've brought in good grades before, but this is better than a four-inch rain in July to me and your mother." He looked at Mattie until the silence filled the room and brought chill bumps to Jake's arms. "This is good for all of us. Proves we can make it out here."

Rance waved the envelope until it bent at the corners and fluttered like a wounded sparrow. "But this ... you never brought home anything like this before. Do you know what it says?" He handed the note to Jake.

Jake shook his head and sat up more, switched on the small lamp on his headboard, and removed a blue card from the envelope.

Jake is an excellent student. It is a pleasure to have him in my class. I expect he will grow up to be a great success at whatever he tries. Thank you for encouraging his studies.

D. Finnegan

Chill bumps spread across Jake's shoulders again, and his face warmed. He did not know what to say. He placed the card back into the envelope and tossed it on the bedspread. "He's a retired Navy guy. I sorta like him. A good teacher. Probably puts those notes in with most of the report cards."

Rance smiled at his son and walked out of the room.

Mattie followed. Jake clenched his fists in the air, rolled over on his stomach, and put a pillow over his head.

Jake was surprised to see no cattle grazing when he returned from school the next day. He could not believe that the cattle had already been there over three months. Will Tom Sunday had picked them up while Jake was at school. Jake saddled his horse to investigate what was attracting buzzards in the road beside the wheat field. Scar hesitated as they got closer to the circling birds. Jake stopped him in front of a rotting cow carcass. Back home, the wind would have carried the smell all the way back to the house. Here, Jake might have ridden by without noticing it if not for the vultures and his horse. Jake had let a cow die and had not even known it. At supper, he asked Rance what Will Sunday had said about the dead cow. Rance's mind was on something else. "That cow was sick when they brought him, Jake. Didn't you notice it?"

Jake had not. "How come it didn't smell?"

"Dry air. Walk close enough; it still smells."

11 Though Jake had found almost no new close friends at Hereford High, he knew a few students well enough to have occasional conversations. The bullying had stopped, and Jake felt confident enough to take notice of some girls, but the notice was not reciprocated. By late April, he was considering staying at Hereford rather than starting all over at a new school in the fall. That changed during a bus ride in May.

Nocona Wells poked him in the ribs and nodded toward the front of the bus. Jake had already seen him—or sensed his presence. Mike Drager walked down the aisle toward them with Steve Weston. Jake had seen Steve around school and knew he was on the boxing team. He seemed like a nice-enough guy. They dropped into the seat behind Jake and Nocona. The bus was a few miles out of town before Drager broke the tense silence.

Mike nudged the base of Jake's neck with a knuckle. "Tell your buddy I want to talk to him."

Jake turned and stared at the boy they called Snake, afraid that his voice would reveal his fear. Jake wanted to find something wrong with this bully, some weakness. Perfect

79

white teeth, chiseled features, and nice clothes that fit a muscled body well stared back at him. "What buddy?" Jake's question was sincere. He had never thought of Nocona as his buddy, just a misery-loves-company mentor of sorts.

Mike, still slouched in the seat, nodded toward the back of Nocona's head. "Who do you think, Dipshit? Indian Nooky there."

"Tell him yourself." Jake saw Nocona cut his eyes slightly toward him, saw his clenched teeth behind lips parted into a wide smile.

Nocona did not acknowledge Mike's presence until Mike nudged his shoulder with the knuckles of his right hand. Nocona leaned forward, away from the nudge, and slowly turned. His smile grew broader as his black eyes looked directly into Mike's blues. "Excuse me, I thought your sister was nudging me."

"Funny you should mention my sister. That's what I want to talk about. She tells me you been talking nasty to her on the bus every day."

"That right?"

Mike stayed in his slouch position. "You stay away from my sister. She ain't goin' out with no redskin. Don't speak to her; don't ask her out; don't even sit close to her on the bus. We all clear on that?"

Nocona smiled. "I'm all clear. You might want to check with her, though. She's been known to fight for a seat close to me."

Mike sat up straight, his nose only inches from Nocona's, hands on the rail above the seatback, knuckles turning white. "I only give warnings once, Indian. Stay far, far away from my sister."

The smile left Nocona's face as his left fist pressed slowly against Mike's nose. His middle finger made a slapping sound as it collided with Mike's forehead. "Or what, asshole?"

Mike leaned back against his seat and took a deep breath.

His expression was resigned and relaxed. A smile flickered at the corners of his mouth. "I like to take care of things like this sooner rather than later. I'll meet you at four o'clock tomorrow afternoon in the gym—center court."

"We gonna beat each other with basketballs, or what?" Nocona turned to face the front.

"That wouldn't be a fair contest." Mike nodded toward Steve Weston. "Steve, here, is sweet on my sister. He's gonna kick the shit out of you tomorrow."

Nocona turned toward Steve. "Marquis of Queensbury rules and all that, I suppose?"

Steve seemed confused. "Any rules you want, Chief."

As soon as the bus stopped and their feet touched the ground, Jake turned to Nocona. "Ain't this the last stop? Why are they still on the bus?"

"They stayed to intimidate me. Weston lives in town. He just does whatever Drager tells him."

Jelly had not heard the conversation between Nocona and Drager. "Where was his sister?"

"I imagine he told her to skip the bus today."

Jake saw their Ford making dust as it approached from the north and the Wells' Chevy approaching from the east. "Why are you fightin' Steve instead of Snake?"

"Steve's main problem is that he's stupid. Thinks he's gonna impress Drager's sister by whippin' my ass. He believes whatever Snake tells him."

Jake watched the departing bus. "Can you box?"

"I been in a couple of scrapes."

"Yeah, but ... Weston's some kinda champion boxer ... and he's taller and bigger than you are."

Nocona's mother scooted over to allow Nocona to take the wheel. Nocona put his hand on the door handle and winked at Jake. "I wadn't in the ring when he won those fights."

Jake smiled as he took the wheel to their Ford and

watched Nocona pull away. Mattie waited for Jake to put the car in gear. "What are you grinning at?"

"Nothin'. Just somethin' Nocona said."

Jake was disappointed when Jelly was the only one waiting for the bus the next morning. "Where's Nocona?"

"He talked Daddy into lettin' him drive his car today. Made up some kinda story. Made me ride the bus just so I could tell you to meet him at the gym at four o'clock. Said you would know why."

Jake watched his mother drive away. "I can't do that. Mother will be here to pick me up. Without a phone, I got no way to let her know I'm not riding the bus." The phone company had said it might be two or three years before phone lines reached them. They stepped onto the bus.

"That's what he said you would say. Said to tell you that he would drive you home and have you here before the bus."

Mike Drager, Steve Weston, and three of their friends stood at center court when Jake stepped into the gym after his last class. No sign of Nocona. Jake hung back behind the bleachers, hoping that they would not notice him. But the door clanged behind him, and they did. Drager pointed at him. "You come to watch, or you want some of what's left after we finish with the redskin?"

Jake tried to ignore him. He sat on the bleachers and wondered if Nocona had tricked him again. He jumped when he felt a hand wrap around his ankle. "Come back under the bleachers, Jake." A welcome sound.

It was dark under the bleachers, and Jake stumbled on a pair of boots. "Don't stomp all over my new Justins."

Jake's eyes adjusted as Nocona moved toward him. In the bleacher shadows, Nocona looked naked. Rays of light between the bleacher seats struck him as he approached Jake, revealing fringed skin-colored buckskin pants and shirt over a pair of moccasins. Nocona's regular school clothes were in a heap beside his boots. Nocona picked up the heap, boots and all, and stepped out on the gym floor. Jake hung back, unsure of what to do.

Drager and his friends laughed and made war-whoops. One did a little mock-dance around the mid-court circle, making Indian chanting sounds. Steve Weston looked confused. Nocona turned and smiled at Jake as he lowered the pile of clothes and boots to the gym floor. He pulled a red bandanna from the pile and tied it around his head. Jake noticed for the first time that his hair had been cut into a flattop. It had been pretty long the day before.

From just under the first bleacher seat, Nocona retrieved a stick a little smaller in circumference than a baseball bat and a little above waist high to Jake. A feather was tied to one end, and part of an antler protruded from the business end. Colorful beadwork and rawhide surrounded the body of the stick. He handed it to Jake. "That's a coup stick. If anybody tries to help Steve, you hit ` em with it."

Nocona read the hesitation in Jake's expression. He put his hands on his shoulders, and their black eyes met. "Are we friends?" Jake nodded. Nocona turned to look at the boys at center court. "Steve will fight fair, but that prick Drager will do anything to win. If I get the best of Weston, Drager and his friends will pile on. That's why they're here."

Jake's face still held a question. "I count five of them and one of me."

Nocona winked. "That's why you have the stick. You got balls, Jake. I saw it when you jumped on Drager. Ain't ten kids in this school woulda done that."

Jake stared at the boys and tried to keep the tremor out of his voice. "I never hit anybody with a stick this big. I only jumped on him because I was too scared to do anything else ... plus I didn't know who he was."

Nocona chuckled softly. "Hell Jake, you probably won't

have to use the stick, but I need to know that you will if you have to. Hit ˋem right across the nose or anyplace you can get in a good lick ... hard as you can." Nocona didn't wait for an answer as he walked toward center court. He turned after a couple of steps. "These bastards want to see an Indian show; let's give it to ˋem. We'll still be friends, even if you can't use the stick. Just don't let the bastards kill me. Just run for help if you can't do anything else."

Jake nodded and walked alongside Nocona. He was more frightened than he could remember, but what Nocona had said made him feel good enough to keep his feet moving. The boys continued to snicker. "Two little Indians. Why didn't you bring the whole tribe? That red rag your war bonnet? You bring along a second for the duel?" Drager and Weston kept quiet as the other boys made their jokes. Nocona stepped into the circle and faced the boxer. Nocona smiled. Steve winced.

Steve extended a pair of boxing gloves to Nocona. "I brought these for you. Don't mean you have to fight by the rules."

Nocona shook his head.

"Mind if I wear a pair?"

"Suit yourself."

"Might be easier on your face if I use these." Steve pulled on the gloves and Drager helped him with the lacing

"Thanks. I apologize for thinking you were just protecting your knuckles."

Steve lifted his gloved fists. "Ready?"

Nocona left both hands open as he crouched. Jake took a deep breath. Maybe Nocona knew Judo. Steve bounced on the balls of his feet and moved around Nocona. Nocona slowly followed him, keeping his crouched stance. Steve feinted with his right and landed a left to Nocona's forehead. Nocona's head jerked, and he stumbled a little as he stepped back. He shook his head and resumed his crouch. The second shot hit him in the nose, and his head snapped back again. Two more quick body punches and a right cross dropped Nocona to the gymnasium floor. He crawled toward Mike as he struggled to rise, putting his hands just below Mike's feet. Steve stepped back. "You hurt, Wells?"

Mike looked at his feet. "Too late to beg now, Tonto. Get up and fight like a man or stay down."

Nocona struggled to his feet, put his left hand on his bent knee and took a couple of deep breaths. He reached his right arm high behind him as if he were stretching. The arm came forward in a rising motion as Nocona's grunt echoed through the building. His open right hand slammed against Mike's crotch and stayed there. Mike screamed before Nocona's left thumb pushed against his Adam's apple. He picked Mike up and slammed him down again with both hands squeezing. Mike screamed and flailed helplessly. The other boys pranced around the two locked combatants and shouted. "Fight fair, you sumbitch. Turn loose."

Nocona moved his mouth close to Mike's ear and eased his thumb off his throat. "Want me to stop squeezin' your balls?"

Mike managed a nod.

"Then call off your stooge and say you're sorry for calling me names."

"Back off, Steve. Sorry."

"And you won't ever do it again."

"Won't ever." The words came out as a squeak.

Nocona turned him loose and jumped to his feet. "Throw me the stick, Jake." Nocona waved the stick in front of him, feather flying, as he slowly backed away. He returned the stick to Jake, picked up his clothes, and ran out the door. The Chevy was parked just outside.

Jake looked at his watch as they pulled away. It seemed like hours to him, but the whole thing had lasted less than fifteen minutes. "Damn, Nocona. Never saw anything like that before. They're gonna want to get us back."

"Don't think so. That sumbitch won't ever bother me again. He knows I won't let him whip me." Nocona smiled his wide grin. "By the way, we can call him Worm instead of Snake from now on."

Jake figured that what Nocona said was true, but he was more concerned about Drager and his friends taking their revenge on **him** for what Nocona had done. Doing eighty, they passed the school bus halfway home, and Jake breathed a little easier, knowing that his mother would not worry when he did not get off the bus. He examined the buckskins that Nocona was wearing. The beading along the seams was beautiful, and the leather looked soft as cream. "Where did you get the buckskins?"

"Christmas last year—coup stick the year before. Mother usually buys me some Indian stuff every year. Wants me to remember my heritage."

"Your heritage?"

"Don't tell me you ain't noticed I'm adopted. I'm a full-blood Comanche."

"You named after the town?"

"No, dumb-ass—after the Indian chief. Mama claims I'm a descendant of Peta Nocona and Quanah Parker. That's probably all bullshit, but it makes her happy to keep me in Indian stuff."

Jake had heard of both but knew little about the famous Indians. "I knew you and Jelly weren't full brothers, but figured it was none of my business."

"I'm adopted. He's not."

"So you never saw your mother or daddy? You don't know what they look like?" Jake regretted the question as he saw Nocona's expression.

"Nah. Who gives a shit?"

"Why did you ask me to meet you today? You must have known I wouldn't be much help. Any of those pricks could whip me easy."

"You might be surprised. Steve Weston is the only one of
that bunch that's willin' to fight anybody his own size. Drager
just suckered him by telling him a lot of crap. You take him
away or catch any one of them by himself; they don't want no
part of fightin'. That's why I grabbed Drager by the balls and
not Weston."

"Yeah, but why me?"

"They wanted an Indian show. Figured we would give it
to `em."

"I still don't know what you're talkin' about."

"You ain't noticed that you look about as much like an
Indian as I do? You got black eyes and the same color skin.
Hell, you're more red-skinned than I am."

Jake studied his hands. Copper-colored, like his father's.
He had heard about Indian blood in his family but had not
paid much attention.

Nocona laughed. "Hell, I just did you a big favor. Ain't
nobody gonna mess with you the rest of the year."

"Why not?"

"By the time we get to school tomorrow, what happened
today will have grown. They'll say that Indians fight dirty.
We'll use sticks and knives, hit somebody in the balls and
squeeze like hell, maybe even cut throats."

Jake asked the question he had been holding. "Why **did**
you fight dirty?"

Nocona laughed. "Hell, you think it's fair for a trained
boxer to whip hell out of somebody who never boxed in his
life? I gave it my best shot. When it was clear he was gonna
turn my face into meat loaf, I decided to put a stop to it.
Only fighting I ever did was no-holds-barred. I couldn't whip
Steve Weston in his kind of fight. I knew Drager couldn't
whip me in mine. Just hoped that Steve wouldn't help
Drager."

"So you knew going in that you were going to fight dirty if

you had to?"

"Hell, yes. That sumbitch would have beaten me to a pulp with boxing gloves. Ain't nobody gonna do that to this pretty face."

Put that way, it sort of made sense to Jake. He did not feel right about it, but he felt safer somehow. He could fight dirty if he had to.

12 When they stepped off the bus the next morning at school, Principal Meadows was waiting. He waggled his index finger and beckoned them to follow. Inside the office, he put his elbows on the desk again. "You boys are intent on causin' trouble. You're hereby expelled from riding the bus for the rest of the year. You can report to my office after the last class and take your licks or bring your parents in tomorrow morning at eight."

Nocona spoke first. "What are we being punished for?"

"You know very well. Don't play games with me, Mr. Wells."

Jake shifted in his seat. "I don't know."

"Myra Drager's parents have filed a complaint against both of you for using foul language and talking dirty to her on the bus."

Jake and Nocona raised their eyebrows. It had been months since Jake had asked Myra why her brother was called Snake. When he found out the answer, he had avoided her ever since. He looked at Nocona with a question. Nocona shrugged.

The principal was impatient. "Right now, it's just the bus,

but you boys are on the verge of being expelled from school. If that happens, you'll have to repeat this year."

That got Jake's attention. "I didn't ..." Nocona squeezed Jake's arm.

"What's it gonna be, boys? Time to get to class."

Nocona stood. "I'll take my licks."

Jake nodded. "Me, too. How are we supposed to get to and from school?"

Principal Meadows pointed to the phone on his desk. "Feel free to call your parents. I'll be happy to explain the reasons why you're being thrown off the bus to them."

Jake stopped Nocona as he started down the hall to his first class. "How many licks are we talkin' about?"

Nocona shot a finger at the principal's office door. "At least ten. Maybe more. Be ready, `cause that bastard can hit one out of the park."

Jake was worried about the licks but was more worried about getting kicked out of school and having to repeat his freshman year. After English class, he approached Mr. Finnegan for advice. The Navy man pointed a pencil at Jake. "Take the licks and that will probably be the end of it. Mike Drager is bad business. He probably put his sister up to it, but you can't be sure. You've hooked up with another bad one in Nocona Wells. You're makin' some bad choices, Bucko."

Jake nodded. "What if it ain't the end of it? What if they try to kick me out of school?"

"*Isn't* the end of it, Mr. Rivers ... *isn't*. If you have only done what you told me, your grades will keep you from being kicked out. Keep your nose clean, and I'll come to your defense if necessary."

Jake felt better. Now he only had to worry about the whipping.

He ran from his last class to beat Nocona to the principal's office. If he cried, he did not want Nocona to see it. Principal Meadows obliged his request for speed. Jake gripped the desk, and the principal picked up the paddle like a baseball bat and swung for the fences. Jake's grip on the desk held until the third lick propelled him across it, splitting his lip. The fourth lick felt as if it had traveled through his testicles to his eyeballs. The pounding seemed to go on forever. His eyes were watering against his will, and he was getting dizzy as he heard Nocona come in to witness the ninth and tenth. Jake stood and wiped the drool from his mouth, ignoring his wet eyes.

Nocona whispered that Jake should stay and watch how to take licks. Jake, buttocks numb, but starting to come back to life with painful tingles, watched in awe as the big principal assumed the batter's stance again and swung with both arms. It was clear that he felt challenged to move Nocona's grip and propel him across the desk. Two coaches stood outside the door and watched. Jake figured there was a bet going. If they bet against Nocona, they lost. His eyes were watering, but he never lost his grip.

Knowing that it was over gave Jake a strange sense of elation as he and Nocona started walking out of the schoolyard. He had taken his whipping and survived. They stopped at a service station and bought Cokes and Butterfingers before calling Nocona's parents. Nocona blurted out the whole story on the phone—his way of insuring that he would get the keys to his car back. Nocona's mother picked them up a half-hour later. She was a gentle woman who took their side in the mess. She was not angry, only unhappy that an unpleasant situation had developed for her son and his friend.

Jake's euphoria dissipated when he saw Rance's pickup at the bus stop. He had hoped for his mother. The bus had already come and gone when Jake closed the passenger door of the pickup and took a seat beside his daddy. Before Rance could ask him why he was late and not on the bus, Jake told him about the whipping. He figured on getting some sympathy for the ten licks before telling about getting kicked off the school bus.

Jake watched his daddy's hat move back on his head as he tightened his scalp and clenched his jaw. A bad sign. "Damn, Jake. I thought you were all straightened out at school. Why did you get ten licks?"

"I don't know."

"We're not gonna do the I-don't-know-dance again, are we? No teacher is gonna bust your butt without tellin' you why."

"He said me and Nocona were talkin' dirty to one of the girls on the bus."

Rance's expression softened. "And were you?"

"Nocona teases her a little every once in a while. He may have said some sex stuff. Didn't seem too bad. I thought they were sweet on each other."

"Never mind Nocona. I asked **you**."

"I said something to her once on the first day of school. I can't remember saying anything since. I probably laughed when Nocona teased her. She's the kid sister of the boy that I got into it with on the first day."

"You couldn't handle the brother, so you took it out on the sister?"

"No. I didn't even know she was his sister when I said something."

"Jake, I haven't got the time for all the bull. Just tell me the whole story. If what you tell me is true, I'll be at the damn school first thing in the morning. This ain't right."

Jake's voice was urgent. "Please don't do that. I just asked her why Mike Drager was called Snake. That's all. Mike got on the bus the other day, and he and Steve Weston challenged Nocona to a fight. Nocona asked me to go with him for the fight. I did. I figure that's the real reason we're getting punished ... the real reason we got kicked off the bus for the rest of the year."

Rance's head snapped toward Jake. "They're saying you can't ride the bus anymore?"

"Yep."

Rance wheeled the pickup into the yard and stopped. "We'll see about that. I'll take you to the bus tomorrow. If the bus driver says you can't get on, I'll get on with you and see if he'll try to throw me off. Then we'll have a little talk with the principal. I'll make that son-of-a-bitch drive me home on the damn bus."

It took Jake and Mattie the rest of the night to convince Rance that his going to school the next day would only make things worse for Jake. With less than a month of school left, Jake was thrilled when they agreed to let him drive the GMC the rest of the year. "Can I take some of the junk out of it?"

Rance was still not pleased with what had happened. "It's a farm truck, Jake. We're gonna keep using it that way. It's bad enough you'll have it during the time I'm planting maize. I don't want to load and reload it every day."

"I'll do it."

Mattie touched Jake's arm. "Leave well enough alone, Jake. The truck is fine as it is."

Rance put on his hat to go outside. He had begun to spend his evenings working in the shop when he was not in the field. "I just overhauled that truck, Jake. I catch you hot-roddin' it, what that principal did to you will be like a pimple on a gnat's ass. I'll slap a knot on your head that'll whistle like a ten-penny nail."

Jake washed and waxed the battered, ten-year-old GMC. With its bed full of fuel cans and farm tools, it rattled him back and forth to school the rest of the year. Mattie supplied a worn-out quilt to put over the greasy, worn seat covers. When his father had to have the old pickup, Jake rode with Nocona in his '55 Chevy.

School dismissed for the summer at noon on the last day

of May. Jake and Nocona walked to their cars together. Nocona noticed the water bag hanging from the pickup's front bumper. He grabbed the rope handle and shook it. "You don't like the water fountains in this school?"

Jake smiled at himself for forgetting to remove the bag. "Never know when you're gonna be stranded in the desert out here."

Filled with euphoria, Nocona wanted to race Jake and the GMC home, but Jake just smiled. He knew the six-cylinder had little chance against Nocona's big V-8—he also remembered throwing a rod. As he opened the pickup door, something caused him to look toward a second floor window. Duff Finnegan stood at the window with his hands in his pockets. Jake waved and Duff gave a Navy salute.

13 Jake had begun to take solace in the sound of the wind turning the blades and the creaking of the windmill tail. The stock tank goldfish had survived the winter under a hard layer of ice while he survived a hard freshman year at Hereford. Mattie found him leaning against the pump house, soaking up the sun's warmth, secure in the knowledge that he had three months of freedom. "Better get changed and find your daddy, Jake. He's cutting irrigation ditches. Said for you to bring those irrigation tarps in the shop. He's gonna show you how to irrigate."

Jake snacked on peanut butter and crackers and watched his daddy cut an irrigation ditch at Section Nine. Rance stopped the tractor at the end of the ditch, stepped off, and walked behind the big wheel and out of Jake's view. Rance had never urinated in Jake's presence, so he figured that he had neither seen nor heard the GMC when Jake arrived. He started to look away until he saw his father bend at the waist and retch. He emerged from the tractor wheel wiping his mouth with a handkerchief. Back in the tractor seat, he noticed Jake. He lifted the plow and drove toward him.

"Bring the tarps?"

Jake removed the tarps from the pickup bed and dropped them on the ground. He waited in vain for Rance to say something about throwing up. "You sick?"

The question surprised Rance. "Why do you ask?"

"Looked like you were puking."

"Been having a little stomach trouble lately. Nothin' much. Comes and goes."

Jake recalled his mother's questions about whiskey. "What do you reckon is causin' it?" His tone was sarcastic.

"You bring the tarps or not? If you did, bring one over to the ditch, and I'll show you how to make a dam in the ditch. We don't need to water yet, but you need to know how, just in case I'm out of pocket when the time comes."

Jake followed his daddy to the freshly dug irrigation ditch. There was something different about the way his daddy walked. Rance wasn't swinging his arms and walking fast the way he usually did. His pace had slowed, and he held one hand inside the bib of his overalls against his stomach.

"There's a bunch of old suction tubes lying over by the fencerow. Go get one and I'll show you."

Jake trotted toward the fencerow, but saw nothing but tumbleweeds. He turned and made a questioning shrug in Rance's direction.

Rance pointed. "They're under the tumbleweeds."

Jake was pulling back big tumbleweeds and throwing them out into the field when he saw something dark draped across one of the metal tubes. Instinct pulled him back a couple of steps. "Rattler!"

Rance came running with the shovel, but stumbled to one knee. Jake ran and picked up the shovel before Rance could get to his feet. He used the shovel to push back the remaining tumbleweeds until the rattler was uncovered, coiled, and rattling. He let the snake strike the shovel twice before he managed to trap its head. When the head was cut off, Jake took a deep breath.

Rance took the shovel from Jake and began poking around the irrigation tubes. "They like to warm themselves on hot metal this time of year. Shoulda warned you."

"I'll sure know from now on." Jake saw more movement as he spoke. They used shovels to pull the irrigation tubes and the rest of the tumbleweeds back, revealing a nest of small rattlers. Rance killed them all.

He took out his pocketknife and cut off twelve buttons from the big rattler. "Didn't Papa tell you to get him some rattles for his fiddle?"

Jake nodded, took the buttons, and tossed them in the floorboard of the GMC.

Rance picked up an irrigation tube. The tubes were shaped like giant snails with a hump in the middle of two tails. He held the tube by the hump and slapped it hard against his brogans. "The fellow who farmed this place before us got snake-bit. I'll show you how." Rance dropped one end of the tube into the ditch and draped the hump over the mound on the side of the ditch, leaving the other end dropped into a row of maize. "Imagine there's water in the ditch, Jake. You pick up the tube, put your palm over the end out of the water, and pump like this. Two pumps and you can drop the end in the row. It'll run in the row for about twelve hours."

Jake barely heard the instructions. "So how did the guy get snake-bit?"

"He forgot to slap the tube like I did. A rattler had crawled up in the warm tube and bit him on the hand when he did that first pump."

Jake shivered a little. "I'll pray for rain. Maybe we won't have to irrigate this year."

Rance stayed in the shop while Jake ate his supper alone. Mattie banged on her ironing board and shook the stoppered

Dr Pepper bottle furiously as she sprinkled the clothes. The tension and noise made Jake irritable. "Why are you banging the iron like that?"

"That's what ironing sounds like, Jake."

"No, it ain't. What are you mad at?"

Mattie started to sniffle. "Just thinking about old times and home." She put the iron down and burst into tears.

Jake had not seen his mother weep since Tuck's funeral. People had said she did not cry enough to properly heal. Maybe they were right.

"We haven't sat down to a meal together more than a half-dozen times since we got out here. He misses dinner most days and comes in after bedtime for supper. I don't know how he survives on what he eats."

Jake rattled ice cubes in his glass. "Yeah, but he's here for breakfast every morning."

"He just stares into his coffee cup at breakfast. You know that. You won't talk in the morning because you're always in a bad mood about school."

Jake had seen first-hand some of his father's problems, but he had been too absorbed in his own to notice his mother's life. "You said yourself he was under a lot of pressure."

"I hope that's all it is. He's not himself. He's lost a lot of weight. Have you noticed him drinking any?"

An image flashed across Jake's mind that brought a wave of sorrow. Rance had drunk a lot when Jake's little brother had died. Jake had known most of the places where his father kept small stashes of whiskey. He had never agreed with his mother's intolerance for alcohol, and sharing his father's secret seemed to bring them closer. He loved sitting with his father, grandfather, and uncle as they "mellowed" by a blacksmith forge or in Dad Flanagan's store. Now, the thought of his father drinking again brought a confusing sense of fear and dread to Jake. He blamed his mother for the fear. He spoke harshly. "No, Mother, I haven't smelled or seen any whiskey."

Mattie took a chair beside Jake at the table and wrung her hands. "JD's always got a bottle with him. Makes me so mad that he brought that stuff back into our lives."

"Uncle JD drinks it in his own house. If you wadn't so dead-set against it, maybe Daddy wouldn't have to sneak around."

Mattie leaned back as if Jake had struck her. "You might want to ask Bess about drinking and whiskey before you spout off about things you don't know anything about."

Jake had not had a serious argument with his mother in months, and his anger flared. "You admit you don't even know if Daddy has been drinking. Have you seen him take a drink? Has he come in drunk?"

Mattie's face contorted as she held back tears. She shook her head. "No. I just know that something is wrong."

"You're the one who told me the pressure he's under. You both lost a son, but Daddy also lost his best friend when Hack died. Why don't you lighten up on him yourself? You're already blamin' him for somethin' he ain't even done."

Jake hated to see his mother cry. He felt anger, pity, and fear at the same time when Mattie cried. It made him angry with her and with himself, because he was more concerned about what her problems meant to him than what they meant to her. He rose and stalked out of the room. "I'm gonna shower and go to bed."

He opened a window in his room and listened to the wind, still surprised by the coolness of late May evenings in the Panhandle. Bob Lee had told them that nights would remain cool until the hottest days of summer. Even then, their attic fan would pull breezes through the house to cool them. Jake would not miss East Texas humidity or water-cooled window fans. He listened for sounds of his mother crying and was relieved when he heard none. He tried to imagine why she was so upset as his mind drifted back to happier times.

The Rivers had grown up together as a family of six—seven if you counted his grandfather. Jake thought of how much Tuck's death from scarlet fever had hurt him, but he could not fathom the depth of his parents' pain. To him, Trish's marriage had been a celebration. He missed her, but she had made him an uncle twice, and he liked being an uncle. Maybe Mattie saw her marriage as the loss of another child. She did not get to see her grandsons much, either. Gray Boy's departure for the Marines brought her losses to three. Her family had been cut in half at the same time she moved away from most of her sisters. Jake began to understand that she probably felt worse than he did starting in a strange school in a strange place with strange people. He pushed back the sheet and put his feet on the floor. He was reaching for his jeans to go in and apologize to his mother, but his father's voice stopped him. He would do it tomorrow.

14 Jake learned to drive their bobtail grain truck during wheat harvest. Rance promised him that he could drive a combine the next year. He took pride in mastering the changing of irrigation dams and tubes. Water coming from the deep irrigation wells was always fresh and cool. Rance had added wire handles to an ale can, and Jake enjoyed catching water fresh from the earth, drinking it and pouring it over his head. Always alert for rattlers, he never found one in a tube.

In East Texas, farming for Jake had been all about backbreaking work in cotton fields and removing cow manure from dairy barns and lots. Here, he was allowed, even expected, to run grain drills and sow the crops as well as tend and harvest them. He was involved from start to finish and began to understand, despite his lack of true interest, the agricultural process. Work was hard, but not backbreaking, and it gave him a small measure of competence.

He had earned his second pay as a cowboy when String hired him to work the bank's cattle. They had penned the small herd in a fence corner on a cool, sunny Saturday morning. String roped each one and tripped it. Jake's job was to hold the rest of the herd while String did whatever had to be done to each head. When Jake had to hold a big steer or help with a vaccination, Pink, reins tied to his empty saddle, held the herd. Jake watched with awe as Scar mimicked the other horse's actions. Riding back at sunset, covered with sweat and dust, Jake felt almost like a man. Almost like a cowboy. Twice during the summer, he and String had roped and tied a few calves.

He was pouring wheat seed into a grain drill when he saw a tall plume of dust traveling behind a moving vehicle on the dirt farm-to-market road that ran a mile south of their house. The car moved across a mirage-lake of shimmering August heat waves like an apparition. Jake could see it, but could not hear it. He smiled, figuring it was Bob Lee's black '57 Chevy— the turd-hearse. Bob Lee and the Chevy knew one speed— wide open. The car seemed to slow little as it approached the road that ran beside the wheat field and Jake's house. Jake turned back to pouring wheat seed, figuring the car was going to pass.

As he closed one seed hopper, he heard the first dull sounds. The rooster tail of dust grew thicker as the car made a ninety-degree turn, and Jake recognized the rumble of twin pipes. Not the black turd-hearse, but a cherry-red '55 Chevy. Nocona Wells slowed his approach. The wind drifted the dust away from the Chevy, as if God was protecting Nocona's fresh wax job. He killed the engine and let the dust settle before he rolled down his window and motioned for Jake to join him. Jake's hands were busy, so he jerked his head to invite him into the wheat field. He was a little peeved that Nocona had not dropped by all summer.

Nocona stepped out of the car wearing new starched Levis and an emerald green shirt with red piping stitched around a custom-made yoke that traveled all the way to his belt. He gingerly picked up a black felt hat off the seat beside him. Holding it by the crown, he brushed off the brim with his sleeve and pulled it down on his head. He stepped over the two-wire fence and yelled at Jake. "What's it gonna be, Cowboy? Whitefaces or Matadors?"

Jake filled the last hopper. "If you mean Hereford or Adrian, I ain't decided yet."

Nocona moved his Doublemint and held it between his front teeth before pushing it back. "Ain't decided yet? What's to decide? Your mama and daddy talk you out of it?"

"Naw. They say it's up to me. It's just I already know a few people and some teachers at Hereford. I took drivers' education there this summer. Wadn't too bad. Hate to start all over again."

"Hell, you'll know more people on the first day than you met all year in Hereford."

"Easy for you to say. You already got friends there. I don't."

"You want to meet all the kids at Adrian High before school even starts, come to the party at Gabe's a week from Saturday night. There ain't but about forty kids in the whole high school."

"Who's Gabe?"

Nocona put a hand on the grain drill and pointed southwest with the other. "You ain't met the Lowrys? Hell, they don't live more'n ten miles from you as the crow files. Probably your closest neighbor."

Jake noticed that his hand was darker than Nocona's. "Think Daddy may have mentioned the name, but I don't know Gabe."

"Well, Gabe's the same age as you. He's a friend of mine, and his mama is throwin' a party before school starts. Everybody will be there."

"I ain't goin' to any party I ain't invited to."

Nocona waved his arms in a gesture of defeat. "Hell, I just invited you."

"Ain't your party." Jake threw another sack of wheat seed

over his shoulder.

"Gabe told me to invite you. You know where Overstreet Road is by that big cottonwood on the way to Section Nine?"

"The one that's growing in the middle of the road?"

"That's the one. Turn left there, go about three miles, and turn at the first right. That's the Lowrys' driveway."

Jake coughed away the wheat dust. The thought of meeting new people and being rejected again scared him. "Just come by myself?"

Nocona laughed. "Hell, yes. You got your license, don't you? I guess you could bring your mama if you need her."

"My license should be in the mail any day."

Nocona turned toward his car. "Gotta go." He turned after a couple of steps. "Oh, yeah, Jake. Don't wear them damn loafers. All the boys at Adrian, and I mean all the boys, wear boots."

"I may not get to come then, 'cause I outgrew my only pair of good boots. Work boots are about worn out."

"Get your mama to turn loose and buy you some." He thumped the brim of his hat. "Maybe one of these, too. We can wear 'em to school at Adrian."

"You get to wear hats to school there?"

"Yep." Nocona turned to go again. His Chevy disappeared into the heat waves, leaving Jake feeling empty and envious.

Jake and Mattie had supper without Rance again. Jake told her about the party. Mattie refilled his glass with iced tea. "I hear the Lowrys have one every year. You going?"

"When were you gonna tell me about it?"

"Gabe was supposed to ride over on his horse one day this week and invite you."

"You know Gabe?"

"I met Nelda, his mother. He passed through the yard when I was leaving their house one day. Big cowboy kid with black hair. Good-lookin'. His mama keeps him decked out in those fancy-yoked shirts."

Jake already disliked Gabe. He was big, good-looking, and had failed to invite him to the party. "I don't much like those shirts with yokes that zig-zag all the way from your shoulders to your belt."

Mattie looked stricken. "I thought you liked those. I hired Nelda to make you a couple, and they cost a small fortune. One should be ready in time for the party."

"Really?" Jake really wanted one of the shirts but had convinced himself he did not like them because he figured he would never have one. "Reckon she makes String's shirts, too?" He really preferred the kind of shirts that String wore, with material that looked like a combination of ducking and denim. They had yokes that sort of laid over his shoulders like capes. They looked good enough to wear to a dance, but tough enough to work cattle.

Mattie shook her head. "I don't know, Jake. All the kids are wearing the kind I ordered for you."

"I'm not so much worried about shirts as I am about boots."

The next morning, they had a rare good rain, and Rance told Jake and Mattie they could take the day to get clothes for school. They started for Adrian just after daylight. Jake turned west on the farm to market road. "How far is it?"

Mattie's expression was puzzled. "You don't know?"

"How would I know? I can't drive by myself unless I'm goin' to school, and I haven't got any friends to come and get me. In case you ain't noticed, I haven't been anywhere all summer."

Mattie's lips made a straight, tight line. "You went to the picture show in Hereford a couple of times. Do you know how to get to Adrian?"

"Thought you did."

"It just never occurred to me that you had never been. I thought your daddy would have taken you sometime when he went for supplies."

"I'm usually in the field when he makes those trips. Anyway, he buys most of his stuff in Hereford."

After a quarter hour of driving in silence, Mattie giggled. "What if we get lost?"

"I know the general direction. Will Sunday told me that Adrian was on 66 that first night I drove out here from home." Jake nodded north just as they approached a T and a paved road. "66 is over there." In another fifteen minutes, they were driving down 66 with Adrian in sight.

The Mother Road ran along the south side of the town. A hodgepodge of trading posts, service stations, garages, and cafés had sprung up on the north side to give 66 travelers a chance to fill up their stomachs and cars before heading farther west into even more desolate country. Some had signs that said *Last Chance.* Jake could not imagine a town more isolated than this one. At the Bent Door Trading Post, someone had drawn an arrow with two heads on the window. Chicago was printed on the arrowhead pointing east, Los Angeles on the one pointing west, with 1,139 miles printed in the center. Jake saw another *Jesse's Café* sign and thought of the pie Will Sunday had bought him.

Conflicting emotions washed over Jake as he slowed to get a better look. Garish colored plastic and glass clashed with stucco, wood, brick, and rock buildings along route 66. The clash was even greater across the railroad tracks that ran beside the highway. Huge grain silos, what Will Sunday had called elevators, sat along the tracks. North of the tracks, Adrian embraced the railroad that took its grains to market, but refused to concede the modernism brought by Route 66.

He let stray cars pass him as he drove slowly on the highway until he saw a sign that said *Glen Rio, New Mexico, 24 miles.* Will Sunday had said he might end up there if he did not pay attention. Jake turned around and came back. The clock turned back as he crossed the railroad tracks into the

town. To Jake, Adrian reminded him of old Mexican desert
towns that he had seen in picture shows. Most of the houses
looked a lot like the one he lived in, except most had stucco
sides. Few trees shaded the yards, and blades of grass were
rare. Even on this wet, cloudy day, Adrian looked desolate
and dry. It was just past seven when they stopped in front of
Adrian Mercantile.

Jake looked up through the front window of the Ford.
"Looks like an old hotel out in the west."

Mattie opened her door and walked toward the general
store. "I think I remember JD or Bess saying it started out as
a hotel—rooms upstairs and a lobby and saloon downstairs.
"Suppose those are buffalo hides?" Mattie turned up her nose
at a dozen or more fresh hides, with hair and blood showing,
stacked on a wooden slab in front of the store.

"Cows, I imagine. Buffaloes been gone a long time, I
think. They don't seem to smell too bad. Wonder if they tan
`em and make boots right here?" A small bell tinkled as Jake
opened the door. A man of slight build with delicate features
looked up from pushing red oil-dust with a push broom across
a plank floor worn slick from decades of steps. The place
smelled of leather and oil-soaked wood mixed with horse and
mule feed, wet tow sacks, cotton fabric, and salt blocks.
Shelves as high as eight feet spread out under a taller ceiling.
They were filled with a haphazard assortment of groceries and
supplies. Horse liniment mingled with vanilla extract, potato
chips, and aspirin.

Naked bulbs in the back revealed harness and saddles
stacked on stands. More leather and tack was piled in the
floor. The man leaned his broom against a counter that was
cluttered with paper sacks, wrapping paper stands, and candy
jars. "Good morning, folks. Name's Caleb Pirtle. Can I help
you find anything?" His voice was small and gentle, almost a
whisper.

Mattie wasted no time. "We need to see some boots for

this boy."

"Yes ma'am. What size?" Jake liked this kind man. With his soft gray hair and smooth skin, he looked more like a preacher or traveling salesman than a clerk in a general store in raw country.

"Not sure. He just outgrew some, but he's got a narrow foot like his mother."

The man looked at Jake and patted his arm. "You going to the Lowrys' party?"

Jake nodded.

"You must be Jake Rivers. Nocona was in here yesterday picking up a new hat and said to expect you. Come with me." He put out his hand to Mattie before heading to the back of the store. "You must be Mrs. Rivers. I'm Caleb Pirtle."

"Call me Mattie."

"It's a big country, but we generally know when someone new arrives."

They followed the man past windmill blades, pump jacks, bolts of fabric, women's panties, bras, and shoes. Jake tried on eight pairs before Caleb's face showed defeat. He winked at Jake. "Well, our motto is that we have it or we can get it." He handed Jake a Justin catalog. "Page 16."

Jake put the book on the floor under a naked light bulb suspended from the high ceiling. He dropped to his knees to examine the beautiful boot pictures. He saw none like his uncle JD's. The man kneeled beside him and put his finger on a pair. "These are what most of the boys are buying this year. Stovepipe tops with a diamond-stitch pattern. Notice the Justin toe-bug and the way the pointed toe slants back. You can recognize that Justin toe anywhere." His knees popped as he stood.

Jake stood and straddled the catalog, comparing the cheap, worn-out boots on his feet to the picture. "How much?"

"Thirty-one ninety-five."

Jake heard his mother take a deep breath. With hope in his eyes, he looked at the man. "You got any cheaper ones? Maybe an off-brand?"

"Yes, I do, Jake, but I don't have a better value, and you won't be happy with them. Most of the cheaper boots don't come in the right width for you. I could probably order a cheaper pair, but these Justins are about the only thing I can get here in time for the party."

Mattie put her hand on Jake's shoulder. "You get the same kind the other boys are getting."

Jake felt a tingle of anticipation as he stared at those boots. He started to look forward to the party. He wanted the brown ones, but decided black would be safer.

He felt Mattie pressing a wheat Lee Rider jacket against his shoulders. A pair of wheat jeans was folded against her chest. "Let's see now, we have boots, jeans, shirt, and jacket. You're about covered."

Jake smiled as he fingered JD's hundred in his pocket. "Not quite. Mr. Pirtle, you got any Resistol hats?"

"This way, Jake." Caleb Pirtle picked up a wooden stick about six feet long with a piece of flat, sloping wood glued to the end. He pointed to a stack of hatboxes on shelves reaching to the ceiling of the store. "I assume you want black?"

"Yessir."

"What size?"

"Seven and three-eighths." Jake knew his hat size because it was bigger than the rest of him.

Caleb slipped the stick under a box lid and pulled it from the stack. He placed the box on the counter, opened it, and removed a black hat with the crown still open and round. Jake's smile disappeared. "You don't have any that are creased like Nocona's?"

Caleb Pirtle chuckled. "We'll shape it to your specifications." He put his fist inside the crown and began walking to the other side of the store, calling as he went. "Sage. We have a customer who wants one of those new low creases."

A skinny brunette with full, bouncy, bobbed hair and big glasses with plastic frames the color of butterscotch met them at the steamer. She took the hat and smiled at Jake. Jake kept his eyes on the XXX Resistol. The girl, who looked about twelve to Jake, was cradling it under her arm as she switched on the steamer. He shot a helpless glance at Caleb, beseeching him with his eyes to steam and shape his hat, but Caleb and Mattie were off on a search for vanilla extract and a bolt of fabric.

Sage smiled at Jake again. "I haven't had any complaints so far. If I mess it up, you don't have to pay."

She had a sweet expression, but she was just a kid, and her nose turned up a little too much to suit Jake. He smiled back, trying not to look too relieved. He wanted to show her he knew a thing or two about hats. "This is a beaver felt, right?"

"Yep. Rabbits are too flimsy to crease. They wilt under the steam." She pointed to the three X's printed on the sweatband. You won't see those on a rabbit hat."

Jake marveled as she calmly ran her fingers down the middle of the crown to make the initial deep crush. She rolled each side over the dent she had made, waved it a couple of times with both hands to let the felt set, then held it in front of her to make sure it was straight. Her big glasses had steamed over, and Jake suppressed a grin. Flustered, she dropped them on the counter, revealing eyes as black as Jake's. "How much turn-up do you want on the brim?"

Jake had a quick answer. "Not quite as much as Nocona's. Did you crease his?"

"Sure did. He won't let anybody else touch his hats." She steamed the brim, brought it to her knee and worked it gradually up to keep from making a wrinkle. She held it toward Jake. "About like that?"

"Looks good."

She brought the freshly steamed brim front to her chin and gave it a slight upward push against her chin. "I usually duck the front a little lower than the back. Keeps water from running down the back of your neck."

Jake nodded as he took the hat. He felt the firmness of the brim as he placed the still-warm hat on his hat and walked to the mirror. He liked what he saw there. If the crease needed changing, he did not know how to tell the young girl what it needed. "I never had a beaver felt hat before. Always wore wool ones until I got a rabbit felt Christmas before last."

Caleb appeared behind him. "You'll like the way this one holds a crease. I'd wear it the rest of the day. Lets it conform to your head quicker."

Jake's face warmed. "Guess I should have asked the price before I had you crease it."

Caleb smiled. "Twenty-three fifty." Jake winced.

"That's a three-X beaver, and beaver is getting expensive. And these are factory seconds. Firsts would run you eight or ten more."

Jake picked up his hatbox and followed Caleb and Sage to the checkout counter. Sage was wearing a pair of Wranglers and a pair of plain, natural color, soft-looking calfskin boots with a walking heel. Jake noted that her jeans needed a little filling out in the seat, but she walked good for a twelve-year-old kid. He walked back to get her glasses for her.

15 A full week after his fifteenth birthday, legitimate drivers license in his billfold, Jake felt a little stiff and maybe a little too noticeable in his new yellow cowboy shirt with brown piping around the yokes. He had cleaned the '55 Ford with rags and toothpicks and plenty of his mother's furniture polish, but a coat of dust had already settled on the dash. More drifted in the windows as he made his turn at the big cottonwood. He knew where he was going, because he had ridden Scar on an exploratory mission the day before. Jake started to pass by and wait for cover of darkness to make his entrance, but he looked at his new boots on the clutch and accelerator and made the turn. It was now or never.

He climbed the hill to the house and felt better when he saw Nocona's red Chevy parked in the side yard with an assortment of other cars and pickups. Some of the pickups had horse trailers attached. Support stumps were visible under the house's porch, making it look like houses in East Texas. It needed paint, but not as bad as the Rivers' house did. A barn and several outbuildings surrounded a side yard larger than the Rivers'. The setting sun illuminated dust clouds being stirred from a long barn to his left. No sign of

any kids. Jake was reminded of those open yards where Roy
Rogers and the Sons of the Pioneers serenaded at sunset after
a hard day of rounding up outlaws.

The strains of Hank Williams singing "Cold, Cold Heart"
drifted through the thin air and warmed Jake as he walked
toward the music. He traced it to a long, low building just
behind and south of the house. The windows and door
were open. He heard voices singing along with the music,
shouts of laughter, giggling, and loud talk. His hat crown
struck the low doorframe as he entered to the stares of a small
bunkhouse full of boys and girls. His hat felt cockeyed on
his head, and he imagined that the crown had been mashed,
making him appear foolish. He dragged the hat across his
head and examined it. The crease had not been hurt.

A big boy was changing forty-fives on a small record
player. He looked over his shoulder at Jake. "Hope you like
Hank Williams. I ain't got any of my own records. Borrowed
these from Daddy." He pointed at the hat in Jake's hand.
"Throw it on the bed with the rest." The boy wore a shirt
made exactly like Jake's except it was red with blue piping
around the yokes. "Nice lookin' shirt, but yellow's unlucky
for cowboys."

All six feet of the boy stood after putting the needle on
the record. His hat would have struck the low ceiling if he
had been wearing one. He had broad shoulders and fresh-
cut, shiny black hair that was long on top. Jake envied the
sideburns that reached to the middle of his ears. He had
never been able to grow them. If not for a weak chin, the boy
would have looked good enough to be Gregory Peck's stunt-
double.

Jake smiled weakly. "Guess somebody forgot to tell either
your mother or mine about yellow bein' unlucky." Jake
stopped staring long enough to see two bunk beds covered
with a sea of black hats. Two more bunk beds were in the
back of the long room. He hesitated, recalling that in East

Texas, putting a hat on a bed was bad luck. Well, he wasn't in East Texas now, and these kids obviously considered it bad manners to wear a lid inside. He laid his hat on the bed with the others.

"Name's Gabe Lowry. You must be Jake Rivers." Gabe's voice was low and rumbling, but he slurred his words a little and talked like he had too much spit in his mouth. He rolled his tongue around his mouth and pushed it against his jaw with each sentence. He was wearing new boots exactly like Jake's.

Jake was glad that Gabe had a weak chin. "You nailed me. Nocona said it would be all right for me to come. Appreciate the invitation."

"He's out by the arena. We got some little bulls out there he wants to ride, but he's afraid to get his clothes messed up."

Afraid that he would not be able to identify it later, Jake kept watch on his hat out of the corner of his eye. The others had cards stuck in them or names written on sweatbands. He saw a feminine hand lift his hat and turn it over. Sage looked through her butterscotch frames and frowned at Jake. "Never lay a hat on its brim. Ruins the crease."

Jake felt properly chastised and humiliated. "I knew that … just nervous, I guess." She was wearing a western shirt the same color as his, but without the fancy yokes. There must have a lot of yellow fabric at Adrian Mercantile. The words came before Jake could collect his thoughts. "Thought this party was for high school kids."

She colored a little. He had thought of her as a bold kid, not shy. "As of next Monday, I will be a high school kid."

"You're a freshman?"

"Just one year behind you." She handed him his hat. "Put that on and follow me. Daddy said I should introduce you to the other kids."

Jake pulled down the Resistol and followed her out the door, taking care to bend down. Nocona was crawling over the arena rail fence as they approached. He looked up at Jake and smiled. "Well, well, my Indian friend, and Little Sage. Damn, Jake, you look better in a hat than I do. Sage, here, says that my face is too wide."

Jake could not take his eyes off the leggings that Nocona was unbuckling. It was getting dark, but Jake could still see that the batwing chaps were a soft, crinkly, dark green. He was still staring when Gabe joined them. Nocona finished unbuckling the legs and reached for the belt. As he carelessly flopped them over his shoulder, Jake reached out to touch the glove-soft leather, his envy spilling out on the dust. "Where'd you get those chaps?"

Nocona patted them. "Birthday present from my parents. I won the bullriding up at Dalhart in July wearin' these babies. Green's my favorite color. They brought me good luck."

Gabe put his arm across Nocona's shoulders and looked at Jake. "While you and me been plowin', this boy's been on the rodeo circuit all summer."

Jake's eyes showed surprise. "You really ride the circuit? You never said anything about that before."

Nocona jerked a thumb toward Gabe. "He's exaggeratin'. I made three rodeos is all. First time I ever entered anything other than a high school rodeo."

"And you ride bulls?" Jake tried to swallow his envy.

"All the rough stock events."

As they walked back toward the bunkhouse, Jake took the time to really look around. The setting sun illuminated a deep gorge behind the house and barn compound, rising to a stone bluff on the western horizon. It was the first break in eternal flatness Jake had seen in the Panhandle. Just to the side of the bunkhouse, couples had started dancing to "Moments to Remember". One of the girls had brought her own records. The hair on Jake's neck stood up and a little chill ran down his spine as he saw the little swirls of dust kicked up by their boots as they danced. He felt as if he had found the gold at the end of the rainbow—a collection of kindred spirits. He decided then and there that he was going to be a Matador.

As the sun dropped completely behind the rock bluff, Jake felt a soft hand in his. Someone flipped the forty-five to "Love is a Many-Splendored Thing" as he felt himself pulled to the couples. He resisted weakly, trying to get a clear glimpse of who was pulling him. She was taller than Sage, and the seat of her Levis was nicely filled. Her hair was dusty-blonde and flipped up on the ends. She wore a musky cologne that Jake did not particularly like, but felt drawn to. He also detected a hint of sweat. The combination drew him like flies to pies. He was not used to smelling a girl caught sweating. He caught a glimpse of a cheek as she snuggled confidently against his shoulder. Her hair, bringing the scent of a recent shampoo, tickled Jake's nose.

He had never danced with anyone other than his mother or sister and felt clumsy, but no matter what moves he made, she glided with him across the hard ground. Firm breasts pressed boldly against his own, and Jake aged a year or two before the Four Aces finished their beautiful song. Trish and Mattie's dance lessons had paid off.

When she finally stepped away, Jake got his first look at her face. His breath caught in his throat. She was gorgeous. Deep brown eyes—hair that bounced—dark, well-defined eyebrows that rose to a nice point in the middle—full lips that needed no lipstick—a face full of mischief and fun. Jake knew by now that she was firm all over and moved like his sister—an athlete. Jake felt his face warm when Nocona and Gabe whistled wolf calls as they walked back toward them.

Nocona had a redhead under his arm. "Jake, meet Texie Malone. Looks like you already met her best friend." Texie, a look-alike for Shirley MacLaine in *Sheepman*, stuck out a freckled hand to Jake and giggled as she winked at the girl still holding Jake's hand. Hank Williams was tuning up again with "Your Cheating Heart".

Nocona did the introduction. "Loretta Knight, meet Jake Rivers, the toughest kid at Hereford High last year."

Loretta stood eye-to-eye with Jake as she smiled all the way through his eyes. "You mean he fights, too? Most boys who fight are too dumb to dance, and this boy can dance." The voice was mellow and sweet and communed perfectly with her fragrance and appearance.

Nocona turned to Gabe. "Gabe, you might want to introduce Jake to the toughest kid in Adrian. He'll want to whip his ass the first day and get it over with."

Gabe took off his hat and scratched his head. "Well, that would probably be me, unless you take over for me this year."

"Naw, I mean besides you and me."

"The only kid I wouldn't want to mess with is Burt Donovan."

Gabe turned to Jake and laughed. "Sorry, Jake. Burt ain't here tonight. Not the social type. You'll just have to wait until Monday to show him he's been replaced."

Jake was almost certain that they were kidding him, but not quite. "Guess I'm all done with that. It didn't work out too well for me at Hereford. Who's the smallest freshman? I'll pick on him." Loretta was pulling him toward the dancers.

Before the song was over, Loretta pulled Jake off the dirt dance floor and led him to the back of the bunkhouse. She gently backed him against the building. Jake had kissed a girl once before—inside the Tunnel of Love on Rural Youth Day at the State Fair of Texas; he had been bold enough to press his lips against some part of Annie Black's face in the darkest part of the tunnel. He had not been sure if he had kissed her lips or her nose. This was different. Loretta put both hands on his face and tenderly touched moist lips to his, deftly parting his lips before she pressed her body against his. This was not her first kiss. Clumsy at first, Jake was surprised at how quickly he got the hang of it. Loretta touched him in places he had never been touched before. She seemed very thirsty, and Jake was more than pleased to provide her a drink.

Jake was tingling all over, and his ears were ringing so loud that he barely heard Gabe's mother ring the dinner bell—a signal that the party was over. There were more whistles when they emerged together. Texie pulled Loretta away and pushed her into Nocona's Chevy. Jake felt confident and transformed as he cranked the Ford. A hand on his shoulder seemed natural. Sage put her elbows on the open window. "You got off to a fast start."

"How do you mean?"

Sage smiled. "You know what I mean."

"You mean Loretta?"

"Who else?"

"She seems pretty sure of herself. How old is she?"

"Older'n you."

Jake felt the air go out of his balloon. He had never thought of dating an older girl. "How much?"

"She's a senior, but old enough to be graduated."

"She fail?"

"Nobody knows why she's a year behind."

Jake was sinking deeper and deeper. "Why would she have anything to do with me?"

Sage sighed with impatience. "In case you haven't noticed, there are only three senior boys, and she's already been through all of them and most of the juniors. Boys from Vega are afraid of PK."

"PK?"

"Preacher's kid."

"Loretta is a preacher's kid?"

Caleb Pirtle drove up in a beat-up Dodge pickup and parked beside Jake. He signaled for Sage to get in. She waved and turned away from Jake. "You better be a Baptist."

16 Jake forked the last bite of fried biscuit and dragged it through the confection sugar syrup. He felt really good for the first time in a long time as he washed the biscuit down with orange juice. His first plate of fried biscuits had been made better because he was sitting beside Nocona and across from Gabe in a booth at the Bent Door Trading Post. Three black Resistols—three pairs of black Justins. He still could not believe it was a school day and that there was plenty of time to make the first class. He looked across 66 toward the school and felt confident. Tomorrow, he would have to ride the school bus, but today, he was riding with friends.

Nocona parked the Chevy in front of the school. Jake tried not to notice the lack of grass, trees, or anything of color around the drab little building. He liked it because it looked about the size of the Klondike school. Gabe and Nocona hung their hats on the long hat rack in the hall, and Jake followed suit. He checked to make sure the little card that said *Hands off! This hat belongs to:* was still in the sweatband. They had stopped at Adrian Mercantile to pick the card up before school. Jake had printed his name and Route 4,

Hereford, Texas, under the warning.

Nocona and Jake walked to the principal's office together. Nocona's defiant attitude was gone as they sat across from the pale, balding, sixty-ish man with round glasses. He looked so out of place in this severe ranch and farming country that Jake felt a kinship with him.

By last period, Jake had met most of the kids in high school and a large number of elementary school kids. His real test came the next day. A pair of new black Converse shoes hung over his shoulder when he gathered in the gym with all four grades of high school boys. He joined the others as they scrounged through piles of white athletic shorts and shirts dumped on the gym floor. Jake was lucky enough to find a pair of shorts and a shirt that fit. In the locker room, he felt a sense of camaraderie and tension as they all shucked jeans and boots, pulled on shorts and tee shirts and laced up their gym shoes. As individual style gave way to uniformity, Jake felt almost equal for the first time since leaving East Texas. He might not match them with a rope, in the rodeo arena, or driving a tractor, but Jake felt a soothing comfort returning from an old life as he stepped on the hardwoods.

A young, handsome coach with dark, coarse hair and eyebrows and perfect white teeth assembled them in a straight line across the gym floor. Jake tried not to notice, but the young coach reminded him of an older, darker, Snake Drager. The skin on his face seemed to be pulled back, stretching his eyes. He had the tall, lean build of a basketball player. A man in his fifties with light-brown, thick hair, and a spare tire around his waist walked in front of them, examining each boy as he strolled. Veins swept across his face like a cobweb. From a clipboard list, he started calling roll. When all the names had been called except Jake's and Nocona's, he stopped in front of them.

"I see that you boys are new. Transfers from Hereford."

Jake and Nocona nodded.

"If you didn't have different last names, I would have thought you were brothers."

Nocona laughed. "Not a chance."

"I'm new here, too. I have records and stats on the other boys, but nothing on you two. Ever play any basketball before?"

They nodded. Jake spoke first. "Played in grade school is all."

Nocona spoke up. "Played my freshman year at Hereford." Jake shot him a surprised look.

"That's a big school. You get any playin' time?"

"Junior varsity first string till mid-season."

The coach tapped the clipboard with his pencil. "What happened at mid-season?"

"Got kicked off the team."

"What for?"

"You gonna hold it against me?"

"Depends."

Nocona shook his head. "Got caught with beer in my car on the school grounds."

Ignoring the snickers, the coach nodded and turned to Jake. "Both of you got the bodies to play ball. We'll soon find out if you got the heads."

He stepped back and addressed the group. "My name is Alton Gee. You can call me Coach Gee. I'm sure you all know Ken Watson, my assistant. It may not look like it now, but I played college basketball and baseball. Course, that was a long time ago. If you do what I say, I guarantee we will win more games than you won last year." Snickers. "Today, we are going to learn to jump rope and start getting into shape for basketball. My guess is that you played out of shape last year. Even an old man like me can beat you when you're out of shape."

Gee and the young coach brought gunny sacks full of jump ropes and dumped them on the gym floor. Jake picked

Jim Ainsworth

up a rope and looked at the other boys. They seemed as bewildered as he was. He had not jumped rope since first grade. Girls jumped rope. He was snickering with Nocona and Gabe when Coach Gee blew the whistle. "We'll start with a hundred jumps today, then double it every day until we get to a thousand or so."

Gabe looked at Jake and silently mouthed "A thousand?" They both laughed.

Within minutes, ropes were tangled around legs and wrapped around necks. It was pratfall time in the gym. Jake began the familiar skip, jump, skip he had seen the girls do in the schoolyard. He was feeling pretty superior until he saw Coach Gee standing behind him. "You always do things like a girl?"

Jake's mirth and pride disappeared. "What do you mean?"

Gee took the rope from him. "Everybody listen up. I'm only gonna do this once. Hell, once is probably all I can do it." He jumped the rope several times like a boxer in training, leaving out the skip. After a dozen jumps, he crossed his hands in front without missing a jump. He jumped the rope backwards a few times for good measure. Jake noticed that the inner tube around his waist was bouncing. Coach Gee, breathing hard, handed the rope back to Jake. "Think you can do as good?"

Jake shook his head, but after a few misses, he was jumping the rope without skipping. He reached a hundred jumps within minutes. He did another hundred while the other boys caught up. After a few laps around the gym and some wind sprints, a whistle called them to a stop. Coach Gee slapped a volleyball down in the center circle of the court. "We have about twenty minutes left. Anybody know how to play dodge ball?" Most nodded. "All right. Last man standing wins."

There was hesitation until a young freshman swooped in

and picked up the ball. He slammed it against the head of
another freshman and picked it up again. He had put out
three boys before Gabe stole the ball on his last hit. Within
a few minutes, only six boys were left in the game. Some sat
on the sidelines with bloody noses and red eyes or cheeks.
Jake soared with confidence. His size had changed from
disadvantage to advantage. He recovered the ball from a pile
of boys and put out two more. Only Gabe, Nocona, and a big
kid stood between him and victory on his first day of school.
He recalled Mike Drager sitting on his chest in the school
auditorium at Hereford as he took out the big kid with a solid
smack to the face. Nocona and Gabe grinned until he took
them out, too.

Most of the other kids had already gone to the showers
when Jake was last man standing. It diminished his first
victory at anything in a long time. The big kid pushed him
from behind, and Jake dropped the ball. The kid picked it
up, cocked his arm, and stalked Jake. Jake backpedaled.
"Aren't you already out? I hit you before I took out Gabe and
Nocona. There's still a red spot on your cheek." He was
answered by a volleyball aimed straight for his nose. Jake
caught it, ran behind the big kid, and slammed him squarely
in the nose with the ball when he turned around. "Now
you're really out." Blood poured from the boy's nose, and
Jake offered him a towel. "Hey, I'm sorry. Guess your nose
bleeds easy."

The boy held his shirt to his nose and ignored the towel.
Cold eyes stared at Jake over the white shirt that had turned
blood red. Jake meekly followed him into the locker room.
Nocona was waiting at the door. "How did you know who he
was?"

The boy disappeared into the locker room. "Who?"

"The kid whose nose you just bloodied. That's Burt
Donovan, the tough kid Gabe and I told you about."

Gabe joined them. "I thought Nocona was just kiddin'

about you taking out the meanest one first, but it looks like you really aim to do it. If I were you, I'd skip the shower. Want me to go in and get your clothes for you?"

Jake declined the offer. Inside the locker room, he took a seat on the bench beside his locker and wiped sweat from his forehead with a towel. Elation to despair only took seconds. He had done it again. Only a few kids remained in the group shower as he put his towel on the bench outside. Trying not to stare at the naked bodies, he took a deep breath when he realized that Burt Donovan was not there. Jake tried to be nonchalant about his first shower with schoolmates, but he was in and out of the water and had a towel wrapped around his waist in less than two minutes. The tap on his shoulder came as he reached inside his locker for his underwear. The tap startled him, and his towel dropped to the locker room floor. Jake stooped to pick it up.

The long arms and big hands of Burt Donovan faced him as he rose. The arms were just as Gabe had described them. Brown and sinewy with bulging veins, they almost reached to his knees. Knuckles bulged like knots on huge hands that seemed to face the wrong way. Fear clutched Jake's heart and froze his tongue. Burt was staring at Jake as if he were a foreign object that he could not figure out. From the smell of him and the way his shirt clung to his chest, Jake knew he had skipped the shower.

Burt spoke behind a serious overbite and crooked teeth. "Guess you and me ain't done, Sheepherder. I think I need to whip your ass."

"Why's that?" Jake hated his meek whimper.

"You made a fool out of me in there." Burt jerked his thumb toward the basketball court.

"I been playing dodge ball since I could walk. It's just a game. Makes everybody look silly."

"When and how do you want it?"

"What's that?"

"Your ass-whuppin'."

Fear almost made Jake forget his nakedness. He needed time to think. He turned his back to Burt and stuck his legs through his underwear and jeans. His head was a little clearer as he buttoned his Levis. Still shirtless, he faced Burt and stuck out his hand. "Name's Jake Rivers."

Burt stared at the hand, recalling the way it had bloodied his nose, before returning a cold stare to Jake's eyes. The boy never seemed to blink.

"Look, Burt. I'm new here. Nocona and Gabe told me your name and that you were the kid who could whip anybody in the school. I just didn't know who you were when we played dodge ball. Otherwise, I would have never hit you twice, especially in the face."

Burt's large ears sat low on his head. Somehow, that eased Jake's fear a little. Burt's eyes were still confused, but they seemed to soften a little as he spoke. "Damage is done. I got you figured for a sheepherder, and I don't see any way out of this thing except to whip your ass in front of everybody who saw you make a fool outta me."

Jake's mind raced for a way out. "Maybe not." He reached for his shirt, tucked it in and began snapping the snaps. "I want to be friends, but I ain't takin' a whippin' without fightin' back. Ask Nocona Wells if you don't believe me. I been fightin' my brother since I was six, and he's about as strong as you are and one helluva a lot quicker. I never whipped him, but it got to where he had to bring his lunch to whip me."

Burt doubled his fists and pushed Jake against the locker. "You sayin' you think your puny ass can whip me?"

Jake's temper flared for a second, and he pushed back. Taking his whipping inside the locker room away from curious eyes briefly crossed his mind. "What I'm sayin' is that you're about a foot taller'n me and fifty pounds heavier. You're at least two years older. You're going to have to whip me really

127

good to save face. If I just get in a couple of good licks, you're gonna look like a loser even if you win ...which I'm sure you will."

Burt studied Jake's words. His silence gave Jake enough courage to put a finger lightly into Burt's chest. "And I guarantee you I'll get in a couple of licks." He thought of Nocona's fight with Steve Weston. "And I'll fight dirty if I have to ... and what's this sheepherder bullshit about?"

Jake saw more confusion in Burt's eyes. He stuck out his hand again. "Look, probably most of the kids in school are tougher than I am. Why waste your time on me? Let's walk out of this locker room together and start all over." Burt walked away without shaking his hand.

Coach Ken Watson was waiting as Jake exited the gym. Jake nodded and tried to walk around the coach. Watson grabbed his arm and pulled him back. "I know some of the coaches in Hereford. They tell me you and Wells were trouble. You startin' off on the same foot here?"

"No, sir."

The coach poked Jake's chest with a hairy finger. "You been here two days and already trying to start fights and mess with my best basketball player."

"Didn't know Burt was your best basketball player."

"I'm talking about Loretta Knight. You little snot-nosed boys always runnin' her and takin' advantage cause she's a preacher's kid. Keeps her head messed up for basketball."

Jake shook his head, his anger returning. "Hey, I just met Loretta last night. Doubt if she even knows my name." When Watson did not reply, Jake jerked his thumb toward Nocona's car. We all done? I need to catch my ride home."

He dropped into the seat beside Nocona and blew out breath that he seemed to have held for an hour. Nocona cranked the Chevy and backed out. "You gonna have to fight old Burt?"

Jake smiled as he shook his head. "I think I talked him

out of it. Had a worse time with the girls' basketball coach. What's his problem?"

From the back seat, Gabe began telling the story of the coaches. Ken Watson, the handsome young coach, had been boys' basketball coach the previous year. Adrian boys had won two games all year, none of them in district play. "School board wanted to fire him, but his wife is grade school principal, and everybody loves her. The girls' coach quit, so they gave him that job so they could keep Miz Watson."

Nocona crossed the railroad tracks and headed down 66 with pipes rumbling. "Wish she taught high school. She's better lookin' that any of the girls except Loretta."

Gabe leaned forward. "Better not let Texie hear you said that."

Nocona put up his middle finger without taking his eyes off the road. "Texie's got her own good qualities—and you know better than to repeat anything I say." As they turned off 66 onto the farm-to-market toward home, he pushed the Chevy to ninety. "Need to get home and practice. This damn rope-jumpin' has got me stiff already."

Jake still had his mind on Burt Donovan. He was still a little shaky from the close call with another school bully. Aside from Burt, his first two days had been good ones. "Practice for what?"

"I got a barrel stretched between two posts in the yard. I ride it every day. School rodeo is in three weeks. You entering?"

"What would I enter?"

"Calf roping. Gabe's gonna enter the ropin' and the bulldoggin'. I plan to ride barebacks, saddlebroncs, and bulls."

"I can't rope and I sure as hell can't ride in the rough stock events."

Gabe rolled down the back seat window, stuck his head out, and hollered through the wind. "String says you can."

"He said that?"

"Says you need some more practice, but that little Shetland-lookin' horse you got can do it."

"He's twice as big as a Shetland and he looks better'n that jughead you ride. Why did Burt call me a sheepherder?"

Gabe laughed. "Around here, that's a general insult that covers just about everything. This is cattle country."

For three weeks, the boys went through exercises they had never done before in addition to hated familiar ones like climbing the bleachers, the crawl, wind sprints, and simple laps around the gym. Without breaking out a basketball, the new coach had them setting picks, maneuvering around screens, rebounding, running fast breaks, pivoting and executing complex plays—all done without a basketball. More often, they drilled to build strength. When they complained about not actually playing, Gee told them they could play when they *got their breath*. "Teams may beat us on skill or size, but they will not beat us on stamina."

They started each day with jump ropes, and Jake was beginning to feel like a boxer who never threw a punch. He could cross the rope in front and back and had picked up a few other tricks. He was ready to pick up a basketball and see what he had lost since missing his freshman year. He liked Coach Gee and felt liked by him. The boys grumbled about constant exercise and mind-numbing drills every day, but the soreness had begun to wear off, and they started to take pride as muscles grew and bodies took on new shapes.

Jake was taking his turn at ten-slaps-on-the-backboard under Coach Gee's watchful eye. "Rivers, I expect you to touch the rim before the first game if you want to start."

Using his thighs and knees the way he had been taught, Jake slapped the backboard for the tenth time before relinquishing his place. As he went to the back of the line, he studied the rim. Being a sophomore-new-kid-starter had only been a dream. At the beginning of school, he could barely reach the net. Now, he was expected to touch the rim. He understood why they had been jumping rope. The muscles in his upper and lower legs were now pronounced and firm. When it was his turn again, he took a running start and grabbed the rim with one hand.

17 Jake stepped out of Rance's pickup at the rodeo
arena just outside of Adrian and walked toward
Nocona's Chevy. The car door was open, and his
green chaps lay across the front seat. An open can of bootleg
Coors sat on the floorboard. Nocona was seated on the dirt,
his legs splayed out in opposite directions. He was alternately
touching each boot toe with his fingers. His usual glibness
was missing.

"When do you ride?"

"I drew the first bareback." Nocona's tone indicated
that we wanted to be left alone to focus. Feeling left out,
Jake wandered off. All of his new friends had entered the
one-night rodeo. Ashamed that he was not really a cowboy,
Jake avoided Loretta and the other girls. He did not want to
hear them yell for his friends or see his envy. He took a seat
beside the only boy in school who neither played basketball
nor entered rodeos. Cecil Newberry was a skin-and-bone boy
who was said to have Bright's disease. He sat in the bleachers
while Jake and the others worked out in the gym each day.
Jake now understood how Cecil must feel sitting on the
sidelines. He made idle conversation with him until Nocona's

name was called.

Loretta and Texie screamed when Nocona rode his bronc for the full eight seconds. Nocona had been thrown from his saddlebronc but had won second in bareback. A hand touched Jake's knee as the calf roping was about to start. "How come you aren't entered up?"

Jake had not noticed Coach Gee sitting below him. "No rope, no chaps, no riggin', no bronc saddle, no bull rope, no trailer, not much horse, and even less cowboy. Plus I'm no good." Jake knew the answer by heart. He had recited it to himself and to others plenty of times.

"I feel so sorry for you; I think I might cry. String tells me you can rope."

Jake wondered how String had met the coach. "I have to borrow calves, a rope and a piggin' string every time I practice with String. Not good enough to compete."

"Sure it's not because you can't stand to lose? Got to stick your neck out if you want to play basketball for me." The coach turned to watch Gabe ride the black gelding he called Stud into the box. Jake watched him call for the calf, watched the rope curl as it circled the calf's neck. Gabe jerked his slack, ran down the line, and flanked the calf. He used the piggin' string to take two wraps and a hooey around three of the calf's legs and held his hands in the air to stop the clock at just under twenty seconds. Jake took a deep breath. Roping and tying calves was one of the most beautiful athletic feats he had ever witnessed, but it almost made him moan with envy when he saw his friend do it. He hated his envy, hated himself for not entering.

String slid onto the bleacher seat on the other side of Cecil. He reached across Cecil and spoke to Jake. "You could have done that in sixteen."

Jake's eyebrows arched. "You ever time me?"

"No, but I got a feel for it. Gabe's a good, all-around hand, but you're quicker on the dismount and running down that line. You got better hand-eye coordination for tying, too."

Jake watched Nocona take first in bull riding and choked on his own jealousy when Gabe got a new rope for second place in calf roping and a buckle for first in bulldogging. Nocona won a buckle for best all-around cowboy. Jake suppressed his true feelings and forced a smile and handshake for Gabe, Nocona, and the rest of his schoolmates who had competed. He barely interrupted their jubilation. Jake was even jealous of the boys who had missed or been thrown. Dejected and ashamed of his feelings, he kept his head down as he drug his feet through the sand walking back to the pickup.

Loretta was lying in the seat when he opened the door. Seeing her brought mixed emotions. His first encounter with Loretta had brought him plenty of grief at school. Every kid he met asked if he was *new meat for the PK.* Dating an older girl just did not seem right to Jake. He had also heard about her father. The Reverend Floyd Knight was said to be six feet, five inches tall and to weigh about two-eighty. The gentle giant watched his daughter like a hawk.

Tonight, Jake needed consolation, and Loretta knew it. He looked around to see who was watching. "What are you doin' here?"

She shushed him with a finger to her lips. "Get in and drive."

He cranked the Chevy and pulled out on the farm-to-market. "Where to?"

Away from the arena, she sat up, scooted close, and laid a hand on his inner thigh. Jake squirmed a little. "Where do you usually take your girlfriends?"

Jake turned to look at her. "What girlfriends?"

"Where did you take them back in East Texas, or wherever you lived before?"

"I didn't even have a drivers license back there, but I used to ride along with my brother when he took his girls to the woods. He'd make me lie in the floorboard in the back, but I sure got to hear a lot of interesting stuff."

"Woods, huh? We call it going to the bushes around here. I don't know why, though. Not even any bushes to get behind out here."

"Where do you go to make out?"

"Out on the Matador, honey. You just drive till you are so far out that nobody can get close to you without your seeing them first."

Jake knew that a cattle guard crossing to the Matador Ranch lay less than a quarter mile from Adrian school. Nocona had taken him across after school one day. Jake had stared in awe at the wide-open spaces that represented a tiny slice of 400,000 acres. The grandeur of being on part of the old XIT in moonlight excited him almost as much as Loretta's hand on his thigh. "Wanna go?"

She put her head on his shoulder and sighed. "You come prepared?"

Jake tried to imagine what his brother would say. "I'm always prepared."

"Show it to me."

Jake pulled the car over, took a deep breath and looked at her. "You really mean that?"

Loretta cackled. "Not that, Jake. I mean show me your rubber."

Jake expelled the breath. "Don't have one."

She squeezed his arm. "I'm just jackin' with you, anyway. I want to go, but I can't. Not tonight. I'm supposed to be at Texie's. Daddy will be checking on me in about twenty minutes."

"No time for a Coke at the Bent Door or Jesse's?"

"Nope. Can't even be seen with a boy. Especially you."

"Why especially me?"

"Cause you haven't been properly introduced to my

parents. Especially my daddy."

They stayed far away from the Baptist parsonage as they rode around Adrian. Loretta, between strokes of his thigh, showed him where some of his schoolmates lived.

Jake looked at his Timex as they stopped on the dirt street in front of Texie's house. "You got about five minutes before your daddy comes lookin'."

Jake's ear tingled as she made a kissing sound in it and breathed heavily before putting her knees in the seat and sliding out the passenger door. She blew him a kiss before turning away. "See you on the Matador. Come prepared next time."

18 Jake slapped his leg all the way home. He had failed at rodeoing and at his first real date. The bellowing of cattle greeted him when he pulled into his yard. Still drowning in self-pity, he followed the noise. The quarter-moon provided just enough light for Jake to see cows milling in the lot. *I wonder why String didn't say anything about rounding them up when I saw him at the rodeo?*

"How was the rodeo?" Rance's voice startled Jake. Jake found the glow from a cigarette and followed it to his father's outline in the sparse moonlight. Rance was sitting on the top rail.

"Okay, I guess. Gabe won the doggin' and took second in the ropin'. Nocona won second in bareback, first in bullridin'." Jake's voice was flat. "He got all-around cowboy, too."

Rance nodded and took another drag before mashing the roll-your-own against the corral board. He shredded it and let the pieces fall from his hands. "How come you didn't enter?"

Darkness gave Jake the nerve to stare boldly at his father. He and Rance had never discussed the possibility of his entering the rodeo. Jake had assumed that his daddy would think it foolish and extravagant. The question irritated him.

"Didn't figure you would let me. You never let me rope our calves for practice back home."

"I notice you and String been doin' plenty of ropin' on the bank's cattle. He tells me you can do it. Papa said you could, too."

"Too late now. These cattle don't look like the bank's. Where'd they come from?"

"They're ours, or at least they will be when we pay off the note."

Jake's spirits lifted a little. "Where'd you get `em?"

"I told Will Tom Sunday to be on the lookout for about forty head a while back. He sent word this morning that he had some at a good price. I signed a note at the bank, and Will delivered 'em just before dark."

Jake was disappointed that he had missed Will Tom Sunday, but the prospect of owning cattle washed away some of his self-pity about the rodeo. "What did he have to say?"

"Asked about you, like he always does. Will Tom's a good man, but seems to carry a deep sadness about him. We talked a little about his boy and Tuck." Rance stared at the quarter-moon. "His wound is fresher."

Words failed Jake as he shifted his position on the rail, took out his pocketknife, and began to peel small curls of wood from the gray top rail. They sat without speaking, listening to the low bellowing of the small herd and the creaking of the windmill. The cattle smelled of manure, grass breath, and dust. Different than the wild-onion-milky smell of dairy cattle. "You gonna turn `em in with the bank's herd?"

"Tomorrow. We got to brand and vaccinate first, though. There's some bull calves that need cuttin'. It's a mixed group—a few mama cows that'll calve in the spring, a few steers, a few pairs and some heifers. Cheaper than gettin' a uniform herd. Bank said we could use their bulls."

The mix did not matter to Jake—just as long as they were cattle.

Rance stepped off the rail and started toward the house. "Better get to bed. I'll be callin' you at daybreak."

Jake pulled down his worn-out, cheap hat when Rance knocked on his door the next morning. He wanted to wear the Resistol but was not ready to risk getting it stepped on or worse. He walked into the kitchen in his socks, carrying his old work boots. He sat down and tried to pull on a boot, but the dried, cracked leather would not yield to his too-big foot. Mattie poured cups of coffee for herself and Rance. "Jake, those boots would ruin your feet even if you could get them on. Why don't you just wear those old tennis shoes? You'll just be walking around in cow mess all day." Jake gave her an exasperated glance that said you do not wear tennis shoes when you work cattle.

"Start your breakfast. I'll be back in a minute." She returned with a pair of brown rough-outs with gum soles. The rough leather had been worn slick. "These are Gray Boy's. See if you can wear them."

Belly full of breakfast, Jake walked to the corral beside his father in his brother's boots. The morning was cold and the wind biting. Jake felt redeemed. String, fresh from a bath in the trough, was waiting. "Mornin' men. How we gonna approach this little job, Rance?" Jake looked beyond him and saw both Scar and Pink fully tacked. He felt a little guilty, but a lot grateful.

Rance had stopped at the well house to pick up a five-gallon bucket of supplies. The handle to a branding iron and a Hot-Shot cattle prod stuck out the top. "Need to build a fire first thing, I guess. Ought to be pretty easy. We're just gonna brand `em and vaccinate `em. There's four bulls to cut."

Jake rolled four barrels, rusty and blackened from many such uses, into a corner of the corral to protect the fire from the cattle and vice-versa. He poured a little diesel on the kindling he had gathered and borrowed his father's Zippo to get it started. It wasn't full daylight yet, so the light and the warmth were welcome. Mattie brought three cups of coffee from the house, and she could not keep from grinning when she handed Jake his. He grinned back. Coffee tastes good on a cold morning beside a campfire with cowboy work to be done—even if you don't like coffee.

Rance rolled out a towel on top of one of the barrels and used the light of the campfire to arrange his needles and syringe. "Put that iron in the fire, Jake. Gather some more kindling. You'll need to keep that fire hot till we finish branding." Jake left in a trot.

Rance turned the iron in the fire. "String, I think we can take care of it all from this chute, don't you?"

String nodded. "We'll do 'er anyway you like it, Rance."

Rance turned as Jake dropped a pile of scrap wood beside the fire. "Jake, I want 'em to stick close to the house when we turn 'em out so I can watch 'em a little. I still ain't had a real good look in the daylight. Will Tom said he'd make good anything I reject."

Jake nodded. Will Tom was a man that could be trusted.

Rance tested his syringe with alcohol. "Keep your horse handy. They'll probably head to that corner as soon as we turn 'em out. Ought to be easy to hold there. If one strays, don't get excited; just lope out and bring her back. I don't want 'em stirred up till they get used to the place."

String pointed toward his saddled horse. "Take Pink out there. He'll help you hold 'em. They'll likely stick around till there's more outside than in."

Jake grabbed a handful of Scar's mane with his left hand, the saddle horn with his right and stuck his foot into the stirrup. He pulled himself into the saddle and heard the satisfying creak of leather. Feeling older, taller and stronger, he took Pink's reins and led him around the barn. With reins tied and draped over the horn, Pink took up his duty just outside the corral fence and next to the barn. Jake rode up to watch as String punched the first one into the chute with on old walking cane. The electric prod stayed in the bucket. Rance put a creosote post between the rails to keep her from backing up, picked up his syringe, sterilized the needle with alcohol, and gave her a shot. He picked up the branding iron from the fire. Two wavy lines representing rivers glowed in the predawn light. ⤳⫫ Jake had long admired the Rivers' brand but had seen it used only once before. They had not branded their dairy cattle in East Texas.

The hair on Jake's neck tickled him as he saw the brand's glow move toward its target. His father was John Wayne and he was Matthew Garth from *Red River*. He felt the warmth of the heat from seared hair and hide, smelled the burning. Rance's voice shook him from his trance. "Let 'er out, Jake. Shut the head gate behind her. I don't want any escapes. You can brand the next one."

Jake stepped off Scar onto the chute and stood over the next cow as String moved her forward with the cane. He hesitated when Rance handed him the branding iron without instructions.

Rance glanced up from disinfecting his needle. "Hurry up, the iron's getting' cold, Jake."

Jake stuck the hot iron to the steer's hip and held it firm as the smoke curled under his nose and settled under his hat brim. It was a little crooked, but he had the feel for it now. He jumped down and put the iron back into the fire and stirred the coals. "All done with him?" He did not know if Rance had vaccinated or not. Rance nodded as he prepared the next shot.

Only four small bulls were left in the corral when Mattie brought lunch. She had been watching from the kitchen because she also carried a small pan to hold the bulls' testicles. Jake saw her coming through the gate as he and Scar returned a few head that had decided to investigate things in the north pasture. The smell of freshly fried ham mixed with the smell of burned hair and hide as she sat a large basket on one of the barrels close to the fire.

Jake felt the smile exchanged between his mother and father as Rance spoke. "Just need to cut these bulls, and we'll stop to eat."

Mattie grimaced. "Sure it won't spoil your appetite?"

Rance ignored the question as he slipped a post behind the bull's legs and dropped down in the chute behind him. "Jake, come over here and hold up his tail."

Jake grabbed the shitty tail and pulled it up with both hands, wishing he had worn gloves, trying not to notice the little drops of runny manure dropping on his collar and sliding down his back. Rance had his pocketknife in one hand as he pulled the scrotum between the bull's legs. The bull bawled for his mother as the always-kept-sharp pocketknife neatly removed the bottom third of the scrotum and dropped it into the dirt. Rance allowed the scrotum to drain for a few seconds before pushing the first testicle through the opening. Jake winced as he saw his father pull the spermatic cord to an impossible length before cutting it. Mattie placed her pan on the ground just outside the chute and looked away as Rance dropped the bloody, slimy glob into the pan. Jake's hold on the tail involuntarily tightened as his father repeated the procedure for the second testicle. Jake was out of breath from tension when they released the still-bawling first bull—now steer.

String had already trapped two more bulls in the chute and had to use the prod to ease them forward. "They don't seem to wanna dance at this party. Musta noticed what happened to their compadres."

Rance turned them into steers within minutes. The final bull seemed to know what was in store. He banged his head against the corral rails and frantically searched for an escape hole. Failing to find one, he made a run and tried to jump the top rail. He managed to get his front feet over before falling back. Rance poured alcohol over his knife blade and wiped it against a pants leg. "Get your horses, boys. Let's see if we can get him in the chute before he kills himself."

Jake hustled to do his first real horseback work of the day. His grandfather's words echoed in his ears. *Never do work afoot that can be done horseback.* String rode Pink to the end of the corral, stopped in a corner, and nodded toward Jake. Jake felt his face warm, knowing he was about to be tested. He eased the bull into a corner behind the trap lane, hoping he would calm down a little, but the bull was having none of it. He rammed the fence with his head before turning to face his foe.

Jake felt Scar crouch under him. Mattie looked at Rance as he seemed to be speaking to himself. His voice was not raised, but it carried through the thin air to Jake's ears as if it had been shouted through two generations of Rivers. "Be a good passenger, Son. Let the horse drive."

Jake look a light grip on the saddle horn and let the little gelding have his head. The bull saw an opening and took it, only to find himself nose to nose with Scar. He raced to the other side. Same result. Jake felt as if he were sitting on a spot no larger than a dime, legs loose and easy, body floating with the horse's graceful movements. For the first time, Jake heard the music his grandfather had always described. Creaking leather; hooves trampling and sliding on hard ground; small bellows of protest from the bull; effortless exhalations of satisfied air from Scar's nose combined for a beautiful symphony Jake had never heard before. Even the rising dust seemed to find a voice and bring a satisfying crescendo to the music. Scar blocked every escape route the bull tried, and Jake tingled when the bull finally gave up and went into the lane. He took a deep breath and stifled a shout of exultation but could not keep the corners of his mouth from turning up. Rance slipped the post behind the bull's legs and turned to smile at Mattie as the sound of slow clapping came across the arena. String was putting his hands together and smiling. Jake acted as if he did not hear the clapping, tied his horse to a snub post, climbed the chute, and pulled up the bull's tail.

19 Jake pulled both pickups into the pasture and stood a couple of broken gates between them to serve as a temporary holding pen for the recently worked cattle. They sat on the pickup tailgates and had ham sandwiches and iced tea. Cattle trying to escape through the gaps were quickly discouraged by Pink. Finished with lunch, Rance took his equipment to the shop and his remaining vaccine to the house refrigerator. Mattie carried her basket of empty glasses and sandwich wax paper to the kitchen. String sat on the ground and leaned against the GMC's front tire. Jake leaned against the back. "How long you think he'll hold ' em here?"

"A man likes to look at his cows when they're new. Calms him."

"Daddy's been pretty tied in knots since we moved out here. The cattle did seem to calm him, didn't they?"

"A man gets a lot of satisfaction out of doin' somethin' he's good at. Rance is right at home with these cattle, but I guess farmin' out here is pretty new to him."

Jake felt a hollow feeling in his stomach, fearing that String was about to criticize his daddy. He was still trying to frame a response when they saw Rance approaching with his checkbook. "Sure much obliged, String. No use in tyin' you up any longer. How much I owe you?"

String stood and brushed at the seat of his jeans. "Tell you what, Rance. I been eatin' hot food from your table pretty regular. How about loanin' me Jake and his horse for the rest of the day? We'll call it even."

Rance watched his small herd grow restless as they finished the few blocks of hay Jake had thrown on the ground. "Guess we can let `em go if you two got other business. Till you're better paid, then."

"Jake and I can follow `em to the back side of the place. Make sure they locate the water back there and all. I just need to throw a couple of the bank's cows. One's shakin' his head like he's got an ear tick or somethin'. Got a big heifer that needs a shot. We missed her the first day. Bitch jumped out of the trailer, over the loadin' chute and ran off before we could stop her. May need some help with her. She's flighty."

Jake caught his breath as he waited for his father to answer. Rance put his checkbook into his bib overalls and snapped the pocket shut. "We don't charge for food in our house, but it's fine by me if it's all right with you and Jake."

Jake and String eased the cattle through a gap and let them find their way to the rest of the pasture. It was late afternoon when String loosened Jake's loop around the wild heifer and let her get to her feet. She ran toward the herd as Jake coiled his kinked old work rope and laid it over his saddle horn. "Kinda just dawned on me that we didn't rope a single head this mornin' when we worked our cows."

String tightened Pink's cinch and took a comfortable seat in the saddle. "That bother you?"

Jake felt a tinge of embarrassment for his daddy that had become too familiar since they had moved out here. Something he had never felt at home. "I didn't know what to expect, I guess. It's just that I like the way folks out here work cattle better than the way we worked `em back home. Ropin' and draggin' `em to the fire seems more cowboy. Daddy's got his ways and he don't change too easy, though."

They rode in silence until the house and outbuildings could be seen in the distance. The chirp of saddle crickets did not stop as String spoke. "Jake, it ain't none of my business, but I've sure taken a likin' to your little family. Guess it's got something to do with my daddy and your granddaddy being friends."

Jake felt warm and nodded.

"So, I hope you won't take it hard if I offer some free advice."

"Nope."

"Well, I know you don't mean to, but it sounds like you're tryin' to apologize for your daddy bein' what he is."

Jake started to protest, but String help up a hand to stop him. "Just hear me out. We worked them cattle this mornin' about as slick and quick as three men can do it, Jake. Out here, we usually rope and drag `em to the fire. We like the old ways, but the old ways usually takes more men. The smaller ranches get together and help each other out. When you just got three cowboys and a workin' chute, Rance's way was the best."

Jake was ashamed of what he had been thinking but could not scare away another thought. *Does Daddy have enough friends out here to call when he has cattle to work?*

String seemed to hear his unspoken question. "Oldham County can't make up it's mind if it's gonna be ranching or farming country. Nowadays, only the big ranches work roundups together. The Rivers place sure don't qualify as a big ranch. The few farmers that run cattle are either hirin' lots of cowboys for day work or doing it like your daddy did it this mornin'."

Jake felt better. "I get it, but I still like the old ways. I like the life you live."

String signaled Pink to stop with his legs. He leaned

forward and put an elbow on the horn as he turned to face
Jake. "How do you mean, Jake?"

Jake felt his face warm and wished he had not said it.
"Don't mean to get personal, but I mean, you wear nice
cowboy clothes, ride a good horse, drive a nice pickup. You
work, but seem to be free, too. You got time to go dancin'
and things like that."

String shook his head. "You need somebody to admire,
all you got to do is bend your neck a little." String looked up
and Jake followed his line of vision.

It was twilight, and he could barely make out his daddy's
dark silhouette against the fading sunlight. He was standing
on the windmill tower. "What do you reckon he's doin' way
up there?"

"Greasin' the windmill, most likely. You ain't noticed the
squeakin' has been getting' louder lately? Keeps me awake
some nights."

"I kinda like it."

"Well, your daddy noticed."

"I didn't figure he knew how to grease a windmill."

"He may not have, but Rance is a man that figures things
out. He's already turned this place from the piece of crap that
he leased to a fairly respectable farm."

Jake stared at his daddy's fading profile. His movements
on the windmill ledge were barely discernible.

String eased his horse forward. "Jake, don't think I don't
want your respect, even admiration. I do. Right now, though,
I ain't much to admire. Sure, I dance and work kinda when I
please, but I got nobody but myself that counts on me."

"What's wrong with that?"

The words came hard, and it was obvious. "I lost a good
woman once and sort of went off track. Since then, I been
avoiding responsibility and attachments. I spend all my
money on myself, all my time however I feel like. Pretty damn
selfish."

String nodded his head toward the windmill. "Rance there, he wears overalls with holes in `em so you can have a good pair of boots. Your mama starches and irons a good pair of Levis to settle down over them boots. Me and you—we're vain. Rance, he's a man comfortable in his own skin. He wears clothes because they're easy to work in, not because of how they look. He probably don't seem excitin', the way he keeps his nose to the grindstone, but he's a man worth lookin' up to—a damn sight better role model than me."

String squeezed Pink forward. "You think your mama will cook those calf fries tonight?"

20 Coach Gee had an important, but vague appointment the day the basketballs came out. Coach Watson lined the boys in single file and dumped the balls in the middle of the court. The boys stared like cats watching a herd of mice as the balls bounced and rolled across the hardwood. Nobody made a move to touch one. The coach picked one up and spun it one finger, rolled it down his arm and across his shoulders to the other hand. He palmed the ball and then spun it again in front of Jake's nose. "I think it's about time we did what a basketball team is supposed to do. What do you think?"

The line of boys shuffled feet and looked at each other. After a silence, a few started mumbling affirmations and nodding their heads. Jake, Nocona, and Gabe kept still. The coach moved the spinning ball closer to Jake's nose. "What about you, Rivers? They play with basketballs in East Texas or y'all just roll watermelons?"

Jake cut his eyes in Nocona's direction before answering. "We played a little."

The coach stopped the spinning ball and bounced it off Jake's forehead. Jake felt his face grow hot, felt something hot and bitter rise in his throat. He looked directly at Gabe and Nocona as if for guidance, but mostly to buy a little time. Nocona had his teeth clinched in that familiar way. His expression said that the coach's behavior was not acceptable, but his shrug said he did not know what that Jake should do. The ball came toward Jake's forehead again, and Jake grabbed it. His stare was level with the coach's chest.

Nocona stepped out of the line. "How about a little two-on-one, Coach Watson? Me and Rivers been talkin' and we think we can take you."

Coach Watson smiled and back-pedaled to the top of the key. "Okay, boys, plot your strategy and bring it on. You inbound it first. Rebounds have to be taken to the backcourt on each change of possession. First one to reach twenty wins."

Nocona pulled Jake to the baseline and whispered. "Can you shoot?"

"I ain't shot a basketball in a year or more. Used to be pretty good from the outside. You?"

"Never could shoot worth a damn from outside. I can rebound and make close shots, though. You shoot, and I'll rebound. I got to start in Hereford cause I know how to play rough. I'll see if I can elbow the sumbitch and break a rib or somethin'." Nocona ran and stood next to the coach before Jake could reply. Jake in-bounded it to Nocona without interference from the confident coach. Nocona passed it back and ran toward the goal, drawing the coach with him. "Shoot it, Jake."

Jake dribbled to the top of the circle and shot an air ball into the coach's waiting hands. Coach Watson dribbled to the backcourt and turned to drive easily past Jake. He stopped just short of a lay-up, faked Nocona, and bounced one off the backboard for an easy two points from three feet back. His feet never left the court. He pointed two fingers at Nocona and turned toward the other boys. "Anybody wanna bet ten bucks they don't score more than six points?"

The Wells-Rivers team repeated the game plan except Jake
dared to go to the free throw line for a jump shot. The coach
swarmed him with speed and slapped the ball away as it left
his hand. He dribbled to the top of the key, feinted left and
went by Jake's right side. Nocona defended the basket, leaving
Watson all alone at the free throw line. Swish. 4-0. Watson
help up four fingers. The boys were outplayed four more
times on both offense and defense. 12-0.

Nocona shrugged and held out his hands in a gesture of
helplessness. Jake took the ball out as the coach smothered
Nocona under the basket. Jake knew a pass was going to be
impossible. Watson let him dribble to the corner and take a
set shot without interference. The shot did not have enough
arc, but bounced off the backboard, rolled around, and
dropped through. Jake took a deep breath. 12-2. Jake stayed
back and crouched when Watson drove toward him from the
backcourt. He was ready for the fakes, got a hand on the ball,
and knocked it away. Nocona stole it and immediately passed
to Jake.

Watson came to him this time, put a big hand on Jake's
hip, and shoved just enough to keep him off-balance. Jake's
anger surfaced as he stopped dribbling and held the ball.
"Who's calling fouls?" He looked toward the audience of boys
for help.

Ken Watson smirked. "You mean you can't play with
somebody touching you? You wouldn't be even be able to play
in this Podunk school if that bothers you."

Nocona walked toward them. "That's okay, Jake. Let's
play a little looser than normal. It's just practice."

Jake nodded and walked the ball back to center court.
The coach stayed back at the free throw line. Jake dribbled
directly toward him, feinted right, then switched to his left
hand. Watson's knee shot out and stopped Jake, but he got
the ball around the coach just enough to make a bounce
pass to Nocona under the basket. Jake fell over the knee as

Nocona make an easy lay-up. 12-4.

Watson stopped at the top of the circle and dropped one in for two more. 14-4. Adrenaline from the pain in his knee drew Jake into the game and hate for the big man who had humiliated him pushed aside his self-consciousness. Watson let him take his own shot from the top of the key. It went in without touching the rim. Nocona grinned. 14-6. "Ain't you glad nobody took the bet, Coach?" No response.

The pace of the game accelerated, but it seemed as if it had slowed to Jake. He and Nocona swarmed the coach in the backcourt on the next possession. Nocona liked playing contact basketball. He put a hand on the coach's hip and applied firm pressure. Jake stole the ball and took it in for an easy lay-up. 14-8. Both boys were prone on the floor when the coach scored again. 16-8.

Coach Watson missed a corner set shot on his next possession, and Nocona rebounded. The smile on Nocona's face and the accelerating roughness and pace of the game sent Jake's adrenaline through his skull and down his arms and legs as he drove to the right of the free throw line for a jump shot. 16-10. The coach missed again.

Jake and Nocona knew that Watson would now have to leave the frontcourt and come to Jake to keep him from taking easy shots. When he did, they executed rapid passes and faked shots until the coach got out of position, and Nocona bounced one off the board for an easy two more. 16-12. They were all sweating and breathing hard, but Ken Watson was gasping as he dropped two more. 18-12.

As Jake took the ball out, he felt a hand on his shoulder. Coach Gee's whistle blew in his ear. "Huddle up."

The entire team huddled around the coach. He sank to one knee and looked up at his team. "What are Rivers and Wells doing wrong?"

Shrugs.

"They're letting Coach Watson use his size to his

advantage. They need to use his size against him." Heads
nodded, eyes showed confusion. "Nocona, when he pushes
back against you, push back, then step away and release. Pull
him off balance. Jake, you head straight for him like you're
gonna crash into him, then do that stutter step and head fake
you been doing, dribble back, fake a jump shot. When he
goes up and forward to block you, wait a split second. He has
to come down."

Jake nodded. "How long you been watching, Coach?"

As Jake took the ball out at mid-court, his lost love for
basketball returned, and he was on the Klondike court again
with a supportive crowd in the stands. He did not usually
sweat much, but droplets rolled down his brow and dropped
from his eyebrows onto the hardwood as he crouched to
charge the coach. He and Nocona were behind, but they had
already won. Now Coach Gee was there to protect them
from reprisals. Gee's instructions were carried out exactly.
Jake faked—Watson left his feet—Jake met him going up as the
coach came down. Jake's eyes never left his target. The ball
rolled off his fingertips as he broke his wrist with the release,
rolled in the air to a satisfying arc, and dropped through
the net without touching the rim. 18-14. Hesitant applause
erupted from the other boys.

"Traveling!" Watson pointed at Jake's feet. Your feet left
the ground on that fake."

Coach Gee made a short whistle blast. "No, they didn't,
Coach."

Coach Gee looked at Jake and at Nocona before turning
back to his assistant. "I'll decide when the boys start handling
basketballs. Go get the jump ropes, Coach." He blew his
whistle a long blast. Two-on-one was over.

21 The principal's office was empty, and the phone was off the hook when Jake walked in. He eyed the heavy black receiver warily before picking it up for his first long distance conversation. "Hello?"

Gray Boy's voice echoed over the miles and states. "Hey, Little Brother."

"What's wrong?"

"Nothin'. Just called to wish everybody a Merry Christmas."

"When are you gonna be here?"

Gray's voice softened. "Not gonna make it this year, Jake."

"Why not?"

"Leave got cancelled."

"Why?"

"Don't you know any words besides why?"

Jake did not answer.

"Ah, hell. It was either miss Christmas with the folks and spend it on guard duty or spend two weeks in the brig."

"What for?"

"Fightin'. But don't tell Daddy or Mama."

"What do you want me to tell `em?"

"Just tell `em I'm on some sort of special duty.  Make it sound important.  Tell `em I'll be home first chance I get."

"What about your presents?"

"Just hold `em till I get there. They'll keep."

"Mother is gonna be pretty upset. Trish is not coming, either."

"Can't be helped. You playing any ball?"

"Only played two games, but I'm startin' point guard so far."

"Sophomore starter. Must be an all-girl school."

"Very funny."

"Any good-lookin' women?"

Jake saw the principal coming down the hall. "I do all right. Principal's comin' back."

"Okay. Merry Christmas. Tell the folks I love `em."

"Merry Christmas. Bye."

"Hey, Jake ... tell `em I'm sorry, too."

Jake hung up and nodded at Mr. Alderman as he left.

Christmas was lonely. Jake got his mother a canister set and his father a pair of coveralls. Mattie mailed presents for Trish, Pete, and the two boys. Jake got a new rope with a rawhide burner, a piggin' string, a jerk line with a metal ring, and a tie down for Scar. As he pulled each roping item from separate packages, he glanced at his father. Rance smiled, nodded and looked at Mattie. Gray Boy's presents, alone on the floor, shouted loneliness.

22 The girls' game was in the third quarter, and Jake was already in uniform, standing at courtside as Loretta worked her magic on the court, when he saw his parents enter the gym. The season was half over, and they had not seen Jake play a game. He tried not to resent it, but he knew that they had never missed any of Trish's or Gray Boy's games. They had not told him they were coming, so Jake was not prepared when he saw his father shake hands with Coach Gee. He tried to read their lips from across the court.

"Jake's a good shooter from the outside. Excellent hand-eye coordination for a sophomore." Coach Gee watched Loretta sink a jump shot.

Rance nodded. "Want to know how he got it?"

"Good genes?"

"Nope. I built the kids a basketball backboard and put up a goal in the yard by the house. Wound up being in the middle of a cow lot after we stared dairying. Jake got tired of wiping cow manure off his basketball and wading mud to play. He cut the bottom out of a Mrs. Tucker's lard can and nailed it to the side of our old smokehouse. His cousin gave him some tennis balls to shoot with."

"How big a bucket?

"Just a gallon can."

"Tennis balls and a gallon lard bucket?" Jake could hear his coach's laughter across the court but could not make out the words. "Maybe I might change some of my coaching methods."

"Jake played himself every day. He laid out a half-court with rocks and played imaginary games."

"How long did he do that?"

Rance grinned and looked at Mattie. "How long, Mattie?"

"Did it till we moved. I'd say about six years. He knew he had to follow his sister and brother on the Klondike basketball court." She kept her eyes on Jake.

Rance jingled the change in his pocket. "Didn't think we knew about the imaginary games. He would stay outside until he could make consecutive shots from the corners, the quarter points, the top of the key, the free throw line, and under the bucket."

Coach Gee nodded toward the basketball court. "That's eight shots. From how far?"

"I've seen him make as many as twenty in a row from twenty to thirty feet out. It was entertaining to watch—just as long as he didn't see me. If he knew anybody was watching, he couldn't hit a bull in the butt with a bass fiddle."

"That answers the question I was going to ask."

"What's that?"

"Jake's averaging about six points a game. About right for most point guards, but he could make us more of a threat if he would shoot more. His percentage is real high. We need him to draw the defense out and free up the taller forwards."

"That's probably my fault, I guess. Our family was always taught not to show out."

Mattie spoke up. "Plus, Jake's awful self-conscious. He'll agonize over a missed shot for a week."

"That's why I sent word for you to come. I hope you'll help me bring him out of that. Most boys take bad shots, but it's hard to get Jake to take good ones. He's probably too small to ever play college ball, but he can sure as hell be a factor in this little district."

Rance's face grew serious. "Been stayin' away because we thought it would be easier on him. He may not play as well with us here."

With his parents watching, Jake scored eight in a three-for-four performance from the field. He also collected a rare foul. In a one-and-one situation, Jake dropped both through the net. He also had four steals in a game that Adrian lost.

The team traveled over a hundred miles to Texline for the final game of the season. The Matadors won, but Jake scored only four points and had one of his worst defensive games of the year. He also had the ball stolen from him twice.

Coach Alton Gee gave a locker room speech after the game. "We won more than half our games this year. I'll be back next year, and so will most of this team. You're a young team, and we just got to know each other this time around. We're gonna run some track, play some volleyball, and stay in shape the rest of this year. If you boys can come back in good shape in the fall, we'll take it all next year."

Jake's new letter jacket had snow on the shoulders when he boarded the bus and snow had covered the ground during their game. Coach Watson headed in the wrong direction as they left the Texline school grounds. Jake looked around to see if the car caravan that brought the girls team was following. No sign of them. The bus stopped in front of an old two-story house a few blocks from the school. Coach Gee turned in his front seat. "Lowry, Wells, and Rivers. You boys bring your stuff to stay the night?"

Jake thought of the toothbrush and change of underwear and socks in his bag. "Yes, sir." Their combined shouts bared the excitement that had begun to build when they turned in the opposite direction from home. When the teams traveled by bus instead of in family cars to Texline, they usually stayed the night to avoid a dangerous late night trip back home. Texline families opened their homes to the Adrian players. On this last game of the season, however, they had planned to return to Adrian unless there was bad weather. Coach Gee had an important meeting the next day. Snow answered the boys' prayers. They liked staying overnight.

"You boys get off here. Family's name is Sherwood. They're old folks, so keep it down, stay out of the refrigerator, and be ready to leave at eight in the morning." Coach Gee grabbed Jake's arm as he stood on the last step of the bus. "These people are opening up their homes to us. They're friends of mine. Show them you boys got a little sense. Don't disappoint me."

Nocona pressed the doorbell beside a twelve-foot door. When nobody answered, Jake trotted toward the departing bus and waved for it to stop. It was dark, but he imagined Ken Watson looking at him in his side-view mirror as he drove away. He gave up in the middle of the street and walked slowly back toward the big house, dribbling an imaginary ball and taking imaginary shots. The ever-present wind took a short rest to let quiet and snow have their moments. Jake thought of the time that he and Tuck had played in the snow and wondered again how snow usually made things quiet. He stopped at the sidewalk and looked down the street. A row of cottonwoods had been planted to separate the field crops on the east side of the street from the houses on the west. A few scattered trees that looked distressed from lack of water dotted some yards, but the snow was falling on hard dirt, not grass lawns.

A horse bowed-up against the snow stood beside a small tin barn in the middle of the mostly-small, mostly-stucco houses. The porch where Nocona and Gabe stood was the only porch within sight, and it was attached to the only two-

story house. The wood exterior had been painted recently.
His two friends had turned up their collars and hunched up
against the cold when Jake stepped back on the porch. He
looked through the frosted glass in the front door to check
for movement. The glass had been etched with some sort of
wildflowers that resembled tumbleweeds. He knocked lightly
on the glass. Nothing. He prepared to knock louder as the
door opened.

A smiling, gray couple stood at the open door in pajamas,
gown, and robes. The man, not much taller than Jake, spoke
first. "Me and Mama had given up and gone to bed. We
figured you boys had gone on home, after all." The man's
voice was cheerful and welcoming.

The woman's youthful beauty shone through the wrinkles
of time. Her eyes showed memories of youthful merriment.
"Fred forgets his manners. I'm Winnie and this is Fred
Sherwood. You boys come in out of the cold. We'll have
some hot chocolate."

Jake started to say no thanks, but Gabe beat him with a
low, rumbling, "Thank-you, Ma'am. Hot chocolate sounds
real good."

Nocona lifted his eyebrows as he smiled at Jake. Within
minutes they were seated on the living room couch with mugs
of hot chocolate in their hands. Jake looked around for the
fireplace but found clanking wall radiators instead. Wood for
a fireplace would be scarce in this almost-treeless country.
Fred and Winnie were schoolteachers who had spent their
entire careers teaching in Texline. He had retired as a
principal but had also coached. She had taught all grades of
elementary school in one room. "That was when the town
was still getting started," she said.

Fred rose and stood in front of the boys. "I rooted against
you boys tonight, but all is forgiven. I like to see good
basketball played anytime, and some of the best in the world is
played in small gyms like the ones at our schools. I bet you

boys are proud to play for Alton Gee."

Gabe felt a reply was courteous. "Yes sir. He's a good coach, I reckon. We sure did a lot better under him than we did under Watson. Uh ... Coach Watson."

The old man's stare was quizzical. "You boys don't know about Coach Gee, do you?"

The boys shrugged.

"Alton has three trips to the state tournament under his belt. Two championships at big schools."

Nocona was the only one brave enough to speak. "He never said ... ."

"Alton Gee is not one to brag about his accomplishments. He builds a team from the ground up. Give him a year or two and a little cooperation; you boys can go to state. Playing on a state championship team is one of the best things that can happen to you. Nobody can ever take it away."

Gabe stood and backed up to the wall heater. "Why would he come to Adrian? We don't get that kind of coach out here."

Fred Sherwood looked at his wife. "I never asked; he never said. I expect he's got his reasons."

As Winnie led the way up the stairs, Fred put a hand on Jake's arm. "All you boys played well out there, but I'm always partial to the little ones, Jake. I saw a hint of a fine basketball player out there tonight, but he kept it well-hidden."

Jake winced. "I know I played terrible tonight."

The old man rested his elbow on the stair rail. "Well, there's terrible and there's terrible. The only thing terrible is to hide your talent under a washtub. Bring it out in the light so we can all enjoy it. Nothin's as pretty as ball-handling, crisp passing, and fine shooting."

"Wish I could just do one of those things well." Jake followed the others to a loft bedroom. Three single beds were pushed against the wall. Jake could feel the excitement in the room as the couple left the boys alone.

Nocona raised the room's only window and stuck his head out. "Smells real good and clean out there. What say we take a look around this little town?"

Gabe walked over to join him. "How you gonna get down?"

"Easy enough. Just drop over that ledge, swing down to the porch post, and shinny down. You comin'?"

"If it was Adrian, I would. Always something happenin' on 66. This little town is probably shut down tight as a drum. Besides, it's still snowin'."

Nocona put one foot out the window and onto the porch roof. "You're goin', ain't you Jake?" Jake had sneaked out with Nocona on an overnight stay once before. They had prowled the streets of Dalhart all night and slept all the way home on the bus.

Jake shook his head from the edge of the bed closest to the window.

Nocona's grin looked almost lecherous in the moonlight. "You don't wanna dip your wick? I think I know where Loretta and Texie might be stayin'. You think Loretta's gonna waste this time away from the preacher? It's either you or that tall kid who played post for Texline."

Jake tried to smile, but his anger and jealousy surprised him. "We never found 'em last time. Besides, they came in cars with families. They've already gone home." He tried to focus on what Coach Gee had said about respecting the Sherwoods. He shook his head again, and Nocona turned to leave.

Jake was stretching out on the bed when Nocona stuck his head back in. "Be sure and leave this window cracked a little so I can get back in. One more question, Jake. If I find Loretta before I find Texie, is it okay if I....?"

Jake raised his arm and flipped out his middle finger.

Nocona smothered a laugh. "Only in case of emergency, you understand."

23 A soft knock awakened Jake from a fretful sleep. He had dreamed about Nocona, Loretta, and the tall kid who played post. Fred Sherwood's mellow voice came through the cracks around the door. "Coach Gee said he would be by to pick you boys up at eight. Winnie has hot chocolate and coffee ready."

Jake swung his feet to the floor. "Be there shortly, Mr. Sherwood." He yawned and stretched as he looked at the other two beds. Nocona was back, his head completely covered by quilts.

Gabe yawned and stretched his arms toward the ceiling. "How much did it snow, Jake?"

Jake bent to look out the window. "Can't tell. Looks like about a foot."

Teeth brushed and faces washed, Jake and Gabe walked into the kitchen together. Winnie handed each a cup of hot chocolate. Gabe stared at his cup. "Appreciate the chocolate, Ma'am, but could I have some coffee after I finish it?"

"Of course. How about you, Jake?"

"No Ma'am. Hot chocolate suits me fine."

Fred ushered them into a dining room where they sat at a large table. "We would be pleased to feed you boys breakfast, but Coach Gee asked us not to. Said you always ate out. The Branding Iron downtown has good, hearty breakfasts."

Jake and Gabe were almost to the bus when Nocona finally joined them. "Why didn't you assholes wake me?"

Gabe pushed a black strand of hair off his forehead. "Hell, we did wake you. Twice. Ain't our fault you went back to sleep."

Jake nodded. "We didn't take you to raise." He wanted to ask what had happened the night before and if the girls had stayed over, but did not want to give Nocona the pleasure.

Coach Watson drove the bus away as Coach Gee handed each of them a BLT. "Sorry, boys. This is breakfast. Snowstorm headed toward us. We got to get home."

Jake looked out the window at a world of white and thought of the hot breakfast Winnie Sherwood would have cooked. "Looks like we already had a snowstorm."

"This is nothin'. Just snowed about eight inches. Weatherman says we may get two more feet before nightfall— and it won't be fallin'. It'll be comin' right at us like a chargin' bull."

Jake did not want to ask the question but could not resist. "Where are the girls? They gonna follow us in cars?"

"They went home last night."

Jake glanced at a smiling Nocona.

It started snowing again as they crossed Mustang Creek. As they pulled into Dalhart, the wind picked up a little. They stopped at a service station, and Coach Gee went inside to get a report on the weather. Watson kept the bus engine running while the attendant filled it with gas. Only boys who needed to use the restroom were allowed to leave the bus. Gee and Watson huddled in the front of the bus, but did not try to keep their voices down. "Looks like if we stay the night again, we might be here a few days. In bad blizzards, this old boy says the road down by the Canadian River might not clear up for a week. We have to decide to try and make it home or try

to find something here. This guy says the only hotels are full
to the brim. He says the houses in Texline where we stayed
last night are already fillin' up."

Watson looked down at the shorter, older coach. "I say
we try to make it."

Jake knew that Coach Gee had mentioned an important
appointment, so he was not surprised when the coach
nodded. Visibility was measured in feet, and the cobweb of
red lines in Coach Gee's face started turning blue as they
passed through Hartley. Watson's grip on the wheel was
turning his hands white as their progress slowed to a crawl.

Nocona leaned back and fell into an easy slumber, and
Jake was enjoying the excitement until he saw the look on
Gabe's face. "Ever seen a blizzard, Jake?"

"Guess not."

"Well, you're in one now. I just hope that Watson can
drive a bus in a blizzard and keep it on the road. Otherwise,
we may be spending the night in this old pile of junk. I ain't
too fond of freezin' to death."

"Where are we?"

Gabe looked out at the wall of driving snow. "Best I can
tell, we just passed through Channing. I think I saw a Quien
Sabe Ranch sign a ways back. We're headed toward the
Canadian. Watch out the left side for Old Tascosa and Boys
Ranch."

Jake stared out the window and thought he could make
out Saddle Rock in the distance. They had played a couple
of games at Boys Ranch. He liked the thrill of the snow but
regretted not being able to see this part of the trip. From
Tascosa to Vega on 385 always reminded him of Monument
Valley and *The Searchers*. One day, he would ride Scar through
those hills and pretend he was John Wayne, slinging a fringed
rifle scabbard to the ground before rescuing Natalie Wood.
Jake always wondered if Ethan Edwards returned for that
scabbard. It kept his mind off of what Gabe had said about

freezing to death.

Weaving through abandoned cars at crawl speed, they stopped seven times on 66 between Vega and Adrian to pick up stranded travelers from cars that had either stuck in the snow or driven off the road. Most of the boys had given their seats to families and were standing when they limped into Adrian by mid-afternoon. The old bus had heated up with the exertion and idling and the radiator boiled, smoked, and hissed as they stopped at Whitey's Service Station on 66. The boys waited while the stranded travelers exited.

Coach Gee stood in the aisle. "How many of you boys can fend for yourselves to get home?" All raised their hands. Out of habit, they stood in line outside the bus and stared at what had been a thriving highway. It was now a white parking lot scarred only by tracks from the bus tires.

Jake looked at Gabe and Nocona, the ones who lived nearest to him. "How **are** we gonna get home?"

Nocona snickered. "Who wants to go home? Let's make us a little easy money."

Gabe followed him into the service station and Jake fell in behind as the other boys began their walks to homes in town or got into cars with parents who knew to wait at a service station or café after snowstorms. Others headed for the nearest telephone. Weary travelers stood in small groups around the station's only stove. A station attendant in a blue grease-covered shirt with matching blue pants, also grease-covered, rested his elbows on a glass countertop, taking bored puffs from a cigarette. Jake noticed that a long ash was about to drop to the floor. *Whitey* was embroidered just above his left shirt pocket.

Nocona wrapped his knuckles on the counter. "Hey, Whitey. Wake up. Same deal as the last snowstorm?"

Whitey shook his head. "I don't know, Nocona. Don't much like to have wild Indians driving my truck in the middle of a blizzard."

"What's not to know? Blizzard is over. Just a nice gentle snow out there now." Nocona rapped the knuckles again. "Listen up. How many of you folks got cars buried on 66?" Most hands went up. "How many would give $50 to have those cars unburied?" The same number of hands went up.

Nocona turned back to Whitey. "That old wrecker still run?"

Whitey nodded as he lit another cigarette.

Nocona opened his hand for the keys. "Same deal. Twenty to you for the use of the wrecker, thirty for us."

"I seem to recall it was thirty-twenty last time."

Nocona nodded toward Jake. "Well, we got a new man this time. Twenty won't split three ways. With more help, we'll pull out more cars, and you'll make more money, anyway." The logic of the argument worked on Whitey, and he dropped the keys into Nocona's hand. Jake looked down 66 to the other service stations and cafés. There was no sign of Rance's pickup. He knew they would be worried, but without a phone at home, what could he do?

24 Jake borrowed a pair of rubber boots from Whitey big enough to pull over his Justins. The boys dug through snow with their hands to reach under the bumper of the first car, a '57 Pontiac Star Chief that sat in the middle of the highway. Jake stood back as Nocona winched it up. The undercarriage was packed with huge chunks of snow and ice. "I could understand slidin' off in the ditch, but why do they just stop in the middle of the road?"

Gabe walked under the lifted car and tried to pry loose a block of ice. It would not budge. "See that? Won't move. These new cars are slung low. This one probably started carrying a little snow about Clarendon or somewhere, and it built up till it was just more or less sliding along. Finally, the snow wins when it stops the wheels from turnin'."

Each time they brought in a car, Jake watched for his daddy's pickup. He knew Rance would not let the snow stop him. He decided that Rance had found out what was going on from someone with a phone and knew that Jake was safe. The rationalization made him enjoy the day more. By the time the boys stopped for supper at the Bent Door Café, they had hauled in five cars and made fifty bucks each. Jake splurged on chicken-fried steak and french fries. The sun had

175

come out, and he could not remember being as hungry or as happy. He had money in his pocket, a new home, a new school, a new team, and two good friends who were sharing a day that none of them would ever forget.

They worked under the full moon until clouds covered the sky again. The temperature warmed some, but it seemed colder. They unhooked the last car in complete darkness, and Whitey asked for the keys to the wrecker. Going back for more cars would be dangerous, he said. Hands in their pockets, fingering their wad of twelve ten-spots, the boys seemed to run out of steam. Jake was ready to go home. He had not slept much the night before and working in the cold all day was starting to catch up. "How we gonna get home?"

Nocona started walking toward 66. "Hell, it's too late to go home tonight. My car is parked at the school, but it probably wouldn't make it, anyway. Out here, Jake, a man can freeze to death if he's stranded."

"Where we gonna stay?"

Nocona slowed, but did not turn. He waved a backward wave. "Gabe knows where I'm goin'. You boys are on your own."

Gabe spat in the snow and grinned. "He's going to Texie's. He sleeps in the bedroom next to hers and sneaks over during the night."

Jake was starting to worry. "I'm real proud that he's gonna have a warm place to sleep and a bed partner, but what about us?"

"I'm sure you can find lodging in the Baptist church ... or the parsonage. Might find something crawling under the covers with you, too."

Jake half smiled. "No thanks. I've seen the big preacher."

Gabe scanned the few lights that flickered in Adrian. "Power's out. Most folks operatin' with lanterns or coal-oil lamps. Used to put travelers up in the rooms above the Mercantile. That old building was the Giles Hotel once. Caleb and Sage live up there now. Stranded travelers probably took all the spare bedrooms in town. I think we're stuck with the gym." Gabe started working toward the school, and Jake followed.

Jake watched his step as they crossed the icy railroad tracks. It looked like a train had barreled its way through the snow, leaving ice-covered rails. "That old gym is drafty. Think they'll have any heat? Do they set up cots in there, or what?"

"Church and women's groups set up roll-away beds and cots. Last time, travelers trashed it up pretty good. They stopped up the toilets and showers in the locker rooms."

Jake really longed for home as he turned to scan the cars parked along 66. He was about to give up when Whitey opened his garage door to pull his wrecker inside. An aqua-blue '56 Chevy pickup was parked just inside the door. Jake turned back and yelled. "Gabe, there's Daddy's truck. You want to ride home with us?"

Gabe shook his head. "You forget what me and Nocona said? Too dangerous to go home in the dark. Go get him and bring him to the gym. I'm freezin' my ass off. I'm goin' on."

Jake turned back and trotted across 66. He knew Rance would not let a little snow stop him from coming to get him—or taking him home. He hollered to Whitey. "Hold up a second, Whitey." Whitey kept his hand on the garage door and waited.

"That's my daddy's truck. You know where he is?"

Whitey moved in front of the truck. "Reckon I might. How do I know he's your daddy?"

"Never told you my name. I'm Jake Rivers. His name is Rance."

Whitey kept his protective stance. "What's he look like?"

"Black hair ... wears bib overalls mostly ... I expect he's wearing coveralls in this weather ... probably wearing a cap or hat ... black hair with little flecks of gray in it." Jake made a move toward Whitey. "Somethin' happen to him?"

"Your daddy came lookin' for you last night. We visited a spell, and I offered him a little something to take the chill off. We got to be right friendly, visitin' bout farmin' and East Texas and such. I'm from Waxahachie, you see."

"Where is he?" Jake was getting impatient.

"It ain't my fault. I didn't know the feller couldn't hold his liquor. He got sick on me. I let him move that pickup in here so he could sleep it off. He's been asleep more'n twelve hours." Whitey nodded and made a low bow to affirm his good intentions. "I's just about to wake him up and buy him a little supper."

Jake strode past Whitey and threw open the pickup door. The smell of stale beer, whiskey, and vomit emptied into the garage like an ill wind. Jake stepped back and swallowed hard to keep from losing the chicken-fried steak when he saw his father. Rance was curled in the seat in a fetal position. He raised his head, revealing bloodshot eyes and gray stubble. His lips were crusted with something white. His hat was in the floorboard, holding an empty bottle of Jim Beam. "Son."

Jake slammed the door in his father's face and half-walked, half-ran out the still- open garage door. He looked up and down the row of service stations and cafés to see if anyone was watching. Whitey called after him. "What do you want me to tell him?"

"I don't give a damn. That's not my daddy." Jake stopped to catch his breath in front of Adrian Mercantile. He turned to see if his father had left. The garage door was closed. He was not ready to face spending the night in the company of strangers in a drafty gym, but he started walking toward the school. He turned again when he remembered he had left his gym bag in the wrecker. He wanted to be home, but now there was no home again.

"Jake." The young female voice carried through the still night. "Where you headed?"

Jake turned toward the voice. Sage's head and one arm were braving the cold air while the rest of her remained inside Adrian Mercantile's front door.

"Y'all still open?"

"No, but you can come in and get warm if you want to." Sage pulled the door back.

Jake had not realized how cold he was until he stepped inside. The oil stove was boiling. "Just headed over to the school for the night. Me and Gabe and Nocona been pulling people's cars out of the snow all day and ... ."

Sage put her hand on his arm. "I heard. You wanting to go over to the gym to be with somebody special?"

"Gabe's over there."

"You like sleeping with Gabe?"

Sage's smile brought one to Jake's face. "Slept with him and Nocona last night."

"If you're interested and don't want to walk another mile, we have an empty half-bed. Not much and probably a little musty, but it's warm and dry."

Jake looked toward the second floor. "Gabe said you didn't have rooms anymore."

"We got one couple upstairs with us, but we still have the basement." She opened a door and pointed toward a cabinet. "See if you can reach that cabinet door up there. There's bedding on the top shelf."

Jake stuck a set of sheets, a quilt and a blanket under one arm and a pillow under the other and followed Sage and her lantern down the stairs. At first the basement reminded him of the storm cellar back home—without the smell of mildew and wet earth. This basement smelled of dust, old wood, and dry leather. Caleb's stash of harness and tack spare pieces in the corner was providing the leather smell. Sage's lantern washed the dust-covered plank floor with light.

She took the sheets from him, shook them, and allowed them to fall neatly across a single bed with an iron bedstead like Jake's bed back home. The sheets smelled of Twenty-Mule-Team Borax. Jake stood dumbly as Sage moved efficiently from side to side of the bed, tucking corners and spreading the quilt first, then the blanket. She fluffed the pillow and put it at the head of the bed. The room was cool, and the bed looked inviting.

Jake felt comforted, welcome, and safe, but inadequate. He still considered Sage to be twelve, though she was only a year younger than him. "You do that like you been doin' it a long time. Your mother teach you?"

"Mother left before she could teach me anything. Sorry about the dark, but Daddy doesn't like to leave lanterns down here; he's afraid of fire."

"Sure don't blame him for that."

Sage took the first step up the stairs. "There's a flashlight on the floor beside the bed. You can use it till the electricity comes back on. Anything else you need?"

"Just to say thank you. I sure do appreciate this."

"You need to go, you can come up and use the one in the store or just go out back."

Jake's face warmed and a smile flickered at the corners of his lips. "Out back?"

Sage hurried up the stairs. "Last man that slept in that bed just hung it out the back door and let 'er fly. Didn't care who was lookin', either."

Jake's hand was on the railing when she closed the door.

25

Jake got up and dressed as soon as sunlight filtered through the basement window. Thankful that his hat covered his hair and wishing he had a toothbrush or even a mirror, he waited for the sounds of footsteps before climbing the stairs. The pleasant smell of coffee brewing greeted him as he opened the door and walked into the store.

Caleb Pirtle was already waiting on a customer who had trailed snow down the aisle. "Mornin' Jake. Grab yourself a cup off that post over there and help yourself to the coffee."

Jake did not want any coffee, but he obliged. The warmth felt good in his hands. He strolled around the store, looking for Sage but he did not see her. He finished the last of the coffee as the customer left with an armful of supplies. "Guess I better go find Nocona and Gabe and get on home. Seems like I been gone a week."

"Two-bits says you can find `em over at the Bent Door eatin' fried biscuits. They may not be there now, but they will be."

Whitey was working a gas pump as Jake walked through the station's office to the garage. He was relieved that Rance's pickup was gone. He took his gym bag from the wrecker. Whitey met him in the office. "Told him you said you had a way home. None of my business, but your daddy came through thirty miles of blizzard to get you. My old man wouldn't have put a water hose up my ass if my guts was on fire." Jake returned a look that said he did not want any advice and stalked through the snow to the Bent Door.

Gabe had already ordered when Jake slid into the booth across from him. Gabe laid the menu on the table. "Thought you went on home. Where did y'all stay?"

"I stayed at the Mercantile. That wadn't Daddy's pickup. Made a cold trip back to Whitey's for nothin'. Sage stopped me when I was passin' back by. Stayed in her basement. Where's Nocona? I need to get home."

As if he had heard his name, Nocona appeared at the door, looking fresh from a good night's sleep. Gabe's mouth dropped open slightly as he stared. "You shaved. You smell like talcum powder and aftershave. You showered. Those are clean clothes."

Nocona smiled. "I got an image to keep up. Don't expect me to walk around lookin' like you two, do you? Is that body odor I smell?"

"Kiss my ass. Where'd you get the clean clothes?"

"My woman keeps a few stashed away for such occasions. I been forced to spend the night there before."

Jake was pretty sure he did not smell, and he did not have a beard, but he did feel dirty. "Texie's parents let you keep clothes there?"

"Her parents know I'm an innocent boy who only has their daughter's best interests at heart."

Jake had a sick feeling about his daddy and could not eat. The thought of seeing him curled up in the seat of that pickup was gnawing all the way to his backbone. He drummed his fingers on the table while his friends finished their breakfasts.

Nocona noticed. "You're kinda fidgety, ain't you?

"I didn't have a nice shower or brush my teeth like you did. Left my stuff in the wrecker. Didn't sleep too good in that basement last night, either. Don't mind admittin' that I'm lookin' forward to my own bed."

Skies had cleared again during the night, dropping temperatures to the single digits. Snow had formed a hard enough crust to drive on. To Jake's surprise, Nocona drove sensibly and with skill all the way to Jake's yard. He enjoyed his new friends, but two days and two nights with them was enough. He groaned when he saw Bob Lee's black '57 Chevy parked between Rance's pickup and Mattie's car. The hood was missing from the Ford. Snow had covered the engine.

The heat seemed stifling as he stepped inside, making him even more irritable. "Well, the prodigal son returns." Bob Lee's voice usually made him smile. Today, its cheerfulness was like sandpaper across his brain. Mattie, Rance, and Bob Lee sat at the kitchen table. Jake thought it discomfiting that they could be so relaxed while his whereabouts and safety remained in question. He had expected to be met with outrage tapering off to welcome-home joy.

Mattie was not good at hiding her elation. "Well, you finally remembered you have a home and family." Jake did not know how to reply. Rance stared into his coffee cup as he rolled a cigarette.

Bob Lee grinned. "Heard you been haulin' dumb Yankees off of 66. Me and some other old boys used to do the same damn thing. You boys are smarter than we were, though. Tore the transmission out of one of daddy's pickups trying to pull cars all the way back to Adrian. We saved at least one family from freezin' to death."

Jake felt strong fingers dig into his shoulder. He turned and faced his brother. Jake grinned and stepped back. He felt the room's clammy heat dissipate and his irritability slip away. "What are you doin' here?"

"When did you get big enough to stay out all night two nights in a row?"

"Snowed in at Texline the first night. Adrian the second. Ever been in a blizzard?"

"Did you see the car? Blizzard took the hood right off."

Rance frowned, cleared his throat and stood. "You boys visit. I'll be out at the shop." He poured his coffee into the sink and walked out.

Gray Boy shook a Winston out and lit it with his Zippo. "You win the basketball game?"

"We won. You never said why you're here."

"Got four days. On my way to temporary assignment down at an Air Force base in San Antonio. Marines dropped me in Amarillo and Bob Lee flew me here."

"Flew?"

"That black bitch Bob Lee drives will mortally fly."

Mattie dropped all pretenses and hugged Jake as she picked up his gym bag. "I heard the girls won district."

Jake nodded as she dropped his basketball suit and other dirty laundry into a basket and took his toothbrush and duffel bag into his bedroom.

Jake sat beside his brother at the table. "How'd y'all know what I was doin'?"

Bob Lee answered. "We got a telephone. Called around till I found out, then came over here to tell Aunt and Unc. Knew they'd be worried."

Jake could not splice the pieces together that had brought Rance into Adrian looking for him, but he did not want to ask more questions in front of Bob Lee. He just wanted to erase the memory of his father in that pickup seat. "That really what happened to the car hood?"

Gray Boy looked to see if Mattie was returning. Bob Lee spoke first. "That little green Ford will run nearly as fast as the turd-hearse. Fast enough to blow the hood right off its hinges."

"Y'all were racing in this snow?"

"Might as well tell him the whole damn thing. You already told the worst part."

Bob Lee giggled as he warmed to the story. "I picked him up at the bus station in Amarillo. Tried to talk him into cruising a little. You know how he is with women ... that uniform and all. Best muff-magnet I ever saw. I'm just happy to pick up what he throws away."

Gray Boy waved the coffee pot in Jake's direction, and he shook it off. Gray looked at Bob Lee. "Tell him I did the right thing."

"Sure did. Made me bring him right home. Didn't do us a bit of good, though. Lights were out here. Nobody home."

Gray Boy flicked an ash at the ashtray. "I took a shower in the dark and found the keys to the Ford. We found Mother at Aunt Bess's, and she said Daddy had gone to look for you." Gray Boy lowered his voice. "Told Mama I had a date in Amarillo, and she let me borrow the Ford. Bob Lee followed me to Vega. He tried to pass me and that's when we lost the hood. It was just dustin' snow here then."

Bob Lee was laughing so hard his face was red, and tears were running down his cheeks. "The turd-hearse was about to get it done until that hood flew off. I slowed down after that, but Gray Boy didn't. I never caught up till we got to Vega. Turns out we didn't have to drive to Amarillo." He put a hand on Gray's shoulder. "Old Stud here had two girls in that Ford inside of an hour—without the hood."

Jake smiled but did not find the story as funny as they did. The Ford was what he used for dating. Rance usually had the pickup when he needed it and always ruined his wash jobs the next day. He had also converted it to run on farm propane. Use of farm propane for non-farm driving could get a farmer into trouble. "So, where's the hood?"

Laughter slowly subsided. Gray Boy clicked the Zippo lid. "Couldn't find it on the way home. It was snowing pretty good, though. We'll go back today and get it."

"You gonna put it back on?"

"Damn right. May have to order some new hinges, though. We'll wire it up till we can get `em."

Jake turned in his chair to look out the window toward the shop. "What did Daddy say?"

"Just shook his head. Say Jake, where you keep your rubbers? I went through all your drawers and couldn't find a one."

"You went through my stuff?"

"Just needed a rubber. Used to keep mine taped to a drawer bottom. I know you're getting' it. I can see it in your eyes. Take my advice. Don't be knockin' up any of these split-tails out here. Their parents will run your ass clean out of the Panhandle. Even the other girls will turn against you."

"I need a shower and some sleep." Jake walked to his room.

26 When Bob Lee and Gray Boy left for the Amarillo bus station in Bob Lee's Chevy, the Ford still had no hood. Jake had hidden his anger about the car during his brother's visit, but as soon as they left, it welled up. The school bus was late, so he cranked the car to melt the snow still covering the engine. The car's old purr had changed to a loud, rough rumble. Jake was staring at the motor as if he would will it to sound better when Rance appeared on the other side of the car. "I imagine Gray Boy blew out the glass packs. Sounds like a lifter is stickin'. Lucky he didn't blow the engine. Kid ain't ever gonna grow up."

Jake nodded. Few words had passed between him and his father since that night in Adrian. With Gray Boy gone, it would be harder to avoid conversation. "What about the hood?"

Rance chewed lightly on his lip. "You're welcome to drive it to school and look for it on the way home if you want to."

Jake took the long way to school, driving the road to Vega. No sign of the hood. Loretta was standing on the school front steps when he pulled into the parking lot. "Everybody sure knows when you're coming in that Ford, Jake. Why so loud and where's the hood?"

"Long story. Let's just say my Marine brother can do a lot of damage in a short period of time."

"My daddy heard about your rescuing people on '66 the other day. Says you're a Good Samaritan."

Jake knew some of the Good Samaritan story but felt uncomfortable talking about the Bible with a preacher's kid. "That right?"

"Yeah. I didn't tell him you made money doin' it."

Jake was taken aback. Taking pay that day had not seemed wrong at the time.

"Anyway, maybe he might let us go get a Coke sometime."

"Good."

"You goin' to the dance at Simms next weekend?" Simms was a community twenty miles south of Adrian. A traveler knew he had passed Simms only when he saw the sign for the grain elevator and the community center building. There were no other buildings.

"Are all the kids at Adrian invited?"

"That's who the dance is for. Kids who live at Simms go to school here."

"Haven't asked my folks, but I guess I'll probably go." Jake pointed at the Ford. "Probably have to go in that, though." He walked past her to the school front door. With his hand on the knob, he turned. "You goin'?"

Loretta was watching kids step out of a school bus. "Me? You kiddin'? Baptists don't dance."

"Could have sworn that was you that taught me how to dance out at Gabe's last summer."

"I didn't teach you much you didn't already know, Honey. Dancing out at Gabe's is different than dancin' at Simms. Lots of parents there. PK's not allowed to enter, much less dance." Religion and churches had always made Jake nervous. He did not want to say something wrong to a girl who had spent her life in Sunday School. Loretta walked past him and through the door. Her eyes glistened. Jake could not tell if it was tears or the bright sun's reflection.

On the way home from school, he stopped in the area that Gray Boy had described. He walked the ditches for a mile in both directions looking for the car hood. No luck. That night, Jake waited in vain for his father to mention the lost hood or its replacement. They seemed to have reached a cold truce, speaking in dead voices and only when necessary. The incident at Adrian hung over them like a vulture on a dead tree limb.

Jake cleaned up the Ford for the dance, but his heart was not in it. The greasy engine stared through the windshield with every furniture-polish swab of the dash. He wiped the air cleaner cover and the inside fenders but gave up on the rest of the engine. Nothing was going to make it look good. When the Ford was clean, he took a shower and splashed on some Aqua-Velva. He arrived late at Simms Community Center on purpose and pulled the Ford to the back of the building. He planned to come and go without the missing hood being noticed. Those plans were dashed when Nocona, Texie, and Loretta emerged from the shadows.

Nocona peered at the engine. "You do some kinda custom work on this Ford, Jake? I don't see any chrome three-barrel carbs or anything."

"Funny. Just like to show off a greasy engine. You should take the hood off your Chevy. What are y'all doin' on the dark side of the building?"

"Waiting for most of the parents to drop off their kids so Loretta can go inside and dance. Gabe's mama is chaperone, and she won't tell."

"Somebody mention my mama?" Gabe walked around the side of the building and stared at the missing hood's hinges. "What happens if it rains? Bet that engine will drown right out."

"Thanks for bringing that up, Gabe. With my luck, it'll probably rain before I get home."

"I wouldn't worry about it. Hardly ever rains out here. Loretta, Mama says you can come in now. She'll keep a lookout."

The thumping sound of music began to change to recognizable songs as they walked toward the front of the building. The sounds of the Drifters singing "There Goes my Baby" made chill bumps on Jake's arms as he walked into the dimly lighted big room. His eyes were still adjusting when Loretta moved under his arm. She gently swayed against him to the beat of the music. Jake remembered what his grandfather had said about the flow.

I especially like the feeling you get when your hand is resting in the middle of a woman's back before the music plays. Then the sound of music courses through your blood and sweeps you both across the dance floor.

Encouraged by his grandfather, Jake moved his hand to the middle of Loretta's back. They finished the first song and were well into the second when Loretta felt a tap on her shoulder. Texie stepped into Jake's arms to complete "Sixteen Candles". Her hands were a little rough for a girl and her body was slimmer and a little firmer than Loretta's. She even smelled of the same cologne—but she could not dance like Loretta. Jake felt clumsy when he stepped on her toe. "Sorry."

The music stopped, and Texie stepped back and smiled. "Not your fault. I get no practice with Nocona. He won't set foot on the dance floor."

Jake's confidence grew as he danced every slow song. When they finally played a fast one, he drifted to the punch bowl. Sage handed him a glass of punch. "You're lookin' like Gene Kelly out there."

Jake tried to hide his pleasure by putting the punch glass to his lips. "You dancin' or just handin' out punch?"

"I danced once. Harvey's boots stomped out any desire I

might have had to do it again."

Jake looked at her for the first time in the dim light. The butterscotch glasses were gone. Dinah Washington began "What a Difference a Day Makes". "Would you dance with me?"

"You just askin' because I put you up on a cold night?"

Jake answered by taking her hand and leading her to the dance floor. "Can you see good without your glasses?"

Sage frowned but her eyes kept their smile. "Forget what I said about Gene Kelly. He would never have asked such a dumb question."

"Sorry. I was trying to give you a compliment. You just look so pretty without `em."

"He wouldn't have said that either."

They danced without conversation after that. Sage did not move in close like Loretta and Texie had, but Jake found her almost easier to dance with. She responded to the slightest touch of his hand on her back and seemed to know his moves in advance by watching his eyes. Jake could not see Loretta's eyes when he danced with her because she snuggled against his cheek. Sage was just a kid, and Jake handled her like a fragile doll, but the confidence in her eyes made her seem like his oldest dance partner of the evening. She moved a little closer as Dinah crooned, "the difference is you". As they walked back to the punch bowl, Jake felt her arm against his and smelled shampoo mixed with the scents of Adrian Mercantile. It was comforting.

When the girls announced a Sadie Hawkins dance, most of the boys stepped out on the front porch to avoid being chosen. Jake wanted to keep dancing, but he lacked the confidence to stay inside with the girls. Burt Donovan was lighting a cigarette as Jake opened the door. He nodded and grunted a little. Their truce had held. No sign of Nocona or Gabe.

"Well, Fred Astaire, you abandonin' the ladies?" Coach

Ken Watson's voice grated on Jake's nerves, but he managed a tentative smile.

He tried to think of a clever reply, but could not. "Out here keepin' an eye on your team, Coach?"

"That would be right, Rivers. This girls' team could beat you boys on most days. I expect we'll win state if I can keep the team together. You little horny studs don't help matters much."

Jake turned away from the coach's stare and made small talk with Burt until he heard it.

Burt did, too. "What the hell is that?"

"Sounds like my car."

"Your car sound like a threshing machine?"

Jake had already hurdled the porch rail and was trotting to the back. The Ford was cranked and idling. Loretta was behind the wheel. Her boldness irritated Jake. "What are you doing?"

"Take me for a ride, Jake."

Jake pushed her over and killed the engine. "Thought you wanted to dance."

"I love to dance, but I feel like everybody in there is judging me. I feel like talking—like being alone. Let's go out on the Matador. We can talk—maybe fool around."

Jake was having the time of his life at the dance, but he could not think of a reason to say no. As they crossed the cattle guard and entered the Matador, Jake got that been-here-before feeling again. The full moon made the narrow winding trail look like it led to the edge of the earth. He turned off the radio, got out and rolled down all the windows. He loaned her his letter jacket and got an old Levi jacket for himself out of the trunk. He drove slowly for about a half hour, wishing for a hood to muffle the sound of the engine. He saw no sign that any thing other than horses or cattle had traveled the road before or that it led anywhere.

Loretta continued the soft hum she had begun while Jake

was rolling down the windows. Finally, she squeezed his arm. "Pull over here." She pointed at a solitary mesquite tree in the middle of an abandoned corral. The land was flat, but the corral sat on a little knoll. Prickly pear cactus grew all around and through broken fence rails. A buckboard with one wheel missing listed in the moonlight, blown sand drifted past the axles. A soft wind whistled, reminding Jake of the cowboys who had once branded and loaded cattle here. Jake imagined that he could smell the cattle, but their lowing was in the distance.

Loretta stepped out. "They say this used to be the southern loading pen when this was part of the XIT. They'd do the spring works here, then shipping in the fall. My daddy says that was back when they used a chuck wagon."

Jake stood beside her. Something about the place stirred him. Maybe his great- grandfather or grandfather had worked cattle here. Maybe Jake had been a cowboy in another life. Loretta leaned back against him and began that soft hum again. She took a deep breath and released it before turning to face Jake. She kissed him like she had back in the summer, but with more urgency. He tasted the salt of tears, smelled a change in her scent.

"You come prepared this time?"

"Are you crying?"

"Just the wind and the dust. Did you?"

Jake thought of the single Trojan that Gray Boy had shown him in the trunk of the Ford the day he left. He opened the trunk and groped around in the corner until he found it. Gray Boy had taped it just behind the taillight. He had figured to call her bluff, do some heavy petting like before, return the rubber to its hiding place, than go back to the dance. There would be promises to return.

Jake liked those promises, but as he rose from the trunk with the condom in his hand, he saw her boots, socks draped over the tops, sitting next to the back tire of the Ford. Loretta was already wriggling out of her jeans. She folded them and placed them on the front seat, dabbing at her eyes with the backs of her fingers. Jake noticed how delicate her fingers were. He took an involuntary deep breath, rubbing the plastic wrapper on the Trojan with his thumb, feeling the outline of the small balloon inside, wishing that he had actually seen an open condom before. There was fear and a feeling of being tested as he imagined Gray Boy looking over his shoulder. His mother's face walked across his mind, but he would not allow her to talk.

Barefoot, Loretta walked toward him in her panties and blouse. Jake noticed her small feet, the red polish on her toenails. She rose to her tiptoes, put her hands on his cheeks and pulled him to her. He felt her slick panties pressing against him. A need to disguise his innocence caused a sense of urgency, a need to rush before she could discover his naiveté. Putting the condom in his pocket, he put a hand on each of her buttocks and pulled her closer. She slowed him by stepping back a half step and drawing his hands to the buttons of her blouse. Sensing his nervousness as he undid each button, she pulled the blouse off her shoulders and tossed it toward her jeans. It hung on the steering wheel. She reached behind to unhook her bra, hesitating a split second before allowing it to fall away from her breasts. Almost shyly, she handed it to Jake without looking directly at him. Marveling at how her small, firm breasts differed from the ones he had seen in his brother's magazines, he inhaled the fragrance of talcum powder and her cologne as he promptly dropped the bra in the dirt.

She giggled a little as he picked it up, shook off the sand and laid it carefully on top of her jeans. Jake accepted her guidance as he pulled her panties down to her knees. He bent to his knees and held the panties away from the dirt as she stepped out of one leg, then the other. Raw sensory emotions enveloped him as he ran his hands back up her legs and to her

buttocks, inhaling her fragrance with each breath. She
pushed him back and let him look at her in the moonlight—
the first naked girl he had ever seen.

"Now, you." She said softly.

Jake flung his boots in the dirt, his clothes across the
windshield and cab of the Ford. He stood in front of her as
she lay back on the back seat, tears running down both
cheeks. Her voice cracking, she whispered, "You have to put
it on, Jake."

He retrieved his jeans from the windshield and returned
with the condom. She took it from him, dropped the plastic
cover in the dirt, and handed it to him. When his hands
trembled as he tried to put it on wrong-side-out, she took it
from him and gently guided it on. The touch of her hands,
the sense of patience, intimacy, and tenderness flooded Jake
with desire and sent his breathing into spasms. He blocked
out what his mother would say and thought only of what his
brother would do. There was no going back—no thinking
after that—no consideration of consequences—just urgent
pressing of his body against hers.

The never-experienced physical sensations, the pungent
fragrance of her body, her soft moans and the feeling that she
wanted him overwhelmed Jake and carried him away. It was
over before he could think of anything beyond wanting and
being wanted. Finished, he stood beside the car, suddenly
embarrassed, feeling out of control—as if this important event
had happened without his permission—without being able to
look forward to it or to contemplate it—even to enjoy it. He
apologized for being clumsy and fast as chill bumps came up
on his arms and legs.

She reassured him as she walked naked, shivering, to
retrieve her panties and jeans. Feeling guilty and awkward, he
pulled up his underwear and jeans as he made a mental note
to dispose of his underwear before going home. The first
button of his Levis reminded him of the rubber. It seemed to

be missing. He looked on the moonlit ground, walking in circles. Desperate to be dressed again, he asked her to help. "Do you see it?"

She searched the seat of the car and the ground beneath. Nothing.

Jake got down on his hands and knees and ran his hand across the ground. "That's impossible. It has to be here."

She squeaked a little as she kneeled down to help him search. "No use looking, Jake. It disintegrated. I can feel it inside me. How long have you had the damn thing?"

Jake felt it just as she said it. Nothing left but the ring. He rolled it off and threw it away. "I've only had it a few days. My brother gave it to me. I guess the heat in that trunk ...."

Loretta leaned against the car and began to cry. Jake thought he might be sick. "Is it that bad? It don't necessarily mean that we're in trouble for sure, does it?"

"With my luck, it ain't good, Jake."

"What do you mean, your luck?"

Loretta's scream hit Jake like a gust of wind in a sandstorm. It burned his eyes, his ears, and pushed him back. He looked around the deserted place as if they had an audience. "Damn, why are you screaming?"

She wiped her eyes and tucked her blouse into her jeans. "I come out here by myself sometimes, mostly so I can scream. Sorry to do it without warning you. It's just that I don't ever want to go through that again."

"Go through what again?"

"I've been pregnant before, Jake. Nobody told you?"

Jake felt stupid, frightened, and betrayed—like everyone at Adrian knew except him. "No. Who else knows?"

"Everybody. Or nobody ... who knows?"

"When were you pregnant before?"

"When I was fourteen. The year before we moved here. That's why we're here. My daddy had a big church in Ft.

Worth before I ruined it for him."

"You got pregnant when you were fourteen?" Jake's tone indicated that she might as well have committed murder.

Loretta slipped Jake's letter jacket back on as she walked to the buckboard and leaned against a broken wheel. She patted the ground beside her. Jake sat. "Nobody really told you, Jake?"

He shook his head, suppressing the urge to run as he pulled on his Levi jacket.

"I never told, but I assumed most of the kids knew. One of the church deacons does, and that's usually enough. Figured they had me pegged for a slut, so I acted like one."

"What happened?"

Loretta picked up a handful of dust and let it sift through her fingers. The wind moved it slightly as it drifted down. "I have a daughter."

Jake got as far as his knees before suppressing the flight urge again. "You got a kid?"

"I had a kid. I saw her for a few minutes before giving her up for adoption. I missed a year of school. I'd be out by now if not for that. That's another reason I figured everybody knew."

"Have you ever told anybody before?"

"Nobody before you. Not even Texie. I don't know why I told you."

"I won't tell."

She started to cry again, and Jake offered his handkerchief. She wiped her eyes, blew her nose, and handed it back. Jake wondered what his mother would say if she found lipstick on it or smelled perfume. He would lose his underwear, a handkerchief, and his virginity in one night. He searched for words. Finding none, he put his arm around her and she put her head on his shoulder. He still could not get his mind to accept what he had just been told. "What did your daddy say when you told him?"

"I have nightmares about what it did to my daddy and mother. We lived in a parsonage that was connected to the church sanctuary by a long hall. Daddy went down that hall screaming 'goddammit, goddammit.' I can still hear it. Never heard him use the Lord's name in vain before or since. Never said anything worse than darn before."

"Him bein' a preacher, it must have been double-tough."

"Yeah. He stopped screaming when he went into the chapel. Mama said he stayed on his knees in front of a picture of Jesus on the cross and prayed all night. Next day, they took me to a home for unwed mothers. I lived there until the baby came. Daddy gave up his church. Said Jesus told him to. When the baby was born, we moved here and started over. Now, I guess I'll put him through it again."

"Do you know where the baby is?"

"No, but I dream about her a lot."

Jake guessed it to be midnight when they finally dusted themselves off and walked to the car, but he was relieved to see 10:15 on his wristwatch. It had taken less than two hours to ruin both their lives. A small shiver ran down his spine, and he slapped his leg before starting the Ford. This bell could not be un-rung.

27 He eased back into his old parking space back of the Simms Community Center and killed the open engine. They knew it would fool nobody, but Jake and Loretta decided to go inside separately. Jake stood hidden at the end of the building while Loretta walked up the porch steps. A creak of a rocking chair and a low voice startled him. "Loretta, let's go home." Jake thought the big man would never stop unfolding to his full height as he rose from the chair. Loretta stopped. He put his arm around her and walked her to his car. Jake leaned against the porch for a long time, shrinking, as they drove away.

He wanted to go home and pull the covers over his head and never come out, but he did not want to wait until Monday to face his tormentors. More importantly, he needed to see how much trouble he had caused Loretta. The answer might be at the dance. He slipped in the door. Elvis Presley singing "A Fool Such as I" gave him some cover, but not much. Elvis was singing to him.

Caleb Pirtle stood beside the door. He nodded. "Jake." Sage looked at him without expression as she followed her father out the door, taking her information about Loretta and

199

her father with her.

Jake sat in a metal chair beside Gabe. "Where you been?"

Jake shook his head. Maybe nobody knew that he and Loretta had been together. "You ain't dancing?"

"I already told you and Nocona. I save it all for Betty Boop." Betty Baker was Gabe's Channing girlfriend, and Gabe enjoyed saying he was a one-woman man.

Jake stared at the floor until a pair of black penny-loafers appeared next to the toes of his boots. He looked up to the outstretched arm of Mary Ann Stafford. "Next one's another Sadie Hawkins, Jake. Dance with me?"

Jake looked at Gabe. He shrugged and looked away. Mary Ann had beautiful olive skin, pretty white teeth, and cat-green eyes. Problem was, she was a junior and taller than Jake. Much taller. Jake tried to see her eyes in the dim light. "Sure, Mary Ann. Could you just give me a minute? I was just tellin' Gabe something, and I need to finish it. Wait for me by the punch bowl?"

"Okay." Mary Ann skipped across the dance floor in time with the music.

Jake turned in his seat and faced Gabe. "What harm would it do for you to dance just this one with Mary Ann? Betty will never know. She wouldn't care even if she found out. I'm feelin' a little sick right now."

"She didn't ask me."

"You know damn well she would have if you didn't run around all over the school braggin' about being a one-woman man." Jake looked across the room. Mary Ann was watching him. He sighed. "She's got to be six feet tall."

"Five-eleven and a half." Gabe folded his arms and smiled as he shook his head. "Mama says that she may not be the prettiest girl in school now, but she'll make the most beautiful woman."

Jake looked again, trying to take a fresh perspective. "Who used to dance with these girls before I came? I never even had a girlfriend before I moved here. Girls in Hereford wouldn't give me the time of day."

"Told you before. There's a shortage of boys and a surplus of girls in Adrian. Besides, you're like a shiny new nickel. I been here since first grade. I'm just a rusty old quarter to these girls. Mary Ann, there, was my first sweetheart. To her, I'm all used up. You're fresh meat."

Conversation and dancing was stiff. Jake liked to listen to Fats Domino sing "I Want to Walk You Home", but he could never hear a beat to dance to. He was surprised when Mary Ann said she had brought the record from home. Jake looked up into her eyes. "Why?"

"Thought somebody might take a hint. I've danced to that song three times tonight and nobody has taken it yet."

"What hint?"

"Don't you boys ever get your mind out of the gutter long enough to listen to the words of songs?"

"You mean you want somebody to walk you home? Where do you live?"

"Fats Domino says walk; I say ride. Nobody walks anybody home out here, Silly. I live on a ranch a few miles west. Miz Lowry says this dance is over at eleven-thirty. My brother won't be here till midnight to pick me up. I bet him that I would find a ride before he got here."

Nelda Lowry unplugged the record player, allowing the needle to strangle Fats Domino's last words and scratch Mary Ann's forty-five. The silence was embarrassing as the lights came up and Jake looked up at Mary Ann. "Uh, I guess I could take you home. I'm already late, and our old car ain't much, but if... ."

"May as well. Your old car couldn't be any worse than ours."

Gabe winked at him as he and Mary Ann left Simms Community Center. Jake mouthed "kiss my ass". Following her directions, Jake headed west. Cursed with little sense

of direction, he had learned to find his way around the
Panhandle by distance. He noted the odometer reading as he
struggled for conversation. "Watson may be mad at you for
riding home with me. Thinks you girls can go to state if he
can keep the boys away."

Mary Ann smiled. "Did he say that? I don't think he was
talkin' about you and me."

"Who then?"

"Loretta. I'm the tallest, but she's the court magician.
She's team leader."

After fifteen miles of listening to Mary Ann and thinking
of Loretta, Jake slowed. "Where'd you say you lived?"

"See those big posts up there? Turn between them.
That's the ranch my daddy manages." This was going to be
easier than Jake thought. He checked his odometer again as
he turned between the posts. A low fog crawled along the
ground as the Ford rattled over the cattle guard.

"Never saw fog out here before. You?"

"Every so often. Takes just the right conditions, I guess."

Twenty-eight miles and three cattle guards later, Jake came
to a gate. He turned to Mary Ann, who had scooted over to
his side when they entered the ranch. Dim light from the
instrument panel illuminated an outline of her hair and face.
"Guess this is the gate to your yard?"

"Not yet. Just a little farther." The fog rolled above the
door bottom and into the car as Jake stepped out to open
the gate. There had been several turns along the way, and
Jake was starting to worry about finding his way back. Fog
came over the headlights and danced over the hood like a cat
stalking a mouse as he eased the car through the open gate.
When he returned from closing it, Mary Ann was not in the
car. He switched on the interior lights and looked in the
floorboard and back seat. No Mary Ann. He stepped outside
and shouted her name.

"Turn off that light and stay on your side of the car.

Something about that gate makes me have to go every time. My brother usually does, too. If you need to, go ahead."

Jake turned out the car lights, killed the engine, but turned the key to allow the radio to play. He walked a few feet away into the fog, grateful for the chance to keep from wetting his pants. The voice of Connie Francis and "My Happiness" drifted through the haze as Jake buttoned. He heard Mary Ann singing "whether skies are gray or blue, anyplace on earth will do", before he saw her leaning against the Ford's trunk. The fog was caressing her legs like a puppy wanting his belly rubbed.

She took his right hand and placed it in the middle of her back. "We didn't get to dance a slow one." She moved inside his arms and pressed her tall, thin frame against him.

Jake stiffened as the awkward scene with Loretta and the Matador worked its way into the song's lyrics. He had ruined enough people's happiness for one evening. Mary Ann's body was supple and her movements graceful, not seductive. Jake felt himself escaping into the moment in spite of his guilt and sadness. The fog, the music, and the scent of a beautiful young girl made Jake forget how tall she was. It even took his mind off Loretta for a few seconds. Inside the car again, she smiled, kissed him lightly, plopped back into the seat, and straightened the folds of her dress. "Whew. That's better. I was about to bust. Home, James."

Jake laughed and felt a little easier for the first time since leaving the Matador. "I see a light over there. Is that your house?"

"Nope, not yet. Daddy's brother lives there alone."

Fifty-nine miles from Simms Community Center, Jake saw a single light in the middle of the road. "Damn. We're meetin' a car. First car we've seen since leaving the dance."

Mary Ann smiled. "That's not a car. It's my house. Road ends right at our front door. We live on the edge of the ranch. If there wasn't fog, you could see into New Mexico behind the house. Lonesome out here, but pretty after you get used to it."

Jake glanced at Mary Ann's profile as she picked up her Fats Domino forty-five. Her chin was lifted, and she was smiling. She really was beautiful. And fun. Too bad she was so tall. "You play that record a lot?"

Mary Ann giggled. "Only at dances or at somebody's house who has a record player. We don't have one." Jake did not have a record player either, but it sounded sad when Mary Ann said it. Living way out here, even more isolated than the Rivers, she had to be lonely. He pushed the light switch halfway in, leaving only the fog lights on. A tall, dark man stood in the doorway, holding the screen door partially open. He had a little paunch and a well-worn felt hat was pushed back on his head.

Jake wondered why the man was wearing his hat inside this late at night. He stepped outside the car, intending to do the right thing at least once during this mistake-filled day. "I'll walk you to the door and meet your family."

She reached over and pecked him on the cheek. "Nope. I have put you out enough for one night. I'm sorry I didn't tell you how far I lived. You made me feel desirable tonight, Jake." With her hand on the door handle, she seemed to want Jake to have the last word.

"You made me feel six feet tall. And you are desirable." Jake looked at the man standing in the doorway, trying to make out an expression. "You in trouble?"

Mary Ann looked toward her father. "No, I can handle my daddy. He trusts me. My brother may be in a tight spot, though. He lost the bet. Thanks for that, Jake. I had fun." And she was gone.

28 It was past midnight, and Jake knew he was at least eighty miles from home. He was going to be in trouble when he got there, but trouble at home was not his major concern—gasoline was. The gauge was leaning against the E and looked ready to drop flat. After an hour of driving, he knew he was lost. He had made it fine to the gate that had to be opened and closed, but all the cattle guards looked alike, and he could not remember where turns had been made. Fog kept him from seeing anything that he might have noticed on the way into the ranch. Heading in what he thought was the general direction of home, he hoped for the best. Surely this method would eventually take him off the ranch and onto a road with signs. He wished that he had heeded Mattie's warning to always fill up before leaving the house.

Two hours of wrong turns later, he found the road to Simms and headed home. He rolled down the windows and drove fifty in the fog, feeling sensible for the first time tonight. He killed the Ford in the Rivers' driveway at just past three in the morning. Rance and Mattie were in the kitchen. Mattie flew on him like a hawk on a field mouse.

"Where have you been, Jake? You had us worried sick. Your daddy drove over to Simms and all the back roads. Even went into Adrian looking for you."

"I got lost in the fog."

"Everybody else get lost in the fog, or just you?"

"I did a favor for a girl and took her home. She didn't tell me that she lived nearly all the way to New Mexico."

His revelation was met with stunned silence by Mattie.

Jake tried again. "Besides, I thought we had agreed that y'all were gonna trust me."

Mattie threw up her hands. "Trust you? It's not a matter of...

Rance started to untie his brogans. "We'll work this out in the morning. Right now, I need some sleep. I got to work tomorrow."

Mattie was smothering fried chicken when Jake dragged himself out of bed the next morning. She did not look up when he walked past the kitchen. The spring sun was unusually warm as he walked toward the red barn. Pleased that String was not home, he leaned against the north side of the barn and absorbed the sun. He never liked Sundays back home—and they were worse here. Sabbaths were days of guilt. If he went to church, the preacher filled his head with warnings of hellfire and damnation. He had always thought himself a bad sinner; now, he knew. If he stayed away from church, he felt guilty for not going.

His sister and brothers had been there on East Texas Sundays. Days-of-worship were usually interrupted by visits from cousins and aunts and uncles. After dinner, Jake could escape to the woods or creek bottoms or ride Scar to Papa Griff's. If cousins came, twilight brought homemade ice cream, watermelon, and games of Kick the Can or Red Rover. If company did not come, Mattie often made fudge and they listened to Dr. Sixgun on the radio.

Panhandle Sundays were all the same. Only Mattie's

fried chicken interrupted plowing, planting, harvesting, or repairing. Even the chicken was store-bought rather than being fried fresh from the yard. This Sunday showed every indication of being one of the worst. His best hope was that he would suffer only for a month before finding that Loretta was not pregnant. He dared not think of the alternative, just that he would never take such a risk again.

There was little conversation at the dinner table until Mattie served lemon meringue pie, Jake's favorite. He saw it as a good sign, but it was the only indication that things were getting better. She did not return his smile of gratitude. Jake was hooking up the water hose beside the shop to wash last night's layer of dust from the Ford when Rance came out the back door. "Fog and dust don't mix too well, I guess."

Jake continued washing. "Nope."

Rance turned off the faucet and walked into the shop. "Come in here and sit down, Jake."

Jake sighed deeply and dropped into a rickety chair that had been discarded from someone's kitchen. Rance leaned against the workbench and folded his arms. "We can't have anymore of this coming in at three in the mornin', Jake. It's killin' your mother. We went down that road with Gray Boy and we're not travelin' that way again."

Jake stared at the shop floor. "I told you what happened."

"It's been happenin' too much. It shows a lack of respect."

"I thought we talked about me having to drive a long way to go on a date or to a school event. Sometimes it's hard to get home before midnight. You said you were gonna trust me."

"I said I was going to give you plenty of rope. You seem to forget that I'm still holding the end of that rope, Jake ... and I'll jerk it if I have to."

Jake shook his head. "You and Mother don't see the way things are out here. They're different."

"You think we don't know that things are different out here, Jake? You haven't noticed that they're different for us, too?"

"What do you want me to say?"

"Let's get this out in the open. You've been surly since that night in Adrian. It's like a dead carcass between us. The longer it stays, the worse it smells. Let's get it out in the open and bury it."

Jake averted his father's stare. "Fine by me."

"Is your mind made up, or do you want to listen to what happened?"

He looked up into his father's piercing black eyes, a place he seldom visited. "I know you were drunk. What else do I need to know?"

Rance stiffened, and Jake cowered a little. "If you're lookin' for me to beg for your forgiveness, forget it."

"Never said anything about begging."

"You know I've always liked the taste and feel of a little whiskey in me. Never had a problem with it until Tuck died. I know we made a pact that I wouldn't do it again. I've kept my word."

"A little whiskey? Hell, Daddy, you were curled up in that pickup seat like an old drunk wallowing in his own puke." Jake was surprised at his own boldness. He had never raised his voice to his father before.

Rance responded in kind. "I had two drinks with that old boy at the garage—Whitey. Must have had some type of reaction to it. I had a good dose of Pepto-Bismol beforehand, but whiskey is about the only thing that eases me. But it made me sick as a dog that night, and I passed out. Don't know if it was bad whiskey or my stomach. I been havin' a little stomach trouble." His voice trailed off at the end.

Jake remembered the time he had seen his father throw up behind a tractor tire. "That start when we came out here?"

"Before."

"What did Dr. Olen say was causin' it?"

"He doesn't know. Remember when you and Tuck stayed with Seth and Tillie for a week? He sent me to some doctors in the Medical Arts Building in Dallas. Stayed a week, and they still didn't know what's causin' it."

Rance took out his pocketknife and used his thumb to open and close the blade. "Papa used to say that doctors are like birds. You let one peck at you a little here and there, and it don't do too much damage; but if he keeps it up, he'll eventually kill you. If you get a whole flock after you, they'll peck you to death pretty quick. I just got tired of the peckin' and came on home."

"They didn't have any idea?"

"Best guess is ulcers. Doc says the only way to tell for sure is to cut me open."

"Dr. Olen tell you it was okay to drink whiskey?" Worry softened Jake, and he wished he had not asked it.

Rance looked through the shop window toward the house. "He said it could kill me, but hell, anything could kill me if they don't know what's causin' the hurt."

Jake felt weak and afraid. He had felt superior—even righteous, when he slammed that door in his daddy's face. The long-suppressed memory of his father leaving for Medical Arts crossed his mind. Now Jake knew why he had suppressed it. Rance had lined up all his children like little soldiers to say goodbye. Trish and Gray's weeping had frightened Jake. He knew that they knew something he did not. When Rance hugged him and kissed him on the cheek, he knew that whatever his sister and brother knew was bad. When he and Tuck drove off with Uncle Seth and Aunt Tillie, Jake had wondered if he would ever see his father again.

Rance stood and turned to leave. Through the open shop door, Jake saw the spring late afternoon sun low in the west behind his father. The brightness made his father look like a silhouette. Rance's shadow put out a hand and leaned against the doorframe, staring at the sun. "Jake, you remember when we used to listen to fights on the radio together?"

Jake smiled. "Yeah. I sure remember Rocky Marciano. I remember when he beat Joe Louis. Remember Archie Moore, too. Remember Wednesday Night Fights at the Clicks?"

"Yeah. Don't know what made me think about that."

Jake did not get up when his father walked away. In a few seconds, he was back. "I hear Floyd Patterson's gonna fight Ingemar Johansson again sometime soon. Maybe we can listen together again—if it's on the radio." Rance stepped away without waiting for an answer, and then stepped back into the sun's rays. "Jake, this stomach thing ... it ain't somethin' you need to worry about."

29 Jake sat on the last seat in the back of the bus the next morning, feeling like he had that first day at Hereford. He just thought he had problems then. Now he really did. To his surprise, nobody teased him about Loretta at school. By last class period before athletics, he decided she had stayed at home—probably with morning sickness. Mary Ann smiled at him in the hall, but he was afraid to ask if Loretta was at school. As he stepped into English, Loretta waved at him from the end of the hall. She looked sad. Jake felt a strange sense of relief.

He took his usual seat and awaited the arrival of Mrs. Boucher, the English teacher. After a five-minute wait, students started to whisper and walk around. They had progressed to throwing erasers, spit wads and pencils when Mr. Alderman cleared his throat at the back of the room. "Students, take your seats and quiet down. Mrs. Boucher will not be here today. Unfortunately, she has decided to take early retirement due to failing health."

Jake's yoke of shame grew heavier. Mrs. Boucher had come out of retirement after her husband's death to teach English one last year. The students had made her life hell. When they found she was too nice to apply discipline or call the principal, they behaved like sharks when there is blood in the water. Jake laughed at the crude pranks at first, but his memory of Duff Finnegan stopped him. He had worried a little about missing a whole year of English, but not enough to stand up to his classmates and help an old lady. Last Friday, a freshman had stapled a "kick me" sign to the bottom of her dress as she walked down the aisle in her classroom. Too deaf to hear the stapler click, she had worn it all day. It had probably been the last straw. Jake envisioned the old woman removing that dress, finding the note, and sitting down on her bed to cry. The principal's voice and the sound of a familiar name brought him back to the classroom.

"Reverend Floyd Knight has graciously consented to finish out our school year. Besides being a Baptist minister, Reverend Knight is an experienced English teacher. I am sure he will receive your complete cooperation." Principal Alderman led polite applause as Floyd Knight walked down the aisle beside Jake's desk. Jake's momentary sense of relief was over.

Jake had never seen Loretta's father up close. He had expected a fat man, but Floyd Knight was not fat. The preacher had played three sports at Baylor and looked ready to deliver a crushing tackle today. He sat in Mrs. Boucher's chair and folded both arms across the desk. His skin was lighter than Loretta's, and his hair was a red hue that had been bleached by the sun. Jake wondered if she was adopted. Floyd Knight's short-sleeved white shirt revealed arms covered with reddish-blond hair. The arms were bigger than Jake's legs. It was easy to forget that he was a preacher. When Mr. Alderman left, Reverend Knight leaned forward, smiling at the class of sophomores for what seemed like a long time as restlessness and awkwardness filled the room.

"I guess we all know why Mrs. Boucher is in bad health. We all know the real reason she left in the middle of school year. I'm disappointed in all of you, especially the boys—and particularly this class. I understand you were the worst. I can't believe that a whole class of students would be willing to miss out on an entire year of learning English just so they could pull pranks on a helpless old woman who wanted to teach them something."

Reverend Knight stood and walked down the aisle on the other side of the room from Jake. "Now, because of your laziness and lack of respect, we have to cram a full year of learning into less than three months. But ... I think we can do it. Do you?"

Heads jerked and nodded. Some grunts of assent.

"I want you all to refer to me as Mr. Knight, even those of you who know me as Reverend Knight or Brother Knight. At school, I am a teacher—not a preacher. Understood?"

Yessir's bounced off the walls and echoed down the hall.

"First assignment. Get out some paper and write a theme of at least two pages on what you did this weekend."

Jake felt, rather than saw, Gabe turn in his seat to look at him. Without looking up, he opened his spiral notebook and stared at the blank pages until he felt Burt Donovan's tap on his bowed head. "Rivers, loan me some paper. I ain't never brought nothin' to English before. Don't think I even know where my book is." Burt was a junior taking sophomore English.

Jake kept his eyes down as he tore out two sheets and handed them back to Burt. If Burt was going to write something, surely he could. His pen was a little unsteady as he wrote "What I Did This Weekend" at the top of the page. *Is this assignment especially for me? Does he know?* He heard the rustling of pages as the other students began to write, even Burt. He looked over his shoulder at Burt's paper. "Ate supper. Fed hogs. Went to dance. Fixed flat on tar. Had chicken-fried stake for dinner." Burt's scrawling and spelling made Jake feel better and gave him an idea. He titled his first sheet. "Marines and Car Hoods". He was feeling good when he titled the second sheet. "Lost in the Fog". When the bell rang, Jake wrote two more lines to fill two pages. He bounced them on the desk as if they were a book manuscript before looking up. Floyd Knight was standing at his desk with his hand out. The other students had left. Jake handed him the sheets, and Loretta's father smiled.

30 Jake got an A+ and a nice note from Mr. Knight on his first theme the next day. He also got a whipping. Mr. Knight asked each of the students if they felt they deserved punishment for what they had done to Mrs. Boucher. Everyone raised a hand. The boys got to choose between reading a book chosen by Mr. Knight or licks. The girls' choices were the book or cleaning up the school grounds for a month. Jake wanted to choose the book, but took the licks along with the rest of the boys to prove his manhood. Mr. Knight could swing a paddle as well as the principal at Hereford, but he only swung it three times and seemed to take no pleasure in it. Jake did. He knew he deserved more than three licks from Loretta's father. The sting from the licks made him feel better about himself than he had since that night on the Matador.

Not to be outdone by the new popular teacher at Adrian High, Coach Ken Watson delivered ten more licks to Jake, Nocona, and Gabe that afternoon. He caught them huddled in a back corner of the schoolyard next to the building. Smoke was curling from the threesome. They were late for the second track practice. Nocona was the only one smoking, but they all took their licks. Coach Watson seemed to enjoy it. With a sore butt, Jake ran the hundred and the two-twenty that day. To his surprise, a freshman passed him and beat him by two steps in the hundred. A junior beat him by a yard in the two-twenty. He ran the four-forty the next day and came in third. He ran last in the eight-eighty the next day.

"How you expect to win any track meets when you can't even beat your own teammates, Rivers? Thought you were a hot shot—fast on your feet." The girls had lost their bi-district game the night before, and Watson was irritable. He seemed to be taking over as head track coach. Coach Gee hardly observed from the shade of the building as the boys ran on the sand track beside a dilapidated baseball diamond.

Jake thought he knew what was wrong, but he could not tell the coach. He was distracted, wondering why Loretta had been benched at the half in last night's critical game. "What am I doing wrong?" Jake thought sure he could at least win the hundred-yard-dash. He was always ahead at ninety yards, but not at a hundred. *What good was there to being small if you were also slow?*

"Wrong? You never were the jock you think you are."

Jake was pleased to see Coach Gee approach. "Think you can pole vault, Jake?"

"Never tried it."

"Go in that equipment closet by the locker room and see if the pole is still there. Bring it out, and we'll take a run at it."

Jake expected to see the pole when he opened the door to the closet. It was not leaned against the wall or in plain sight. He lifted duffel after duffel of basketballs and volleyballs before he saw it. As he lifted the last bag to uncover the pole, a baseball rolled out and came to rest at Jake's feet. He sat down on the bag and picked up the baseball. He had not touched one in more than a year. It felt good in his hands. He tossed it up a couple of times, rolled it in his hands, felt the seams. He stood the duffel on its end and pulled out

a catcher's mitt and facemask. He jumped at the sound of
Floyd Knight's voice.

"You like baseball, Jake?"

Jake nodded and smiled. "Used to play a little."

"Any good?"

"My daddy wanted me to be good, but I think I
disappointed him."

"Where's that damn pole-vault, Jake?" Coach Watson's
sounded hollow as it bounced off the metal lockers. He stuck
his head in the closet door. "Scuse my language, Reverend
Knight. Didn't know you were in here."

"Floyd will be fine, Coach Watson." Reverend Knight
looked in Jake's direction. "Jake here, says he used to play
baseball."

"Well, I hope he can play baseball, cause he sure can't run
track."

Mr. Knight nodded. "I understand Adrian used to field a
baseball team a few years back. Still got the equipment, I see."

"Not many schools in our district play baseball anymore.
Too windy and too much dust out here, I guess—wind will
blow a homerun back to the pitcher's mound sometimes.
Plus, it's too far to travel during crop season. Some of these
boys' daddies want 'em in the fields right after school this
time of year—not on the road playin' baseball."

Coach Gee met them as they were leaving the locker
room. He extended a hand to Floyd Knight. "Floyd. You still
willing to help us out a little?"

"I'll do what I can, but you know football and baseball
were my games, not track. Couldn't even throw the shot
far enough to qualify in field events. According to Coach
Watson, Jake seems to have the same problem with track and
field. He likes baseball. Any chance of us fielding a team this
year, Coach?"

"Kinda had that on my mind after I clocked these boys in
track."

Coach Watson did not like the way the conversation was headed. "Who we gonna play on the outside chance we can pull together a team this late?"

Coach Gee took the baseball from Jake's hands. "Several teams south and east of here still play. I think Hartley does, too. Hedley, Happy, Lazbuddie, Bovina ... a few more. We might have to play a couple of big schools, but I can find some games."

Coach Watson picked up the pole and examined a small crack that ran most of its length. "What about track? These boys got their hearts set on runnin'."

"You got one boy that's likely to win anything in this district. Terry Creitz could go to state in the mile." Coach Gee turned to Jake. "Rivers, tell the boys to huddle up. We'll see if we got track stars or baseball stars."

The boys were more than willing to stop running and sit on the shaded dirt outside the locker room. Gee asked for a show of hands for baseball. All but one sweaty hand went up. For track, only one hand went up—Terry Creitz's. Coach Gee turned to Coach Watson. "You work with Terry. Coach Knight and I will concentrate on the baseball team."

"Coach Knight?" Watson was perplexed.

"He's a preacher and a teacher. He won't mind one more hat. Will you, Coach?"

Watson would not let it go. "So, if we play baseball with teams outside of our district, what will we be playin' for? We can't win a district title."

Coach Knight tossed a baseball in the air and caught it. "For joy, Coach. And for the love of the game." He picked up the duffel and emptied it in the middle of the huddle. "All right, boys. How many have played baseball before?"

Four hands shot up. Jake looked at Gabe. "You never played baseball?"

"You ever dog a steer?"

"I get your point."

Coaches Knight and Gee had the boys in position on
the dusty field in a matter of minutes. Three boys stood at
shortstop with Jake; nobody was at catcher. Coach Knight,
holding a ball and bat at home plate, looked behind him.
"Nobody catches?" No response. "Anybody ever catch ...even
in practice?" Jake reluctantly held up his hand. "Okay,
Rivers, get the mitt and get back here."

Jake more stumbled than trotted to home plate. "Coach
Knight, I only filled in for the catcher in some practices in
Little League. I never actually played catcher."

"You wanted to play baseball, Jake. Can't play without a
catcher. What's it gonna be?"

They traveled to Bovina for their first game. Jake had six
passed balls, missed two easy pop-ups at the plate, allowed
four boys to steal second, two to steal home, and threw the
ball away twice on simple returns to the pitcher. He could not
stop blinking when the bat was swung, could not peg second,
and stayed too far away from the plate. Nocona pitched,
ignoring most of Jake's signals. Bovina 12–Adrian 0. Not a
single Adrian player reached first base. Jake popped up for
the last at-bat. He picked up the catcher's mitt and mask and
slung it in the duffel.

Coach Gee shouted. "You played like a girl, Rivers.
You're afraid to squat in there close to the batter. You're not
talking to the batters. You missed easy pop-ups. You're the
only thing we have for catcher, and you just about lost the
game all by yourself."

Jake was angry and mortified as he saw Floyd Knight
approaching. He did not like wearing shin guards, the chest
pad, or the facemask. He especially did not like using a
catcher's mitt to catch pop-ups. "I told Coach Knight I had
never actually played catcher before. I just caught while the
real catcher batted. I can play shortstop better than the kid
who's out there, though. Let him play catcher."

Coach Knight put his hand on Jake's shoulder and

smiled. "I thought Jake was just being modest when he said he couldn't play catcher, Coach Gee. Turns out he was being honest." Both coaches laughed. Coach Knight squeezed Jake's shoulder. "Jake, I played catcher in college. By the end of the season, I'll have you pegging second without ever getting out of a squat. By our next game, you'll stop blinking and know how to use that mitt."

He was trying not to, but Jake liked Floyd Knight a lot. He was every bit as good a teacher as Duff Finnegan—a good coach, too. He wished that they had met before he took Loretta to the Matador. Jake lived for his English classes and baseball. They were the only things that took his mind off Loretta. She dominated his thoughts when he was driving a tractor or doing anything on the farm. She passed him in the halls daily, shaking her head to indicate that their fate remained uncertain. By the time the team traveled to Lazbuddie for their second game, Jake had stopped blinking at swinging bats and had moved closer to the plate. The first batter sent Jake's mask flying to the pitcher's mound. Jake barely felt the jerk when the mask was picked cleanly off his head.

Coach Gee walked out to speak to him as he retrieved it. He was chuckling. "When I said you needed to sacrifice your body for the team, Jake, I didn't mean it literally. Move far enough back to keep your head from becoming a watermelon." Jake nodded and smiled. He was starting to like the mask, the mitt and the pads.

By the final game of the season, Jake felt like a field general. He called pitches, signaled the number of outs, calmed pitchers, positioned outfielders, and harassed the other team's batters. He gave up on pegging second in a squat, but he mastered throwing off his mask, standing, and putting runners out at second. He wondered how he had ever felt satisfied at shortstop. His teammates had not grown up with baseball as he had, but that did not lessen Jake's happiness.

Happy was their final chance to win a single game during the 1960 season. Jake wanted his daddy to see him play, but he knew that Rance was getting the fields ready to plant maize. He had to put in extra hours because Jake seldom arrived home before dark on game days. Also, no games had been played at home because of the poor condition of Adrian's field.

In the top of the eighth, Jake was up to bat in Happy. A south wind had gotten up and was rolling dust clouds across the diamond. Happy had been wise enough to face their field north, so the wind was at Jake's back. He had gone two for two, and the score was tied at one-one. Gabe on second. Two outs. As Jake swung two bats in the on-deck circle, he heard a familiar voice.

"Look right, Jake." The voice was conversational in tone, but loud enough to be heard. Jake turned and nodded toward his father. He was standing at the end of the bleachers. *How long has he been here?* Jake had his mind on left field. He was an early swinger, and almost all of his hits went toward left field. He liked swinging early and felt more power if he hit the ball to that part of the field. Happy players had noticed, too. They had moved left. Even the first baseman was playing halfway to second.

Jake positioned his body into an unfamiliar stance to try to hit toward the open spot. He foul-tipped the first pitch. He stepped back from the plate and looked at his father's expressionless face as the ball spun harmlessly on the ground toward the Happy dugout. He swung a little late on the second pitch and hit a line drive over first base. As he rounded first, he saw Gabe heading for home. Jake was gaining on him. He looked over his shoulder as he rounded second and saw the out-of-position right-fielder pick up the ball after it bounced off the fence. Gabe headed for home, and Jake headed for third. He was surprised to see the third baseman's eyes anticipating the ball. The kid in right field must have shot it from a rifle. He heard the ball pop in the third baseman's glove as he began his slide. The glove and ball passed six inches above him. A triple. He was brushing his uniform off, wondering what his daddy was thinking, when Coach Watson grabbed his arm and pulled him off the field.

"Get your pads on, Rivers. That's the last out."

"Who's out?"

"You are. You ignored my signal to hold up at second."

"I didn't see your signal, but I was not out. The guy never touched me. You know that." Jake pulled the arm of the Happy third baseman. "You know you never touched me." The player shrugged and walked away.

Jake was furious as he walked toward the home plate umpire. "Who called me out?" The umpire pointed toward a man leaning against the left field fence a few feet behind third base. Jake looked toward his father as he made his way toward the man. Rance moved a level hand back and forth—the safe signal. He walked on the other side of the fence parallel to Jake as they approached the man. He was dressed in a khaki shirt and silver-belly hat with a cattleman's crease. The third base umpire shook out a Winston and shielded his Zippo from the wind.

"Sir, did you make that call at third?" Jake was overstepping and knew it, but Rance seemed to be backing him.

"Yeah, I guess I did."

"I'm sorry, Sir, but did you even see the play? He never even got close to me with the ball."

The man pointed his lighted Winston toward Ken Watson. "To tell the truth, Kid, I let that man sway my decision. I didn't really see it. When a coach puts up an arm and a thumb on his own man, that's good enough for me. I just followed his lead."

Jake slumped as he looked at his father. Rance shook the

man's hand and turned to Jake. "Shake it off. Watson was probably trying to teach you to watch the base coaches. I saw him give you a hold-up signal."

"We haven't had a third base coach all year. Watson coaches track. This is the first game he's even been to. I ain't used to watching anybody when I run bases."

"You learned a hard lesson. I don't see punishing the whole team to teach you a lesson, but you do have to learn to watch for signals."

"Would you have held me at second?"

"No, but I didn't know that kid in right field had a major league arm. Maybe your coach did. Get over it. You had a good hit—drove in a run. You're ahead. Hold them for two more and you can win."

Jake ran for his pads and mask just as Coach Gee came out of the dugout to get him. Coach Knight was warming up the pitcher. Adrian won its first and only game of the season—two to one.

31

Jake was helping Coach Knight unload baseball equipment from the bus when he heard her voice. The entire baseball team had stopped to greet her as she made her way to her father. Memories of the last girls' basketball game would not go away. "How come you sat out the last part of that game, Loretta? Y'all could have won if you had stayed in." Like she always had, Loretta shook her head at the questions, briefly rewarding them with a flirtatious smile as she made her way toward her father.

"Daddy, any chance Jake and I could go get a Coke? He'll bring me home before dark." Floyd Knight was bent over a duffel full of bats and balls. He looked over his shoulder at his daughter, then at Jake. Jake felt his face getting darker.

"No harm in that, I suppose."

Jake knew he had been hiding from the problem that should be dominating his life. Baseball had been a warm refuge, but it was now over. He had been able to block her out of his mind during games and during some classes, but he could sense her presence, even smell her, all day. He chose to sit across from her rather than beside her in a booth at the Bent Door. His breath was ragged as the waitress brought the Cokes. Jake focused on the two straws that Loretta placed between her lips. She looked up as he saw her throat move with the first swallow. "Jake, I just wanted to tell you we don't have a problem."

Jake took a deep breath and let it out. "So you're not ... ."

"I should have said something earlier, but with basketball playoffs and you being with Daddy every time I see you, I just couldn't find a way to get you alone."

Jake wondered how long she had known—how long she had let him suffer. "I thought sure when you sat out the last half of a bi-district game that it meant somethin' bad. Didn't know what. Just bad."

She stared into the dark Coke. "Guess that was my last basketball game." Tears welled in her eyes as she looked up.

"Yeah. Watson says you girls could have beat us boys on nights when you were on your game."

She dragged the Coke back and forth across the tabletop and made a half-smile. "I was always on my game, Rivers. Wanna do some one-on-one?"

It wasn't the first time she had looked deeply into his eyes, but it was the first time there was no mirth or playfulness in her stare. She reached across the table and took Jake's hand away from the glass. Their hands were cold when they touched, but Jake felt the familiar surge of warmness that Loretta always drew from him. Guilt and fear had suppressed that feeling since that night on the Matador. He did not know what he would say if she were to invite him there again. The confusion and fear must have shown.

"Don't worry, Jake. We're gonna be good from now on. Just tell me one thing. Would you have ever asked me out on a real date if I had been the same age or younger than you?"

Jake answered without thinking. "In a heartbeat. You're the prettiest girl in school. All the boys want to take you out."

She laughed. "I just needed to hear you say that. Someday, you'll see how silly you were to let a couple of years come between us."

"I'm already startin' to see it, I guess." He looked toward the Baptist parsonage and thought of the Reverend Coach Floyd Knight. "Changin' schools twice in the last couple of years sort of threw me off. I think I must have had some sort of plan about which girls I would ask out back home. There were all younger than me."

"I'll just bet none of them had kids, either."

He reached across the table for her other hand. They sat like that until the tinkle of the little bell above the bent door made them aware of the moment. "Course, I was scared of your daddy, too. And I was a little scared of you. Couldn't figure why a girl as pretty as you would have anything to do with me. Come to think of it, I still have never had a real date."

Loretta laughed. "And your reputation is already almost as bad as mine." She slid from the booth and stood beside him. "Better go. It's gettin' dark."

Jake parked in front of the parsonage and stared at the light inside. "First time I have ever actually stopped in front of your house without sneakin'."

"You like him, don't you?"

He turned toward her and smiled. "Yeah. Yes, I do."

"Everybody does. He likes you too, Jake. I promise you I'll never do anything to change that." She squeezed his arm. "Gotta go."

"Could I walk you to the door?"

They walked across the yard and stood under the porch light. Loretta leaned against the door, her hand on the doorknob behind her. He caught her scent as she ran her fingers lightly across his jaw. "I hope we'll always be good friends, Jake." She opened the door and backed inside before he could reply.

32 Jake knew that his first experiences with girls had
courted disaster. He knew they would be part of
his life again in the fall, but pledged to stay away
from them for the summer. Rance made it easier by handing
him a list of chores each morning. He and String roped every
night after supper. If there was moonlight, they stayed at it
until bedtime. He was happy until the first night String was
not home. He saddled Scar, but left him standing idle as he
roped the dummy until bedtime for three nights in a row.
He remembered what Will Tom had said about cowboys not
knowing how to say goodbye. Jake did not know when String
had left or when he would return.

The fourth day with String gone was a Saturday. Jake
drove the grain truck fifty miles to Adrian after unloading his
last load of wheat at the Ford grain elevators. He wanted his
friends to see him driving the big truck. Wheat harvest made
things festive in Adrian, even across the railroad tracks from
Route 66. He drove up and down 66, enjoying shifting gears,
without seeing any cars or people he recognized at the service
stations, garages, or cafés. He stopped at the Bent Door.
Same results. He caught a glimpse of himself in the side
mirror as he pulled himself back into the big truck. His face

was covered with wheat dust and dirt. Mattie had told him
that it was time to shave, and the wheat dust highlighted the
beginnings of a beard—just enough to make him look more
like a kid who could not grow a real beard. He headed the
truck home.

He showered, shaved with a new single blade Schick
dispenser razor, splashed Aqua-Velva on his face, sprayed
Right Guard under his arms, and added a dash of Mennen
Skin Bracer to his arms and neck. Mattie seemed glad to see
him drive off in the still-hoodless Ford. His vow had lasted
a little over three weeks. At Adrian, he walked through
the Bent Door again as if he were looking for somebody in
particular. He drove up and down 66, then through the
streets of Adrian. He told himself he did not want to see
Loretta, but drove slowly past the Baptist parsonage. Just
before closing time, he stepped into Adrian Mercantile.

Caleb Pirtle nodded, but he did not speak. Busy with
another customer, he was probably not happy to see Jake at
ten minutes before closing time. Jake pretended to be looking
for something as he roamed the store. Nobody. He was
starting to believe that he had dreamed his sophomore year at
Adrian High School when he heard Sage's voice coming from
the back storage room. A customer followed her. She nodded
in Jake's direction. He waited for the customer to leave.

"Hey. Good to see a familiar face. Where is everybody?
Nobody comes to town during the summer?"

"Some of 'em will be here in a little bit. Staying in the
fields late for harvest. How did you get away?"

"Took the last load of wheat to Ford. Daddy will haul the
one that the combine is harvesting now. Won't be time to get
another one." The explanation made Jake feel good about
himself. He wanted Sage to know he was big enough to drive
a grain truck.

"You seen Nocona or Gabe around?"

"Nope. I hear they're spending a lot of time in Vega.

Nocona's fightin' with Texie."

"Really? How about Mary Ann Stafford?" Jake did not know why he asked about Mary Ann. He wanted Sage to think he was on a mission of sorts, not just killing time.

"Mary Ann doesn't get into town much. It's about seventy-five miles to her house from here." Sage grinned a little. "Course, I guess you know that."

Jake ignored the jab. "What have you been up to since school turned out?"

Sage waved an arm. "You can see what I've been up to. Same old thing."

Jake knocked on the counter with a knuckle. "Yeah, me too. Listen, you wanna ride around a little after you close?"

Sage looked as if he had slapped her. "I'd like to Jake, but Daddy won't let me."

It was Jake's turn to look slapped. He nodded too much and too fast. "Okay."

He stood outside, wishing that he had not asked Sage. She was too young. What was it Loretta had said? *You'll see how silly you were a few years from now.* Loretta was too old; Sage was too young. Actually, Sage was just right in years. It was just that she seemed so young. He had only asked her as a favor to let her get away from that store for a while. *Was Caleb just an excuse? Thought Caleb liked me.* He looked south at 66 and north down the street. Texie lived a few blocks away. He was curious about what had happened between her and Nocona ... and he was curious about Loretta.

He drove past Texie's house several times, hoping she would notice him and come out. After four drive-bys, he gave up and decided to go to Vega to look for Gabe and Nocona. He was easing past Whitey's garage when he saw Texie standing beside her daddy's car while Whitey checked under the hood. Jake pulled up beside her.

"Hey."

Texie folded her arms and leaned against the car. "Hey,

yourself. You're brown as a biscuit. A burned one."

"I hear you and Nocona are having a little spat."

"You could say that."

"What about?'

"I imagine you know what about. Same as always."

"Nope. I really don't know. Haven't seen Nocona since school let out."

"I only saw him once. Caught him red-handed with some little slut from Vega."

"Sorry I asked. Well, I guess I'll head on home. Nobody to talk to here."

Texie stood and feigned disgust. "Thought you and me were talking."

"You know what I mean."

Texie moved to Jake's side of the car and put both elbows through the open window. She smelled of gasoline, wildflowers, and Juicy Fruit. "You afraid to talk to me cause I'm Nocona's girl?"

Jake kept his eyes straight ahead. "I'm talkin' to you, ain't I?" He turned to face her and smiled. "But me and Nocona are friends."

"Besides, I'm too old, right? Loretta and I laughed about that."

Jake's face warmed, and he reached for the ignition. Texie's hand covered his. "You might not want to be so particular. You're gonna have a hard time gettin' a date in Adrian after what you did."

"What did I do?"

"I saw you driving by the parsonage."

"So?"

Texie grabbed the doorframe and leaned out, arching her back like a cat stretching. "You know she's gone, don't you?"

"Who's gone?"

Texie's eyes started to turn red as she looked away. "Loretta and her family. They all left."

Jake felt weak, empty and betrayed. He had convinced himself that he had not come to look for Loretta. "What do you mean, gone?"

Texie, still stretching and staring at the ground now, managed a nod. "I mean gone."

"Where'd they go?"

"Only a few people know, and they're not tellin'."

"I get the feeling that you are one of those people."

"I got a good idea."

"Well, then ... why ... and where?"

Texie came out of her cat pose. "Because of you, that's why."

Jake was getting mad. "What the hell are you talkin` about?"

"She didn't tell me anything, but I heard my parents talkin' about it. Loretta's in trouble. Everybody in this town loved Floyd Knight. They're gonna hate you just as much as they loved him." She turned and walked away.

Jake wanted to go home and hide behind the barn, but he headed for Vega. He figured Gabe or Nocona would know what really happened to the Knights and would not beat around the bush telling him. He saw the Lowry's pea-green '56 Chevy parked in front of a small Burger Hut on 66. Gabe had put green plastic tape that clashed with the pea-green on top of the side windows to cut down on wind noise. Six counter stools and two small tables at each end allowed the small joint to seat only fourteen when it was full. Gabe, perched on one of the stools, was the only customer. Jake took the stool beside him. "What are you doing in here by yourself?"

A blonde with cat-eye glasses appeared in front of Jake. "What's for you?" Jake ordered a root beer.

Gabe held up an empty sugar dispenser as she turned to fill Jake's order. She stood in front of him and smiled. "Sorry, we ran out of sugar. My boss is due back with a sack any minute. Coffee not sweet enough?"

Gabe's smile was awkward. "I usually take a teaspoon of sugar with my night coffee. Take it black in the mornin', though."

The girl put an index finger in his coffee and stirred it. She put the finger in her mouth and sucked off the coffee. "That sweet enough?"

Gabe took a long pull from the cup and smiled. "Just right."

The waitress left to fill an order at the drive-in window, and Gabe turned to Jake. "Now you know why I'm in here by myself."

Jake laughed in spite of the way he felt. He looked toward the girl. Not his type. "What about Betty and all that loyalty bullshit you been talkin' about ever since I met you?"

"Me and Betty are takin' a break. I still expect to marry her, but we need a little time off."

Jake whispered. "This girl ain't as pretty."

"You ain't seen her come out from behind that counter."

"What's her name?"

"Charlotte."

Charlotte placed the root beer in front of Jake and took a dime and nickel from him. "You know you're sittin' on Elvis' stool, don't you?"

"Nope. Didn't know Elvis had a stool of his own in here."

Charlotte pointed at a picture hanging on the wall behind Jake. A man with dark hair and sideburns seemed to be sitting on that very stool.

Jake turned on the stool. "So that's Elvis?"

"Yep. Big white Cadillac parked right out there one day last summer. He sent an old man in to order a cheeseburger basket. Then he decided to come in and eat it right where you're sittin'."

Jake's nod was hesitant. He felt his leg being pulled but was not sure. A little late, he stuck out his hand. "Jake Rivers."

She grasped it firmly. "Charlotte Redman. Nice to meet you, Jake Rivers."

A round, short man with gray, thinning hair appeared behind the counter just in time to unlock Jake's eyes from Charlotte's and make them both forget Elvis. "Hello, Boys. Charlotte, you can fill the sugar dispensers now."

Charlotte took the bag of sugar, lifted a board at the end of the counter and stepped through. She bent to pick up the sugar jar at the first table. Jake leaned behind Gabe to look at the well-filled short-shorts and long legs. Gabe smiled and Jake shook his head as if to chase away the diversion. "What have you heard about the Knights?"

Gabe's smile faded. "Probably the same thing you did."

"Why didn't you come by to tell me?"

"Figured you knew. Besides, I been ridin' a tractor or a horse from can-till-can't same as you. When I first heard it, I figured they were just visiting relatives or somethin'. Figured the rumor was just bullshit. Then Texie and Nocona peeked in the window of the parsonage. It's vacant."

"You know why they left?"

"Heard talk."

"What talk?"

"Why don't you just come right out and ask me what you want to know? Was Loretta knocked up? I don't know. Are folks blamin' you? Let's just say you ain't gonna be elected deacon in the Baptist church this time around. Probably need to be comin' to Vega to find your women for a while. You already been out with most of the good ones in Adrian, anyway."

"Something ain't right about this. Loretta told me ... ." Charlotte's filling of the sugar dispenser cut him off. He decided not to finish the sentence.

3 3 Jake guarded the mailbox for a week, hoping to hear from Loretta. He alternated between hauling grain and driving a tractor during the day and roping by himself all night. He roped the dummy from the ground and from the horse every night until it was too dark to see. He limited his conversations with Mattie and Rance, fearing that they could read the guilt on his face or in his voice. On Saturday afternoon, Rance let him off early.

He found his way to Mary Ann's house without missing a turn. He would have turned around when he saw they had company but figured he had already been seen. Some sort of celebration was taking place. The sun had created enough shade from the house to fill in the blanks left by two mesquites in the front yard. Two-by-tens twelve feet long had been laid across four sawhorses to make a table. Jake guessed that there was food under the white sheet draped across the checkered tablecloth.

The rumble of hooves on hard ground announced the arrival of dust clouds that drifted irregularly over the house's roof and around the sides. The occasional bellow of a steer was usually followed by grunts or shouts from deep voices. Jake recognized the sounds and smells of a roping. He looked behind him and saw a trail of dust approaching from the same road he had taken. He knocked on the screen door. No answer. He peered inside. Nobody.

The source of the dust, a two-horse trailer pulled by a 1955 Buick Roadmaster, stopped just behind his Ford. Two cowboys emerged from the dust cloud left by the Buick and quickly unloaded two saddled horses. Jake returned their nods and followed them to an arena behind the house. The Ford's radio had said it was over a hundred in Amarillo, and the sun was squatting on the horizon like a giant yellow beach ball on a lonely desert. Jake climbed the arena fence, sat on the top rail, and let that been-here-before feeling wash over him.

The wind had settled, as it sometimes did at sunset, and each boot, each hoof, left its own little trail of dust as the cowboys led their horses toward the front of the arena—where the action was. They kept their heads bowed to let brims shield them from the sun's glare, painting a picture of doomed men marching into the hottest part of hell. Jake knew that their march was to a place more like heaven.

He noticed the way the cowboys had buckled their spur straps—listened for, but could only imagine, the jingle of the spurs. One man wore his spurs a little high; the other sat his directly on the spur ridge of his boots. One wore his jeans inside his boots to show off the tops, the other let his Wranglers nestle over. Leather skid boots for the horses were strapped to stirrups for later use. Each man carried a rope in his hand, and an extra one was thrown across each saddle horn. Both pairs of boots had sloped, tall heels meant more to keep them from slipping through stirrups than for walking. *Never do work afoot that can be done horseback—Griffin Rivers.* Both pairs had achieved that nearly-worn-out-but-not-quite look that Jake could never achieve with his boots. Jake watched the twelve trails of dust rise and settle like small dust devils, observed the way the men handled their ropes. The horses kept their heads down but snorted occasionally with anticipation—they knew what was about to happen, too.

The two cowboys were exchanging rope halters for bridles and strapping skid boots on their horses at the back of the arena when another steer was turned out. Jake was surprised to see two mounted cowboys chasing it. The first threw a perfect loop that hit the steer just behind the sweet spot between the horns. The loop curled around the right, swirled around to get the left before making a figure eight across the steer's back. The cowboy jerked his slack, pulling the rope tight across both horns, and took a dally. Their movements seemed precise, not jerky like Jake's when he was roping.

He checked the steer easily, raising its head to let it know he was in control, and turned it due left. The other cowboy, swinging the biggest loop Jake had ever seen, effortlessly dropped the loop in front of the steer's back feet, let the steer step into the standing trap, drew his slack, and dallied across his saddle horn. The two mounted cowboys faced each other, the steer stretched between them, in a dance that rivaled tie-down calf roping in its beauty.

A tap on his butt brought Jake back from heaven. "That's my daddy on the big sorrel. Old Red is sorta big-headed and Roman-nosed, but Daddy says he's never seen a horse that loves to rope more."

Jake spoke to Mary Ann without taking his eyes off her father. "Is that team roping?"

"Sure is. Never seen it before?"

"Heard about it, but never saw it before now." Jake took a deep breath. "And that's your daddy."

"That's him, all right. What are you doin' out here? Not that I'm not glad to see you."

Jake jumped down from the fence and was rudely reminded that Mary Ann was still taller. "Sorry to just drop in, but neither one of us has a phone."

"All of our visitors just drop in. You picked a good day.

We'll eat when that old sun drops off that cliff."

"I gotta get on back. Could I just talk to you in private for a few minutes?"

"Sure, but Mama's already seen you. You have to stay and eat. Otherwise, she'll find you kinda suspicious."

They watched the roping until the sun went down. Mary Ann introduced him to her mother and father. Both had Mary Ann's black hair, olive-colored skin, and dark brown eyes with long eyelashes. Jake thought they might be Mexican, but he could not tell for sure. Mary Ann did not look Mexican. The meal was definitely Mexican. Mary Ann had to show Jake how to build a burrito and explain what a tortilla was. Jake had heard of them but had never actually seen one.

Jake made a hit with Mrs. Stafford by asking her for recipes. He had never tasted better food. Jake felt Mr. Stafford's eyes on him, but the man never offered more than a nod and a grudging smile. If he had not been so bashful and nervous, it would have been one of the most memorable nights of Jake's life. It was getting dark when Mary Ann followed him to the mesquite trees as the two cowboys loaded their horses in the two-horse trailer. The big Buick squatted under the weight and floated away on a cloud of dust.

They chose separate mesquite trees and leaned against them. She spoke first. "I know you didn't come just to see me. You want to talk about Loretta."

Jake shook his head and then nodded. "Both. Did you know the whole family was leaving? It ain't just Loretta. I thought Coach Knight might say something to me, too."

"They didn't say anything to anybody, Jake. Not you—not me. Loretta and I were pretty close, but she and Texie were like sisters. She apparently didn't even tell her."

"I talked to her at the Bent Door just a few days before the end of school. I been rackin' my brain tryin' to figure if she was tryin' to tell me somethin' that night. Thinkin' back on it, I think she might have been."

"Like she was carryin' your baby?"

Jake stared at his boots. "How much do you know?"

"Just guessing."

"She said she wasn't."

"So it's possible she was? Some folks in town are blaming you, I hear. Folks loved Loretta because she could play basketball about as well as any girl ever played it in this little school. But they idolized her daddy."

"I liked him, too."

"So you screwed his daughter to show it?"

"I didn't know him then."

"So you did screw her."

"I thought we were friends, Mary Ann. I came for advice and help, not to get the third degree."

"I'm just trying to find out what kind of friend I've got. What were you going to do if she had said she was carrying your baby?"

"Hell, I don't know. I meant to do what's right, but I could never figure out what that was. I ain't even sixteen yet. Can't make a living or support a wife and a kid."

"Then you need to keep that thing in your britches. Whose fault was it?"

"What do you mean?"

"You point that thing at her and push it, or did she pull you in?"

"Don't guess that matters."

"Good answer, I suppose. I know that Loretta got a lot more blame than she deserved." Mary Ann walked a few steps closer. "Okay, we'll be friends again. Sounds like you were just young, stupid, and horny. You may have dodged a bullet when Loretta left town."

"What do I do now?"

"Just lay low for a while, I guess. Sooner or later, somebody will let slip what really happened. If adults in Adrian find you guilty for causing them to lose their favorite citizen, teacher, preacher and coach, you're gonna have a hard time getting any parents to let you take out their daughters."

"What about you?"

"My parents don't pay much attention to what goes on in town and almost none to gossip."

"You think it's gonna be that way till I graduate?"

"The only way to work your way into the good graces of people at Adrian is to be a top hand or play as good a brand of basketball as Loretta did."

Jake looked at her to see if she was kidding. She did not seem to be.

34 String returned just as he had left—without announcement. He always seemed to return just in time to save Jake from himself. They practiced roping every night for two weeks. When the second Saturday rolled around, Jake stepped out of the house to saddle his horse in time to see String dropping into the stock tank. He had started wearing a pair of loose overalls when he bathed in daylight on the slight chance that Mattie might be looking out of Jake's window. The overalls still allowed him to reach all of his parts with a bar of soap. Jake turned his back. "You usually wash up after dark—after we rope."

"Man feels the need to go to town every once in a while, Jake. Tonight's one of those nights. As I recall, I felt the same calling when I was your age. You been stayin' home too much. Got woman problems?" String ducked his head under the windmill pipe to rinse with fresh, cold water.

"What makes you say that?"

String dropped the overalls in stages as he stepped out on a board and began drying with a towel. "I heard the talk. Figured it was just that—talk."

"Got any advice?" Jake turned his back until he heard the sound of String's Wranglers coming up.

243

"Some folks would say, and they'd be right, that you've come to a mighty poor source for advice about women. I never been much count when it comes to the opposite sex."

Jake heard the snaps as String snapped his shirt. "You ever have this kinda problem?"

"Not at your age, Jake. Guess it ain't fair that you drew the wildest bronc in the string for your first rodeo. Floyd Knight was probably the most honored man in this little community. Adrian's always been welcoming, but sorta suspicious of preachers. Floyd overcame that in short order. Loretta, well, she proved herself on the basketball court. Don't seem to matter much what else you do around Adrian if you can play basketball or make a good hand with horses and cattle."

"Yeah. Bad luck. But what do I do?"

"Looks like Floyd Knight took that decision right out of your hands. I imagine he knew what he was doing."

"So just do nothing?"

"Nothing you can do. Best to tiptoe around for a while. It'll blow over. Everybody knows you're just a boy and that Loretta was a wild child."

"I can deal with all that. I just don't know if I can deal with not knowin' if I got a kid somewhere." Jake turned to walk toward the house. "Thanks."

String headed for the barn to finish dressing. He turned as Jake was opening the gate. "I imagine your grandpa would say *don't make the same mistake* twice. Best advice I got on such subjects came from my daddy. Sorta crude, but it makes sense. You got two heads, just be sure that the one between your legs don't do any more thinkin' for you. He said that boys start shootin' real bullets too early. Just remember that the next time your brains drop between your legs."

Soon after their talk, String left again. Jake replayed his last conversation with Loretta hundreds of times, trying to convince himself that she was not really carrying his baby.

A whole community was blaming him for things out of his control. Nocona was away at rodeos most weekends, and Gabe had returned to Betty. When he did see his two best friends, they seemed unsympathetic, absorbed in their own lives. He felt helpless—antsy.

Near summer's end, a rare rain took Jake away from sowing wheat at Section Nine. Rance had dropped him off, so there was no way to get home except to drive the tractor. The Super M's tires slung mud over his back and head all the way home, but Jake was exhilarated by the rare wetness and sudden coolness. He left the tractor outside, walked into the shop, and sat down in the rickety chair to watch the rain fall, imagining wheat seeds coming to life with the moisture. The rain made him feel cleansed and sowing wheat gave him a sense of new beginning.

When the mud started to dry and pull on his skin and hair, Jake went to the house. Showered, powdered, and smelling of Aqua Velva, Jake was sitting in the Burger Hut before dark. He ordered coffee and asked Charlotte to stir it. When she got off at nine, Jake took her up and down 66 and through the streets of Vega. It felt good to be a boy again. Stirring coffee and riding in Vega became a regular thing.

Their dates were regular, but Charlotte also introduced Jake to her friends. She did not seem to mind when Jake dated them, too. When a condom dropped under Mattie's ironing board as she shook out his wet jeans, he picked it up and walked away. Mattie frowned but did not say a word.

Jake's confidence had returned by the beginning of the school year. He was almost defiant during the first days of school. Upholding a long tradition, September was devoted to the school's annual rodeo. Coach Gee urged him to enter. "I saw the yearning on your face last year, Jake. Hurt your confidence all year because you didn't. I don't give a damn about rodeo, but I need your leadership on this basketball team."

Jake still needed more convincing. "Probably make my confidence worse if I make a fool out of myself."

The coach shook his head. "You're hard-headed. Winnin' is better, but it's having the guts to try that counts. Enter the damn thing."

Something changed when Jake wrote his name on the entry form and entered the calf roping. Loretta and Floyd Knight's presence, dominant during the first weeks of school, seemed to dissipate. He roped the dummy every night until his hand hurt, wishing for String's return. He started looking at Scar through a stranger's eyes, wondering if the little horse with a long mane and tail would be laughed at—wondering if he would embarrass the horse and himself by missing.

On rodeo night, Jake's little gelding drew some smiles and stares during the grand entry. Jake wondered if it was Scar's long mane and tail, the old saddle and bridle, or both. Most of the other boys rode ranch horses with roached manes and tails trimmed to the hocks. They were decked out in tack that was new or used just enough to be soft. Jake had saddle-soaped and oiled all his tack and was holding a new rope in his hands. Still, he was painfully self-conscious and almost wished he had not entered—but not quite. He eased a little when they announced the roping would be a two-header. He would have two chances to at least catch a calf. Missing would not eliminate you, but it counted as sixty seconds.

Scar sensed his nervousness and took charge as he rode into the box and backed into position—close to the butt-bar but not touching it. Jake, numb with fear, had offered no assistance or instruction to the horse, but Scar knew the drill. His ears perked forward and laid back as if he were signaling for release of the calf. Jake did not wait for him to get impatient. He nodded for the calf, felt himself jerked backward and out of position as Scar lunged forward. He almost lost a stirrup, but his muscle memory kicked in enough for him to swing his rope and throw it.

The small, slow calf helped him by almost putting his head through the poorly-thrown loop. Jake did not tag his horse, but had the presence of mind to pitch his slack and dismount. Scar pulled up without the tag. Jake ran down the line, flanked the small calf, grabbed a front leg, and looped it with the pigging string pulled from his mouth, pulled the two back legs to make a V with the front leg, took two wraps and a hooey, and raised his hands. Twenty three seconds flat—not a good time, but he had caught and tied his calf. He remounted and eased his horse forward to create slack in the rope. The cooperative little calf did not even fight being tied until the judge signaled the time was good. String handed him his pigging string and patted him on the leg. Jake felt good.

"You got lucky. Might want to think about helpin' your horse next time."

Jake found Rance and Mattie standing by the fence and rode his horse beside them. "I messed up, didn't I?"

Rance watched Gabe back Stud into the box. "You got one down. Consistency is the most important thing on a two header like this. Just catch and tie the next one and you should win something. Just two other boys have caught so far. Let's see if Gabe makes it three."

Gabe nodded for the calf, and it took off like it had been shot from a gun. Gabe's loop fell harmlessly on the ground as the calf entered the back chute. Stud had been unable to put him in position to rope.

Rance shook his head. "Good thing you didn't draw that little speed demon."

"Tell me what I did wrong. I can take it."

Rance turned to face him. "You let the horse do all the work. You acted surprised that Scar was going to chase the calf after you nodded. What did you think was gonna happen when you nodded? It's hard on a horse when the rider jerks back like that. You gotta be in those stirrups, leanin' forward over his withers and swingin' that rope when that calf hits the barrier. Your head wasn't in it."

Jake nodded. "I froze."

"It's a natural thing. Get over it. It's your first time to rope in front of a crowd."

"I'm still nervous."

Rance walked over and put his hand on Jake's boot. "What are those?"

"Uh, spurs."

"I can see that. Where'd you get `em?"

"Borrowed `em from Nocona."

"What for?'

Jake shrugged. He thought it made him look more cowboy.

"Those are bronc spurs, Jake. Not ropin' spurs. You been ridin' your horse with spurs in practice?"

"No, but I figured ... ."

"You figured you would look real cowboy and use spurs for the first time on a horse that don't need `em in your first real competition." Rance looked up as if seeking help from a higher source. "That about sum it up?"

"I guess."

"It's not you **or** the horse, Jake; it's you **and** him. Stop thinking that he has to be **made** to do your bidding and start thinking he **wants** to." Rance put a hand on Jake's leg. "A horse will do pretty much what you expect him to. Expect bad behavior and you'll likely get it. Expect great performance and the horse will work his heart out trying to give it to you."

Jake was removing the spurs as String walked up. "This thing is yours to win, Jake. Gabe was your toughest competitor, and he drew a bullet. Catchin' is the main thing now."

Rance nodded. "Tell him where his strength is, String. He won't listen to me."

Jake wondered how his daddy knew so much about his roping.

248

"It's like I've said before. Your strength is on the ground. Get your horse into position before you throw. Take an extra swing if you need to. Then run down that line and tie her up good and quick. You can tie quicker'n me."

"What if I draw the bullet?"

String looked at Rance and winced. "Don't think about the draw. Just rope whatever it is."

String hustled back to the arena. Rance rubbed Scar's nuzzle. "I figure just one of the boys out there is better mounted. You never give this little horse enough credit. Now go find a spot by yourself and get your head on straight."

Jake wondered what he meant, and his face showed it.

"Roping, like most things, is mostly in your head, Jake. After you practice enough, your muscles will pretty much do what they've been taught. It's your head you gotta keep in control. If you can see what's gonna happen ahead of time, and you expect it to happen right, it usually will. Go out there and map this thing out in your head. Picture it like you were in a picture show watching yourself. See yourself backing into the box, roping the calf clean, flankin' and tyin'. Your head was in the stands on that last run; keep it in the arena."

"Every time I do that, I see myself missing or falling off my horse."

"If you asked Annie Oakley why she was such a good shot, she'd say because she could see where the bullet was goin' before she pulled the trigger. Block out everything else; see where that rope is goin' before you pull the trigger."

Scar shivered under Jake like he did when flies landed in the middle of his back. Jake wondered if he was trying to say something. Rance made it sound easy. Jake was in the dark, trying to follow his father's instructions and will his grandfather's comforting presence when he heard his name called. With the fastest time in the first go-round, he would be the last to rope. He trotted to the arena. He glanced at the lane where calves were lined up and counted back to his draw.

Jake recognized the white topknot on the otherwise all-black, big calf. He had drawn the bullet. He could feel his father's anguish and visualize the hopeless look on String's face when they saw what he had drawn. Jake took a deep breath as Gabe tied his second steer in seventeen flat—faster than anyone in the first round. Only Jake could beat Gabe now. When his name was announced, he rode into the box, asked Scar to back up without touching him, and nodded.

The big calf exploded and so did Scar. The little horse seemed to have recognized the steer. He put Jake in position to rope halfway down the arena. Jake replayed what he had visualized minutes before. Everything was going just as he pictured, and it was going in slow motion. He threw a perfect loop, pitched his slack, and tagged Scar's neck to let him know that it was time to stop. The little gelding folded his legs under him, stuck his long tail in the dirt, and began to slide as Jake dismounted. The big calf caused a strong jerk as Jake ran down the line. He flanked a calf that he would not have been able to lift on most days. As he reached for his pigging string, he heard the groan. First from Scar, then from the crowd.

Scar's back legs had crumpled and he dropped to his belly, his front legs splayed. His head stayed up as he struggled to do what he had been taught—to keep the line taut while Jake finished tying the calf. Jake dropped his string and looked directly into his horse's eyes. They were starting to roll back. He cut the rope with his knife and ran back to his horse. String was already there. Rance was coming over the fence. Another groan, an expulsion of air, and Scar laid his head down.

Jake rubbed the horse's jaw. "Easy, boy. What's wrong?"

String put a forefinger under Scar's left jawbone. He looked at Jake, then Rance. "His pulse is slowin'."

A small group gathered around the horse and waited in stone silence. Even the crowd was quiet. Only an occasional

whinny or bellow interrupted the terrible hush. String tried
the pulse again before standing. "He's gone, Jake, Rance. I'm
sure 'nough sorry." The wind whistled.

Jake stood, took off his hat and slapped it against his leg.
His voice cracked. "It's my fault. Should never have asked
him to rope that big calf. He wadn't big enough."

Rance took a deep breath and looked away. "Not your
fault, Jake. He was big enough. His heart was damn sure big
enough."

The gray roping judge's knees creaked and popped as he
leaned down and touched Scar with gnarled fingers as if he
were holy. His voice was a whisper. "Saw a horse die like that
one other time in all my years. Up in Wyoming. Probably
ruptured an artery. They said he roped his heart out."

Bob Lee put a hand on Jake's shoulder, his usual
exuberance stifled. He looked at Rance. "Uncle Rance, if
you want to bury him out on the place, I can go get a dump
truck and winch him."

JD and Bess, Will Tom Sunday, String, Coach Gee, Gabe,
and Nocona were waiting in the dark when Bob Lee, Jake,
and Scar arrived in the dump truck. Will Tom had brought
his backhoe and Rance was using it to dig Scar's grave north
of the red barn. Jake winced at the rough treatment
necessary to drop his horse into the grave. Will Tom stood
beside him as Rance lowered Scar and began covering him.
"It's hard to be gentle about burying a large animal, Jake."

Jake had not uttered a sound since announcing that is was
his fault. He still did not trust his voice. He kept his eyes on
Scar until the horse was completely covered. Then he
watched the dirt until the mound was smoothed over. He
dared not look at any faces.

Will Tom understood. "Most men never own a horse as
good as that one, Jake. He'll stay with you the rest of your life.
He gave you everything he had tonight, and more."

Jake held his hat in his hand as Rance smoothed out the

mound on the grave. "It cost him his life. He died because of me."

Rance stood with a rake in his hand, watching a sudden wind gust blow the small clods on the grave as Jake walked away.

35 Sunday—another guilty Sabbath. Seeking solitude, Jake found his saddle, bridle, blanket, rope and other equipment draped carefully over a fifty-five gallon drum inside the shop. Nocona's spurs rested on the saddle horn—evidence of his father's work. Jake felt a surge of gratitude. He had completely forgotten about the tack and could not recall seeing anyone undress his dead horse. The inanimate drum was a grim reminder. Rance and Mattie had spent the morning trying to convince him that it was not his fault, but they did not understand. They thought Scar had died from roping and stopping a big calf—Jake knew he had died for his own sins. God was punishing Jake for fathering a child and not accepting responsibility for what he had done.

He could have stayed home from school without any argument from his parents on Monday, but he did not. At school, students and faculty avoided him. He got sympathetic nods, but little conversation. Nobody knew what to say. Only Gabe came forward at day's end. He handed Jake a small box. "This is yours."

Question in his eyes, Jake opened it and looked at a silver buckle with a mounted calf roper and calf soldered to it. *Champion Roper–Adrian High 1960* was engraved under the images. Jake handed it back like it was burning his hands. "No, this ain't mine. It's yours." Jake wanted it so bad his mouth watered.

"You won it fair and square. You roped both calves clean."

"Appreciate it. Really do. But I didn't finish that run. It's yours fair and square." The offer thawed the cold feeling Jake had held since Scar had died. He took it to mean that Gabe now considered him his equal—a worthy competitor in roping. He even smiled as Gabe dropped the buckle into his back pocket. "Hey, won't that buckle make you ineligible for basketball?"

"Nope. Coach says this is like a small trophy we might get in basketball. Money or high-dollar gifts are outlawed, not this little buckle."

Mary Ann, Sage, and two of their friends waved and smiled as they left the school. Jake felt accepted again. Strange that it took Scar's life to do it.

A definite nip in the air made Jake feel that new-beginning tingle he always got during fall's first cold snap. A baby blue four-door '60 Ford sat in the '55's usually spot when he stepped off the school bus in early October. Nothing had been said about trading in the old Ford. Jake examined the shiny car. It was plain vanilla as cars go—hubcaps instead of wheel covers—four doors—but it had a hood. He peeked through the window. His heart picked up a beat or two when he saw the standard shift. Rance did not care for automatics. That meant the car was probably theirs. He looked around, getting the definite feeling that he was being watched.

Mattie's approach confirmed it. "How do you like my new car?"

"Nice." Jake opened the door and got behind the wheel. The new smell soothed him. "Thought we were broke."

"Still have to have a way to get to town and back. The old Ford wouldn't crank this morning. Just the sight of that missing hood has been making your daddy irritable for months. He still wants to whip Gray Boy's butt, but he's too far away and too big."

Jake wondered if the new car was partly for him—to make him feel better about losing his horse. If that was true, it worked. Rance appeared from the shop and lifted the hood. "Nothin' fancy. Their smallest V-8."

Jake tried to talk man-to-man—hiding his exuberance. "How'd you get the old one cranked?"

Mattie placed a hand on Rance's shoulder and answered for him. "You should know by now that your daddy can crank just about anything,"

Jake pushed in the clutch, futilely turned the radio off and on. "Can we afford it?"

Rance nodded. "Never bought a car I could afford, but we made a pretty good crop. We'll manage to eat."

"When can I drive it?"

Mattie ordered plastic seat covers from Fingerhut, and Rance installed them under protest. The next Saturday, Jake picked up Nocona, and they drove to Amarillo. Jake's life savings were in his billfold. They returned with light blue floor mats, extra speakers installed in the back window ledge that could be controlled by a small knob under the dash, two flipper wheel covers on the front and two moon wheel covers on the back. Jake had to settle—not enough money for four flippers. Nocona talked him into buying decals for the back window. A sack of horse and mule feed for the trunk took his last three dollars. It made the little blue car sit lower.

They were installing the decal letters on the back window when Rance drove in from Section Nine. Jake held his breath as his daddy circled the car. "What did you do with the hubcaps?"

Jake installed the last letter and pressed it down carefully.

Jim Ainsworth

"They're in the trunk."

"Couldn't find four wheel covers to match?"

"Didn't have enough money. They said they would take the moons in trade when I saved up enough to buy another two flippers."

Rance looked at his son for a few seconds before nodding. He walked behind the car and looked at the decals. "What does Searchin' mean?"

"Jake looked at Nocona, who was staring at his boots. "Uh, it's part of a song." He hoped Rance would not make him scrape it off. Choosing between dreamin', hopin' and searchin' from Johnny Burnette's "Dreamin'" song had been difficult—and Jake liked his choice.

Jake breathed a little easier when Mattie joined them. Rance put his arm around her. "Well, Mattie, how do you feel about going to the grocery story in a car with mismatched wheel covers?"

Mattie laughed. "Now, Rance, you have to admit those are prettier than the hubcaps that came on it."

He took her hand and walked her to the car's rear. "Okay. How do you feel about having *Searchin'* on your back window? Think that will cause talk at the grocery store?"

Mattie's smile faded, replaced with a quizzical stare.

Jake took his chance to speak. "Nocona's got *Comanche* on his back window."

Mattie held a hand to her throat as she silently mouthed "Searchin'". "Well, then I guess "Searchin'" will be just fine." They all laughed.

Jake could hardly wait to hit the streets of Vega. He stopped at Nocona's to let him get dressed. Jake was in a hurry. "Don't do like last time. I'll wait, but I ain't waitin' on you to powder every inch of your body and drown yourself in after-shave."

"I ain't rushin' the process. Never can tell where a girl's nose is likely to wind up. Better for you to go on, anyway. I

256

like to have my own car there in case I run into some sweet
meat that likes privacy. I'll see you in town."

Jake did not argue. It was Charlotte's night off. He
followed his usual route down 66 and through Vega's
downtown area. He stopped in front of her house and
honked—she did not like for him to come to the door. She
peeked through the screen door, waved, and blew a loud wolf-
whistle. "Five minutes."

Jake smiled and nodded. He sat back and listened to
Jimmy Charles sing "A Million to One". He knew those were
the odds for him and Charlotte. That made their relationship
more fun. Charlotte lived alone with her truck-driver father.
She had spent two years in California with her mother after
their divorce. Jake had asked several times why she had
returned, but her standard answer was "wide open spaces."
Their small house was made of native red stone. Doors and
windows showed neglect. The picket fence that enclosed a
dirt yard needed paint. Jake was wondering what the Rivers'
house would look like on a town lot when Charlotte opened
the driver's side door. He stepped out and let her slide across
the plastic.

Jake could not see the flippers turning, but he imagined
how they must look. He imagined himself in a car behind
his own—reading *Searchin'* on his rear window. Occasionally,
he would see a reflection in a filling station window as they
rolled down 66. If two flippers looked that good, four would
be perfect. He was cruising about fifteen, arm hanging out
the window, watching the car's reflection in a service station
window, when he heard a rough-running engine behind
him. The sounds reminded him of the '55 Ford. A black
'49 Hudson, right on his bumper, appeared in the rearview
mirror. He speeded up to thirty, then forty-five, but the
Hudson hung close. He turned around and headed east
on 66—the Hudson followed. When he turned down a side
street, the car followed again.

Charlotte squirmed in her seat and kept her eyes on the black car that looked like a big boat turned upside down. "Get back out where the lights are, Jake. We don't want to be caught down here in the dark."

Jake felt the black car nudge his back bumper. "Damn. The sumbitch is comin' up my tailpipe." In first gear, Jake slammed the accelerator, punching it into overdrive, turned sharply down a side street and left the old car in the dust. He was heading west on 66 when the Hudson appeared again. Jake stopped at the only stoplight in Vega and the black car roared as it started pushing him through the light into oncoming traffic. Jake saw a car coming full speed down 385 from Hereford, ready to cross through the green light—right into Jake's door.

He slammed on his brakes, but the car kept sliding. In desperation, he clutched and ground it into reverse, pushing the black car back until the light turned. He shifted into first and took off. The Hudson turned down a side street. He turned toward Charlotte. "You know who that was?"

Charlotte chewed her lower lip. "I don't know for sure."

Jake heard before he saw the black apparition again. It pulled out beside him from just off 66. He heard sickening thuds along the side of his car and was horrified to see a huge man with shoulder-length black hair flopping in the wind as he leaned out of the old Hudson, slamming his passenger door against the side of the Rivers' new baby blue Ford. The big man was screaming at Jake. Jake swerved across oncoming traffic and pulled into the Burger Hut's gravel parking lot. The Hudson followed and stopped within inches of Jake's door. When Jake started to get out, the man slammed his car door against Jake's and penned him inside.

The longhaired man, still screaming, finally stopped hammering Jake's door. Jake could now hear the words and see their source. He was sure that Charlotte could hear his heart beating. His fury had turned to fear. The man's skin was swarthy-red and pockmarked—his eyes were yellow-red where they should have been white—and his face was dark with fury. He squeezed his bulk out of the Hudson and stumbled a little as he slammed the door and reached for Jake with arms that looked like corner posts. Jake smelled him before he felt rough hands brush his throat—whiskey, rancid body odor and puke. The big man was so drunk and so enraged that he was drooling.

"What's this *Seachin'* bullshit on your back window? What the goddamn hell you mean, backin' into my car? I'll cut your little punk-ass up and feed you to my goddamn pigs."

Jake pulled away and pushed a frozen-Charlotte out the passenger door. "Run inside and call the cops."

Jake recognized the rage and helplessness he used to feel when his brother whipped him, then held him down and spat in his face. This piece of garbage had wrecked his new car on the first night—and he was now sitting in it. The monster drunkenly fumbled with the keys, trying to start the Ford. Jake opened the passenger door and managed to pull the keys away without being grasped. The man started banging his hand on the dash. Jake expected the instrument panel to flop out onto the front seat with each hit. He screamed in desperation. "You crazy? Get away from my car. Cops are comin'."

The man stopped beating the dash and turned toward his challenger. Jake jingled the keys. "Get your lard-ass over here and take the keys if you can." It sounded weak and girly to Jake's ears, but he had to get the monster out of his car.

He knew he was making idle threats out of fear, but Jake could clearly see himself putting a bullet in the big man's forehead—if the .22 had not been left in the GMC. He hated himself for not having a weapon of any kind in the car. Even the tire iron was bolted to the spare. He looked on the ground and all around him—nothing but small pebbles. The red-faced man stepped out. "You're a cocky little bastard, ain't you? You little spoiled-ass rich cowboys come off them big ranches around Adrian, thinking you own the goddamn town. You think you got big balls? How's it gonna feel goin' home without ` em?" The switchblade clicked and the blade reflected off the Burger Hut lights. "I aim to cut you up enough to slop my hogs, then cut that baby blue piece of shit to pieces."

Jake frantically tried to remember what his father and brother had told him to do in such situations. *Use his size against him—don't get in close.* He also remembered Nocona's strategy. *Fight dirty if you have to.* The knife changed things. Only one thing gave him some semblance of hope—the big Indian was drunk. Charlotte and her boss were screaming from the Burger Hut for Jake to run. He wanted to, but he could not leave his car. The man would destroy it.

Jake backed slowly away, daring the man to follow. Anything to save what was left of the Ford. The big Indian followed a few steps and then stopped. Jake beckoned him with his fingers. "What's wrong, panty-waist? You afraid?" The man lunged with the knife, and Jake stepped aside and behind him. He hit him as hard as he could in the kidney, hurting his hand. The knife swung back and barely missed Jake, but the blow had given Jake confidence. He circled him over and over until the man stopped following. Jake knew he could safely stay away from the drunk until help arrived. He just had to keep him focused on himself and away from the car.

Jake crouched and bounced on his toes, daring the man to come to him. When he lunged, Jake averted the blow and wound up behind him again. When he delivered a kick to the crotch, he felt two big hands grab his boot. The man twisted Jake's foot until he fell on his back. He stood over Jake, a firm grip on his foot and leg. He had dropped the knife. Jake could not see it, but he recognized the comforting melody of the red Chevy's twin pipes. Dust swarmed over him as it stopped. Its fender brushed the big man's leg. Nocona's voice was heavenly.

"You pickin' on somebody half your size, ain't you, Yellow Eyes?"

Yellow Eyes did not take his eyes away from his prey or his hands away from Jake's foot. "Nothing to do with you, Nokey."

Nocona pressed a thumb against Yellow Eyes' Adam's apple and wrapped his fingers around the back of his neck. "Afraid you're wrong about that."

Yellow Eyes strained his neck against the thumb to look toward the spot where he had dropped his knife. "Lookin' for this?" With his left hand, Nocona held the blade tip just under the big man's chin. A trickle of blood formed at its tip. "Now turn everything loose, Yellow Eyes. Move slow. Wouldn't want to cut your drunk-ass throat."

Jake scrambled to his feet when he felt the big man release. He put his hands on his knees and struggled for breath. "Thanks."

Jake stumbled to the driver's side of the Ford and examined the black spots in the sparse light. "Dammit!" He was on the verge of tears. "Look at what that son-of-a-bitch did."

Jake ran to Yellow Eyes and delivered the kick he had meant to before, kicking so hard that he fell back. The Indian dropped his head, projecting vomit out on the gravel.

"Damn. You sorry bastard. You puked on my good boots." Nocona pulled the knife away from his throat and pushed him forward. Yellow Eyes fell into his own vomit.

Jake kicked him again and again in the ribs. "Damn you to hell. Damn you to hell." He looked up at Nocona. "Gimme the knife. I'm gonna cut his damn nuts out."

Nocona smiled between clenched teeth. "Damn. He pissed you off, didn't he?"

261

"I'm damn tired of taking shit off of assholes like this. If I don't kill him or disable him, I won't ever be able to show my face here again."

Nocona folded the knife and tossed it to Jake just as the Hudson drove off. They stared at it, then at each other. "Hell, who was driving?" Jake stared in stunned silence as the black Hudson tore down 66 and north on a side street. "Guess I thought the car was driving itself when he was banging my car from the passenger side. Did you see who it was?"

"Pale face—light hair. That's all I saw. I didn't know anybody was in the car."

This changed everything. Nocona nudged Yellow Eyes and looked up at Jake. "Well, you gonna turn him into a tub o' guts or not? I hear the law comin'." The night constable's siren could be heard coming from the courthouse.

Jake had lost his nerve. Now he had two enemies to worry about. "How the hell am I gonna explain what happened to the car to Mother and Daddy? Can you believe this shit?"

Gordon Wilson, Charlotte's boss, a bent, overweight, gray, polite man clucked his tongue as he looked at Jake's car. "Yellow Eyes—he's bad business when he's drinkin'. Harmless during the week, but an outlaw on the weekends."

Jake clicked the switchblade and pointed it toward the prone body. "Who the hell is he, and why is he mad at me?"

Charlotte took Jake's empty hand into hers. "Town drunk. Garbage man. Somebody probably put him up to this—fed him some bad whiskey, I imagine. He doesn't usually cause trouble on his own. They call him Yellow Eyes because ... well, I guess you saw why."

Nocona ran his hand over the scuffmarks. "Bring it by the house. I got some rubbin' compound and wax."

Relief and hope swept over Jake. He took Charlotte home and followed Nocona to his house. In the Wells' lighted shop, he saw the first black paint disappear under the rubbing compound. Jake ran his hand along the back bumper, checking for dents in the sparse light. He was home before midnight.

36 A vision of Yellow Eyes shocked Jake awake just after dawn. Sunlight announced another guilty Sunday. He dressed quickly and walked through the seldom-used front door to get the first look at the Ford in daylight before facing his daddy. As he peeked around the corner of the house, he knew he was too late. Elbows out, fists pressed against his waist, Rance's hat brim curled against the strong wind as he stared at the car. The cool air seemed to take on heat as Jake got closer to his daddy. Jake had seen his daddy's wrath stirred before, but this time he understood it. It was the same rage he had felt against Yellow Eyes the night before. Rance had never struck him in the face and it had been a long time since Jake had felt a razor strap across his buttocks. But he kept his distance.

Attracted by the rubbing compound and wax, dust settled over the Ford's driver's side a lot heavier than on the rest of the car. It did not look as bad as Jake thought it might, but the remaining black paint and worst scuffmarks and shallow dents were more visible in the morning sun. Rance finally spoke against the wind's whistle. "What happened?"

Jake had his lie ready. "Left it parked at the Burger Hut last night while I rode around with Nocona. It had black

265

Jim Ainsworth

scuffmarks all down the side when I came back. Looked like somebody drove beside it, banging a door or something all the way down."

"Anybody see it happen?"

"I asked around. Nobody would own up to seeing anything."

"You got any enemies in Vega?"

"Some of the boys don't like me dating Vega girls. Figure it was one of them, but I don't know which one." Jake knew he could not tell him about Yellow Eyes. Rance would definitely look up the big Indian to collect damages. More importantly, he would know that Jake had allowed another bully to get the best of him.

They stood a long time, the wind blowing Rance's hat and Jake's baseball cap. Little particles of dust stung their faces and caused them to blink away tears. Rance finally put his hands in his pockets. "Gray Boy blew out the back window on the old car with a firecracker about two months after we got it. How long did we keep this one looking new—a week?"

Jake did not even bother to shrug. "I'll finish waxing the whole car."

"Uh huh."

Jake washed and waxed the Ford all over and was glad for the diversion. Waxing gave him time to think—time to make important decisions. Yellow Eyes had delivered some sort of message that he dared not ignore. Jake decided that he would stay away from girls and from Vega. Trying to return to his daddy's good graces, he washed and waxed his pickup. By the time he finished, he had decided that his earlier resolution might be too hard to keep. He resolved instead to stop driving the new car. That would be his self-imposed punishment.

It was almost dark when he began washing and waxing the GMC, his new dating vehicle. He tried to put the flippers and moons on the old pickup, but they would not fit.

266

Besides, they had already left ugly marks on the Ford's wheels. Even waxed, the GMC was still a dead color of green with rusty hubcaps, torn upholstery, and lots of dents.

He waited almost two weeks before he dressed to go out again. He let the GMC engine idle next to the back door a long time, expecting Mattie to take pity on him and beg him to drive the Ford. She did not. He cruised Adrian without being recognized and without seeing any girls before he headed to Vega. He was nervous when he passed the city limits sign on 66. He made two passes through town looking for the black Hudson before pulling into the Burger Hut. He parked on his usual stool, ordered a cherry coke and watched Charlotte stir it.

They visited long enough for Jake to relax and start to feel the pieces of his life come back together. Charlotte did not seem to think of him as a coward. She was cooking burgers in the kitchen for a haggard-looking husband and wife traveling 66 headed for Los Angeles, when Jake felt the wind caress his back as the front door opened. He did not turn. The stools were all screwed to the same wide board, and Jake felt the long board move, heard it creak, as someone took the stool next to him. It irritated him that someone would take a stool so close when all the others were empty. He and Charlotte would have to suspend their flirting until the customer left.

Jake felt a big arm brush his own and was aware that his stool partner was very large and smelled of Old Spice. Jake cut his eyes just enough to see braided hair draped over the man's right shoulder and a pockmarked cheek. When he saw Charlotte's expression as she came out to take his order, he knew he was sitting next to Yellow Eyes. She stared at Jake as she placed a cup of coffee in front of the big Indian. Jake knew she could see the fear in his eyes—wondered if she could also see the slight tremble in his hands.

Yellow Eyes took a long sip of his coffee and kept his eyes focused on the menu just below the ceiling. "You belong to a light blue sixty-model Ford?"

Jake took a deep breath. "Used to. Not anymore."
Yellow Eyes cut his gaze toward Jake. The eyes were still
yellow, but not quite as red as Jake remembered—certainly not
as wild and angry. It gave Jake some courage. "You belong to
an old black Hudson?"

"Used to. Up on blocks now."

Jake felt a little glow of satisfaction as Charlotte delivered
the burgers to the tired couple, but he said nothing.

"I drink some ... get a little wild if it's good whiskey ...
a little crazy if it's bad. I guess it's true what they say about
Indians and firewater." His tone was soft, almost whispered.

Jake turned on the revolving seat. "Why me?"

"Can't remember what got me started on you exactly.
Barely remember some big kid driving my car. He had the
whiskey. Told me something that got me riled at you, I guess.
I do recall it pissed me off when you pushed me backwards."

"You pushed me into the intersection first. I was trying to
keep from getting' killed. Who was the kid?"

Yellow Eyes shook his head. "Never caught his name.
Still got my knife?"

Jake nodded. It was under the seat of the GMC, along
with a baseball bat.

"Keep it. Just don't ever use it."

"Why not?"

Yellow Eyes stood and walked toward the door. He spoke
without turning as he opened the door. "Look at me."

Jake watched him as he plodded across the parking lot and
down the shoulder beside 66. When he turned, Charlotte
was across the counter from him again. "What did he mean
by 'look at me'?" Jake asked.

"Probably just that his life was ruined because of violence.
I think Yellow Eyes spent some time in prison for using a
knife like the one you and Nocona took from him. Rumor
around here is that he almost scalped his wife. Think his real

name is Joe Horn or something like that."

Jake felt a sense of elation as he drove Charlotte home
from work. He had faced his mortal enemy and survived.
The threat of Yellow Eyes seemed to be over. It was cool
enough to roll up the windows on the GMC, and he and
Charlotte were breathing hard enough to fog the windows
when they heard a car. They jerked up from lying in the seat
just in time to see a white '59 Chevy pull across the GMC's
front, immediately followed by a pink '55 Olds across the
back. A tall boy emerged from the Chevy holding a tire iron.
Jake felt a bitter taste in his mouth when he recognized him.
"Damn. That's Snake Drager."

Charlotte squinted toward the boy. "Snake? We call him
Mike." She turned in the seat to look behind. "And that's
Bobby Bullard's pink Olds."

Jake found her voice a little too chirpy as Drager tapped
his window with the tire tool. Jake rolled it down.

Drager poked Jake's shoulder with the sharp end of the
tool. "You a little far from home ain't you, Rivers?"

Jake pushed his door as hard as he could and stepped out
before Drager could put a knee against it. "I'd say that you're
the one far from home. Adrian's closer than Hereford. What
business is it of yours anyway?" Jake could see about a car
length's view of traffic passing on 66 and wished for a glimpse
of Nocona's red Chevy.

Drager pointed the tire tool at Jake. "I'm makin' it my
business. Ain't that many girls over here, and we don't need
you Adrian boys comin' over takin' whatever you feel like.
You already broke up Bobby and his girl."

Jake saw Bobby Bullard sitting behind the wheel of the
pink Olds. He was about Jake's height and size, maybe a few
pounds heavier. He and Jake had been matched at point
guard last basketball season—good sport—nice guy. Jake was
not afraid of Bobby, but he was afraid of Mike Drager.
"Who's Bobby's girl?"

"Don't matter who she was. You crank that piece of crap you're drivin' and haul your ass west. We see you in Vega again after sundown, you'll wish we hadn't."

Jake looked at Charlotte. Her elbows were draped over the GMC's door, and her chin rested on her hands. Jake thought she looked too content—too entertained.

"Why doesn't Bobby Boy speak for himself? And what's **your** problem with me?"

Drager glanced at Charlotte. "I told you what my problem is. Now get in your damn truck and get the hell out of town and don't come back."

Jake tried to calm himself—tried to remember what Nocona had said about Drager—something about his not being willing to fight if he was alone. Jake did not want to test that theory, but he was either going to be disgraced in front of Charlotte and all the Vega boys or take a stand. "Sure takes a lot of you Vega boys to run one little Matador out of town."

Drager seemed caught off guard, so Jake decided to press the point. "Don't it?" No response. "All them brave boys in that tittie-pink Olds carrying weapons, too?" Jake expected them all to pile out of the car at his words. When they did not, he felt himself calm a little and decided to test Nocona's theory a little more.

"Since you seem to be the one with the problem, how about just you and me talk it over? You get rid of the tire tool and tell your friends to go back to whatever they were doin'. If you still got your heart set on whippin' my ass, then we'll just get it on."

Drager seemed a little ashamed of the tire iron as he put it behind his leg. He jabbed a finger into Jake's chest hard enough to make Jake take a step back. He moved close enough to whisper in Jake's ear. "You show up in Vega again, they'll find you face down in the Canadian River." Drager made the air sing with a swift swing of the tire iron as he walked back to his car. Jake admired the mellow rumble of twin pipes, the red pin striping around the fender skirts and down the side of the Chevy as it rolled past him. The Pink Olds' lake pipes were louder as Bullard backed up, spun the tires and followed.

Jake was drained and shaky but breathed a little easier as they drove away. His feelings were different than they had been after Yellow Eyes had threatened him. There was less rage at his tormentor and more anger toward himself—more shame. Nobody could blame him for what happened with Yellow Eyes, but this could be his fault. What had he done to bring such hatred from the Vega boys and Mike Drager? At least he knew who had been driving the Hudson for Yellow Eyes.

Charlotte cleared her throat, and Jake turned to face her. "Suppose you been goin' out with that asshole."

Charlotte looked up from her hands. "Just once. You know we said we wouldn't ask about other boys or girls. You run around with almost all of my friends."

"Which one is Bobby's girl?"

"I think he was talking about Marty, but she and Bobby never went steady."

Jake's friendship with Charlotte had always been fun. There was no talk of love or even going steady. There was no sex. Jake felt obliged to try but was secretly relieved when she stopped him. He knew that other boys called her a prick-tease, but he figured it was just her way of handling things. It worked well. Tonight, however, her voice and manner were irritating. She seemed to be enjoying herself at Jake's expense.

"Why do the Vega boys let Drager come over here from Hereford while they try to run me off?"

Charlotte stepped out of the truck. "I thought you knew. He goes to school here now. Switched to Vega last year after they threw him off all the sports teams in Hereford. Something about vandalism. He stayed out the whole year, figurin' he'd gain an extra year of eligibility. He's finishing here, so he can play his senior year."

Jake picked up a rock and hurled it against the back of an abandoned tin building across the street. "So I guess he'll be playin' us this year?"

"All the boys say he's a stud basketball player."

Jake had seen the intense rivalry between Vega and Adrian during last year's game. Vega had won a close one, and the crowds had almost spilled onto the Adrian gym floor over each whistle blown or basket scored. "So why's he after me? Can't be that bullshit about me breaking up Bobby and his girl. Drager doesn't care about anybody but himself."

"How do you know so much about him? He had to ask who you were."

Drager's whisper played itself over and over in Jake's mind on the way home. He could almost feel his peppermint breath against his ear. He had threatened to kill him. Jake had uttered his share of empty threats, including the ones he shouted at Yellow Eyes. Boys did that type of thing for show. But this threat had been whispered, not shouted for bravado. Jake also thought about what Charlotte had said about Drager having to ask who he was. Jake had grown a little taller and put on some weight since that terrible day in the Hereford auditorium. Maybe that was it. He was wearing his hat and boots. Maybe that was it. No ... the truth was that the worst humiliation of Jake's life was not even a ripple in the stream of Mike Drager's life.

37 "So Worm is playing at Vega this year. Means we'll will face him in the grudge match." Nocona smiled through clenched teeth. He and Jake were standing with the rest of the basketball team at center court in the Adrian gym. Coach Gee had just announced their election as co-captains. Elated at being chosen by his teammates, Jake's warm glow erupted into loud laughter when he heard Nocona refer to Mike Drager as Worm. Two months of jumping rope and lifting weights had shifted a couple of pounds from Nocona's frame to Jake's.

After-school practice and other school activities gave Jake an excuse to stay away from Vega after Drager's threat. He felt welcome at Adrian again and a new crop of freshman girls and maturing sophomores added new excitement to school functions. When he did go to Vega, Nocona went with him. Drager had not shown himself again.

Coach Gee's whistle interrupted them as he dropped a bag of basketballs on the gym floor. The coach had also put on some weight and the cobweb of blue lines in his face seemed more pronounced. His nose and ears seemed to have turned a reddish-blue. "I think you boys are in shape to play. Let's see if you can handle the basketballs as well as you handle jump ropes." Jake liked him even better than last year.

They were three victories into the season when Coach Gee failed to show up for a workout. Coach Watson's whistle drew them into a circle at mid-court. "Coach Gee had a stroke last night around midnight. He's in the hospital at Amarillo. They don't know a lot yet, but he may have to have physical therapy for a few weeks after they release him. It will be after Christmas if he returns at all this season." Watson waited for the news to sink in and the mumbling and soft groans to cease. "We have a game Friday night and I'm sure he would want us to carry on. Line up for crip shots." Jake's heart sank as he shared knowing glances with Nocona and Gabe.

His worst fears were realized at Thursday's practice. Coach Watson stopped the light scrimmage by grabbing the basketball and putting it under his arm. The team formed a huddle around him. "I'm making some changes into tomorrow night's starting lineup. I scouted Hedley for Coach Gee last week. They have a big boy playing point guard that's tough as raw meat. I'm moving Wells to point guard and inserting Donovan into his place as forward. Gabe will stay at center."

Jake's eyes were burning, and he kept his head down. The rest of the team also stared at their shoes until Nocona stepped forward. "Rivers is point guard, Coach."

"You coaching this team now, Mr. Wells?"

"No sir, but Rivers is point guard. He's co-captain of the team. Ain't right to bench him."

"How'd you like to sit on the bench with him?"

"I can't shoot from the outside and can't handle the ball or set the plays like he can."

Jake punched Nocona with his elbow and shook his head.

He sat beside Nocona on the school bus that afternoon, his head leaned against the window. Talking did not help, so they kept silent for most of the trip. When he stepped off the bus, he heard the unmistakable sound of hogs. His already sick stomach rolled again. He walked toward the sound until he matched a smell to it. Hogs for sure. His daddy and his uncle JD were walking among pigs in the barn corral.

Mattie's car was gone, and she was not in the house. He dressed in work clothes, walked to the red barn corral, and stood below where his daddy and uncle were sitting on the top rail. He peeked through the rails. An irrigation tube had been set in a trough to pump water into the lot so the hogs would have a mud wallow. JD looked down at Jake. "What do you think, Jake?"

"What do I think about what?"

The terse reply brought a glance from Rance. JD laughed. Jake caught the smell of whiskey. "Whassamatter, Jake? You don't like fresh pork?"

"I like fresh pork well enough. Let's get started and butcher all of `em. They stay here very long, cattle and horses will probably never come in this corral again. String will never come back for sure."

"Me and Rance thought we'd make you and Bob Lee partners on these pigs. Bought `em at a hell of a price. You take care of `em for us, we'll split the profit when we sell `em."

Jake's anger at being benched and at the hint of a whiskey-ruled pig transaction spilled out. "No thanks. I ain't takin' care of no hogs. How much y'all been drinkin' when you bought these suckers?"

Rance stepped down from the rail. He had been drinking, but he was not drunk. "Feed's over there in the feed room. Fill those troughs."

Jake stared directly into his daddy's eyes for a few seconds before he crawled the fence. A big sow charged him and

knocked him down as he started through the mud. Nobody
laughed as Jake got up and kicked the sow.

Playing second string in practice each day, Jake was always
matched against Nocona at point guard. He played with
vengeance, stealing the ball from his friend so often that
it started to bother Nocona. Second string was outscoring
first string too often to suit the coach or the players. The
Matadors lost two of the next three games. At night, Jake
fed hogs. His spirits were lifted when Trish arrived with her
sons for Christmas, but he could not bring himself to tell her
he had lost his place on the team. Gray Boy was not granted
leave to come home.

Two days after Christmas, the big sow that had attacked
him had a litter of pigs. Jake started to soften as he watched
them nurse. When he returned from school that afternoon,
he caught the sow devouring one of her own piglets as he
dropped into the lot. He rushed across the mud and pulled
the quivering pig from his mother's mouth. Too late. Jake
kicked the old sow, the feed bucket and each trough, and
then slid down the feed room wall and pressed the heels of
his palms against his forehead. The sow started on another
piglet as he came out. Jake found an axe handle and beat the
sow until she turned loose. Too late again. Jake chased her
around the corral, beating her with the axe handle, until she
broke a rail trying to escape.

He found an old rope, roped her around the neck, tripped
her, and tied her legs. He wound bailing wire around her
snout and pulled it tight with a pair of fence pliers until it
broke the skin. "Now, try to eat your babies, you old bitch."
He kicked the hogtied cannibal sow again for good measure.
Jake was sick enough to throw up as he walked to the house.
After washing his hands and staring at his supper for a few
minutes, he grabbed the .22 and walked to the barn. He

placed the end of the barrel against the sow's head and pulled the trigger. The big hog squealed once and dropped.

Rance heard the report of the .22 and seemed to appear before the hog uttered its last squeal. "What the hell are you doing?"

Jake's stare was blank. "I hate hogs."

Rance saw the two half-eaten piglets. "She been eatin' her litter?"

Jake stared at the dead sow without speaking.

Rance brought a hammer and a handful of nails from the hay room. "Better fix that hole in the fence or they'll all be out in the morning."

Jake took the hammer and ten-penny nails, held up the broken rail and drove the first nail in. His anger and frustration exploded when he hit the second one a glancing blow. He heard the whistle as the nail whizzed past his head and now knew what his father meant when he said 'whistle like a ten-penny nail'. He was reaching for a replacement when he heard his daddy make a sound deep in his throat unlike any sound that Jake had ever heard. He turned to see Rance on his knees, both hands covering his right eye. Jake fell back in horror when he saw the nail head protruding between his daddy's fingers. A small trickle of blood followed.

Jake yelled loud enough to bring Mattie out of the house. Rance grabbed his arm. "Calm down, Jake. This may not be as bad as it looks. I need for you to stay calm and help keep your mother calm. Just an accident. Not your fault. Just get me to a hospital."

Rance's voice soothed Jake only a little. He knew it was his fault. He had struck the nail in anger without paying attention to what he was doing. He hadn't cared that he only hit it a glancing blow. Now his father had a nail buried in his eye.

Mattie sat in the back of the Ford with Rance as Jake drove. He kept taking his eyes off the road to stare at his father, expecting blood to gush at any minute. Rance assured him that the pain was not that bad and gave him clear directions to the hospital.   Jake wondered if he had been there before.

Doctors tried to keep Jake out of the emergency room, but Rance insisted that he be allowed in, correctly sensing Jake's need to stay with them. He got his first look at the nail when Rance dropped his hands to allow the doctors to examine him. It was neatly driven between his right eye and his nose as if Jake had driven it in with a hammer.

Jake dug his fingers into his palms as he stared at the nail for almost an hour while they waited for a specialist to arrive. The tall, lean, handsome, and young surgeon took only seconds to arrive at his diagnosis. "The eyeball is ruptured. It will have to be removed to save your sight. Otherwise, you stand a chance of losing both eyes to infection."

Jake got all dead inside. A small whimpering groan escaped repeatedly from his throat without his permission. His mouth was full of cotton and he had difficulty swallowing. He had killed his horse and now had possibly blinded his father. Death would be preferable to what he felt. He felt a hand on his shoulder but did not look up. Bob Lee, JD and Bess were in the room and seemed to be saying something, but Jake could not hear them. He sat motionless and deaf while the doctor punched a hypodermic needle into his daddy's arm and applied some sort of ointment around the nail. Mattie and Rance spoke to each other, then to JD and Bob Lee. The nail was still there when they walked out the door.

Cold air in the parking lot awakened Jake enough to feel Bob Lee shaking him like a rag doll. "You got to pull yourself together, Jake. Uncle Rance says he wants you and Aunt Mattie to go with us."

"Where we goin'?"

"You hear anything that went on in there?"

"Guess not."

"I'm gonna fly y'all to Cooper. Uncle Rance won't let anybody touch his eye till he sees Dr. Olen." Bob Lee did not wait until they got to the airport to fly. Rance put a calming hand on Mattie's shoulder each time the black turd-hearse seemed to be leaving the ground. He parked a few feet from a shiny four-passenger plane. Bob Lee had called ahead and the little Beechcraft Bonanza was fueled and ready. He left the keys in the Chevy and they were off the ground quickly.

Jake took the first deep breath he had taken since the ten-penny had whistled. There was no real reason for it, but he began to feel life stirring inside his numb body. The lifting sensation when the plane left ground look away some of the heavy weight he had felt since it happened. The plane's small interior closed around him and his family, giving them cohesiveness and strength. And if anybody could save his daddy's eyesight, it was Dr. Olen Bartlett. The ringing in his ears softened.

Jake's airsickness began about the time he asked the question that had lingered since takeoff. "I never knew you could fly a plane, Bob Lee. How long you been flyin'?"

Bob Lee leaned back with one hand on the controls and smiled at Jake. "Got my solo license last week. I been takin' lessons off and on for a good while."

Jake swallowed hard. "This your plane?"

"Naw. Me and a couple of buddies just lease it. It's the same type of plane that Buddy Holly and the Big Bopper died in."

Jake kept his eyes straight ahead.

"You're lookin' a little peaked, Jake. Barf bags are over there in that little side-pocket."

The little plane bounced only a little when Bob Lee sat her down at the Commerce airport. JD had worked his telephone magic, and Seth and Tillie, Rance's brother and

Jim Ainsworth

Mattie's sister, were waiting at the little pasture airport to drive them to Cooper and Bartlett Clinic. Tillie patted Jake's shoulder all the way to the hospital.

Dr. Olen met them at the door as if it were regular office hours rather than the wee hours of the morning. He glanced at the nail, then up and down Rance's frame. "How much weight have you lost, Rance?" Without waiting for an answer, he took his friend by the arm and escorted him down the hall to his office. Hand-in-hand, Jake and Mattie followed. Bob Lee, Seth, and Tillie stopped in the waiting room.

A familiar feeling of safety came over Jake when he entered the office. The sights and medicinal smells of Dr. Olen's office and the sound of his voice had always comforted him. He could tell that his parents felt the same way. No words or time were wasted. Mattie handed him the written notes from the Amarillo doctor. He scanned the notes. "Uh, huh." He laid the sheet of paper on his desk and turned to examine the nail. Without hesitation or warning, he picked up a small instrument that looked like shiny pliers to Jake and pulled the nail out. A collective sigh could be heard all the way down the hall. He held the nail under his office lamp. "Looks like you used a pretty new nail. Hardly any rust."

Rance asked the question he had been holding across Texas. "Can we save the eye, Doc?"

Dr. Olen waved his hand in front of the damaged eye, and Rance blinked slowly. He laid him back on the examination table and examined the puncture closely. "We'll save the eyeball, Rance, but you're gonna lose sight in that eye. It'll be a problem for you at first, but you'll learn to use one eye."

It was terrible news, but Dr. Olen delivered it so matter-of-factly and confidently that they all felt better. Dr. Olen sat down on his rolling stool and observed Rance's skin and body. "Now, how about the weight loss? Looks like about thirty pounds. A lot of weight for a man who wasn't ever fat. I don't like your color either."

Rance just stared. Mattie stood beside him. Dr. Olen turned
to Jake and tousled his hair. "Almost didn't recognize you,
Jake. You must have taken the weight your daddy lost. Why
don't you go out there and tell Seth and Tillie what you
heard. Let me catch up with your mama and daddy."

Jake was glad for the errand. Olen Bartlett had an almost
magical effect on him. Two sentences had almost redeemed
him—made him feel bigger—more grownup—ready for
responsibility. The doctor had not even mentioned the nail
being his fault. Bob Lee had him almost grinning with dirty
jokes for the few seconds he forgot that he might have blinded
his father.

Mattie came for him shortly. The flood of tears she had
been holding back burst as they walked back down the hall.
Dr. Olen was waiting in his office. Rance was gone. "We're
getting your daddy set up in a room, Jake. We have to find
out what's causing his stomach troubles. This is not the time
I would have chosen, but I don't think we can wait."

Mattie put a hand on Jake's shoulder. "Your daddy has
had a lot of pain for a long time, Jake—even before we moved
to West Texas."

She seemed to read the question in Jake's mind that he
dared not utter. "Dr. Olen says whiskey is about the only
thing that gave him any relief—wouldn't take pain pills. He's
going to do surgery to find out what's causin' it and fix it."
Uninvited, a vision of himself slamming the pickup door in
his daddy's face entered Jake's mind.

Jake nodded dumbly and was led from the room and up
the stairs to Rance's room. Both of his daddy's eyes were
covered with gauze. Rance called him to the bedside and
reached for his arm. He pulled on his shirtsleeve. "Jake, I
need for you to go back with Bob Lee and take care of things
till I can get back. It may be a while. You got to get that dead
sow out of there and keep those hogs and cattle fed. You
know what needs to be done. I'm countin' on you. You can

drive the Ford to school so you can get home earlier. Use it to go back and forth to catch rides to the ballgames, too."

Jake had not told his parents he had been benched. "Ballgames don't matter. I'll look after things." He stopped to swallow and regain his voice. "Daddy, I'm sorry."

"Not your fault, Jake. Anybody to blame, it's me. I've sent many ten-penny nails flying. I knew better than to be standin' where I was."

38 The change in engine speed woke Jake woke from a dead sleep. The plane was circling as he looked out the side window. "We there already?"

Bob Lee studied the ground from the pilot-side window. "A hundred and fifty miles an hour covers ground pretty quick. Already been over your house once. Think you can walk from the main road? The road by your house ain't long enough for me to take off, so I aim to drop you on the farm road."

"You mean you're gonna land on a dirt road?"

Bob Lee giggled. "I landed on the highway over by Simms right after I started learnin' how to fly. Nothin' to it."

"What if a car comes by?"

"They damn well better get out of the way—cause I sure as hell can't. Prob'ly scare the livin' shit of `em to see an airplane headed straight for `em."

Jake took a deep seat and held his breath as the plane touched ground and bounced a little on the rough road. Bob Lee shouted some instructions over the engine noise as Jake hopped out. Jake could not hear them, so Bob Lee just waved goodbye. Jake watched as the Bonanza swirled dust and left the ground, banked, and headed east for Amarillo. He watched until the plane went out of sight and listened as the engine's roar changed from a hum to silence. Nothing left to do but look toward the house. The sun said it was mid-morning. Heavy weariness returned as Jake trudged down the road, dragging his boots in the dust.

At the back door, he listened to the creak of the windmill for a few minutes as he stared at the red barn that he had admired when he first saw it. He wondered if he could bear to go out there again. The thought of the trussed-up dead sow brought a slight burn to his throat. He went inside, showered, and plopped down on the bed in his underwear. He would haul off the sow before dark.

The honk of the afternoon school bus horn awakened Jake. He had not meant to sleep the day away. He stalked into the kitchen and found some cold biscuits and sausage. He stuffed one in his mouth as he headed outside, wishing that all of the pigs were sausage sandwiches. The sow looked worse in daylight, and the rest of her litter was dead. The other pigs had nudged them through the mud. The first kernel of remorse from killing the sow entered Jake's conscience. No time for that. He picked up the rope around the sow's neck and pulled. The sow barely moved. Wrapping the muddy rope around his hands, he dug in his heels and slid her a few feet. He fought off the anger and frustration that welled up. No time for that, either. He was responsible for the whole farm now, and he must start to think like his father.

He could almost feel Rance's influence as the Case cranked on the first try. He opened the lot gate and backed the small tractor inside. After hooking a log chain to the hog rope, he dragged the sow out without a single hog escaping. He returned with a small trailer for her piglets. After dropping the last one into a small gully in the north pasture about a mile from the barn, he sat down on the edge of the ravine and looked at his handiwork. Back home, a north

wind would bring the smell of rotting carcasses all the way to
the house. He was grateful for the dry air out here.

He had seen many calves and cows die—seen the buzzards
do their work—seen coyotes and possums jumping back from
the open belly of a cow. Harsh, but understood—a part of
nature. Pigs lying in that gully did not look like nature—more
like a multiple crime scene—one where Jake had committed a
murder and followed it with a heinous act that might cost his
father his sight. He wished for his horse as he drove the Case
back to the house. Riding Scar to check cows might have
cleansed the blood from his hands.

Jake took his father's advice about driving to school, but
he decided on the GMC. Driving the Ford and its flippers
seemed wrong, somehow. People avoided him again. Bob
Lee's news pipeline had already reached Adrian. Everyone
seemed to know what had happened. He left before
basketball practice that day and did not return to the gym for
a week, missing two games and five practices. Nocona and
Gabe told him that Coach Watson had thrown him off the
team and named Gabe as the new co-captain.

"Who gives a shit?" he said. He found a small pig dead
that afternoon and dragged it to the gully by hand.

Bob Lee was waiting in the yard when he returned.
"Mama sent me to get you. Think she's got some good news
from Unc."

"What is it?"

"Just said it was good. Stopped me at the door and sent
me flyin' over here to tell you."

JD was standing by the door when they returned. He put
his hand on Jake's shoulder. "Bess just talked to your mama
a little bit ago." He gestured toward Bess with his other hand.
"Whaddya call that tube between the stomach and the little
gut, Bess?"

Bess dried her hands on her apron as she walked into the
living room. "Duodenum. Jake, your daddy's duodenum was

all grown together. Dr. Olen suspected it and found it during surgery. He opened it up, put a tube or something in it, and your daddy's gonna be fine. He'll be able to eat like the rest of us again. No more pain."

Jake smiled for the first time since the ten-penny whistled. "What about his eyes?"

Bess looked at JD. "Well, he won't be able to see out of that eye, but he's gonna have an eyeball, at least. Rance is grateful he can still see out of the other one."

Bob Lee paced around them. "Calls for a celebration, Jake. If we can talk JD out of little money, me and you'll go get a steak." Bob Lee held an open palm toward his father.

JD stared at the hand. "Why the hell you got your hand out to me? You're a grown man. What did you do with your last paycheck?"

"Man's got expenses, Dad." Bess walked to the back of the house. Jake heard a door close in the hall.

"Bullshit. You spend all your damn money on whores and whiskey."

"You never do any whores or whiskey? Work my ass off driving your damn tractors all day. Need a little recreation at night."

"What I do or do not do is none of your goddamn business. All I know is I never put my hand out to my old man. Likely to draw back a stub if I did. You got your goddamn hand out every time I turn around."

"Don't know what to tell you, Dad. Just work hard and save all your money."

"What kinda bullshit talk is that? You ain't so damn big I can't kick your ass into the middle of next week."

Bob Lee put out the hand again. "It's for Jake. He needs a night out."

JD looked at Jake. "Hold out your hand, Jake." JD dropped a twenty into it.

Bob Lee stared at the twenty. "Hell, if that's all you got,

we might as well stay home. We was planning on flying to Ft. Worth to eat at Cattlemen's. They got the best steaks. That won't even pay for the steaks, much less fuel for the plane."

JD took back the twenty and replaced it with a hundred. He looked at Jake but spoke to Bob Lee. "Don't be getting' in that damn airplane and flying anywhere. You might get this boy killed. Hell, you can't drive a goddamn car six months without tearing it up, much less fly a goddamn airplane." He paused to point a finger at Jake. "Jake, you don't get in any damn airplane with his fat ass." Jake stared at the hundred and nodded.

Bob Lee checked his watch as they drove into the steakhouse parking lot. "Thirty-five minutes. I drove it in thirty-two once." Jake tried to figure the average speed for a trip that was probably close to sixty miles, but could not do it in his head with Bob Lee telling one joke after another. Inside, Bob Lee pointed and they were ushered to table by a window.

"Bring me the usual and this boy a big t-bone and all the trimmin's."

Jake had never had a t-bone steak, but had heard JD talk about cooking them. He looked around the room as Bob Lee rambled. Most of the men were dressed in suits or expensive western shirts and khaki pants. Hat lines on the men's hair led him to a four-rowed hat rack of expensive Resistols and Stetsons. He raked his baseball cap off his head and laid it in the chair beside him. Bob Lee's khaki pants were grease-stained and his boots crusted with cow manure. Jake stared at his brother's old boots and slid his feet under the chair. He knew they were crusted with pig manure and mud, but at least he could not smell them. His Levis were faded and stained.

Jake barely had time to dig into the large wooden bowl of salad before the waiter dropped a huge plate in front of him with a rude thud. The t-bone hung over every side. A baked potato so big it needed a plate of its own accompanied the biggest steak Jake had ever seen. An ice-cream-dip-sized dollop of butter steamed from the potato's sliced middle.

The waiter hovered over Jake's shoulder. "What would you like on your potato?"

Jake shot a nervous glance toward Bob Lee, already cutting into his big sirloin. He did not know what else to put on a potato. "Just butter, I guess."

Jake buttered a roll from the cloth-covered basket in the center of the table and then cut into his steak. Blood rushed to the center of his big plate. His father's eye and the dead sow stared back at him.

Bob Lee saw the expression on Jake's face and called the waiter. He pointed at Jake's steak and his own. "I've seen cows hurt worse than that get up and walk off. Herd `em back to the kitchen, kill `em, and cook `em."

The waiter stared at the blood in their plates. "Sorry, Bob Lee. I told the cook the steaks were for Mr. Boggs. He assumed it was your daddy. JD just likes the hair singed off his steaks. As I recall, you like yours medium well. How about your young friend?"

Jake looked up from the blood and nodded. "Just like his."

Full from his first t-bone and the first slice of caramel-covered cheesecake he had ever had, Jake was almost relaxed as he and Bob Lee rolled down the windows and cruised along at ninety. They had made one pass down the main drag in Amarillo before heading home—Bob Lee testing Jake's powers of attraction with women against Gray Boy's. Jake lost. They pulled into Jake's yard just before nine.

Jake recognized Caleb Pirtle's Dodge pickup sitting beside his GMC. Sage sat on one fender of the old pickup she called Goat, and Mary Ann sat on the other. Both wore black hats like his. Bob Lee stared at the girls and laughed. "Here I been feelin' sorry for you all this time—thinkin' you been out here all by yourself—and you been truckin' women out here two at a time. Why didn't you tell me?"

Jake did not answer as he stepped out. Walking toward the girls, he wished for clean clothes, a shower, and his good boots and hat. His home out here had seemed like a completely separate life from his school life. Only Gabe and Nocona had ever been inside his house. He was surprised that Sage and Mary Ann even knew where he lived. Having them here made him feel a familiar warm feeling he had not felt since the ten-penny whistled. He smiled at the girls. "Hey. What're y'all doin' out here?"

Mary Ann answered. "Came to see our favorite boyfriend. We were just about to give up and go home. Hey, Bob Lee."

The whole scene was so good to Jake he could not have dreamed it any better, except for the shower and change of clothes. Bob Lee appeared at his shoulder. "Well, I know these two ladies. Jailbait for me, so I guess I can't help. See you, Jake."

"Thanks for the steak." The turd-hearse left a cloud of dust in its wake as Jake turned back toward the girls. "Y'all want to come inside?" The south wind was bracing, but gentle and not too cold.

They slid off the fender and walked toward him. Moonlight caught them between the shoulders as they approached. Their hats shaded their faces as they moved with athletic grace. Mary Ann contested Texie to replace Loretta as the best athlete in the school. It was clear that Sage would be her successor. Either could handle a basketball or a horse as well as any boy in school. Sage finally spoke. "Can't go in the house with your parents gone, but can we talk in the barn?" Her voice had mellowed away the little-girl shrillness she had when Jake first saw her.

Jake heard the distant grunt of hogs and was thankful that the wind was out of the south. He fawned over their presence and laughed not with nervousness, but with deep appreciation for their company as he led them toward the shop. He opened the sliding door and let the moon slide in. He reached for the chain to turn on the naked bulb above. Mary Ann caught his hand. "We don't have to have that."

The girls moved a few tools and sat together on an old couch that Jake knew had grease on it. He pulled up the rickety chair and sat in front of them. "So. Thanks for comin' out. Gets kinda lonesome out here." The girls nodded. "I got Cokes in the house if ... ."

"No time, Jake. We been waitin' for almost two hours."

Jake regretted missing two hours alone with his favorite female friends. That would have been better than the steak.

Mary Ann leaned forward. "You gonna fight getting thrown off the team by Watson?"

"Why should I fight to sit on the bench?"

Sage stood and walked back and forth in front of Jake.

"Daddy says he'll go to the school board with your parents and get you back on the team. He's got no use for Coach Watson. Says he did you wrong."

Jake nodded. "I sure appreciate that."

"He needs to know if you know when your daddy or mother will be back. Also wants to know if you're willing to take up for yourself and if you can start coming back to practice."

"Watson hates me, but I sure love to play. Yeah, I can make practice unless somethin' goes wrong around here. I expect Daddy and Mama to be back in a week or two."

"Basketball season will be pretty far gone by then. There's a board meeting tomorrow night. You could be back on the team by Friday's game if Daddy goes to that meeting, but he doesn't want to interfere in your parents' business."

"My parents don't know what's happening, but they would be grateful, I know."

The girls' hat brims touched as Sage whispered something in Mary Ann's ear. Mary Ann stood and towered over Jake. "We got some information for you, but we can't decide if we should tell or not."

Jake looked at Sage and thought how pretty she had become. "How can I get you to tell me?"

Sage's stare was direct. "You still in love with Loretta?"

Jake looked down at the grease-stained concrete. "Never was in love, I guess. I still think about her and wonder what happened. Why?"

Sage stood and handed him an envelope addressed to Caleb Pirtle. Jake recognized Floyd Knight's handwriting. A post office box number in Claude, Texas, was in the left hand corner. Jake ran his finger across the handwriting. "I recognize his handwriting. You reckon she's still living at home?"

"We know she is."

39 Jake stood by Caleb Pirtle's side as he made the case before the school board. Coach Watson weakly objected that Jake had not bothered to tell him about his father's injury and had just skipped practices and games without notice. Jake was asked to leave the room and wait in the hall. Caleb came out in five minutes and told him he was reinstated. "Don't miss any more practices without a very good excuse."

Jake shook his hand and thanked him. He suited up for practice the next day and scored eight points for the second string. Nocona did not seem to get angry when he stole the ball and outran him on fast breaks. He knew Jake could not compete against him at forward, but could whip him easily at guard. Jake got in the game for three plays in a losing cause during Friday night's game. He only had time to take the ball down the court once and did not take a shot.

Jake rose well before daybreak the next morning, fed the hogs, and did his other chores. He was dressed and behind the Ford steering wheel shortly after daybreak. The map on the seat of the Ford reminded Jake of his first trip to the Panhandle and how many things had changed in such a short time. He figured it was a little over an hour to Claude—a trip he needed to make.

Jake made one pass through town, watching anyone walking the streets. With no plan, he stopped at a service station and asked about a family named Knight. The attendant was new and did not know them, but handed him a phone book. No listing. He drove around for almost an hour before parking downtown, screwing up the courage to go into a small hardware and feed store and ask about the Knights again. The lady behind the counter nodded hard at his question and pointed. "Loretta passed here less than an hour ago."

Jake felt his heart pick up speed. His luck was changing. "Which way?"

She pointed south. "Probably goin' to the café for dinner. They do it most Saturdays when John Bill can get into town. Just three doors down on this side of the street."

He had hoped to catch Loretta alone, but he would take what he was given. He made a telescope of his palms, pressed it against the window of the Claude Café, and tried to peek inside. A friendly-looking waitress that reminded him of the one in Wildorado beckoned him inside. Jake stepped in and felt woodstove kind of warmth. The walls and eighteen-foot ceilings were covered in railroad car siding. Oak booths ran along both walls of the narrow building. There were no tables. The booth backs came to Jake's neck, too tall to show occupants.

The waitress dropped off two glasses of iced tea at a booth and walked toward Jake. "Slow day. Just take whichever one you want. I'll be right with you. Special's on that blackboard."

Jake glanced at the chalk writing on the blackboard, but the booths kept his attention. He decided to walk beside them rather than ask the waitress. Three steps across the creaking floor planks, he heard her. Her still-seductive voice came from the last booth. They saw each other at the same instant. Her chin rested in her hand as she listened to the person across the table. The chin lifted slightly when she saw Jake. He could not read her expression, so he stopped short, just in case she wanted to wave him away. A long-faced cowboy under a black, dusty hat peeked around the booth's back to see what had garnered her attention. He looked at Jake, then back at Loretta.

Loretta squeezed from the booth and stood. She hesitated long enough for Jake to get a good look before she walked toward him. She was definitely pregnant, but the athletic grace and fluid movement had not completely deserted her. She gave him a light hug, and he clumsily returned it, trying to avoid touching her stomach. She gave him a Mattie-like pat on the cheek. "What in the world are you doing here?"

Her face was a little puffy, but still beautiful. The electricity made Jake feel wet under his arms. His skin started to prickle. He decided it was time to acknowledge the cowboy who was staring at him with malice. He held out a hand. "Jake Rivers." Jake felt his body being pulled forward a step by a larger, rougher hand than his own.

Loretta squeezed her hands. "Sorry. John Bill Garner, meet Jake Ridge Rivers. He's an old friend."

"He the one?"

"No, John Bill, he isn't the one." She turned toward Jake. "John Bill and I are going to be married." She took John Bill's hand away from the vise-like grip he had wrapped around Jake and held it with both of her hands. "Jake was one of my best buddies. Do you care if he and I talk a few minutes about my old girlfriends at Adrian?"

John Bill unfolded his frame from the booth and stood close enough for Jake to appreciate his well-over-six-feet presence. He turned toward Loretta. "I got to get back to work soon. How long you gonna be?" Jake noticed John Bill's face softening and his eyes searching, almost pleading, as he spoke to Loretta.

"If I'm not out in fifteen minutes, go on back to work. I'll see you at the house tonight." Loretta watched him all the way out the door before she slid back into the booth. Jake took John Bill's spot. She reached across the table with both hands and bestowed a familiar smile on Jake. He hesitated before accepting her hands into his own. It was the first time their hands had touched since that day at the Bent Door last spring.

Loretta smiled with matured eyes, and Jake felt like a small boy in her presence. "John Bill is a good guy, Jake. He's going to marry me as soon as the baby is born and adopt it."

Jake blurted out the question he had come to ask. He wanted to get it asked before John Bill came in and caught them holding hands. "Whose baby is it?"

Loretta's smile faded. "I told you it's not yours, Jake. That's all you need to know."

"Yeah, but everybody back in Adrian thinks it is. I can handle that, but I can't handle not knowing myself. How do you know for sure it ain't mine? I been thinkin' that maybe you're trying to protect me because I'm just a kid."

"It's not yours, Jake. Please don't make me spell it out."

"I just got one more thing to say, then I'll leave it alone." Jake squeezed her hands tightly. "If it is, I don't want John Bill out there or anybody else raising a kid with Rivers blood that belongs to me. I'm older now and up to it. Think my parents will help us till we can get on our feet. I'll marry you if I'm the daddy."

Loretta smiled and put her hands, still wet from the iced tea glass, on Jake's cheeks. "Thank you for that, Jake. Believe me, I wish that it could have been yours." She slid her palms across the table and dropped them into her lap. "I'm lucky, really. John Bill is going to marry me. His daddy is a big rancher. Says I can go to college after the baby starts to school."

Jake looked around the booth and saw John Bill's back

leaning against a storefront post. "Guess I better go before I ruin it for you. How's your daddy?"

"He's havin' to substitute teach and do odd jobs for a livin'. Mother keeps books for John Bill's daddy." She wiped at her eyes. "I waited tables here until about a week ago. Doctor said I had to get off my feet till the baby comes. We get by."

Jake looked down. "I miss him. He ought to be teachin' or coachin'. Best one I ever had."

"He misses you too, Jake. He still laughs about you almost getting' your head knocked off playing catcher."

Jake chuckled, and then became serious. "You tell him who the daddy is?"

"He says he'll know after the baby gets here. If he doesn't, I might tell him then. I just can't tell him now. I got my reasons." Loretta slid out of the booth, and Jake stood beside her. John Bill still had his back to them as she brushed Jake's lips with her own. They were warm.

Jake lingered for a second, then turned and walked out. John Bill turned when the door opened. Jake tugged on the brim of his hat and nodded with an expression that he hoped showed gratitude. He did not wait to see.

Jake had the car door open when he heard his name. Floyd Knight, wearing a barber's apron, was hailing him from a barbershop door. Jake walked toward the rainbow sign and shook the big hand. "Good to see you, Coach."

Floyd shook the red and gray hair off the apron and onto the sidewalk. "What in the world? I about fell out of the barber chair when I saw you walkin' across the street. Almost didn't recognize you. How much have you put on ... twenty pounds?"

"Probably still too little to peg second from a squat."

Floyd turned back toward the barber chair. "Come on inside. TJ was just about finished when I stood up on him."

They made nervous conversation for the two minutes it took to finish the haircut. Jake walked outside feeling dwarfed by the big preacher. They sat on a bench under the barbershop sign. "What brings you to the this little metropolis, Jake?"

Jake had tried to come up with an answer to this inevitable question while Floyd was getting his haircut. He knew what would get him sympathy and possibly avoid talkin' about Loretta. "Guess you heard about what happened to my daddy."

Floyd nodded. "Caleb Pirtle wrote me. I was sure sorry to hear it. He home yet?"

"No sir, next week, I think."

"So ... I'm sure glad to see you, Jake, but why'd you come?"

"I been having a little trouble with Coach Watson. Thought maybe you could help me out. You sorta did once before."

"I heard about the trouble, Jake. Caleb tells me you're back on the team, though."

"Back on, but not gettin' to play."

"Did you earn a spot on the first string?"

"Guess you'd have to ask other people to get an opinion that's not partial, but I really think I did." Jake waited in vain for Floyd Knight to give him some encouragement. "I know I ain't big enough to ever be a great basketball player, but I think I can play first string point guard at a little school like Adrian. I think Watson has had it in for me from the first day I set foot on the basketball court. Takes every chance he can to make me eat crow."

Floyd Knight stared into the distance as if he had not heard Jake's long speech. "You see Loretta?"

Jake nodded as he tried to decide about the truth. "Yes sir. Pretty as ever."

Floyd put a hand on Jake's shoulder. "I wish I could do

something for you, Jake ... just like I wish I could do something for Loretta. I pray for guidance, ask for answers, but I admit to being confused and helpless. God has a way of working these things out. If Ken Watson is wrong, I believe it will all come out someday."

Jake flicked a cricket with his boot. "Yes sir, but someday may be after all my basketball playin' is done. I really didn't think there was anything you could do. Just felt the need to reconnect. I appreciate it." He stood to walk to his car.

"Have you been to see Coach Gee?"

Jake nodded. "Ashamed to say just once. They say he is gettin' around a little, but can't speak."

"A shame. Good man. Keep playin' your heart out, Jake. Play better than you can. Things will work out. Don't blame yourself for what happened to your daddy. I'll bet he doesn't."

40 Jake imagined finding the Goat and Sage in his front yard back at home, but was disappointed. A wave of sadness had gradually crept over him all the way from Claude that he could not explain. He should have felt better after seeing Loretta. Returning to an empty house and a large yard where the only occupants were stinking hogs caused a tidal wave of self-pity. He avoided looking toward the hog pen and the red barn. Inside, he plopped down in front of a boring television program, tired of the commercials and turned it off. He turned on the plastic radio in his headboard and was surprised to hear William Conrad as Marshal Matt Dillon in "Gunsmoke". He did not know "Gunsmoke" was ever on radio. He lay down on the bed to escape for a few minutes. Disappointed that he had missed most of it, he changed clothes and went to the hog pen.

His sensory antennae had been on high alert around the hogs since the night he had killed the sow and put out his daddy's eye. Something caused him to break into a run toward the hog pen. He knew why as he stepped on the first fence rail. Dead hogs were everywhere. He counted fifteen before he stopped. Those left alive seemed sick.

JD answered the door in his sock feet, his hat line visible

in his salt-and-pepper hair. Jake had always thought of his uncle as someone bigger than life, but he seemed almost normal standing there nap-interrupted. "What's wrong, Jake? You look pale as a ghost."

"It's the hogs. They're dyin'."

"Shit. Let me get my boots on, and I'll follow you back over there."

The turd-hearse arrived first, followed by the Olds. Jake wondered why they came in separate cars. He sat on the top rail as they examined the carnage. JD stepped in a pile of manure and stepped to the fence to scrape it off. "Goddamn cholera."

Bob Lee joined them, a rifle on his shoulder that Jake had not noticed when he arrived. "Have to kill `em all, Jake. You got any shells for your .22? Don't know if I got enough."

"Yeah. We have to kill `em all?"

"Let's get it over with."

Jake had already heard six shots before he could return with the .22. He stood dumbly and watched the hogs flop down until Bob Lee ran out of bullets. Jake killed the remaining six. Twenty-nine hogs lay dead when the sound of guns was finally replaced with the sound of the wind and the windmill. The tail creaked as if it were a sentinel announcing the latest of terrible events on the Rivers farm. The gunpowder smell of spent bullets mixed with hog blood, pig shit, and mud. Jake wished for his mother as he wondered what his daddy would say about his failure to take care of the hogs. He propped the rifle against his shoulder and leaned against the corral, grateful for darkness to shield the red in his eyes.

"Ain't your fault, Jake. Damn hogs were probably carrying it when we bought `em. Just bad luck all around." JD cupped his hands to light a Camel.

"What am I gonna do with `em now?"

"Hold out your hand."

Jake did as he was told and JD started dropping ten-spots into it. "This is for feedin' and gettin' rid of these hogs. Bob Lee's goin' to Kansas to pick up a load of cattle tomorrow, and all the other hands are off. Too dark to take care of it tonight. Think you can handle it?" He stopped dropping the tens when he reached a hundred dollars.

Jake kept his hand open and let the bills rock slightly with the light wind. The money bothered him, somehow—like getting paid for a crime. "What do I do with `em?"

"Load `em up and take `em down to where you dropped that old sow. Pour diesel on `em and build you a big bacon and sausage fire."

"Is cholera dangerous for our cows? Won't that ruin our pasture?"

"Nothing to worry about if you burn the damn things to ashes."

Jake hated to ask. "What about humans? Can I catch it?"

"Wear you some gloves and a good coat. It won't hurt you. I burned this many once back home. Could smell it in the air for weeks back there. It'll disappear in a couple of days out here."

Jake did not believe it, but he folded his hand around the cash. He was ashamed when two more flippers and a new pair of boots entered his mind.

Jake dreaded what he had to do as he stepped outside the next morning. Another guilty Sunday—this time disposing of evidence. By using a come-along to pull the biggest hogs into the trailer, he minimized contact with the grisly swine. At the gully, he looped two legs with a rope and dragged the hogs off the trailer one at a time. Impatient to be done, he soon abandoned this and started using his gloved hands to throw or drag the pigs into the gully. He returned with five gallons of diesel and a box of matches. On the side of the long hog-filled ravine, he watched the flames start to build. Popping and cracking soon pushed him back. He tried to identify the smell as bacon and sausage, but the dominant smell was of hair, hide and the parts of the hog that most humans would not eat. He moved far enough back to keep from seeing the putrid destruction of the hogs' bodies. Jake figured he would never eat pork again if he watched eyeballs popping and bodies exploding.

The wind never completely died in the Panhandle, but it was calm for the fire. When the fire burned down enough, he drove the Case and trailer back to the house. Calling himself stupid for not having done it first, he returned with the Super M and a box blade to cut a firebreak completely around the fire and build up a small dirt wall to keep the fire from spreading to the sparse grass. At twilight, he sat down again and tried to imagine himself as a cowboy camping on the prairie, the fire as his campfire. But there was no horse, and the smell kept reminding him that this was not a campfire. By midnight, little was left but a few curled pieces of charred hide and some hooves. Jake used the box blade to push the remainder into a pile, added diesel, and burned the rest. Just before dawn, he pushed dirt over what would not burn.

Mattie was sitting on the side of his bed when he opened his eyes just before noon on Monday. Dreaming of burning hogs, he had not heard the school bus honk. "Good morning, Sleepyhead."

The onslaught of emotions involved with the hogs, knowing he had missed school, not being told his parents would be here today made Jake irritable. He felt as if his private domain had been invaded. He jumped out of bed and started pulling on clothes.

Mattie frowned. "No hug?"

Jake calmed himself enough to give her a half-hug. "When did y'all get here? Where's Daddy?"

"Eating his dinner. Come join us."

Jake approached the table warily, hoping that nothing associated with pork was on it. Rance sat at his customary

spot, sipping his coffee from a saucer—a comforting sight. He
looked up at Jake through black horn-rimmed glasses. Jake
stopped and stared. The gaunt look his father had carried for
almost two years—the look that Jake had attributed to whiskey,
cigarettes, and hard work—was gone. Mattie put her hand on
Rance's shoulder. "Your daddy's already gained six pounds
since the surgery. Eats like a pig. But we have to be careful
about putting anything on his right side now. He's already
knocked over a couple of glasses of tea."

Jake took his usual seat. "Speaking of pigs, did you check
on ours?"

"We heard from JD. I've already been to the gully. You
did a good job. I'm sorry those pigs brought you so much
misery. If I had known ... how's everything else?"

Jake tried to examine the blind eye without staring. It
seemed as if his father had a whole new face. The weight gain
and the glasses changed him, but it was the blind eye that
changed him most. It moved like a regular eye, but had a
small fleck of white in the black part of the eyeball. The
piercing stare that had always stopped himself and his brother
in their tracks was gone—replaced with a softer, almost
questioning look that Jake would have to get used to.
"Suppose things around here are all right. Been checking our
cows and keeping hay out. Will Tom's cows seem pretty
content to graze the wheat—not tryin' the fences any."

"What about school?"

Jake looked at his watch and stood. "I'm late. Can't miss
basketball practice. I been goin' every day. Just stayed up too
late last night with the hogs and overslept today is all."

Jake arrived in time for his last two classes and for
basketball practice. He tried to figure what Floyd Knight had
meant by 'play better than you can' but could not. Relieved
that the responsibility for the Rivers' farm was back in his
parents' hands, he concentrated more during practice. He
was aggressive enough to take down a few rebounds and

scored on three fast breaks. Nocona elbowed him on the last
one and whispered. "Lighten up, dammit. You're gonna get
our asses run off. Watson hates it when the second string
wins. He'll make us take thirty laps."

Jake watched his parents sit in the stands for Tuesday
night's game in Adrian. Rance watched the game as if Jake
were playing. Jake knew he was analyzing every play. Mattie
stared at Jake as he sat on the bench, terrible pity in her eyes.
Jake vowed to ask them not to return. Adrian won their first
contest in several weeks against Hartley. In Texline Friday
night, Jake had a different audience. Mr. and Mrs. Sherwood
stopped him on the way to the locker at halftime. Jake was
still in his warm-ups, not a drop of sweat anywhere. He shook
Fred's hand and accepted a hug from Winnie.

"How's Coach Gee? We heard about his stroke."

Jake nodded. "Yeah. Last I heard, he's doin' better,
walkin' and things, but still can't talk."

Fred filled the awkward silence. "If it's any consolation,
he told me you were gonna be his team leader this year."

"Yessir. Thanks." Texline 58–Adrian 46.

It was after two when Jake crawled in the sack after the
game. Mattie and Rance let him sleep on Saturday morning.
Still disoriented by living alone, he seemed almost surprised
to see his mother in the kitchen. A hot breakfast of skillet
toast and hamburger steak seemed an improvement over the
cereal he had been eating. Mattie seemed to understand
about pork. She hummed over the sink as he ate silently.
"Who won last night?"

"They did."

"You get to play?"

"Never left the bench."

"Serves that coach right. What's he got against you?"

Jake shook his head—his signal that he did not want to
discuss it anymore. "Where's Daddy?"

"He's erasing all signs of those hogs, I think." Mattie

draped her dishtowel across the sink. "Jake, we really saw some pretty land for sale when we were home."

Jake examined the probing look in his mother's eyes. "That right?"

"Yep. Lots of trees." She wiped the already-clean table again. "Aren't you angry about the trouble you've had out here?"

Jake did not want this conversation to continue. "I ain't movin' back to East Texas, Mama. Took me too long to get used to it out here. I got lots of friends now, and I know my way around." He finished his last bite and stood. "Can I borrow the car?"

"Better ask your daddy what he has for you to do today before you run off."

He walked outside and followed the sounds of the Super M. Rance had disked and harrowed the lot. The smell of fresh earth was already erasing the smell of the hogs. He waited by the windmill tank until his father pulled the tractor into the yard and killed it. "You got anything you need me for today?"

"Nothin' that can't wait, I guess."

It was late afternoon when Jake returned from Amarillo. He pulled off 66 at the cutoff for home, stopped, and flipped open the boot box beside him. He touched the soft calfskin of the tan Tony Lamas, admired the shiny red tops. He pulled off the black Justins and slipped on the new boots. It had felt good to select his own boots rather than following Gabe's and Nocona's choices like a sheep. He backed out on 66 and headed west for Adrian.

Sage noticed the boots right away. "Nice boots. Where'd you get `em?"

Jake realized his mistake as soon as the question left her mouth. "Uh, my uncle bought `em for me. I helped him work a few cattle. I think he got `em at Teepee's in Amarillo. I always buy my boots from you, of course." Telling a white lie

307

to save feelings seemed the right thing to do.

Sage nodded without smiling. "So, what can I get for you in our little store? We don't carry boots like that."

Jake looked around the store as if he had come to shop. "Just killin' time, I guess." Her smile gave him a little courage. "Think maybe your daddy would let us ride around a little now?"

"Don't you think you should be more concerned about what I want?"

"Sure. I meant if it's okay with you."

She walked over to a hook and put on her blanket coat. "Let's go."

Jake wondered about asking Caleb, but decided not to question his luck.

She got in on Jake's side and slid to the midpoint of the plastic seat covers without noticing the full set of flippers. She smelled good in the car and Jake felt a strange sense of elation he had never felt with Charlotte riding beside him. It lasted until she spoke. "Heard you went to see Loretta."

Jake shot her a surprised look. "How do you know that?"

She ignored the question. "The baby is due any day now."

They rode in comfortable silence through dusty Adrian streets. Neither felt the necessity of idle conversation or the desire to stop for pie or Cokes at any of the cafes along 66. Jake finally stopped at the entrance to the Matador. They got out and walked past the school, the principal's house, and Coach Gee's house. They were surprised to see the coach and his wife sitting on their tiny porch. He waved them into the yard. It was too dark to see him clearly, but it was easy to detect several missing pounds and a slumped posture. He was smiling, though, and his wife seemed to know what he wanted to say. When she did not, he passed her a note—mostly awkward small talk. There was only room for two on the porch, so Jake and Sage stayed in the yard. When Mrs. Gee invited them inside, Jake saw an opportunity to leave.

"Thanks anyway. Got to get Sage in early."

As Jake turned, the coach stood and gestured for him to wait. He wrote a note and passed it directly to Jake instead of to his wife. It said, "Don't give up." Jake read it, nodded and walked away.

In front of Adrian Mercantile, Jake held the door as Sage slid out and stood beside him. He could feel her breath on his neck. He put a finger under her chin, took off his hat, and kissed her.

41 Jake felt lost on Sunday morning without pigs to feed. After breakfast, he cranked the GMC and drove to the north pasture, counting cows. He drove the wheat field fence and checked for any cows off their feet in Will Tom's herd. There were too many to get an accurate count from the pickup, and it was too cold to get out and walk through them.

The Boggs' Olds was in the yard when he returned. He listened to the adult conversation through dinner before asking to use the car to go to Adrian. The mercantile would be open for a few hours in the afternoon. Rance embarrassed him in front of company. "You been chasin' around since we got back. No need in goin' out every night. Two nights for ballgames and Saturday night is enough. Besides, there's something I want to show you later."

Jake pulled his practice dummy from the feed room in the red barn for the first time since Scar had died. He wondered if String would ever return—wondered if he knew about the hogs that had lived under his bedroom. He stood out of sight until he saw the Boggs' Olds head home. Rance intercepted him at the windmill. "Your granddaddy sent you a note. You ain't been still long enough for me to hand it to you."

Jake looked at the Ward's Gro. and Feed envelope from Klondike. "Papa wrote me a letter?" Writing was something Jake had never associated with his grandfather.

Rance clicked the Zippo he held in his hand. "Never knew him to write one, either."

Rance left him alone and Jake unfolded two pages with jagged top edges obviously torn from a Big Chief tablet. The words were printed and betrayed the slight tremor Jake had noticed in his grandfather's hands the last time he saw him.

Jake,

Your daddy has been telling me about some of your troubles out West. I started to come back with him and your mama to have a little chat like we used to, but I hated to ride a bus all the way back. If I know you, you're blaming yourself for your horse dying and your daddy's eye. I know how you feel about them pigs, too. Probably even blame yourself for your coach having a stroke. I figure you did a thing or two out there you regret and you figure The Almighty is swooping down and taking his vengeance on you and everybody around you.

You could be right, but I doubt it. It just don't make sense for Him to spend so much time dealing out punishment for a few bad choices you might have made. I'll bet things ain't as bad as you got them cracked up to be, either. Mattie says your grades are good and you did awful good at catcher in baseball I know you can play a good brand of basketball. You kids cut your teeth on basketballs. Rance says you are making a fair to middlin cowhand and farmhand and roped a calf nobody could catch and had him flanked and ready to tie when Scar gave out on you. Wish I had seen that. That little gelding had a lot of heart. Most men wait a lifetime to own a horse as good. Be grateful. His dying ain't your fault, either.

*I really wish I knew why these bad things happen, but I don't.
I guess we just don't need to know, or we would. I just think
The Good Lord don't interfere as much as most folks think he
does. He just gives us the equipment to deal with what comes
our way and kicks our butt out into the world. I don't think
he beats us up much after that, but helps as much as he can
when we ask for it. As long as it don't mess up things for the
next feller, he might even change things for us when we do ask
Him to. Seems to me, it's up to us if we use that equipment
from The Man Upstairs or not. I want you to start using
yours more. Be happy. Life is short. Everything ain't your
fault. Remember what I told you about appreciating the little
things that come your way.*

Love, Griffin Rivers

Jake folded the letter and leaned against the pump house,
listening to the windmill creaking and water dripping into
the tank until the house lights went out. Mattie surprised
him from the dark of the kitchen when he walked in the back
door. "Come in here, Jake."

Jake sat across from her. "How come you're sittin' in the
dark?"

"Shhh. I think your daddy is already asleep. Did you
know that Gray Boy is coming home next Friday? Says he'll
probably be here in time to see the big game."

"What big game?"

"The big game between Adrian and Vega, of course. I've
been hearing about that game since we missed it last year.
Everybody in Oldham County will be watching to see who's
champion of the county."

"No such thing as county champions."

"You know what I mean, Jake. It's a big tradition just like
we had back home in Delta County. Remember the rivalry
between Pecan Gap and West Delta? JD, Bess, Bob Lee, and a
few of their friends are coming, too. They always go, but they

never had a relative playing in it before."

"I played in it last year."

"I know, but they missed it because JD and Bob Lee were in Kansas. They say Vega has a big kid from Hereford playing this year that half the people in Deaf Smith County will be coming to watch, too. Bet there won't be an empty seat in the house."

"I'll have a place to sit—on the bench. Did you tell them I won't be playing—that I'll be warmin' the bench?"

"I told them, but they're just hoping you'll get to play a little. You know how JD likes to brag. I hear he's bet a hundred dollars on the game. Bob Lee says he bets somebody a hundred every year."

"Probably bet on Vega with Drager playin' for `em."

"Drager? Is he the big kid from Hereford?"

Jake groaned and stalked off to bed. He read his grandfather's letter again before placing it under his biscuit jar.

4 2 With Tuesday an open date for the Matadors, nothing diverted attention from the grudge game with Vega all week. A long week for Jake. Friday afternoon, he stared at the gym floor while Gabe and the other players gave speeches to fire up the student body. During a cheerleading yell, Sage pulled Jake to the gym floor. Embarrassed, he resisted. "Jake, just look." She jerked her head toward the north end of the gym. Jake followed the line until he saw the big preacher walking along the boundary line toward the classroom area of the school. Ken Watson was walking beside him. Jake left the pep rally, walked behind the bleachers and followed. He felt better and bolder just having Floyd Knight back in the Adrian school building.

As the noise from the pep rally abated, Jake watched as Coach Knight opened Principal Alderman's door and followed Ken Watson inside. *Was that a shove? Was Alderman in his office or in the gym with the pep rally?* Alderman's muffled voice answered Jake's question. Without a place to hide, Jake walked down the hall and got as close to the office as he could. The voices grew louder and more intense, but he could make out only a few words. The door opened and Ken Watson stepped out. Jake ran down the hall to the gym and the pep rally, hoping he had not been seen. He considered getting into the GMC and heading for home but decided to tell the truth if confronted—he had followed to see the Reverend Floyd Knight.

Jake was packing his gym bag for the game when Bob Lee burst into his room without knocking. "Ready for the big shootout, Jake? Lotsa money and pride riding on this game. Big tradition around here every year. This big German kid from Hereford is supposed to kick y'all's butts."

"Yeah, Mike Drager."

"You know him?"

Jake nodded grimly and went past him. He gave a cursory wave to JD and Bess and his parents as he passed through to get to the GMC. Gray Boy had still not shown, and Jake hoped his brother would not arrive in time to see him warm the bench.

The Adrian boys gathered on the porch of the Vega gym in twenty-six-degree weather, waiting for Coach Watson. He had forbidden the wearing of hats to ballgames, but fifteen black hats were on the porch. Wanting to show unity when they walked into the gym, the team had decided to defy their coach for this big game. At close to tip-off time for the girls' game, Nocona finally made a decision as co-captain to go inside. "Watson's got to be inside. Got his mind on the girls' game and forgot about us."

The gym felt like a sweatbox and smelled of old gym shoes, popcorn, hotdogs, cigars, and women's face powder. From the Adrian section of the bleachers, a coordinated roar distinguished itself from the din of chatter as the boys walked toward the locker room with their gym bags. The Adrian girls, still in warm-ups, stopped their warm-up shooting and began to clap. The boys returned their applause, and the Adrian crowd joined in. Vega supporters answered with a chorus of boos.

The gym rocked with noise and seemed on fire with smoke as the Adrian Matadors walked down the steps to the basement locker room. The team dropped their bags in the visitors' locker room and walked up the other stairs to a line of folding chairs on a stage beside the court. Both boys' teams would watch the girls' game from separate sides of the stage. Nocona poked Jake as Mike Drager stood and offered a bow-and-smirk to the Adrian team. He clapped until they took their seats. The rest of Vega's Longhorns remained silent.

Drager stood and violated rules by approaching the Adrian team. He stopped in front of Jake and Nocona. "Well, I'll be damned. Two little Indians. I thought I recognized the little one from somewhere. Now I know where." He pointed a finger at Jake. "Remember what I said about the Canadian? Now I got another reason."

Without getting up, Nocona reached out and lightly shoved Drager to the side with the back of his hand, peering around him toward the court. "We appreciate your comin' over to renew old friendships, but your mama shoulda told you it's rude to stand in front of people. I got a girlfriend playin' out there I can't see."

Drager smiled. "Things gonna be a lot different tonight than the last time I saw you two on a basketball court."

Nocona laughed. "Are you sure? Better wear a tight jock strap. I may decide to do it again." Drager returned to his seat.

They could not see the girls' bench from the stage. It was halftime before Jake saw Rance, Mattie, JD, and Bess on the top row of the bleachers in the Adrian section of fans. Bob Lee sat near the top of the Vega cheering section. It was just like Bob Lee to cheer for Adrian in the middle of Vega fans. Jake was watching his family when he felt a tap on his shoulder. Principal Alderman was standing behind him, and most of his teammates were already heading down the stairs to the locker room. When he stood, he noticed Charlotte sitting just below Bob Lee. He turned and followed his teammates down the stairs to the locker room.

Principal Alderman was leaned against a row of lockers, his foot on a metal folding chair as Jake took the last step down the stairs. The principal's round, gold-rimmed spectacles reflected the room's harsh light. He looked hot in his suit and tie. "Boys, Ken Watson won't be here tonight. He resigned his position as coach and teacher effective at the last bell today. I'm coaching the girls' team tonight and for the rest of the season. An old friend has graciously agreed to coach you boys."

A collective murmur filled the locker room as Floyd Knight stepped out of the shadows. "Sorry this had to happen with no notice. I know it's not fair to you boys, but life sometimes isn't fair. Believe me when I say that Mr. Alderman and myself wish that it could have been otherwise."

A few hands shot up. "Please hold all your questions—and I am sure you have many—until the game is over. Right now, let's try to concentrate on basketball. Most of you know that I know baseball a lot better than basketball, so I will be a figurehead tonight. We just can't field a team without a coach. I expect the co-captains to really run this game." Gabe and Nocona glanced at Jake as their heads came to attention. He did not return their looks.

Adrian girls had the game well in hand when the boys left for the locker room at the end of the third quarter. Mary Ann, Texie, and Sage had jelled late in the season. Sage was not Loretta on the basketball court, but Mary Ann and Texie were playing at the top of their games. It was too late for a district championship, but tonight marked five straight victories. Fresh with victory and still in their warm-ups, the girls formed a line on the floor as the boys' team emerged, shouting encouragement for the boys to make it a clean sweep. Jake was in line for crip shots when he noticed Nocona, Gabe, and Floyd Knight in a huddle. He dared not hope, but he did. His hopes were dashed when the usual starters took the floor.

Coach Knight walked to the end of the bench and squatted beside Jake with his back to the other bench-sitters. "This team has been starting for too many games, Jake. I just can't shake it up yet to satisfy your buddies. We have to do what's best for the team and what's fair for the boys who have been starting. If they get into trouble, you'll see some playin' time." Jake nodded, grateful that Gabe and Nocona had supported him. Jake tried not to look at his parents, but he searched for Gray Boy. No sign of his brother, but he did see that String had joined Bob Lee.

Jake tried to think of his grandfather's letter, to concentrate on what he had said to him before about being in the flow, but he could think of nothing but the shame he felt. The pity in his mother's eyes and the pity he knew was in his daddy's heart hurt worse than the shame. He could not bear being pitied. Even outclassed by taller and quicker Mike Drager, Jake wanted to play—wanted his chance to take the field of honor and excel in front of his family for this once-in-a-lifetime game.

He tried to concentrate on the game but found his mind wandering with his eyes as he looked around the old gym. The building reverberated with tension and excitement. Every shot, every turnover brought a roar from the crowd. Farmers and ranchers were not talking about crops or cattle; they were talking about basketball; they were talking about this game and the players in it.

Why? Why had he failed to notice it last year when he played this same grudge-match in the Adrian gym? Was it because he was so caught up in playing safe, embarrassment-free basketball that he failed to notice what was happening around him? Could he have been that self-conscious—that wrapped up in himself? Was he still? And why were these rural people, whose lives mostly revolved around cattle and crops, whipped with fervor about a ballgame between two tiny schools in the middle of nowhere that had no meaning in any record-book?

As the game went into the second quarter, most eyes were on Mike Drager. He owned the court like a champion gladiator in a Roman coliseum. Jake's stomach tightened as he recognized that his nemesis was a great high school basketball player—greater than Jake could ever aspire to be. He could palm the ball, dunk it, dribble with either hand, and shoot from outside or inside. He moved with speed and grace. Drager was moving both teams to another level as the players tried in vain to match his level of play. Even clumsy and slow Burt Donovan played above his head in holding Drager to sixteen points at half-time. He had incurred four fouls doing it. Adrian was down 38–23 when the boys came out of the locker room to start the second half.

43 They were doing light half-time warm-ups on the floor when the crowd noise changed from chatter to murmur. Jake followed the stares as Coach Alton Gee walked around the baseline toward the Matador bench. He walked slowly, but deliberately, unashamed to use the cane. He slapped a clipboard against his leg with his free hand. He took a seat beside Coach Knight and showed him the top sheet on the clipboard as the buzzer sounded.

Jake was already sitting on the bench when Coach Knight called his name. "Rivers, shuck the warm-ups. You're goin' in at point guard. Donovan, great game, but you're in foul trouble. I want you to sit out at least a quarter. Wells, you move to forward for Donovan. Let's see if we can do some damage control on Drager."

Coach Gee folded back the first sheet and showed the second. Coach Knight read it. "They're playing a defensive zone and protecting the basket. We have to shoot outside and bring them out or get ˙em to change to man-to-man. We have to speed it up if we're going to come back."

Coach Gee scribbled again and handed Jake the clipboard. Jake read it and nodded his head once as he handed it back. *Lard Bucket. Play with abandon!* The team did a group handshake and came out of the huddle. Nocona pointed at Jake and smiled through clenched teeth. "Rivers at point guard again. If you whip Bullard's ass like you did mine, we might just win this thing. I'll take Worm."

Gabe pointed at Jake and smiled. "You're co-captain again. Let's kick some ass."

Nobody came out of the zone to smother Jake as he dribbled down the court. He stopped just back of the free throw line and took an unobstructed jump shot for two. Nocona had not been a threat from the outside, so Vega assumed the kid off the bench would not be either. Jake certainly had not been a threat when they played last year. He dropped another easy one before the Vega coach called a time-out.

Jake stole the ball from Bobby Bullard just after the break and tossed it to Nocona for an easy shot under the basket. When Drager came out from his inside position to defend Jake on Adrian's next possession, Jake faked a shot and passed hard to Gabe under the basket. Swish. Eight unanswered points.

Nocona trash-talked Mike Drager, and pulled the hair on his legs. Angry, Drager started missing his shots. Adrian scored twelve unanswered points before Vega realized that momentum had shifted. At the end of the third quarter, the Longhorns' lead was down to eight—46–38. Floyd Knight was coming out of his lethargy and was animated. "We outscored `em fifteen to eight that quarter, boys. If we just repeat that this period, we'll still lose and that ain't good enough. Let's take it up a notch and really stick it to 'em in their own gym."

Jake rushed the ball down the court to the top of the circle and dropped a set shot for two more. Frustration mounting, Bobby Bullard fouled him after the shot. Jake sank his first free throw of the game. Vega 46–Adrian 41. He faked going back downcourt and dropped back while Bullard was in-bounding. He intercepted the pass for another easy two. 46–43. Gabe batted away Drager's hook shot, and Jake and Nocona took it downcourt two-on-one. Nocona dropped another two. 46–45. Drager drove the basket on the next possession, knocking Nocona to the floor. He made the shot and drew a foul, turning it into a three-point play for the Longhorns. 49–45.

Gabe missed a fade-away jump shot on the next possession, and Drager rebounded. He held the ball until everyone retreated across the centerline except one defender—Jake. Feeding on crowd fervor, Drager put on a dribbling exhibition, moving the ball behind his back and between his legs at will. He drove straight at Jake, and Jake fell back on his hands as Drager charged by.

Jake's butt never touched the floor as he whirled and ran up-court in time to get a hand on the ball as Drager dribbled it behind his back again. Nocona batted it toward Jake, and the race to the basket was on. Drager caught Jake on the right side in time to block an easy crip shot, but Jake switched to his left hand and bounced it high off the backboard into the net. He knew it had probably looked clumsy, but he had also known it was going in when it left his hand.

Drager took the ball out, and Jake was there to defend under the basket. "You lucky bastard. No way anybody makes a crappy no-chance shot like that."

Jake crouched and kept his eyes on the ball in Drager's hands. "Scoreboard says it counted." Vega 49–Adrian 47.

Drager took over the Vega team. He shouted instructions for defense, coming down hard on Bobby Bullard for allowing Jake to score at will. Drager scored four unanswered points. 53–47. In a time-out huddle, Nocona looked at Coach Gee and shrugged. "I don't know if I can stop the sumbitch." He turned toward Coach Knight. "Excuse me, Coach, but he's just a damn good basketball player." Coach Gee held up the clipboard. *Rivers - shooting 100%. Feed him the ball. Pull Drager*

*out to free up Gabe. Too slow down-court. Full-court press. Shoot
and steal—shoot and steal.*

Vega, up by six, surprised them with their own full-court
press. The gym was quiet for Jake now, and he welcomed the
Longhorn press. He liked the players scattered all over the
court instead of stacked under the basket. Fast basketball was
made for players his size. He in-bounded the ball to Gabe
and rushed up court. Gabe quickly passed to Nocona, who
caught Jake in the numbers with a bullet pass as he went by.
Jake dribbled down-court toward Bobby Bullard waiting alone
in the paint for Jake to go to the basket. Jake stopped at the
free throw line. Unhindered by a hand in his face, he sank
another easy two. 53–49.

The game now changed to slow motion for Jake as the
Matadors put on their press. He deflected a rushed bounce
pass from Vega's other guard and put up two more as Bobby
Bullard watched helplessly. 53–51—down by two. Frustrated,
Bullard rifled the ball to Drager, who drove it downcourt.
Gabe and Nocona waited under the basket. With thirty
seconds left, Drager stopped at the top of the circle. Nocona
got a hand in his face, and his shot went off the rim into
Gabe's hands. Gabe rifled it downcourt into Jake's waiting
hands. There was nothing between him and the basket when
he crossed the centerline. He was amazed when Drager
caught him at the top of the circle.

Jake slowed but kept dribbling, faked a move to his right,
switched hands and moved to Drager's left to drive the basket.
Drager's knee and long arm cut him off. Committed and
afraid of losing control of the ball or running out of time, Jake
rolled around the knee and Drager forced him to the corner,
his least favorite spot on the court. With three seconds left,
Jake faked the jump shot. When Drager's feet left the ground,
Jake jumped. The big hand was starting its descent, leaving
Jake a clear view of the bucket as he reached the top of his
jump.

The heel of Drager's open hand caught Jake just above his chin, slid across his lips, and raked his nose as Jake fell back. Flat on his back, Jake did not hear the official's whistle but saw his cheeks expand as he blew it, saw the ball swish through the net. He was on his feet before it hit the floor. 53–53. He felt a small trickle of blood running from his busted lip, saw Coach Knight waving a towel in his direction.

Hands on his hips, he walked out of the free throw circle toward the towel. As he slowly wiped the blood from his lips, he looked up into the stands. The Vega crowd protested the stalling. He found Rance's horn-rimmed glasses. His daddy's face had that new quizzical expression, his good eye a focused beam of support for his son. Mattie had both hands around her throat. JD was shouting and pointing a finger at a man two rows down. Jake wondered if it was his betting partner. Bob Lee was laughing as he talked to String. String kept his eyes on the hardwoods. Charlotte was looking around the gym and clapping. Jake did not know for whom. Nor did he care. No sign of Gray Boy. Too bad.

Jake looked at the clock. Two seconds. He could see and feel the floor vibrate with the clamor in the small gym; he could feel heat strong enough to blow out the windows, but he could only hear the wind stirring the windmill at home. The tail creaked as he clearly saw his grandfather leaning against the pump house. As he turned to walk back to the free throw line, he saw Sage, Mary Ann, and Texie on the sidelines, still suited in their Adrian uniforms, Texie pumping her arms, Mary Ann clapping and shouting, Sage quietly focused. Gabe stood on one side of the paint, Nocona on the other. Both were still as statues. Rebounds did not matter much at this point. Their eyes showed support.

Jake stepped to the line and glanced at Drager as the striped-shirt tossed him the ball. He rolled it in his hands, bounced it once, set it in his left palm with his right hand behind it, focused on the Mrs. Tucker's lard can in front of him, lifted the ball with his right hand, rolled it off his fingertips, broke his wrist as it left on a perfect arc. Swish. 53–54. Jake felt the gym floor vibrate again as the crowd clamored. The noise was deafening as the clock started and ticked off two seconds before the buzzer sounded. Jake heard the buzzer–the silence gone.

Mike Drager threw the ball down-court like a football. It bounced off the backboard hard. Drager walked by Jake as he left the floor. "No way you damn cowboys can ever beat us. No damn way."

Nocona heard it. "Nice game to you too, Worm."

Celebrating too long or too enthusiastically was considered bad sportsmanship, so the Matadors made their way slowly through the crowded gym floor to the locker room. Jake smelled Sage's mixture of sweet sweat and shampoo as she squeezed his arm, welcomed Mary Ann's bear hug, acknowledged the pats on his butt and back by nodding his head and smiling. He followed Nocona and Gabe down the stairs, where the boys were shouting and jumping. They quieted as Coach Gee and Coach Knight joined them.

Coach Knight put his arm across Coach Gee's shoulders. "These are Coach Gee's words, boys, not mine." He paused before the shout. "One hell of a game." Another roar from the team. Both coaches shook each player's hand as they walked around the room. Coach Knight stopped as he came to Jake. He waved a clipboard in the air before he brought it to eye level. "Jake Rivers. Eighteen points. Four steals. Three rebounds. Field goal shooting percentage–one hundred; free throw shooting percentage–one hundred." Jake smiled at his bare feet and acknowledged the team shout.

"You boys want to go on celebrating, or do you want your answers now?"

Nocona looked up from untying his shoes. "Tell us now, Coach." Murmurs of assent.

The Reverend Coach Floyd Knight held a hand up for

silence. "If you don't mind, I'd like to say a word of prayer first." He waited for bowed heads. "Heavenly Father, I know you are here and have been here since the beginning. I have always thought you did not interfere in sporting games, but we are grateful that these boys played their hearts out tonight and take home a well-deserved victory. Amen."

Coach Knight's smile dissolved into a solemn expression as he raised his head. "Ken Watson is not here and will not ever return because he betrayed a sacred trust—the trust that parents bestow on teachers when they place their children in their hands. His violation was so egregious that he had to leave at once." The big man took the stairs out of the locker room before questions could be answered.

Nobody said anything until Coach Gee had followed him. Burt Donovan broke the silence. "What does egregious mean?"

Gabe answered. "Bad, Burt, bad. He didn't just bend the rules; he broke 'em, tore up the rulebook, and tossed it out the window."

Talk was confined to the game until the showers were done and gym bags repacked. They had decided to leave the way they came in, as a team. Jake and Nocona were the last to step out of the locker room and onto the gym floor. Nocona, smelling of powder and cologne, whispered in Jake's ear. "I'm getting' Texie and headin' to Adrian. We're all meeting at the Bent Door." Jake smiled and kept walking.

Nocona stood in front of him to get his attention. "You know that sumbitch punched Loretta's ticket and let you take the blame, don't you?" Jake nodded as he walked out the gym door.

44 He pulled the collar up on his maroon wool letter
jacket with black leather sleeves as he stopped
under the gym porch. Jake was surprised and
disappointed that the crowd was mostly gone. Adulation
had been nice while it lasted. The baby blue Ford stood out
among mostly dark cars just a few feet from where he stood.
Rance and Mattie walked toward him. He had to pull a cold
hand out of his jacket pocket to catch the tossed keys.

Rance touched his heart as if the words in there did not
match the ones that came out of his mouth. "We figured you
might want to celebrate with your friends. You take the Ford,
and we'll drive the pickup. Radio says it's in the teens, and
you know this old truck is kinda cold natured. Your mama's
afraid you'll freeze."

Jake stared at the keys and caught the kiss his mother blew
him. "Uh, thanks."

He listened as the GMC engine turned a couple of
extra times before it finally came to life, trying to remember
when he had last checked the anti-freeze. Mattie waved and
smiled as they pulled away. Smoke curled from the tailpipe
of the Adrian girls' team bus as it idled on the parking lot.
Jake figured Principal Alderman was being extra cautious

with some type of departure checklist. He had been overly protective of the girls all night.

The Ford's door stuck a little when he opened it. The GMC's heater did not work, and Jake wondered why his parents had not sat in the Ford to keep warm. Little ice crystals were on all the windows. As he turned the key, he saw a blonde with cat-eye glasses through one of the crystals. Charlotte knocked on his window, and he rolled it down. She flashed her mischievous smile and bounced a little to ward off the cold. "Just wanted to say nice game to the hero." She chattered her teeth a little too much to suit Jake. He noticed she was wearing a Vega letter jacket several sizes too big for her.

He cranked the Ford before answering. "Thanks. Saw you in the crowd. Who'd you yell for?"

"I cheered for you in my heart, but I do go to school here, you know." She looked off into the distance toward downtown Vega and her house and noticeably shivered. The Adrian girls' team bus began moving out of the parking lot. Jake turned the defroster up to high and tried to see through the windshield. Through the thin crust of ice on the side window, he thought he saw Sage looking at them. She did not wave. Charlotte put cold lips to his while he was looking at the bus.

"I'll buy you a cup of coffee and sweeten it for you."

He stared at her until her smile started to fade. Charlotte's smile was fetching. It was what attracted him to her in the beginning. "Sure, but we'll have to make it quick. I have to pick up Gabe in Adrian." Another white lie. He did not want to mention the Bent Door celebration because he was sure she would want to go.

Jake gulped down coffee he did not want and stood before Charlotte's cup was half-empty. She took another sip and stood beside him. "You afraid Gabe's gonna stand out in the cold and wait for you?"

"I told him I'd be there. I always do what I say I will."

Jake was disappointed that Charlotte's father's truck was not parked in front of the house. When he was home, they seldom stayed in the car longer than a few minutes. He killed the engine, gave her a perfunctory hug and stepped out.

She stayed in the car. "Jake, you're hurting my feelings. Never seen you so anxious to get rid of me."

"Told you why. Hate to, but I got to go." He was watching little sparks of static electricity fly from the plastic-covered seat as Charlotte slid across when he heard the rumble of twin pipes, inhaled a little dust and fumes as the white Chevy pulled diagonally in front of him. Its bumper nudged the small picket fence. Jake turned as the expected Pink Olds parked behind him. "Well, shit. Here we go again." He hated himself for not asking Nocona to wait.

Like a bad movie seen twice, Drager emerged with the tire iron held close at his side. This time, Bobby Bullard and four other members of the Vega basketball team stepped out of the pink Olds. In Bobby's right hand, Jake recognized a Louisville Slugger like he had used in Little League. Drager spoke as Charlotte slinked back behind the wheel of the Ford. "You forget what I told you would happen next time we caught you over here?"

"Don't know what to tell you, Drager. Just work hard and save all your money." Jake borrowed Bob Lee's phrase to give him time to think. "My daddy's the only one that gets to tell me where I can and can't go. Beside, you forget we had a basketball game over here tonight?" He licked his split lip and smiled at Drager. "Y'all lost, by the way."

Drager and Bobby each took a step forward with their weapons. Bobby pointed the bat at Jake. "You ain't gonna feel much like braggin' about it when we send you home in a tow sack."

Jake drew small comfort from what he thought was a hesitant, tentative tone in Bobby's voice. He felt sure the part about the sack was a bluff, but it did not take away his fear and loneliness. "Always heard Vega was a bunch of lousy sports, but you boys seem to be takin' it a little far. Hell, you ain't even got the guts to face me without a bat or tire tool with you. Why don't y'all just follow me to Adrian; I'll gather up our team, and we'll kick your asses again."

Drager walked over to the car and tugged on Charlotte's jacket sleeve. "See that? It's mine. I warned you to stay away from our girls."

Jake looked up and down the street, hoping to see the deputy sheriff. He occasionally patrolled the street at night. "Ain't my problem you boys can't hold onto your girls."

Drager slapped the tire iron against one of Jake's flippers and bent it. Charlotte emitted a little squeak as Jake charged him, grabbing the tire iron as they went down. Jake lost his grip when a baseball bat against his throat pulled him back. He could tell that Bobby had left the gym without taking a shower. Drager pulled the tire iron back and stood as Jake fell back on Bullard. Jake was kicking at Drager and pulling on the baseball bat when a long duffle dropped on the ground at Drager's feet.

Jake saw the tire tool spinning through the air, heard it land on the trunk of the white Chevy, slide across, and make a satisfying clinking sound as it hit the back window. A cloud had been obstructing the moon, but it drifted by as Jake looked up into his brother's smiling face. A day's growth of dark beard turned his dimples into dark lines down his cheeks that contrasted with his long, almost-feminine eyelashes. Jake imagined him in full Marine dress, but Gray Boy was wearing an old letter jacket from Klondike and faded, starched Levis. He must have peeled off the uniform as soon as he left the base.

Adrenaline pumping, Jake bounced to his feet with the bat in his hands when Bullard released his hold. The bat felt like an old friend as he swung it and hit Bobby a glancing blow as he ran toward his teammates. Slight pressure from Gray Boy's hip told Drager to stay put. Jake dropped the bat in the dirt and drew several deep breaths before speaking. "Where'd you come from?"

Gray Boy nodded toward the Burger Hut. "Bus dropped me off over at that little shithole burger joint. I called Bob Lee to pick me up. Old man over there said you might be here. Also said you kicked some ass in the game. Sorry I missed it."

Jake nodded. "Sorry you did, too. Played above my head."

Drager regained his voice. "You can say that again."

Gray Boy looked into Drager's eyes as he spoke to Jake. "Who are these assholes, and why are they pickin' on you?"

"This is the starting lineup for the Vega Longhorns. They been trying to run me out of Vega for months now." Jake jerked a thumb toward Drager. "Remember I told you about a big kid jumping me my first day at Hereford? This is him." Jake felt courage drifting from his brother's veins to his own. He had fought Gray Boy more times than he could remember. Recalling those defeats brought heat to his blood again.

Gray Boy kept his eyes locked on Drager, who was looking toward his car. "This is your fight, little brother. You want to just kick the shit out of ` em now? You want the big one first? Damn, look at the size of those feet." Gray Boy put a finger by the side of Drager's eye. "Remember what I told you about chicken-shits? This one is a real chicken-shit. Man pulls a weapon like a tire iron and don't use it right away, he don't intend to use it." Gray Boy ran a thumb down Drager's cheek. "Bet he's made a lot of threats, too. Fighters don't threaten you; they just walk up and knock hell out of you."

Gray Boy turned toward the other boys. "And these other boys, their hearts ain't in it. I can see it in their eyes. Y'all had rather be home with your mamas, hadn't you?" Two heads, including Bobby's, nodded before they could stop

333

them. Gray Boy laughed and turned back toward Drager. "See that white in the corner of his eyes? That's chicken shit. There's so much of it in this big boy, it goes all the way from those big feet and runs out his eyes. Never seen it stacked so high."

Jake pushed Drager away from the flipper and dropped to one knee to examine the damage. "Damn."

Gray Boy kneeled to take a look. "Damn, Jake, you're harder on Daddy's cars than I was. This thing ain't six months old and already skinned up bad." He stood and looked toward the Burger Hut. "Well, I'm getting' tired of messin' with these little dipshits. Do whatever you're gonna do and let's get it over with. If I was you, I'd just send the little one and his buddies on their way. They won't bother you anymore. If they do, just pick one, go straight at him and hit him as hard as you can before he has time to think about it. Don't talk; just kick the livin' shit out of him."

"This big one, though, he's sneaky. He'll do something behind your back. I'd loosen a few of his teeth before I sent him home to his mama. He's pretty big, though. If he starts gettin' the best of you, I'll step in."

Jake stood beside Drager, knowing he was being tested as much as the other boys. His brother wanted to see what kind of man he had become. He was tired of being tested. All of his brother's past admonitions ran through his head. *Don't talk, just fight. Get in the first lick and make it hurt.* He could not keep from thinking about how much his head and hands hurt for weeks after he fought his brother and after his previous scrape with Drager. He recalled Gray Boy's return from boot camp with loose teeth and scabs for knuckles. He thought of the nail in his daddy's eye. Jake did not want to lose any teeth or an eye, but the dented flipper was the last straw. It was either stand up now or endure everlasting shame. He licked his split lip again.

Still standing beside his nemesis, Jake bent forward and

swung backward without warning, hitting Drager in the nose
with the back of his fist. He remembered that Drager was a
nose-bleeder. Blood poured out his nose and into his open
mouth as Charlotte squeaked again. Jake drove his shoulder
into Drager's side, pushing him away from the Ford and onto
the trunk of the Chevy. The rage that only Gray Boy could
tap was released. He straightened and hit Drager in the side
just below the ribs. He heard the breath escape, felt his power
rising, felt the high his brother must feel when he fights.

Gray Boy stepped in the path of the advancing Vega team
and shouted a warning to Jake when Bobby Bullard went
around him and headed for the bat. Jake turned and beat
him to it. He hit Bobby in the side of the knee as he was
retreating toward his car. Bobby screamed but kept limping
toward the Olds.

Jake heard doors slamming and the pink Olds spinning
away as he walked back toward Drager with the bat, intending
to break a knee. If they fought again, it would be on equal
terms. Like he was scattering a group of stray cats, Gray Boy
waved his arms and ran a few feet after the escaping boys
before turning back to Jake and Drager. Drager dodged
Jake's tired swing, and the bat broke a taillight instead of his
knee. Out of breath, Jake managed to knock out a headlight
and slam the bat down on the Chevy's hood as Drager drove
away.

Jake thought it was ended, but Gray Boy's thirst was not
quenched. Adrenaline was pumping too hard to quit now.
Jake's fight had brought Gray's blood to a boil. He opened
the Ford's door and pushed Charlotte over. "Hi, Cutie. Get
in, Jake. He's gettin' away." Jake managed to jump in the
moving car as they sped away.

Jake cringed as the Ford careened through downtown
toward 66. "Where you goin'? He went the other way."

"I know he did, but there ain't nothin' out that way. I'm
bettin' he'll come down 66 and turn on 385 to take his big ass

home. We probably can't catch him if he keeps going west, but if he comes back ... ."

Jake was disappointed when he saw that his brother was right. Drager was coming down 66 from the west doing at least eighty. Gray Boy punched the Ford against the red light and started west in the wrong lane—headed straight for the Chevy. Drager slammed on the brakes and tried to pull off the road, but it was too late. Jake put his hands against the dashboard as Charlotte's scream combined with a sickening crunch. Jake and Gray Boy bailed out in time to see Drager hurdle a chain link fence behind a garage and disappear.

A caved-in passenger door, broken taillight and headlight, and dented and scratched hood and trunk made the once-beautiful Chevy a sorry sight. The Ford fared a little better. The front bumper was bent and showed white paint, but it was not crushed. Jake walked over to pick up a new flipper that had been thrown off in the wreck. It was bent, but possibly reusable. He still had the bat in his hands and started to use it to finish off the Chevy, but it still retained too much of its former beauty to do that. His anger was spent.

Bob Lee, arm hung out the window of his black '57, parked and whistled. "Damn. Daddy says I'm rough on cars, but I do believe you boys got me beat."

Gray Boy was still looking at the fence that Drager had hurdled. "Want to go after the son-of-a-bitch, Jake?" He was clearly enjoying himself.

Jake looked at the carnage and at Charlotte. She seemed as perky as ever. "No. Let him go. I'm done. Get in, Charlotte."

Jake passed Yellow Eyes walking down the shoulder of 66 as he took Charlotte home. The old Indian nodded at Jake. In front of Charlotte's house, Jake reached across her to open the passenger door and looked the other way until she closed it. Feeling sick, he headed home. It was too late to join the celebration—too late to be the hero at his team party.

45 Gray Boy helped Jake and Rance repair the Ford. Except for dented flippers, it looked as well as could be expected after compounding, waxing, and hammering. His brother stayed long enough to see Jake start and play the last two games of the season. Jake increased his level of play and point production a little, but not much. He played like most small point guards playing for small schools everywhere.

He ran into Mike Drager a few times as Snake cruised Vega in his new 1960 dark blue Chevrolet—Charlotte by his side. When they saw each other in the close quarters of the Burger Hut, Jake was relieved when Mike was courteous, almost friendly. Nothing was ever said about the damage to either car. Both knew that further argument would bring physical pain to both. Jake's anger had dissipated, and Drager no longer mattered to him. Maybe his brother had been right when he said to make it painful for bullies, even if you lose.

When Charlotte asked him to take her for a ride, he found an excuse not to. Jake developed a renewed interest in Marty, Bobby Bullard's old girlfriend, and Bobby did not seem to mind. They even laughed about what had happened that night. Bobby expressed gratitude that his beloved pink Olds had escaped damage. Jake wondered if they might have become friends if not for Drager's influence.

Basketball fervor went into hibernation at Adrian when neither team when into post-season play. Crops and cattle always overshadowed volleyball and baseball for most of the community, but not for Jake. He loved them both. His life seemed almost perfect as he played one sport and looked forward to the other. Floyd Knight inspired him as a teacher and coach. Loretta and John Bill even visited the class once and brought along the baby boy. Coach Gee still could not speak, but Floyd became his voice for both boys' and girls' teams.

Jake traveled to Adrian every night that his parents allowed, discovering that the remote little town on the prairie offered endless entertainment if you knew a lot of people and where to find them. He accepted his permanent role as the new kid in town and even began to relish it. When he was not with Gabe or Nocona, he traveled dusty streets and back roads with Sage and Mary Ann. Sage became his regular partner at school events, though they never discussed going steady. Mary Ann went along on most of their dates, looking the other way when they asked her to. When there was not a school function and they tired of the cafes along 66, they parked on the Matador or at Mary Ann's ranch, sat under the stars and talked. There were lots of dances in the basement of Texie's house and a few Coke parties in the basement at Adrian Mercantile.

Jake sensed that this was a special time that must be captured and held like a small bird that would soon fly away. As winter closed, he began to feel rushed—compelled to suck the marrow out of his Panhandle life while he could. He felt the small bird dying a little with every joyous time or new discovery and began to unconsciously squeeze it tighter. He avoided his parents whenever possible but had overheard

enough conversations to know that the decision to return to
East Texas had been made. When Rance and Mattie told him
they would be moving before summer, he stormed out of the
house and did not return until the wee hours of the morning.
He began taking his meals apart from them and plotted
different ways to punish them for failing him. But when he
became too defiant, he always heard the whistle of a ten-penny
nail.

Mattie had already put up the supper dishes when Jake
walked in the back door. It was near dark, and Jake's plate sat
untouched on the kitchen table. Rance's voice interrupted
Jake's direct trip to his room. Rance was pulling a coat and
hat from the rack by the door. "Fences in good shape?"

Jake answered without looking. "Why wouldn't they be?"

"Any cows down?" Will Tom Sunday's cows were grazing
their wheat again this year. Jake checked them twice a day.

"Nope."

"Keep your coat on. We need to go to the north pasture
and check ours. Late norther supposed to be comin' in."

Jake stared out the window of Rance's pickup as they
passed Scar's grave. When Rance slowed at the gully where all
the pig remains were buried, Jake heard the ten-penny whistle.
"Losing that eye bother you a lot?"

"It ain't no picnic. I have a few more headaches, but I can
do most of the stuff I always could."

"Then why are we leavin'? If it's because of your stomach
or eye or somethin' like that ... if you ain't up to farmin' the
whole place, I could help more."

"I'm stronger than I was when we came out here, Jake.
Dr. Olen fixed my stomach problems. No more pain. And I
about got this Panhandle farmin' figured out."

"Then why? Seems like we had some good wheat and
maize harvests. Are we broke?"

"Guess we been pretty lucky with our crops if you leave
out the pigs. I think I even got some money made in the

equipment after I fixed everything that was broke."

"I want to finish high school out here, Daddy. Changing twice was hard. Three times ain't fair."

Rance stopped the pickup. "Life ain't always fair, Jake."

"Fairer to some than others."

"Sounds strange I know, but losin' the eye made me see a little clearer, I guess."

Jake shrugged as he realized that this trip was not to check cows.

"I never could sit down and talk with my kids the way your granddaddy did. Every time I started to tell one of you something I'd learned about life, I'd think of something else that flies right in the face of what I was about to say. I get confused because life is confusing. It's contradictory."

"Sure is to me."

"I've always been a floater, Jake."

"A floater?"

"Remember when we used to swim under the bridges on 24? How I could float on my back with my head and feet out of the water without moving my arms? When Papa told me about the flow, I thought he meant that I could just float along and things would take care of themselves." He smiled at a distant memory. "He let me know pretty quick what he meant by staying between the banks."

Jake laughed. "Means staying on the straight and narrow, out of trouble."

"Yep, but that's only half right. Stayin' in the flow doesn't mean just not fighting the current or trying to swim upstream. I learned that you still have to paddle yourself away from rocks and boulders to keep your little ship of life goin'. Every once in a while, you might go completely under the water or over a waterfall."

"Like losin' Tuck or your eye."

"Or your problem with Yellow Eyes and the Drager kid ... or the preacher's daughter."

Jake wondered how his daddy knew about these things. "Ain't that just bad luck?"

"Never cared much for that word luck. Seems like believin' in luck sorta encourages us to be lazy. We take all the good luck we can get like there's no cause for it, without bein' grateful, then blame bad luck when things happen to us. Keeps us from encouraging the good and doing something about the bad."

A whistle across the windshield announced the norther's arrival. Jake was trying to figure out what this all had to do with leaving a place he had come to love. "Like paddlin' our own boat."

"Yes. My mother used to say that the current of life doesn't ever stop. It slows down, speed ups, goes off course, but we can't stop steerin' ... can't get off unless we're ready to die."

"So you never got in the flow out here? Is that it?"

Rance looked up at the windmill. "No. Believe it or not, I felt the flow when I took that windmill apart and put it back together again. Even hearing that old GMC run smooth after an overhaul put me in the flow. Papa always said it was the ordinary things like that we don't appreciate."

Jake ventured the question haunting him. "So what does this all have to with us givin' up and leaving? You know I won't be eligible for sports my senior year back there."

"I know what I'm trying to say is confusing, Jake. I don't see it as giving up. I see it as steering the boat we're in. Your mother and me are trying to be happy." Rance turned in the seat to face Jake. "I plan on leasin' a little land and runnin' a few cows. This new place we bought has lots of oak trees and the whisper of wind blowing through post oaks puts me in the flow. I can almost hear `em callin' me."

They listened to the wind without speaking, and Jake's mind wandered. "Think I was in the flow during that game in Vega?"

"Only you know that."

"How come I wasn't in it the next two games then?"

"Flow is what happens when that river of life takes us to heights we never thought we could reach. That's special. If it was easy and constant, it wouldn't be the flow."

"So how does Papa stay in it all the time?"

Rance cranked the truck and headed back. "Papa has had a lot more practice than me or you. He told me once that he learned how to do it late ... after his kids had left home and Mama died. Maybe you and me will get as good as he is one day. The thing is to keep on reachin' and tryin'."

"I think that's what I'm tryin' to do, Daddy. Going back east may make you and Mother happy, but not me."

Rance parked the truck in its usual spot. "That's what I wanted to talk about. Your mother and me want you to go back with us, but we know that may not be fair. It may be time for you to steer your own boat ... for a while, at least. Will Tom's buying our cattle. Bob Lee's takin' our lease and buyin' most of the equipment. Says you can stay here till school's out in the spring. Will Tom says he'll even pay you a little to look after the cows. JD and Bess agreed to look in on you regularly. Understand—this is not what we want you to do. You belong with us."

"What about this summer and my senior year?"

"One step at a time."

Jake opened the door and Rance reached over and grabbed his arm. "I've made some mistakes, Jake. I guess we'd both be lucky if you learned as much from what I do wrong as what I do right."

Jake did not sleep much that night. Rance's talk had taken him completely by surprise. Although he had threatened to take a job on a ranch or stay in the bunkhouse at Gabe's, the threats had been empty. This might actually work. At daylight, he braved the north wind and walked to the windmill. He pulled the brake and listened to the creaking as the fan came to a stop. He watched the goldfish for a few minutes until he got cold and walked back, stopping beside the Ford.

The black marks and dents made by Yellow Eyes, the bent flippers from Snake Drager seemed to tell a story—his story. Through the back glass, he noticed that the plastic seat covers had started to yellow and crack around the back ledge. They seemed to be ruining the seat cushions they were meant to protect. Jake opened the door and starting unhooking. When he pulled the last of the plastic covers into the yard, he knew he was going to stay.

His decision cast a pall over the house. Jake heard his parents arguing almost every night. Mattie had agreed to give him the choice, but she had never expected that he would decide to stay. When she acquiesced, her comments always referred to Jake's being gone for a 'couple of weeks' or 'just till school's out'. Jake went along. On the day they left, Bess and Mattie clucked over Jake until the last minute. In the yard, he shook hands with his father and hugged his weeping mother before they drove away.

It was the lack of furniture that struck him first. He expected to miss his parents, but he had not expected to miss the furniture. Mattie might have given in on letting him stay, but she showed her intention for him to follow by taking his bedroom suite and almost everything else in the house. Jake was left with a rollaway bed borrowed from Bob Lee. His folding clothes were in two cardboard boxes. Rance moved an old refrigerator from the shop into the house that could be left behind when Jake decided to follow them. That was it. Jake ate off the same plate and drank from the same glass every meal. He took his laundry to a Mexican lady in Vega. He knew he was being tested and was determined to pass.

Instead of the visits from Sage and Mary Ann he had

anticipated, he usually found Bess, JD, or Bob Lee in his yard every night. Caleb Pirtle knew that Jake was living alone and had taken the keys to the Goat away from Sage. She had to be home an hour earlier every night, but Jake stretched his grocery shopping time at Adrian Mercantile as much as possible. He stayed out long past midnight on the first couple of weekends, but found few friends who could join him. It bothered him to come home to a cold house. Mattie had brought a warmth that he had not appreciated.

46 On his third Friday alone, a late spring snow greeted Jake as he crawled into the muddy GMC to check Will Tom's cows before the school bus arrived. By the time the bus dropped him off that afternoon, a warm south wind had raised the temperature into the upper forties and changed the snow to rain. He stayed home that night, surprised at his fear of getting stuck and stranded. It was still raining when he heard a daylight knock on the back door Saturday morning.

Jake, shirtless and barefoot, opened the door and peeked around the dirty-boot-hut to see Will Tom Sunday. "Mornin' Jake." Will Tom was flanked by String and two other slickered and mounted cowboys. "Somebody told me there was a fair hand with cattle living in this house."

Jake had started to shiver. "Nope. Nobody like that here."

Behind streams from his hat brim, Will Tom's face got serious. "We got to move the cattle off the wheat, Jake. This rain is supposed to keep up for two more days. Any longer, we might not be able to get 'em. They'll tromp hell out of the crop."

"Can you get trucks in here?"

"That's just it. We're gonna drive `em over to 214 where there's a paved road. You've seen the big loading pen over there."

Jake knew where it was. "What do you need me to do?"

"We need another cowboy."

"I ain't got a horse."

String moved forward on Pink, leading a small sorrel mare with a roached mane and a white star and snip. Her tail was trimmed to her hocks. A slicker draped across the saddle. It was cold and wet and the rollaway bed beckoned. Another test. "Let me throw on some clothes and I'll be right out."

The two cowboy-strangers looked impatient when he emerged. The slicker soaked his dry clothes as he put it on. He had searched to no avail for a rain cover for his Resistol. The black Justins were just about to get that look he wanted, but this rain would dry and crack the leather. Couldn't be helped. The little sorrel was clearly unhappy to be working in this kind of weather and bowed up as Jake tightened the cinch. Jake sensed String's influence when the stirrups fit him perfectly. His butt had barely touched the seat when the cowboys rode off. Jake followed, adjusting the slicker over himself and the saddle as he rode. He stood in the stirrups in the vain hope that the seat might dry.

Will Tom had the gate open and the fence down for several yards when Jake rode through. They walked along the edge of the wheat field until they were behind the cattle. A cowboy in a hat with a five-inch brim blew a loud shushing noise through his toothless mouth, followed by blubbering from loose lips. The cattle hardly noticed. Will Tom nodded to a stooped cowboy on a dapple-gray. He pulled a leather string behind his saddle and came up with a long bullwhip in his right hand. He stood in his stirrups, circled it above his head and popped it. "Heeyaaa!" His partner followed suit. A few heads stopped grazing and stared.

The sorrel flinched and shook himself. The vibrating body under him brought Jake to life. He had never seen a bullwhip used to move cattle. It defied everything that his daddy and granddaddy had told him about working cattle.

Will Tom moved his horse beside Jake. "These cows ain't gonna want to move away from their wheat in this downpour. Buford and Drexel are tryin' to get ˈem to move without us having to bog our horses out in that wheat field any more than we have to."

"Buford and Drexel?"

"Buford's the one without teeth. Drexel is his brother. Pretty good old boys from Wildorado. Dayhands. I've used ˈem before." Will Tom pointed north. "Soon as the herd starts movin', go through that north fence and plant your horse on the road to keep ˈem from heading toward your house."

"How am I gonna get through that fence?"

Will Tom pointed to fence pliers resting in a small scabbard on the skirt of Jake's saddle as he pulled away, waving and yelling at the cattle. String held his rope in one hand and waved it. "Heeyah." The cattle complained with bellows as they started moving toward the gate.

Jake recalled helping his father build the two-strand fence as he leaned down from the saddle and cut both strands. He put the sorrel into a fast walk toward his house and did not turn around until he was almost to the equipment yard. He knew the cattle would shy away if he stayed too close to the gate, but he still had to be close enough to discourage them from coming his way. The sorrel showed her impatience as Jake planted her in the road. She knew what was ahead and wanted to get close to the cattle. The first few head glanced in his direction before turning south. A full symphony of moos and bellows drifted through the rain. Jake heard Eddy Arnold singing *Cattle Call*.

Jake knew the direction, but not the route they would

be taking. He fell in behind the cattle as they headed south, hoping that String or Will Tom would give him specific instructions. It was a false hope. Another test.

He knew that riding drag was usually assigned to the greenest hand, so he stayed in that position. Drexel and Buford strung out on the west, keeping the cattle away from the weak fence. The rain slowed a little, and Jake started to relax enough to appreciate what was happening. Will Tom had estimated the distance at twelve to fifteen miles. A hundred and fifty head of cattle were strung out on the road in front of him—a spectacle he had seen only in picture shows. He imagined himself as Matthew Garth, Will Tom Sunday as Tom Dunson and String as Cherry. His imaginary bubble burst when the cattle reached a tee in the road. They had to go east or west. String and Pink were already blocking the west.

The herd was heading east in a trot and picking up speed when he heard a loud whistle. Will Tom and String were standing in their stirrups, gesturing south with both hands. Jake did not know what that meant and held up his hands to indicate his confusion. String hollered and waved hard for him to head east. Jake could not hear him, but the gestures were urgent. He left his drag position and started passing the herd. He held the sorrel to her second gait, fearing that running her by the cattle might cause a stampede. The front of the herd had already passed the road leading south when Jake saw it. He felt stupid for not remembering it was there.

He cut across at the tee and pushed the sorrel into a run. When he was fifty yards ahead of the herd, he turned the mare and started waving his hat and shouting. The cattle looked at fences on both sides of them, and then kept coming straight at him. A hundred and fifty cattle were going to run all the way to 385. Trucks would run into them—people and cattle would die and it was going to be Jake's fault.

Panicked, he crisscrossed the road, waving his arms and

shouting. Most of the herd slowed, but two of the leaders picked up speed. On dry ground, he might have been able to stop one cow if the mare could cut, but there was no way he could stop two on slippery mud. Desperate, Jake charged the leader, a big high-headed Hereford cow with some age on her. He figured the mare would pull aside at the last minute or come to a dead stop on her front feet, and he would find himself sliding down the road on his face. Maybe that sight would stop the herd—or maybe they would run over him. Getting run over was preferable to letting them run all the way to the highway.

Jake was shocked when the mare hit the big cow at full speed, sliding only a little at the last second. The cow stumbled and fell; the mare stumbled as she tried to jump her; Jake fell across her neck, losing both reins and his hat. The leaders stopped and looked around at their options—fences on each side, a cow and horse down in the middle of the road, and a boy lying across the horse's neck. It was the ominous black hat lying several feet in front of the wreck that scared them into stopping.

Jake reached for the reins and righted himself as the mare came up from her knees. He wondered if he would ever have children after that painful collision with the saddle horn. He winced, but managed enough strength to start crisscrossing with the mare again, waiting to see his hat destroyed. The leaders began to turn and head back toward the south road they were supposed to take in the first place. Jake was picking up his hat and wiping mud with his sleeve when Will Tom reached him.

"Guess I should have told you we were going to head `em down this road, Jake."

Muddy reins in his hand, Jake shook his head. "Been living here two years, I should have known we would take the first road south. You just don't think about things when you're in a car like you do when you're horseback. Sorry."

"Buford and Drexel will bring up the rear. I'm impressed with that little mare. Never seen her work cattle before. Think you can keep her on the east side of the herd without spookin' em? There's a stretch about a mile long up ahead where there ain't no fence. You'll need to ride back and forth to keep 'em out of a wheat field. If they get on the man's wheat, I'll be buying me a wheat crop."

"I'll keep ˈem off." And he did.

Jake was way ahead of the game at the next tee. He and the sorrel were in the middle of the paved road ahead of schedule. The tired cattle's bellowing complaints had turned to weary moos. They filled the loading pens and milled. The sun peeked through in the west before it started raining again. Jake was Matthew Garth at the end of the trail.

47 Jake was disappointed when Will Tom decided to hay the cattle and let them rest overnight before hauling them out the next day. He sent Jake home on the sorrel with twenty-five dollars in his jeans—his second time to earn pay as a cowboy. It was after dark when he put the tired sorrel into the red barn and pulled off her saddle. He found a dry tow sack to rub her back and hayed her. He wished for some sweet feed that she sure deserved. He made a Canadian-bacon and cheese sandwich with his only skillet, drank a glass of milk from his only glass, and went to bed.

He was up early on Sunday, figuring that Will Tom would come by for him and the mare to help load the cattle. The rain had stopped. Not wanting to be caught off guard again, he dressed in dry clothes. The mud had crusted on the hat overnight, but the felt was still a little damp. He scraped off as much as he could with his pocketknife. He put black Kiwi on the still-damp Justins, sprinkled talcum powder inside, and pulled them on. No way he was going to risk the new Tony Lamas.

When Will Tom had not shown up by nine, Jake knew they were doing it without him. He drove the GMC down the muddy roads to the loading pens. The cattle were already gone. No sign of Will Tom, String, Buford, or Drexel. He sat on the corral fence, looking east, for a long time. Feeling lost, he headed west on 214 toward Simms. A few miles down the road, he saw a turquoise car hood sticking up in a field beside the road. Jake stopped and walked to the fence. Someone was using the '55 Ford's hood for an irrigation ditch dam. He laughed to himself.

At Simms, he turned north toward Adrian. Adrian Mercantile was closed. He had forgotten it was Sunday until he heard the church bell. In the Baptist Church parking lot, Jake waited. He was leaning against the hood of the GMC when people started coming out. Texie was first, Gabe on one arm and Nocona on the other. Nocona's dark pants and string tie looked good with his polished burgundy boots. Gabe had on new starched Levis and his best white shirt with pearl snaps, but his boots had cracked close to the sole and his sock peeked through. Jake knew there was also a hole in the sole of the other boot. They pointed at Jake and walked over.

Nocona held his palms up. "How come you to stand us up? We came by at ten."

Jake had forgotten his promise to go to church with his two friends. "Figured the roof might fall in if all three of us went at the same time." Texie's parents had made regular attendance at church a new requirement for dating their daughter. Nocona had coerced Jake and Gabe into going along for moral support.

Texie invited Jake over for Sunday dinner. He declined. Nocona and Gabe kidded him about wearing a muddy hat to church and said they would see him tomorrow. They turned and walked toward Texie's house. Jake was watching them walk away when Mr. and Mrs. Floyd Knight walked to their car. He turned in time to see them driving away. Jake wondered how it felt for the former preacher to sit with his former congregation while someone else spoke from the pulpit.

Sage and Caleb were among the last to walk out. Sage's beige dress looked a little pink in the sunlight. She left her father's side and quickened her pace a little as she approached Jake, then slowed as she got closer. She examined him from his boots to his muddy hat. "What's wrong?"

"What makes you think something's wrong?"

"You look different."

"Helped Will Tom Sunday drive his cattle to that loadin' pen over on 214." Jake wanted her to hear that.

"Today?"

"Yesterday."

"In all that rain?"

"Yep."

She stepped back, examined his expression again and smiled. "You're up to somethin'. Never saw you in town on Sunday mornin'."

"Just runnin' an errand close by and thought I would stop and see you."

She lifted his hand and held it with two fingers. "Want to come to dinner with me and Daddy?"

"Guess not. I got a muddy hat. Beside, I have to go. Will Tom will be coming for the horse I borrowed." He reached for her other hand and pulled her to him, played with the tiny band of lace around her throat.

"Jake, we can't be doing this in broad daylight in front of the church."

"S'pose not."

She put both arms around his neck and returned his squeeze.

"Got to go. I'll see you."

Perplexed, she watched him drive away.

Jake stopped at the Bent Door and asked for a hamburger in a sack. He ate it on the way home with a Coke.

At home, he released the windmill brake and watched as the fan came to life. The wind had picked up and was already putting a crust on the wet ground. He walked out to Scar's grave and let the wind speak, realizing that it had come to seem like an old friend. He liked the feel of it against his skin and the sound it made. The ground had almost leveled, and he knew that all traces of the grave would soon disappear. He found enough small stones to line the perimeter. Cattle would soon scatter them, but he wanted them there for a while. As he placed the last stone, he wondered how the little gelding would have handled himself during the cattle drive.

On the way back, he stopped at the corral that had been turned into a pigpen and listened but did not hear, the whistle of a ten-penny na'l. He tried to hear the music his grandfather always heard but heard only the wind. He carried Will Tom's tack to the shop, rolled back the door, and sat on the old couch. When he saw Will Tom's pickup and trailer coming, he slipped the sorrel's halter on, led her to the yard and waited.

String stepped out first. He took the mare's lead rope and put her in the trailer. Jake helped him load the tack into the back of the pickup. Will Tom and String leaned against the pickup for a few minutes as if they could think of little to say to a boy. Will Tom finally spoke. "Jake, me and the wife have a spare bedroom over at our place. When your time is up here, we'd be pleased to have you over there. You can work for me. I saw the makin's of a top hand yesterday."

Jake let the silence hang, enjoying the feeling of being wanted.

String broke it. "You could still go to school at Adrian. School bus don't run out to Will Tom's place, but you could drive your pickup."

Jake stared at his boots. They were starting to get that well-worn, worn-well look that he liked. The wind was blowing hard now and warming some, but his hat did not budge. It had stopped being a fashion statement and had become a tool. "I appreciate that. I really do."

Will Tom stood straight and dusted the caked mud from the seat of his pants. "You been doin' some serious thinkin', Jake. I can tell." He was looking at the biscuit jar, a baseball, an envelope from Ward's Grocery, and a set of rattler buttons on the seat of the GMC. "You're leavin', ain't you?"

Jake nodded.

"I figured. A man has to do what he sees is right. A boy belongs with his people." Will Tom looked left and right as if looking for something on the ground. "When?"

Jake looked at the sun. "Figure I can pack and be there by a little after midnight."

String bent down and rested his arm on one knee. "Was you just gonna leave without sayin' goodbye?"

Jake looked into Will Tom's ocean-blue wet eyes as they shook hands. "Somebody told me once that cowboys don't know how to say goodbye, but you can always count on 'em to show up." He turned to shake String's outstretched, callused hand. "I always wanted to be a cowboy. Maybe I'll surprise you and show up again someday."

Books make great gifts!

To order additional copies of this novel or the first two novels in the *Follow the Rivers Trilogy*— contact:

Season of Harvest
2403 CR 4208
Campbell, Texas 75422

903-886-3293

Order online from www.jimainsworth.com (for signed copies). Also from *www.booksjustbooks.com, www.amazon.com, www.barnesandnoble.com,* selected retailers and other major book websites.

For information on:

Quantity discounts

Book club questions

Speaking engagements

Other information

e-mail the author at *ainsworth@netexas.net* or contact him through Season of Harvest contact information listed above.